Child of Blackwen

An Artemis Ravenwing Novel

Melanie Rodriguez

ISBN: 1499717245
ISBN 13: 9781499717242
Library of Congress Control Number: 2014909908
CreateSpace Independent Publishing Platform
North Charleston, South Carolina

For my mother, Agie, the believer behind the dreamer.

Prologue

B etrayal.

The word repeated in the mind of the warrior woman fleeing her pursuers within the Woodland Realm, the forest of the elves. A chill wind pricked her pale-skinned face; sweat-soaked brown hair stuck to her forehead and neck, her violet eyes wide with terror.

The woman did not dare to glance over her shoulders; she could sense the others trailing her. If she was caught, she would be forced to fight back. Had the circumstances been different, the idea of a clash wouldn't have distressed her so; as it was, she had more important priorities to consider.

She clutched a bundled blanket close to her chest as she ran. Spotting a cliff up ahead, her nerves flared. Tightening her grasp on the bundle, she hesitated a moment before she sprinted forward and leaped off the cliff's edge. In midair, she cursed her overcompensation as she knew she wouldn't get the desired landing. She angled her body and roughly landed on the side of her back.

From the way her clothes suddenly clung to her body, the woman knew she was bleeding. She could smell it as well. She swore under her breath, as she knew her pursuers would be able to also. She felt her eyelids grow heavy, and they involuntarily closed.

Muffled cries tore through the bundle, snapping the woman out of her momentary slip of consciousness. Frantic, the woman unfolded the blanket and sighed in relief once she realized all was well. The little face that stared at her from the bundle, unharmed, stopped its cries.

"I will keep you safe, my love," the woman promised, her voice wavering despite the comforting coos. "I will die before I ever let those bastards harm you. I swear it."

I

*"*W*illow damn you. Willow damn all those bastards to Avilyne's hell!"*

I wanted to stop crying, but found I cried even more the harder I tried. I didn't want to see those two leave. If I watched them go, then I'd have no choice but to accept that I would be utterly alone in a world where I already didn't belong.

Why did there have to be so much fighting in this world? So much hate? Why couldn't they just send someone else into battle to settle the damned matters?

"Artemis!" a familiar voice yelled.

His.

I shook and then buried my head in my knees to muffle the sound of my sobs. Maybe he would miss me if he didn't hear where I was.

As light as they were, I could hear the footsteps. When it was silent, I knew he had found me.

Willow be damned.

I heard a soft sigh and felt gentle caresses along my back. I was running out of mental curses.

"Artemis." The same voice spoke, almost a whisper.

Biting my lip, I finally moved my head and gazed into his warm green eyes; the face that watched my own was lightly tanned, framed by dark blond hair that hung loosely along broad, war-molded shoulders.

To the world of Arrygn, he was the famed Shadow of Ellewynth, a soldier to be feared. To me, he was just Shadow the elf, my dearest friend.

"You found me."

"*You've never been good at hiding from me,*" *he said with a heavy sigh.*

"*You can't leave.*" *I felt another tear slide down to my chin. "*You can't.*"

Shadow looked away, guilty. "I wish I did not have to."

"*Avilyne's hell, wish harder then!*" *I snapped. "While you're at it, wish for Talisa to stay too! Wish for this stupid war to end!*"

Shadow frowned as he sat down beside me. "Artemis, you and I both know that Talisa and I have a duty to the realm and her people." *He grasped my hand and gave it a light squeeze. "I have no choice. I am a soldier of Ellewynth, first and foremost. The elves stationed in Fieros Mountains require my presence on the battlefield now. The faster an end can be reached, the sooner Talisa and I can return.*"

"*Shadow...don't you know what this means?*" *I asked. "The elves will no doubt torture me more than they already have. All because I'm...I'm different.*"

"*I have faith in my kind,*" *he stressed. "You* will *find a friend.*"

I shook my head. "Unlikely."

Shadow caressed my back once more. "I promise, Artemis. I will return to Ellewynth as soon as my service ends."

"*Don't you understand that you could be gone for* years*?*" *I cried. "Goddesses, you're fighting* dragons*!*"

"*I've fought in numerous wars Artemis, and I've fought dragons before,*" *Shadow reminded me. "It's just another nuisance to take care of.*" *He stood while he took my other hand and raised me up. "I* will *return. I swear it.*"

I sighed and fumbled with the ring on my left hand. Taking it off, I gazed at it. It had two birds carved within the silver band, and a small garnet was set in the center. Talisa had given it to me in my tenth year; she called it the "Gift of Peace."

Noting the look of confusion on Shadow's face, I held it out for him to take. He did so.

"*I-I want it back, elf,*" *I explained, while trying to hold back more tears. "It will protect you out there. Until you come back.*"

"*I'll miss you too, my dear.*" *Shadow softly smiled, and held the ring in a firm grip. "I promise to return this to you.*"

I awoke to the sound of the bells ringing deep within the city; they sang with a range of high peals, the very ones that called for the people of

Ellewynth to venture out for celebration. I jumped from the bed and ran to the window; in the distance I watched the elves of the Woodland Realm flood the main square, rejoicing with glee and dancing with one another in bliss. It could only mean one thing—the soldiers that left eight years ago had finally returned home.

Kiare be praised, the war with the dragons was over!

"Thank the goddesses," I said, as I felt the depressing weight I carried for those eight years lift. "Willow be damned for the dream, though."

It was when I looked away from the window that I felt the apprehension. A bundle of bloodstained clothes lay on the ground by the bed. I picked them up and caught the flash of a memory: I was running through the woods, chasing something red.

No…it was orange. Wasn't it?

I smelled the dried blood and got my answer. I had hunted a fox, the animal I preferred to feed on. Avilyne's hell.

I hated what I was. I hated my need for something to sustain—no. I had to keep a peaceful mindset. I had to suppress the dark nature of my heritage.

I hid the bundle for now, making a mental note to burn it all later. It wasn't too long ago that a "slip" like this had happened last. I prayed the next episode wouldn't happen for a prolonged period of time. That damned nature of mine had to have been sated…it better have.

Running to another room, I rummaged through my clothing trunks. Scowling at my lack of "proper" elven garb, I settled on a sleeveless, light green dress with a high neckline—one of the many gifts bestowed to me by Talisa, a witch who served the Woodland Realm and a longtime vassal of the water goddess, Kiare. The thought of her returning brought a smile to my face. I missed her dearly. I'd be lying if I denied missing Shadow more though.

My thoughts returned to the dream I had before the bells woke me. The memory of Shadow's news, of his call to war, still haunted me. He and Talisa were the few true friends I had here in the city, let alone the realm. Who knew that the realm of your birth would make you feel like an irremovable stain on the finest fabric reserved for the nobility?

I was raised away from the cities of the Woodland Realm. I never knew the site of my birth. My mother, Tamina, was murdered when I was still an infant. I never knew the whole story either; neither Shadow nor Talisa would tell me. The two were once close friends with Mother, and they both swore to watch over me, even before the gloomy circumstances.

I spent the first ten years of my life with Talisa, living in her cottage far from Ellewynth, a city that was considered the heart of the Woodland Realm. At the end of that tenth year, I was relocated to Ellewynth and spent more of my time with Shadow. Talisa visited whenever she could to help ease the transition and to ensure her continuing guardianship. I hated living here. The elves quickly rejected me. They would have been more than pleased to cast me out of their borders if given the chance. If it weren't for the Elders, I'm sure they'd have tried to kill me as well.

All of the hatred from the elves was because I was different from them. I am a dhampir, or half-vampire in simpler terms.

My vampiric heritage came from Mother. Full-bloods, her race was called. I wasn't told much about my father, Gavin, other than that he was human. The only other detail I *did* know was that both Talisa and Shadow despised him. I didn't know if he was still alive, and I stopped asking after a time. Angry glances and murmured curses were tiring after a while.

Standing in front of a mirror, I stared at the face that gazed back. I was told by many that I was the spitting image of Tamina; I had her long brown hair with hints of red in the sunlight, but I had my father's hazel eyes. Talisa told me Mother's eyes were violet. I often tried to picture myself with her eyes instead of those I was born with.

Taking a ribbon from my desk, I plaited my hair and twisted the ribbon to bind it. After a sigh, I felt I was presentable enough to venture outside and into the throng of elven society.

As I slipped on a pair of soft brown leather boots, I heard a series of loud, pounding knocks from the main room below. I made my way down the stairs, and I heard a familiar grumbling from the other side of the door.

After opening it, I stood face to face with the only other elf I could call "friend"—even if he was a stitch in my side once in a while.

"Well, good morning, Jack," I greeted him, while folding my arms.

I met Jack several days after Shadow and Talisa's departure. He was the new addition to my archery classes then, and was equally as terrible as I. It was a friendship sent from the goddesses themselves. I never appreciated the strange sense of humor of the sacred sisters.

Like me, Jack was considered an outcast among the elves; he didn't act like the "proper" elf, and to this day he still has little skill with the bow and arrow. Jack made it a habit of skipping weapons training to hide in the library to research spells and other "rewards" of magic, as it was the only thing of interest to him. Jack usually suffered dearly for those antics, mostly at the hands of his horrific aunt. Avilyne's hell, she even terrified *me*. That old crunchy-faced, slack-jawed goat…

Jack was also an outcast because of his appearance: where the Woodland Realm elves had differing shades of blond hair and a pair of either blue or green eyes, Jack was dark haired and had equally dark brown eyes. I was always disgusted with the politics here…if you couldn't blend in, you were sneered at. It was no wonder the other elven realms steered clear from us.

Jack took one glance at my dress and covered his mouth to stifle a laugh. I rolled my eyes as a snort escaped his lips.

"Stop it."

"Since when do *you* wear dresses, Artemis?" he asked, forcing a cough to cover the chuckling. "Soleil burn me, I didn't even think you *owned* one."

Once upon a time, he would have been right about that.

"I didn't have much choice in the 'proper' section of my wardrobe. And I happen to like this dress!" I answered. Studying him, I noticed his hair was pulled back in haste, and his gray robes were disheveled. I groaned once I put two and two together. "You didn't make it home last night, did you?"

Jack laughed nervously. "Well…"

"Oh goddesses, Jack." I covered my face with a hand in disappointment. "Were you drunk again?"

"No! Not this time, anyway," he answered, while rubbing his face. "Look, that's not why I'm here. I thought you'd maybe want to go with me to welcome back Shadow and Talisa."

I raised an eyebrow at first, and eventually nodded as I shut the door behind me. "Let's not keep them waiting."

"Artemis?"

"What?"

"What's that on your hand?" Jack asked.

He pointed to my left hand, and I saw remnants of fox blood on it. Soleil burn me...it must have rubbed off from the clothes. I didn't need Jack's inquiries, not now. He couldn't talk, seeing as his drinking habits were far worse than my dhampir blackouts.

I just needed to work on tightening the leash.

"Nothing," I declared as I moved my palm out of sight.

"Are you—"

"I *said* it is nothing," I insisted as I rubbed my hand along the bottom of my boot. "Let's go already."

Jack and I eventually made our way to the city square, ignoring the grumbles and curses of the elves we passed. I glanced over at Jack and scowled. He was such a mess.

"Jack, for goddesses sake, at least fix your hair!" I scolded. "If *I'm* wearing a dress, the least *you* can do is to look proper yourself."

"There's nothing wrong with slightly messy hair. It becomes me," Jack teased. "As for your choice in wardrobe...maybe you should wear dresses more often. It makes you look normal!"

I glared at him as he guffawed. "If I didn't pity you, I'd cripple you where you stand."

"No, you wouldn't. You'd miss my company and spur-of-the-moment visits," he mused. Before I could snap, Jack held up a hand and pointed straight ahead. "Here come the cavalry. Smile, will you?"

A parade of elven warriors marched from the city gates onward to the square. Some were on foot, others on horseback. Elves from the crowd ran out to those they recognized and partook in teary greetings. I tiptoed over other elves to better my view, and my stomach churned as I couldn't find Shadow or Talisa in the crowd.

Jack grabbed my wrist and helped me move through the crowd; I could feel his own nerves through his grip. There still weren't any signs of Shadow and Talisa, and the stomach twists grew worse. I shook my head to be rid of the thought that they might not return at all.

"Where are they?" I whispered.

"They can't be too far behind, Artemis," Jack assured me. "You worry too much."

"Shadow has already made it into Ellewynth," a voice informed us from behind, startling us both. "Just a little after dawn, if you care for specifics."

Jack and I swiveled around and were greeted with a grin from our former archery-mate, Lilith. She was the same age as us; her light blond hair was unbound and held a crown of white lilies, which matched her flowing white gown. Lilith blinked her bright blue eyes and smiled shyly in Jack's direction. Jack did a terrible job hiding the excitement her presence caused.

Lilith was another one of the very few elves who treated me as a person rather than a monster. It was usually done in secret, however, as her sister, Serlene, was our archery instructor and harbored great disgust for me. Lilith would always be scorned for public kindness toward me; I often felt terrible for the poor girl.

"H-hello, Lily," Jack greeted her, while wringing his hands nervously behind his back. "I w-would hope Serlene made her safe return as well?"

Lilith's smile widened a bit more, and it nearly made Jack fall over. I smiled myself; Jack had had an infatuation for her since the day the two met. I always enjoyed the thought of Serlene ripping her hair out should Jack finally gather the courage to court her younger sister.

"She did," Lilith answered him. "It warmed the heart knowing she made it through her four years of service in the war."

"Lilith, is Shadow at home or did he go elsewhere?" I interrupted, not wanting to hear more about her wretched sister.

"Artemis, please! You don't have to keep calling me by my proper name!" Lilith chuckled. She tapped a thin finger against her cheek. "I'm not sure if he is still at home. If it were me, I'd probably be fast asleep after all the toil and travel."

I nodded in agreement. "Yes, as would I."

"Eight years is a long time for anyone, Artemis." Lilith put a warm hand on my shoulder. "I'm sure Shadow wants to be well rested and presentable before seeing you. A few more hours couldn't hurt, hmm?"

"You do realize you're talking about Artemis, right, Lily?" Jack snorted. "Dhampir or not, she still falls prey to impatience. They have quite the relationship, you know."

"Oh stop it, Jack," Lilith teased, with a light smack to his shoulder. "You would act the same way if your love went off to war."

Jack and I stiffened at her words. After an awkward moment of silence, Jack burst out laughing. I quickly cleared my throat.

"I'm not in love with Shadow," I insisted, while glaring at Jack.

"No?" Lilith asked, blinking her sweet innocence. "Apologies then. I just assumed because you are so fond of Shadow and speak often of him that perhaps you and he—"

"He's a close friend, that's all," I explained, while reaching for Jack's arm. I gave him a sharp pinch. "Stop laughing!"

Jack yelped. He frowned at me, and then focused on Lilith. "What of Talisa? Any news of her?"

"Yes! She's returned safely to her cottage. Serlene helped escort her," Lilith answered.

I breathed a sigh of relief. I was happy knowing they had returned safely, though I still wanted to see them despite their fatigue from the war. I looked at the streets, watching the returning soldiers embrace their loved ones, and felt a twinge of jealousy. Jack jabbed my side, forcing me to pay attention to the conversation.

"Why don't we head back to your house?" he suggested. "I'm sure Shadow will meet you there at some point today. And I may or may not be hungry. You know how that goes."

Lilith chuckled as I glared at him again. "Fine, fine."

"Well, I am sure I will run into the two of you again. A pleasure,"—Lilith reached over and kissed both Jack's and my cheek in farewell— "as always."

I said good-byes for both Jack and myself, as he began blushing like a youngling and was unable to respond. Dragging him away, I gave him a smack to the back of the head.

"You won't win her over if you continue to let your nerves control you," I scolded.

"A lady like her will never share my love, Artemis," Jack said with a deep sigh. "A man can dream though. Such *nice* dreams…"

"I don't want to know!" I chided. "And she does like you, idiot! You just have to work harder. Make her believe that you're more than an acquaintance. And for goddess' sake, do something about the blushing! It's called control, Jack."

"Shut it!" Jack huffed while he folded his arms. "So tell me…you really believe you're not in love with Shadow?"

"I'm not," I groaned. "And do not speak of it again. It's nonsense!"

"Uh-huh. This is coming from the woman who gave away a most prized ring as a 'source of protection.'" Jack stroked his chin in mockery. "If he was merely a friend, you would have just hugged him good-bye, not given him a trinket to remind him daily of you."

"Keep this up and I will not feed you," I threatened.

"You *are* old enough to chase after him now, unless by some miracle he's actually taken to someone who maybe fought alongside him," Jack mused as we walked. "My coin's on you, of course, should you see fit to challenge this new rival…I wonder if Shadow likes a biter?"

I stopped walking and smacked his arm. "Are you done now or shall I have to bite you to shut you up? Believe me, it's a bite you would *not* enjoy."

Jack quickly raised his hands in surrender and followed me home in silence.

2

After a full meal, Jack fell asleep in the main room of my home. Tucking him under a blanket, I rubbed my temples. I was curious why he didn't make it to his home the previous night, but I knew I'd regret asking because it was very likely that the reason was ludicrous.

Once I returned to my room, I settled onto the bed and wrapped my arms around one of the pillows. After I shut my eyes, I felt a bit more at peace than I had in years. My friends were alive, thank the goddesses; things would be far better now that they'd returned.

So I hoped, anyway.

I could hear more festivities taking place from the window. I felt the jealousy return; I would have enjoyed partaking in the fun had the circumstances been different. The elves hated anything with the blood of a vampire—they had their share of wars with them too. They even had a special nickname for me, the bastards: *vampyra.* It was a stupid insult that left plenty of scars behind; it meant "dirty soul defiler." Even dhampirs were seen as soulless corpses, and anyone who shared our company was said to lose their soul to our dark appetite.

Idiots.

Shaking my head at the unpleasant memories, I moved from my bed and sat on the windowsill. The feel of the breeze was comforting. I tucked a few wayward strands of my braid behind my ears.

"If I didn't know any better," a familiar voice said, "I'd say that the young woman currently sitting on the windowsill was once a youngling I left behind all those years ago."

I felt my heart pound against my chest as I poked my head farther out the window.

Outside my doorstep was Shadow. It was as if time hadn't passed. Elves are long-lived, and they age slower than any other being. I have similar traits due to the vampire half of my heritage, but sometimes it spooked me to see such truths.

"Shadow!" I exclaimed, while suddenly remembering to breathe.

"You're not going to make me wait out here all day, right?" Shadow laughed.

I jumped from the windowsill back into my room and raced through the house to open the front door. Before Shadow could say anything, I leaped and hugged him hard. He spun me around, chuckling, and eventually pulled away from the hug.

It was an odd feeling as we both studied one another. Shadow truly hadn't changed; his long dark blond hair was half pulled away from his face, and his skin was still the same tanned shade as when he left. I always remembered him being so tall, yet now I reached his chin.

Giving my hands a tiny squeeze, Shadow tilted his head to the side and smiled. I returned the gesture.

"I've missed you so much," I said. "The past eight years have been miserable."

"So I've gathered through your letters. Talisa and I meant to come back much sooner," Shadow explained, apologetic. "Dragons are...a stubborn bunch."

"More than elves?" I snorted. "Doubtful."

Shadow grinned while he continued to study me. "You know, I almost mistook you for your mother when I saw you on the windowsill. Almost. You took much after her."

"So I've heard." I sighed. "I wish I knew her."

"I know," he said. "This is...your twenty-first year?"

"Yes."

"You'll have to forgive me, it's still sinking in."

"I know." I laughed, and embraced him again. "You don't have to explain yourself."

Shadow sighed. "I've missed so much. Too much."

"We have plenty of time now to catch up." I grabbed his wrist and dragged him inside. "You can start by joining me for tea!"

"I wouldn't have much of a choice otherwise, hmm?"

"Nope."

I let go of him and went to brew peppermint leaf tea, Shadow's favorite. I heard him clear his throat in an odd manner, and I found him standing over the chair Jack was snoring away in. Shadow raised a teasing eyebrow, and I scowled.

"This can't be Jack." He spoke in a low voice.

"Yes, it is."

"The man snores like a drunken human sailor," Shadow teased.

I sighed. "It's normal for him to sleep over here. His life at home is terrible."

"Not much has changed there?" Shadow glanced at Jack and frowned. "I hoped the others would treat him with more respect as well."

"The elves despise him as much as they loathe me." I scowled. "We've grown used to it by now."

Shadow moved to an empty chair and sat down. "I wish things went differently for you two."

I poured the tea and handed him a cup. "It's fine. Such is life."

"So,"—Shadow took a sip of his tea as I took a seat beside him—"how have your studies been?"

"Define studies," I said with a nervous chuckle.

"Archery lessons, for starters."

"Ah! That." I took a quick sip of my own tea, and cursed the burning sensation on my tongue. "It's…going. Going well, actually! Never better."

I didn't have the heart to tell him I'd stopped going to lessons after being thrown out of one at fifteen. There was an unfortunate accident that led to a fist fight—one that I won, but at the cost of serious injury to the elf who initiated it.

The true nature of the dhampir does not like to be, erm, provoked. At least I was able to control the monster enough to prevent worse injuries.

Shadow raised an eyebrow. He could always tell when I was lying. "Artemis."

I sighed. "I stopped going after my fifteenth year. There was a... minor scuffle. *Minor.*"

"How minor exactly?"

"She got into a fight with several of our archery-mates." Shadow and I turned to face Jack, who was now sitting up and lifting off the blanket I had tucked him into. "Welcome back, by the way."

"Good to be back," Shadow answered. I flinched when his gaze sharpened. "Artemis, explain."

"I...I was defending myself," I started. "I shot an elf in the leg!"

"One of our archery-mates snuck up behind her and poked her knee with their bow as she went to shoot," Jack elaborated. "I'm sure you can imagine the response."

"After that, everyone snapped at me. They called me those stupid nicknames," I added. "I...I lost it. The dhampir—"

"Serlene was furious, but did nothing to help Artemis...as usual," Jack interrupted, knowing full well how I felt about my heritage. "It was probably why she volunteered to join the war so fast. The goddesses themselves knew how badly she tried to get out of teaching us both. Too bad they didn't accept her offer until a couple years later."

"She didn't volunteer to fight, she was called into duty by then," I corrected. "And to go back to the incident, *you* just stood there leaving me outnumbered! What a friend *you* are!"

Jack shrugged. "I know better than to get into a fight with dhampirs, friend or not...*control* or not."

Shadow rubbed his brow, and I knew the last comment sunk in. He kept silent on the matter...for now. "Did you win at least?"

Jack and I stared at him, amazed at the question. Jack cackled while he went to get his own cup of tea.

"Oh, she did, all right. One little bite shut the bastard up," Jack explained. "It was an impressive leap too...for a female."

Shadow looked at me, and I felt the guilt return. He surprised me by bursting into laughter.

My jaw dropped.

"If you had lost I would have been very disappointed," he explained, while trying to regain his composure.

"Shadow!" I exclaimed, horrified at the response. "I went into dhampir mode and *bit* an elf! And shot another one!"

"Accidents happen in the world of archery," Shadow said. "And I know you, my dear. You bit in self-defense, not in hunger. Don't be so quick to judge the dhampir's nature."

"I *told* you he wouldn't be upset with you," Jack teased. "Was Artemis always such a worrywart?"

"Indeed." Shadow nodded. "Besides, the fault lies more with Serlene. If she were a true instructor, the incident wouldn't have occurred in the first place."

"Again, that's what I said," Jack said.

"Oh, shut up," I snapped.

"Speaking of faults, I unfortunately have one of my own," Shadow said, taking another sip of tea. "I owe you a ring, my dear."

I froze in my seat. "What happened to it?"

Shadow frowned, his free hand slowly balling into a fist. "I put your ring on a chain and hid it beneath my armor. There were a few close calls before, but in the last year, luck was not on my side. I . . ." Shadow put down his teacup. "During one of the raids, I was in close combat with one of the wizards and we fell to the ground. The chain fell out of my armor, and his sword narrowly missed my neck. The chain broke, and I never had a chance to reclaim it. I searched endlessly for the ring after the raid was over—"

"Stop, stop," I interrupted, now reaching for his wrist. "It's all right."

"I know how much the ring meant to you, Artemis." Shadow shook his head. "I'll repay you, I promise."

"The ring was given as a source of protection, and it did its task. You've returned safely."

Deep down inside, I was heartbroken about the loss of it. Shadow didn't need to know that, however; his life was far more important than a piece of metal and jewel.

After a moment of silence, Jack cleared his throat and returned to his tea. "How come you, Talisa, and Serlene made it back to Ellewynth before the rest of the regiment?"

"We were part of the Elders' escort. The war with the dragons technically ended three nights ago; we were present during the final negotiations with the Woodland Realm Elders and the dragon hierarchy of Fieros Mountains," Shadow explained. "A new dragon queen was appointed, and she declared a peace treaty with us soon after."

"What caused the stupid war to occur in the first place?" I asked.

"Internal disputes that eventually dragged us into it," Shadow replied. "There were separate factions among the dragons of Fieros Mountains. The previous dragon queen's mind was warped by a group of turncoat wizards and dragons. Once we helped the former queen reach a 'peaceful end,' we helped the new queen take the throne. Now everyone can be happy." He tapped his fingers along the arm of the chair. "They better be."

"Just like that?" I asked. "How long do you think before the separate factions could strike again?"

"I worry about that as well, but I pray to the goddesses it won't be for many years to come. We destroyed a large number of the factions that started all this. The rest were exiled."

Jack loudly sighed. "If only I were so fortunate to be in the company of dragons...all the magic I could learn..."

Shadow blinked at Jack, and I hid my face within my hand in embarrassment.

"He has a particular affinity for magic," I explained, while trying to ignore the childlike gleam in Jack's eyes. "He's banned from the libraries for loitering in the magic sections. Personally, I think it's just because he skipped out on most of his weapons training to do so..."

"Is he terrible in weapons training?" Shadow asked, intrigued.

"Far worse than I, if you can believe it," I answered. "I can at least wield a sword, even if I'm still a bit of a novice. His magical abilities are the opposite; he's *very* good."

"Interesting..." Shadow mused. It was as if he knew something I did not. Before I could inquire further, Shadow finished his tea and went to refill his cup. "Jack, have you ever thought of becoming a mage apprentice?"

Jack snapped out of his daydreaming and shook his head. "I-I wish."

"If you're as talented as Artemis makes you seem, you should seek a teacher," Shadow suggested. "Surely you've thought of it?"

"Not with the history we have concerning elves and magic," Jack said, frowning. "I'm sure whatever instructors exist would rather teach Artemis before even considering me, and she doesn't even have an ounce of magic in her blood. You get the point."

"What about Talisa?" I asked. "Can't she take an apprentice?"

"No!" Jack slammed down his tea. "I've heard the horror stories about her and her past apprentices! All the abuse she put them through... Willow damn me to Avilyne's hell before I agree to such a thing!"

Shadow burst out laughing as I grew confused.

"Shadow, what is he talking about?"

"Talisa rarely takes on an apprentice. It's uh, something she does her best to avoid," he explained. "However, I think I'll say a few words to her. It would be well worth the pain, Jack. She is a well-renowned witch even outside the Woodland Realm. She is one of the best in all of Arrygn, especially because she was endowed with a touch of Kiare's power."

"Yes, if I want to live in a new kind of hell!" Jack snapped. He took a deep breath. "It's true that I long to learn all that she knows...the cost however, I'm not willing to pay. At least I know what abuse to expect when I'm with the aunt."

"I'll try to make her reach a compromise. If she agrees, you're on your own after that." Shadow chuckled.

Jack glared at him. I tried to smile reassuringly.

"It'll be fine, Jack," I insisted, while trying to believe the words myself.

I couldn't imagine Talisa being as horrifying and strict as Jack and Shadow made her seem, but I suppose ignorance was bliss.

Shadow stood up and stretched. "I have to tend to a few errands before the day's end, sadly. Perhaps we could catch up more during dinner, Artemis? My home?"

"I'd like that," I agreed. I took the teacup from him, and Jack handed me his as well. "What? You're leaving too?"

"Yes. I have to make sure my home isn't as much of a wreck as I was this morning," he said. "Shadow? Would you mind if I walked a bit with you?"

"Not at all." Shadow hugged me good-bye and moved aside for Jack to leave first. "Until tonight then."

"Until tonight," I repeated, seeing them off.

Shadow and Jack made their way through the celebrating crowd of Ellewynth, and the moment they were finally alone, Jack nervously cleared his throat. Shadow blinked at him, confused.

"So there was a reason you wished to accompany me after all," Shadow stated.

Jack nodded. "Are you really going to speak to Talisa about me?"

"Yes. I think it would be to your benefit to learn from the best," Shadow explained. "You fear rejection from her?"

"Believe it or not, I do." Jack sighed. "I've always loved magic. I've a gift for it, and I can't understand why. Elves aren't normally beings of magical capacity. I mean, I've heard about the elf mages, but I know for a fact that I am not one of them. I'm *not*."

Shadow looked straight ahead in his efforts to avoid eye contact with Jack. He first met him before he left for the war, and Shadow remembered the gossip about the young elf. He had his own suspicions, of course. If Jack was really an elf mage, it was better for Talisa to break the news to him. The elf mages of the past were known to be volatile, whether they wished to be or not.

"Everything happens for a reason, even if we do not understand it at first," Shadow said, breaking the momentary silence. "But I trust that's not all you wish to speak of."

"I know Artemis wrote to you all these years. Did she..." Jack paused a moment. "Did she speak about her blackouts?"

"She did for a time. Even as a child, she feared her heritage. Talisa and I tried to lead her to a safer path for a blood-drinker." Shadow shook his head at their failure. "You can lead a horse to water, bur you cannot make the horse drink. I fear it'll take something drastic to make her realize she must embrace what she is."

"I'm worried about her. I saw blood on her hands earlier today."

"As far as I know, she's only killed foxes." Shadow recalled one of the recent letters stating that she had better control of her blackouts. It appeared she lied. "How bad has it been, Jack?"

"Bad enough that she's stopped being open about it with me," Jack answered.

Shadow shut his eyes. He should have been back sooner.

"I'll speak with her."

"Thank you."

Jack continued to follow him, and Shadow realized there was more he wanted to speak of.

"What else do you need?" Shadow inquired.

"Well…I was wondering about…" Jack began, while wringing his hands. "Artemis is the only true friend I have, and I've tried to understand the feminine point of view on the issue, which is frustrating by the way, but—"

Shadow stopped walking. "Don't tell me you're in love with Artemis."

"Goddesses, no!" Jack choked. "I know better!" He stopped to catch his breath, and mumbled, "And she's in denial of her own love…"

"What was that, Jack?" Shadow asked, now frozen and questioning whether he correctly heard that last bit or not.

"Nothing!" Jack replied with haste. "So…?"

"You're asking *my* advice about the matters of the heart?" Shadow frowned. "Don't you know I've never been involved with a woman before?"

"I refuse to believe you've never been infatuated before," Jack said. "I know of our curse…the one where when we find our mate, they are so for eternity."

It's not necessarily a curse, Shadow thought. "You're wondering if you have found your life-mate?"

"Yes. How in Avilyne's hell do you know?"

"They say you know once you see them," Shadow explained. "When they're all you think about and you feel that twinge within your heart… it's more commonly known as the elven string. Life-mates tend to say they can feel a string-like sensation binding them to one another."

Jack gulped. "Aerios blow me. I'm damned then."

"Oh?" Shadow raised an eyebrow. "Who is it?"

"Lily."

"*Lily?* As in Serlene's younger sister?" When Jack didn't answer, Shadow patted his shoulder. "May the goddesses help you, you poor bastard. That is no easy task."

"I'm very much aware of that. Serlene is a scary bitch." Shadow started walking again, and he stopped once he realized Jack didn't follow. Jack folded his arms when Shadow flashed him a puzzled look. "You really mean to tell me you've never felt an infatuation, let alone the string?"

Shadow took a long time before answering. "All right. It's… complicated."

"How so?"

"It can never happen. Ever." Shadow turned from Jack. "I accepted that a long time ago."

"You mean *you* won't ever let it happen," Jack corrected as he stepped in front of Shadow.

When Shadow didn't answer, Jack's eyes widened with realization. "It's Artemis. Avilyne's hell…you never lost her ring, did you? You couldn't bring yourself to return it to her because it's a memento of a dream you won't allow to become reality. That's not acceptance, Shadow. That's just foolishness."

More silence.

Shadow moved past Jack and kept walking.

"I'll let you know of Talisa's decision when I can." Shadow spoke aloud, and he did not wait for a response.

B

*S*hadow felt agitated as he stepped into his home. He tried to put the last part of his conversation with Jack behind him, but did not have much luck. He had enough on his mind already; there were more important things to pay attention to than what had just transpired.

The first was that of Jack's magical nature. The last time he saw an elf looking like Jack who carried the same curiosity of magic…

Oh, the dark memories *that* brought back.

The scent of peppermint tea wafted throughout his home; it was much too recent. Grabbing a dagger from behind a bookcase in the main room, Shadow moved quietly as he followed the scent to his library.

Dim candlelight lit the room, and a dark figure was seated by the hardwood desk. Shadow gripped the dagger hilt and took a few more steps. A familiar soft laugh stopped his advance; Shadow grumbled as he recognized it.

"You know," the voice started, "if you were an enemy of mine, you'd already be dead."

The chair moved and revealed a tall woman with waist-length black hair streaked with white. She wore dark blue robes common among those who served the water goddess, Kiare. Her pointed, wide-brimmed hat was resting atop several aged tomes. She appeared to be a maiden, but her gray eyes told a different tale; they were eyes that watched many centuries pass by. "Of course, *I* should be the one giving an apology. I let myself in and stole a bit of your tea, after all."

Shadow flipped the dagger, caught it by the blade, and left it atop a book within the shelf. He took one of the empty chairs closest to him and moved it toward the desk, seating himself.

"Fancy seeing you so soon, Talisa. I thought your plans were to lock yourself in that cottage for several moonturns," Shadow teased. "I certainly didn't expect to see you again today."

"I hadn't either," Talisa said, now rubbing her temples. "And my plan *was* to lock myself away after fighting for the realm as long as we did. Goddesses know I *need* my alone time."

"So explain to me why you're sitting here in my library rather than your own."

Talisa deeply sighed. "I was visited by a messenger from the Elders."

Shadow was confused. "And what did this messenger want?"

"To bring more hell upon me!" Talisa snapped as she snatched her hat and crushed the point in her fist. "They mean for me to scout for a disturbance near my cottage."

"This is why you broke into my home?" Shadow rubbed his brow. "You realize it could be far worse, Talisa."

"Oh, but it does get worse. The Elders suspect vampires, Shadow," Talisa explained. Shadow froze, and she handed over a piece of folded parchment for him to read. "Yes, the full-bloods in particular. Apparently, they've become braver by crossing through the Woodland Realm borders. If they are the cause behind a few, erm, mysterious deaths that have been occurring in our absence…well, I don't have to spell the rest out for you."

"It'll mean you and I will be sent to investigate the matter further." Shadow shut his eyes, irritated. "Not even a full day's return and we face the chance of another war brewing. Another damned fight, so soon!"

"We've always fought full-bloods, Shadow, as you well remember. That won't change for centuries to come." Talisa took a sip from her tea and fixed her hat. Satisfied at its less rumpled appearance, she placed it in the spot it had rested before. "But on to happier things. How fares Artemis?"

How predictable of you to bring her up, Talisa. "She's well," Shadow answered aloud. He noticed an odd smile that formed on Talisa's face. "What mischief are you thinking of now?"

"Nothing," Talisa said, quickly getting rid of the smile. "I plan to visit her tomorrow afternoon. I imagine she's fully grown into her mother's image."

"Indeed she has." Shadow frowned for a moment. "Though her eyes are more like her father's than I remembered…"

Talisa chuckled. "I don't believe it bothers you as much as you make it seem."

Shadow raised an eyebrow. "How so?"

"Oh, come now! You've visited the girl and didn't return that ring to her. Don't even bother denying it to me, elf." Talisa crossed a leg atop the other, and mischeviously smiled. "If you were in my shoes, what would *you* think?"

"You speak nonsense, Talisa." Shadow stood up and was ready to leave the room, until Talisa called him back.

"Come back, you ridiculous elf!" Talisa scolded. "It is my duty as your friend to jest. Relax, will you?"

Shadow returned to his seat and remembered Jack. "When I visited her, I saw Jack as well."

"Jack?" Talisa blinked. "The dark-haired elf?" Shadow nodded, and she shifted in her seat. "What of him? Is he causing trouble again? Did he insult Serlene? If he did, I'd like to congratulate him personally. I can never get a rise out of that woman…"

"How do you feel about another attempt at receiving an apprentice?" he asked, ignoring the banter.

He watched Talisa stiffen in her chair. Before Shadow could say another word, she jumped from her seat. The blood rushed to her face, revealing a rare level of fury.

"Are you out of your mind?" she snapped. "Even the goddesses know of my oath to never take an apprentice again! There is no one, alive or undead, that is capable of learning all that I know! *None* have ever finished their tutelage with me!"

"That's because you threaten them away with death by the time they can," Shadow reminded her. "You're no easy master, Talisa. Even *I* would run."

"Then why in Avilyne's hell would you even try to throw another imbecile at me?" she fumed.

"Because,"—Shadow took one of the books lying on his desk and flipped through the pages— "I have suspicions that Jack is of the old elven mage bloodline. I forgot about them until I saw him again today. I refer to the most volatile bloodline, mind you. He can be dangerous, if he continues to figure out his gift without the proper guidance."

"It cannot be." Talisa gaped at him. "My first apprentice had some decent control over magic, but she was no elf mage. What proof do you have that Jack is?"

"His appearance, for starters." Shadow motioned for Talisa to sit. "Don't you dare dismiss that bloodline as a myth, for you and I both remember that one elf mage who shall not be named. He was of the Woodland Realm, and had similar features to Jack—the dark hair and eyes, the lack of interest of weapons training, and a strong need to know all sorts of magic. Artemis told me how gifted he is with it, and how even she can fight with more skill than him when it concerns weaponry. As of right now, he is harmless. How long it will last, I do not know."

"He must be an outcast like she is." Talisa sighed. Shadow nodded. "You understand the elves shun him because that said elf mage caused the first war with the dragons over a century ago...the one you yourself fought in. The younglings mimic the hatred simply because they don't know any better."

"Yes, I'm aware." More so than he cared to admit.

"Then reconsider what you ask of me, Shadow. I won't be the one responsible for him should he repeat the history of his bloodline. I cannot be."

"I won't reconsider." Shadow ignored Talisa's frown. "You are the only one who can help him. You once told me about how you have no memory of your life before coming and serving the Woodland Realm. You could have become a dangerous adversary to Arrygn, if it weren't for Kiare making you a longtime vassal instead...you said so yourself. Jack could use your intervention, and I believe he is capable of being the apprentice you once dreamed of long ago. He could very much use your...harsh discipline, Talisa. His only known vice, drinking, has gotten out of control. Even Artemis cannot continue to be patient with him."

"Oh, wonderful! A drunkard as well!" Talisa said sarcastically. She pursed her lips. "If I do this, you'll owe me *many* favors."

Shadow smiled. "I assumed so."

"I'll collect, Shadow," Talisa warned, while wagging a finger. "*Very* soon."

"Yes, yes, I understand." Shadow teasingly waved his hand. "I take it the first of the favors would be to scout the disturbance for you."

"For starters, yes." Talisa stood up and snatched her hat, adjusting it so that the wide brim cast a dark shadow over her face. "I will return tomorrow and properly converse with Jack. He has to understand that his life will belong to me until I see fit to free him from my apprenticeship. If what you suspect is true, I will have to exert the harshest discipline in my arsenal. For safety's sake."

"Naturally. And just out of curiosity, how long *has* an apprentice lasted under your tutelage?" Shadow asked, also standing. "I could have sworn one survived at least a decade."

"Please." Talisa snorted. "The last one you remember only lasted four years. Four! If any one of those bastards had lasted a decade, I wouldn't so abhor the idea of an apprentice. You'd better pray this one lasts long enough. I'd rather not catch grief from Artemis."

"Neither would I." Shadow led Talisa to the front door and flashed a grin. "I thought you'd like to know that Artemis suggested you to Jack first. If she hadn't, I would have either way."

Talisa tipped the brim of her hat at him out of mockery. "The list of favors continues to grow, elf. I better not hear a single complaint once I begin to collect."

"You may as well call them demands, Talisa." Shadow waved as he watched her disappear from Ellewynth's borders.

"Favors just sound nicer," he heard her say, a whisper along the wind.

He sighed at the thought of Talisa's "favors"; he knew what a few of them would be.

Reaching inside his tunic, he felt thin steel brush along his fingertips. Bringing the chain out into the open, he stared at the ring of carved birds clutching a garnet within the center of the silver band. Rubbing the stone as if it were a ritual, he let it drop against his chest and sighed.

"You are a hopeless fool, Shadow," he said to himself, "a hopeless fool."

The night came quickly that day as I sat in my study, reading through a few books about dragons and other wars of the past. I became interested in the dragon hierarchy after hearing Shadow speak of it earlier. I made a mental note to ask more about it during our dinner.

Feeling my hunger, I went to my room to tidy up before heading to Shadow's house. I found the bundle of bloodied clothes and huffed. I'd forgotten to burn them. I remembered how Jack stared at me when he found the fox blood on my hand, and I frowned; he better not have said anything to Shadow.

You *should tell Shadow*, I thought.

I shook the thought from my mind. I lied to him in the last set of letters about the blackouts. Shadow already had too much going on with the war. I didn't need him to be concerned about me on top of everything else.

I decided not to change out of my dress and instead fixed my braid and ribbon. I found my black cloak, wrapped it around my shoulders, and fastened it with a silver vine brooch.

Stepping out into the night, I moved the hood atop my head so that it cast a shadow over part of my face. I didn't have it in me to deal with hateful comments tonight. It was bad enough that my dhampir senses heightened after the sun set; I needed to keep control of the leash now more than ever.

Taking a more discreet way to Shadow's house, I looked to the sky to admire the stars. I always enjoyed piecing them together to create symbols and faces. Talisa used to join me when I still lived in her cottage. We'd spend countless hours making our own little puzzle in the sky. Sometimes she'd tell me stories about the stars and how the goddesses lived among them. The realm of Eolande, she called it. The ones that shone brighter than the rest, she'd say, represented the sacred sisters themselves—they thought we should see their happiness from the ground and follow their example with our own lives.

I smiled at the memories. I missed those days.

Shadow's house was within sight, and I sped up. He lived far from the main square of Ellewynth. He preferred being close to the city borders so that he might retreat to the more open areas of the forest whenever he wished. I wanted a home near the boundaries for the same reason, but Talisa and Shadow wouldn't hear of it; they wanted me to integrate more with the people of the realm.

A lot of good *that* did.

I reached the door and knocked. I heard footsteps quicken on the other side, and I smiled when Shadow opened the door. He'd tidied up a bit himself; his hair was fully pulled back into a long tail with a ribbon, and he had changed into a darker tunic.

"You're a bit early, my dear," Shadow greeted me.

"I was getting stir-crazy." I winked.

He moved aside for me to enter and held out an arm for my cloak. I scowled at him for being too proper, but I surrendered and handed him my cloak after I was met with a sarcastic stare.

"Am I interrupting one of your errands?" I asked.

"No, I'm done with those for the day." Shadow led me into the main room, and I sat on one of the cloth chairs. "Talisa sends her love, by the way. She promised to see you sometime tomorrow."

"Always a tease, she is." I laughed. "Wait, does that mean you already spoke to her about Jack?"

"Yes." Shadow handed over a glass of wine and sat across from me. "Despite the cost it took on my end, she has agreed to an apprenticeship. She wants to meet with him tomorrow to discuss it."

"Wonderful! And yet, there goes another friend." I sighed. "It'll be good for him though. Maybe it'll help him ease up on the drinking."

"How did it get so out of hand?" he asked, taking his own glass of wine.

"His aunt is dreadful," I started. "It wouldn't surprise me if she herself had first supplied the alcohol to him. Jack has his moments where he drives me to the edge, but I know he can't help his jester nature. It's his manner of defense…to keep sane. He's only seen as a monster by his aunt, so he runs away to the taverns with her coin and drinks to forget the harsh memories she continues to add to. I force him to use the spare room to sleep in because I know he's at least safe with me rather than lying face down on the dirt for others to step on."

"You're a good friend, Artemis."

"I try." I took another sip of the sweet, light wine. "I'll have less to worry about now that Jack will be under Talisa's care."

"Well, you may want to worry *more* now that he'll be Talisa's apprentice." Shadow chuckled. "He's going to have to endure quite a bit these next few years. If Jack can last for more than that, then he'll be considered worthy enough to be called her student."

"His life *is* hers then." I laughed uncertainly. I lightly smacked the armrest after a realization. "Ugh! So much for his chase of Lilith!"

"Ah, so I've been told."

I raised an eyebrow. "You have?"

"I have. Jack was asking me for advice." Shadow stood up and smirked. "Apparently he needed a male point of view, since he had plenty from the female end of the situation."

I stood up as well, frowning at his jest. "Very funny."

"I try."

Shadow led the way out of the main room and into the dining room. There was plenty of food for the both of us on the cherrywood table, and I tried not to rush to the seat; I was hungrier than I first realized. It was comforting to know that I was hungry for *real* food. The blessing of being a dhampir was that I could eat what others could; the curse was that I still needed to drink blood in order to keep up my strength. My refusal to drink blood more than I already do made me weaker, but I did not care. I always wondered how Mother lived with the vampire's curse.

Once Shadow reached his chair, I sat down and quickly took a plate, filling it completely. Shadow was amused at my actions while he took his time choosing his own food. "I wasn't sure if you'd had your 'other' source of sustenance, so I left that well alone."

I couldn't help but shake after that statement. I silently cursed, because I knew Shadow caught the action.

"It's not necessary," I said after a moment's silence.

Shadow watched me carefully.

"Because you already had it," he stated. "Jack informed me about your increasing blackouts."

I cringed.

"I do not drink as often as I should," I started, "and I don't intend to unless I have no other choice."

"That's not wise, Artemis."

"Leave it be, Shadow."

"You are *not* a monster, Artemis," Shadow insisted. "You need to accept what you are. You've only killed foxes…for now. The more you restrain your natural urges, the more they will struggle to take over. There are safer and less complicated ways to deal with this. You know this, my dear."

"I'll say it again, Shadow," I warned. "*Leave it be.*"

Shadow shook his head before taking a bit of fruit from his plate. I was grateful for him backing off. I then remembered an earlier part of our conversation. "What exactly did it cost you for Talisa to become Jack's teacher?"

It was now Shadow's turn to be uncomfortable. "She earns the right to collect on favors I have no choice but to perform. She prefers calling them favors rather than demands."

"Of course she does." Laughing while taking a few grapes, I asked, "Did she at least tell you what they were?"

"I only know of one," he answered. "For the rest, I'll just have to wait and be surprised."

"What is the one you do know of?"

Shadow grew silent, and I felt a twinge of anger from him; I felt uneasy.

"Apologies. You don't have to answer that."

"No need to feel sorry," he said, now smiling again. He rubbed the back of his neck. "I'm just a bit agitated because I've finally returned home after all these years and my plans of rest are interrupted yet again by the Elders."

I felt my heart drop. "Are you being sent away again?"

"No, no," Shadow reassured. I breathed a sigh of relief. "However, Talisa was asked to scout a disturbance that's been occurring near her cottage."

"What sort of disturbance?"

"According to the Elders, there has been an odd string of deaths and attacks within the Woodland Realm. The range has now extended near her cottage."

I shuddered at the thought. "Any suspects?"

Shadow's face darkened. "Full-bloods."

I nearly dropped my wine.

Full-bloods. One half of my heritage. Most of them were red-haired with matching color eyes, and if they did not have it at birth, their eyes would turn scarlet the moment their bloodlust set in. They cannot survive in the sunlight; I never had the problem due to my human half. I heard tales from Jack that full-bloods could turn others into one of them…they needed to be human, however. He probably told me why that was, but I could not recall the rest of that memory. I did have a habit of tuning him out when he was in what I usually referred to as his "scholar mode." I should have paid better attention.

Avilyne's hell…what were they doing here?

"I pray it's not the case," Shadow continued as he sipped his wine and ate more from of his plate. "I don't intend to be sent out to fight for a long time, either. I earned my time to be home."

"What if the full-bloods *are* behind it?" I asked. "What then?"

"Then the regiment will most likely be dispatched again to defend the realm, depending on how dire the situation is."

He barely flinched as I pounded the table with my fist.

"Unbelievable!" I snapped. "Will there not be any moment of peace?"

"There will always be a war, Artemis," Shadow said, his tone sad. "It's only a matter of who the opponent is, and when and where the battles will take place."

"If I could, I'd fight with you," I said. "I'm sick of sitting around."

"You've skipped out on weapons training for far too long, my dear," Shadow pointed out. "Unless you choose to accept your dhampir nature, you would only be hindering the regiment. There's only so much protection Talisa and I could give you."

"Ask me if I care."

Shadow rubbed his chin, and a wolfish grin formed. "Do you truly wish to learn how to fight?"

"Of course I do!" I reiterated. "I refuse to be helpless, Shadow."

"It can be arranged, you know."

"Oh? You know of a good enough teacher who won't hate me at first glance?"

"Oh yes. I know of one who will even put your old teachers to shame."

"And just who would that be, pray tell?"

Shadow folded his arms and beamed. "Me, of course."

After our long dinner I said my farewell to Shadow and returned to the discreet path. I should have kept my mouth shut about my desire of learning to fight again. While it was true that Shadow could put my old teachers to shame when it came to any sort of weapons training, it was also true that I'd rather have Serlene as my teacher again before letting him near me with a sword or bow. There was a reason he was feared in battle.

I should have felt grateful, but shame overpowered it. He wouldn't approve of my lackadaisical method of fighting.

Not one bit.

I saw my home and felt calm again. It was short-lived, as I heard something stumble through the bushes. I raised my guard, and I tip-toed around the bushes to find the source of the noise. Once I grew close, I raised my hand for a striking motion and stopped when I recognized the body falling face first to the ground inches away from my feet.

I groaned, as I was staring at the drunken body of dear old Jack, who looked far worse than he had this morning.

"Jack...Oh, Jack..." I sighed while nudging him with the tip of my foot. "Have we had another long night at the tavern?"

Jack struggled to move himself. Raising his head, he cast a stupid grin from his dirt-clod-covered face.

"Ar-Artemish!" he cried, trying with great effort to stand. "Howwonderful...t-to shee you out here inthish loferly night."

"Avilyne's hell." I rolled my eyes and grabbed his arm to hoist him to his feet. "Unbelievable."

"I...I thought youwent to dinnerat Shadow'sh houshe." Jack let out a belch, making me wrinkle my nose at the acrid smell. "Howish your... yourlofe anywaysh?"

I swallowed the urge to smack him and begged the goddesses for patience. Grabbing his arm once more, I wrenched him inside the house and cast off my cloak. Jack fell onto the cushioned chair in the main room and started giggling.

I hated the person he was when he was drunk.

I rushed to the washroom and unhinged one of the wooden boards from the floor; every elven house in the Woodland Realm had a series of wells beneath it. I filled the washtub with the bucket I kept in the room and grabbed a few washcloths. Casting them to the floor, I went back to the main room for Jack. He grinned as soon as he saw me, but scowled once I gripped his shoulder. In his current state, he couldn't feel the pain a normal person would; I had to grip just hard enough to remind him that he could.

While I led him to the washroom, Jack started whining.

"Artemish...easheup won't you?" he begged. "I'm vefy much...vefy much..."

"Just shut up," I snapped.

"That'shnot necesshary atall, Artemish!" Jack answered, his legs buckling as we walked.

I ignored the rest of his drunken speech as I flung him into the tub. Jack's head snapped to the surface, and he spat Elvish curses at me.

"Shut up before I drown you, idiot!" I threatened, now grabbing his arms and shoving him under the water another time.

"Shtopit!" Jack yelled, while trying to fight me off. "I haf much left-tolif for, damn you!"

Shoving him under the water again, I grabbed him by his loose, soaked hair and forced him to look at me once I pulled him back up.

"Listen to me, you stupid, ungrateful elf," I growled. "You *have* to stop this. I won't always be around to help you, so either you let this be your last night of stupidity or you find someone else to care for your life. I don't give a damn how bad your aunt is to you; be a man! Move out! Take better care of yourself, damn you!"

Jack blinked, and I saw his eyes well up with tears. I sighed as I let him go and allowed him to rest his head on my now soaked shoulder. Loud sobs pounded my eardrums.

"I-I-I'm shoshorry, Artemish," he whispered through his sobs.

"I know." I rubbed his head. "I know, Jack."

Grabbing the washcloths, I wrapped them around Jack as I helped him out of the tub. Leading him to the spare bedroom, I handed him a set of robes he left for whenever he slept over, took the wet clothes from him as he finished changing, and hung them by the window to dry. I tucked him into the bed, and he passed out soon after.

Satisfied that he was still breathing, I made my way to my own room and changed into my nightgown. Releasing my hair from both braid and ribbon, I slid into bed and rubbed my temples. I prayed to the goddesses for a deep sleep to alleviate the headache I now had.

"It can only get more interesting from here on out..." I groaned, shifting beneath the blankets before letting sleep take me.

4

I was running in an unfamiliar part of the woods—far from the borders of Ellewynth, but recognizable enough to be the Woodland Realm. I was clutching a heavy bundled blanket close to my chest; I kept fighting away tears, but without much success. My back ached, and I smelled something both sweet and metallic; blood lingered in the air.

I heard others move in the distance. I was being chased. The scent of blood grew stronger with each stride I took, and I was horrified once I realized the blood was my own. I forced myself to stop running after feeling my chest grow so heavy. I held the bundle in one arm and rubbed my back with the other.

I cursed when I felt blood soak into my tunic sleeve.

The bundle shifted violently as soon as my bloodied arm clasped it; it growled.

"Please be patient, my love," I pleaded. "We're almost to safety."

I was stunned to hear that the voice was not my own; it was softer and…older. What in Avilyne's hell what was going on?

I shifted a part of the blanket, and I looked at a tiny face that seemed oddly familiar. Small hazel eyes brightened the moment they fixated on me; wisps of light brown hair curled atop the pale-skinned head of what I finally realized was an infant.

I tried moving closer to the baby, until I felt a searing pain in my right shoulder, causing me to scream.

I shot up from bed, my hand instantly grabbing my right shoulder. There was no pain, no sensation of blood loss. My nightgown clung to my body in warm sweat, and I sighed in relief, realizing it was only a dream.

Lying back down, I saw it was still night. The moonlight poured through the open window and onto my blankets. The face of the infant wouldn't escape my mind, even when I shut my eyes.

Nerves flared once the realization set in—*I* was the infant. There was no other explanation for it. It also meant that because the infant was indeed me, the person I embodied in the dream was my mother.

She was the one hurt; *she* was the one running while trying to protect me.

"Tamina…" I whispered as I curled beneath the blankets, bringing my knees to my chest. "Mother…help me understand. Help me understand it all."

~

Shadow wandered onto the balcony connected to his bedroom; he was in yet another battle with nightmares. It was one of the unfortunate prices of being a soldier: now and then, he could see the faces of those he had slaughtered not only in the recent war, but in the other battles he'd fought in his lifetime. He learned to ignore most, but some faces managed to break through the barrier and cause the dark dreams. The worst ones had the faces of those he loved and befriended who died in those wars.

"Almost two centuries old…" Shadow cursed, his hand balling into a fist atop the wooden railing, "and you still let them haunt you. *All* of them."

He eventually released his grip. He stared out toward the darkness of the forest and remembered his conversation with Talisa. The part concerning the full-bloods angered him.

What purpose did they have here in the realm? Why bring attention to themselves now? Unless…

"Willow be damned," Shadow cursed as he headed back into the room.

He rummaged among his trunks for his scouting cloak, as well as warmer clothing to travel into the night with.

After he changed into them, he went to his study and grabbed a sheathed elven blade. Pulling the blade from the sheath, Shadow stared at the odd glyphs engraved within the sleek-shaped steel. It was given to him by his long-deceased father, Lord Trystan. It was one of the rare gifts his father had ever given him, and Shadow was never without the sword in war or in scouting missions. Shadow reached for a small bow and a quiver of arrows, and he also made sure to grab a set of reins and a saddle from his stable.

Shadow marched on to the wilderness borders and softly whistled into the night. Stopping, he heard a comforting neigh of a horse and smiled as a large white mare entered his line of sight. The mare eased her trotting as she neared her master; her coat glistened like a jewel in the moonlight, and her golden eyes showed slight irritation. Shadow laughed apologetically while setting the saddle and reins upon her.

"Apologizes, Azrael," he began as his hand gently moved along her neck. "I know it is late, but I wouldn't have called unless it was urgent."

Azrael snorted her disapproval.

"Yes, yes. Once we return from this, I promise to give you the rest you deserve," Shadow pledged as he climbed atop her. "We ride to Talisa's cottage. Once we reach it, I must leave you behind. This is one adventure where I cannot risk your injury if you accompanied me the entire way."

Azrael snorted again, but more in understanding than annoyance. Shadow rubbed her neck once more and gave his thanks as they rode out.

On horseback, Talisa's cottage was half a day away, but Azrael was no mere horse. She had come to Shadow before he set out for his first war; her presence and unusual span of life suggested she was a gift to him from the goddess of earth and the patron of the Woodland Realm, Willow—a gift to help him survive all that was to come. None rivaled Azrael's speed; they would reach Talisa's cottage in moments.

Azrael slowed her galloping once the cottage was in sight. Stopping beside the wooden gate, Shadow dismounted and led her to Talisa's stable. He knew the witch wouldn't mind, especially since he was fulfilling the first of her many favors.

As he patted her one last time, Azrael whinnied. Shadow shook his head.

"I can't, old friend," he said. "I need you here."

Azrael lowered her golden eyes in defeat and pushed his shoulder with her head. Shadow chuckled as he rubbed her neck.

"Yes, I promise to keep safe as well." Reaching the door of the stable, he looked back one last time. "I'll return soon. Behave yourself."

Shutting the stable door as quietly as possible, Shadow shifted the hood of his cloak atop his head and treaded carefully past the cottage. He stilled all thoughts and concentrated on the "music" of the forest. It was said that elves could sometimes hear the voices of the forest itself, but only if they listened hard enough.

After hearing something that did not fit with the environment, Shadow dashed farther into the darkness and found a large ash tree to climb. Satisfied after finding a decent observational post, Shadow peered into the darkness of the forest.

While surveying the grove of ash trees, he spotted traces of blood along the bark of the trees across from him. He just missed a disturbance.

Or so he thought.

Shadow sensed a presence that did not belong in the forest; the aura he felt was undeniably dark. He steadied his stance along the tree branch, and then flinched just barely when a bloodied body fell onto the ground, not far from his tree. Two figures dashed toward the carcass; he heard heavy breathing and the sickening crunch of breaking bones. There was no doubt in his mind that they were vampires. He watched as they feasted on the corpse.

Shadow dared not move lest he give away his position. A vampire's hearing was just as acute as an elf's, and they were far swifter on foot. Looking closely, Shadow recognized the corpse as one of his race; the face was mangled beyond recognition, but he could still see the perfectly pointed ears. Shadow felt his pulse quicken.

He heard a twig snap, and his attention shifted to a new figure that entered the area. Shadow studied it closely and recognized it to be female. Her red hair was unbound, resting atop her shoulders, and she wore a long black leather coat over black clothing. Such a fashion was common among vampire kind. A sheathed short sword hung from her waist, but it seemed as if it were more for show; the woman looked as if she could defend herself well without it. Her dark brown eyes narrowed at her companions, showing disgust.

"Enough," she declared. "Show some respect for the departed."

The figures above the elf separated, and Shadow noted the two were male. They too wore long black coats and black clothing. They did not appear to have any weapons—none that he could see. Their long red hair was bound, unlike that of the woman, and their pale faces were splashed with the elf's now dark blood. The irises of their eyes were red, the sign of a full-blood's bloodlust, along with the elongated fangs.

One of them laughed.

"Mistress Netira," another one of them mocked, bowing dramatically. "To what do we owe the honor of your presence?"

"Indeed!" the first who laughed began, while licking the blood along his lips and clawed fingertips. "Do you care for the sweet, honeyed blood of the elvenkind? It'd be a shame to waste the opportunity."

The one they called Netira moved forward, and she bent to inspect the body they'd gorged on. She kept silent as she rose, and she smacked the nearest vampire hard across the face. She drew her sword and pointed it at the other's throat, keeping him at bay.

"Fools! You bring us unwanted attention!" Netira yelled. "The elves will no doubt investigate and learn that full-bloods now dare to enter their territory."

"Still your nerves, Netira," the one she had smacked said, rising to his feet. "Mistress Arlina ordered us to move within the elven borders. Did you not know this?"

Netira shifted the point of her sword to the other's throat. "Be silent! You disgrace the full-bloods of Blackwen City with your sloppy hunting! If this starts a war, may Avilyne herself stop me from beheading you both."

"Let there be a war," he retorted. "More blood for me."

Before the other full-blood could add to his comrade's comments, Netira swung her sword and beheaded him. The other full-blood was stricken; he hadn't expected it at all.

Shadow shut his eyes momentarily. This did not bode well at all for the woodland elves.

"It appears Avilyne did not favor him." Netira twirled her sword and watched the blood fly off the blade. She glanced at the remaining full-blood and pointed the sword at him again. "You will tell me why the Mistress sent you here or you'll share his fate."

The full-blood gulped and twitched nervously. "M-Mistress Arlina sent for us to scout the elven lands and to listen to their words. I don't know what we were supposed to listen for exactly. We weren't to return until we felt we gathered enough observations worth reporting back."

"How long were you stationed here for?" Netira demanded.

Shadow grew wary as he watched her irises shift color. They weren't turning red, but silver. No full-blood was known to carry that trait; it was one carried only by dhampirs.

"For nearly two full moonturns."

Shadow gripped his bow in anger at these words.

He watched as Netira mirrored his frustrations. Shadow rubbed his eyes, as he swore that Netira's jacket was growing bigger.

"The two of you didn't think to feed on animals rather than the elvenkind while stationed here?" she berated him. "You two jeopardized the safety of our city because you could not keep your bloodlust in check!"

"Apologies, Netira," the full-blood murmured. Then he folded his arms in defiance. "Enlighten me, though. How do you think the Mistress would take the news that her Second not only ran off on her own, but is also a dhampir in disguise?"

Netira shut her eyes for a moment. Upon opening them, she swung her sword and beheaded the remaining full-blood. Ignoring the defiant stare of the dismembered head that was aimed toward her, she wiped the blade along the earth and sheathed it.

"Avilyne's hell...I forgot the damned charm. He'll be pissed."

She sighed as she piled the bodies together and held out a hand. Shadow was amazed as it glowed a bright shade of orange, and the bodies ignited in flame.

Netira removed her jacket, revealing large black wings similar to those of a bat.

"If Arlina keeps this up…" Netira said to herself as she watched the bodies burn, "then the city will truly be damned."

Damned, Shadow thought to himself. *I thought it already was. What is going on over there?*

Netira shook her head and suddenly looked fatigued. Shadow realized Netira did not control natural magic. Those who could did not tire so easily. Before he could speculate further, she spoke again. "It's time. I can't stand by and let the possible destruction of my home happen." Looking once more at the fire, Netira lowered her head. "May the next life serve you better than this one did, elf. This was the least I could do."

Shadow watched her disappear into the darkness. When he couldn't sense her presence any longer, he jumped from the branch and inspected the ash from the fire. Shadow shut his eyes and muttered an elven prayer of passage for the fallen elf. After he finished, he ran back to Talisa's cottage and met with Azrael.

Riding away from the cottage and back to his home, Shadow felt his uneasiness grow. He knew of Blackwen City; it was the largest known full-blood settlement in the world of Arrygn. And yet, a dhampir lived there, obviously in secret, and was unlike the full-bloods she pretended to be. He wondered what this charm of hers was…perhaps it was how she masked her true nature to the others. She had said "he" before, so perhaps she did know a person of magic.

Shadow also knew the Mistress of Blackwen, Arlina Ravenwing. She was Tamina's younger sister…and aunt to Artemis. If what he suspected was true, then not only was the Woodland Realm in danger, but also Artemis.

He couldn't let anything happen to her. No, he *wouldn't* let anything happen to her.

Warmth crept along my face; it was morning. I pulled the blankets over my head, hoping to return to the deep lull of slumber, but it was no use.

Groaning, I moved out of bed and sluggishly looked around for a ribbon. Eventually finding one atop my desk, I tied it along a half-assed braid and walked to the spare room to check on Jack.

Jack wasn't in bed; he was sitting along the windowsill, with his arm hanging from one arched leg and the other leg dangling from the window. He turned and acknowledged my presence with a small nod. Jack slid over for me to join him, and I sat down.

He continued watching the trees rather than meeting my gaze. I knew he felt too guilty to look at me.

"Jack…" I started.

Jack sighed. "I'm fine, Artemis."

"Do you remember last night?"

"Sadly, yes." Jack frowned, still not facing me. "And you're right, you know. I let this get out of control. I keep running away when I should defend myself against that sorry excuse for kin."

"Why can't you just leave?"

Jack finally looked at me, saddened.

"Same as you, Artemis. I don't have anywhere else to go. I'm not brave enough to leave on my own," he answered. "You're a good person, you know. It's a shame the others can't see it. I…I just can't keep coming here and force you to play nursemaid to me. It's not fair to you, nor to our friendship."

"You're always welcome here, you know that," I reassured him. "You know I worry too much about you when you pull these stunts."

"I'm aware of that." Jack chuckled. "Such a worrywart."

"Maybe your apprenticeship with Talisa will help you," I said, nudging him with my elbow.

Jack shuddered. "*If* I get it." He rubbed his arms to get rid of the forming goosebumps. "If I manage to survive this, I won't deny that I'll be drinking a hell of a lot more. Solely for celebratory purposes, mind you."

I patted his back, smirking. Jack grew confused.

"What's with the smile, you evil woman?" he asked, alarmed. "What do you know?"

"Talisa accepted you as her apprentice," I answered, without bothering to hide a smile.

Jack was horrified.

"Wh-what?" he yelled as he jumped off the windowsill. "Lies!"

"Shadow informed me over dinner," I explained. "This means you owe him, by the way. He has to play servant to Talisa whenever she desires."

Jack rubbed his head, stunned. "I'm...I'm afraid, and yet...I can't help but feel excited."

"Now there's the masochistic elf I know and love," I teased. "You *should* be excited! You'll finally get to learn all the magic you've always wanted to! Talisa might even enjoy the 'scholar mode.'"

"I know!" Jack beamed as he returned to sit along the windowsill. His smile warped into a frown. "Oh...I apologize for the tease about Shadow last night."

"I've forgiven you already. I know you have less control than usual when you're drunk."

"And how was dinner with him?"

"It was...interesting." I frowned when I noticed Jack's inquiring glance. "You have a terrible mind sometimes, you know that? I made the mistake of telling him I wanted to return to weapons training."

Jack snorted. "Shame, shame."

"I know," I said. I then explained the possibility of full-bloods venturing into the realm's borders. Jack rubbed his chin and smirked. "What?"

"Good thing Shadow will be teaching you to fight," he said. "You'll need all the help you can get. Pure hatred of them won't be enough."

"Don't act as if you wouldn't fight alongside me if the chance came." I pointed a teasing finger at him. "You wouldn't dare pass up the chance to fight with magic."

"True enough." Jack looked out to the trees again. "When do the lessons start for you?"

"I don't know," I admitted. "I imagine Shadow will drag me out when it's time."

"Talisa will most likely do the same for me," Jack said, growing fearful again. "Make sure she doesn't throw away my soul once I sell it to her, will you? I'll deal with the physical abuse...but I rather like my soul."

I nodded. "Your soul will be just fine."

I spent most of the day lying on the grass outside of the house, staring at the clouds. I was thinking of the dream about Mother; the sudden dream along with the idea of full-bloods hiding within the realm couldn't have been a coincidence. It felt as if something had been trying to unfold since the soldiers returned from the war, and the evil behind it felt far worse than that of turncoat dragons and wizards.

I couldn't get rid of the feeling that somehow *I* would be involved in the next big fight that was to come, and I assumed the dreams would continue. Perhaps it would also explain the increasing amount of black-outs lately...

My thoughts were interrupted by Jack's snoring; he was lying close by. He had gone home to change and returned soon after. Jack had walked out on his aunt, who, as usual, was yelling at him. She yelled at him simply for living.

As much as I wished he would release his anger toward her, I didn't blame him for wishing to avoid her for the remainder of the day. He was too nervous about his coming meeting with Talisa and discussing his future with her. Once he officially became her apprentice, I knew I wouldn't see Jack as often as I did now. I laughed to myself once I realized I would actually miss his daily intrusions and complaints.

I thought about the dream once more and gnawed on my lower lip. I knew I had to talk to Shadow about it; the coincidence of it was not something I could ignore. I thought it was time he told me the whole truth about my mother's death.

"Why is this coming now?" I said aloud, frowning.

"Everything happens for a reason, you know."

I quickly sat up once I heard the familiar voice. Jack's eyes snapped open and he shot up; he too knew the voice well enough.

Standing up and looking behind us, Jack and I were now facing Talisa. Her signature dark blue, pointed, wide-brimmed hat sat atop her long black hair streaked with white. She wore a sleeveless, dark blue robe, one of the many indicators of one in service to Kiare, and it made her fair skin stand out. Talisa blinked her cool gray eyes while smiling.

I leaped and hugged her hard.

"It's so good to see you again, Talisa!" I exclaimed, pulling away from the embrace.

"The sentiment is shared, Artemis." She rubbed a part of my cheek, just as she used to when I was a child.

It was strange now, standing eye to eye with her when I was so used to looking up to the witch. It was just another reminder that too much time had passed by.

Talisa looked over my shoulder and raised an inquiring eyebrow. She was staring at Jack; I could feel his nerves from where I stood.

"You remember Jack, right?" I fetched him to stand beside me.

I shot him a glance to tell him to calm himself.

"Indeed I do," Talisa said, now folding her arms. "You've grown quite a bit as well."

"Y-Yes, it's certainly been a while." Jack nervously laughed. "Talisa. Miss Talisa! Uh—"

Talisa strode beside him and gripped his shoulder, causing Jack to flinch. She laughed while I resisted the urge to scowl at him.

"I see my reputation precedes me." She cast a mischievous smile. "Good. It means you know what lies before you as my apprentice. And 'Talisa' will be just fine. 'Master' just seems far too controlling."

"Don't kill him, Talisa," I teased. "He's one of the few friends I actually have."

"Oh, I won't," Talisa replied, her smile growing as she slapped Jack's back. "I've been convinced that Jack here will prove to be someone of worth. I do have to steal him for a bit, however. You understand, of course."

"Of course." I nodded. "I'll be in my home preparing tea for you."

Talisa tipped the brim of her hat in thanks, and then dragged Jack along with her. Jack looked over his shoulder, terrified. He mouthed the words "help me," and I shook my head. I motioned for him to stop worrying and returned to my home to prepare Talisa's favorite tea.

5

$\mathcal{S}$hadow stopped once he reached the Hall of the Elders. It stood tall in the grove of oak trees, with ornate vines and flowers carved within the woodwork. The bell tower atop it housed three large bells that played only in times of celebration or attack. Shadow prayed he wouldn't have to hear the bells of danger for a very long time.

As he stepped inside, he was greeted with cool air and a mixed scent of brewed teas. A servant greeted him and bade him sit on the benches in the main room. The benches were carved within the walls, with intricate decorations similar to the outside of the hall; the carvings were plated silver.

"With whom do you desire a word, Master Shadow?" the servant asked, while keeping her head low to avoid eye contact.

"Preferably all three Elders," Shadow answered.

The servant now glanced at him, shocked.

"A-All three?"

"Yes."

"But…but o-only o-o-one is here at the moment…perhaps if you would like for m-me to leave a message?"

Shadow suppressed a sigh. The poor girl must have been overworked during the Eelders' absence. That, or she hadn't been around long enough to understand certain protocols and had recently learned the various temperaments each Elder possessed.

"That won't be necessary," Shadow answered, wishing the servant would calm down. "Who is currently in office?"

"The Lady Clarayne, Master Shadow." The servant rubbed the sweat off her brow and composed herself. "I'll see if she'll grant you audience."

"Thank you."

Shadow watched the servant disappear into one of three doors that led to the offices of the Elders. Each door had silver-plated carvings, and the center of each had a different flower that represented the identity of each Elder. The door that led to Lady Clarayne was marked with a rose. It amused him whenever he saw her door.

Moments later, the servant appeared from the door and bade him to follow her. Walking into the room, he heard the door shut and he looked around the study. A large ashen desk was in the center of the office with a large stack of parchment sheets and inkwells resting atop it; bookcases lined the walls, and above one bookcase hung an aged elven blade.

The soft sound of a throat clearing drew Shadow's attention to the window ahead of him; Lady Clarayne had her back to him, as she was window-gazing. She wore a white elven gown with sleeves draped nearly to the ground, and her long, dark blond hair was hanging freely along her back and shoulders; a small silver leaf-and-vine circlet rested atop her hair.

Turning around, Shadow was met with an amused stare that emanated from green eyes like his own. Her skin wasn't as tanned as his, but she flashed a smirk that Shadow often sported. Shadow bowed his head, and Lady Clarayne scoffed.

"There's no need for formalities in private meetings, my dear Shadow." Lady Clarayne laughed, taking a long stride toward him. "I trust you won't object to a hug from your aunt?"

"I do not." Shadow chuckled as he received her warm embrace. "If Uncle were alive today, I think he would be horrified his personal name for you had transformed into your war emblem."

"Perhaps he would. I think he would forgive me seeing as it's a way of keeping a piece of him with me on the battlefield," Lady Clarayne replied as she pulled away. Shadow grew nervous as she stared at the exact spot that hid the chain with Artemis' ring. "I will admit, dear nephew, I didn't expect to see you for a while. I know you wanted to enjoy the peace we've all earned from this ordeal."

"I intended to," Shadow began as he took a seat opposite her desk. Lady Clarayne poured tea for the both of them and took her seat across from him. "However, I fear something is brewing outside the city borders...something far more unpleasant."

"Oh?" Lady Clarayne raised an eyebrow. "What brings you to that thought?"

"There have been a number of odd deaths occurring near Talisa's cottage," Shadow explained.

"Yes, we're aware of that." She spoke, and then took a sip of tea. "We sent a messenger to Talisa yesterday for her to investigate and report her findings."

"*I* went to investigate," Shadow answered. He saw her puzzlement and sighed. "Don't ask."

He remembered Netira and decided to exclude her from his report. She was a mystery he wanted to solve on his own. "Full-bloods are responsible for the deaths, Aunt Clarayne."

She nearly dropped her teacup. "You cannot be serious."

"I wish it weren't true, but I know what I saw...as well as overheard."

Lady Clarayne stood from her chair and quickly paced the office. "I must speak with Lords Celstian and Destrius about this. We hoped it was something else...something less threatening..."

"It gets worse," Shadow continued. "The full-bloods specifically belong to Arlina Ravenwing of Blackwen City. She is behind their sudden bravery of venturing into our realm."

Lady Clarayne's eyes widened. "You don't think..."

"I fear she has learned that Artemis is alive and has been living among us." Shadow put his teacup atop the desk. "If it is true, she will first send an emissary demanding we hand Artemis to her. We cannot do that."

"And if that were to happen and we do not hand Artemis over, you realize more elven lives will be at risk, Shadow," Lady Clarayne explained. "It's not a position I or the other Elders can afford to be in."

"Elven lives will be at risk regardless of what we do!" Shadow stood up. "She'll kill Artemis just as she slaughtered Tamina, and then she'll attack Ellewynth for her own pleasure! You *know* she will. You remember what she's done to us already."

"Of course I do," Lady Clarayne said as her face darkened. "I understand all the possibilities, Shadow, and I know how Arlina thinks. You must realize, nephew, that the choice will not be yours to make in the end."

"I understand, but that does not mean I have to like it." Shadow took a deep breath. "My dear aunt, you cannot let Lords Celstian and Destrius sway you into giving her up to that woman. Please."

Lady Clarayne sighed as she rubbed her nephew's cheek. "Shadow…"

"*Please.*"

Lady Clarayne sighed in resignation.

"I will talk to them once they return." She dropped her hand and returned to the window. "That is all I can promise."

Shadow took this as a dismissal and proceeded to the door.

"Shadow?"

He stopped, but did not turn to face her. "Yes, my lady?"

"Should the moment come and we do hand over Artemis to Arlina… will I be losing a nephew as well?"

Shadow shut his eyes and closed the door behind him as he left the room.

~♮~

I was nearly done preparing Talisa's favorite brand of tea—lemon mint—when she and Jack returned inside from their "meeting." Jack wasn't as pale as he had been before, but he still seemed horrified.

I couldn't help but laugh.

"Jack, even specters have a cheerier disposition than you do right now!" I said while pouring tea.

"Don't be surprised if I end up as one the next time you see me," Jack muttered while grabbing his teacup.

Talisa smiled, obviously content.

"When does the training begin?" I asked.

Jack kept quiet, while Talisa took a long sip of her tea.

"Well?"

"Tonight," Jack finally answered.

I nearly spit out my tea. "What?"

"Tonight marks the full moon of the solstice," Talisa explained. "Magic is most potent at this time. I want to see how well Jack can use his gift. Then, and only then, will I know how to begin his tutelage."

"It's also to make sure I don't go running off to the taverns," Jack added. "As for the aunt..."

"I will be dealing with her soon enough," Talisa said, as her fingers playfully tapped along the table. "You belong to me now. Only I am allowed to abuse you."

Jack cringed while I tried to stifle a cackle. His dream of learning the greatest kinds of magic was coming at a great price indeed.

I'd never seen Talisa be so sinister either. I was lucky to have seen the nice side while I lived with her.

"Well, once he's free from your apprenticeship, he'll belong to Shadow." I smirked, while shaking the thought of a scary Talisa. "You owe him for this."

"Yes, I haven't forgotten," Jack grumbled.

Talisa chuckled. "Ah, that reminds me! I have to come up with more favors to collect from our dear warrior elf. I wonder how many years I can stretch these favors for..."

"That's terrible, Talisa." An idea, however, came to mind. "Could one perhaps be for him to go easy on me during my weapons training?"

"Oh goddesses, Artemis!" Talisa scowled. "You need all the help you can get. Don't think I haven't heard about you skipping out on your lessons." I cringed. "Serlene would never shut up about it. Better for Shadow to be your instructor than me! It wouldn't matter who your mother was, Artemis. I would have you train without sleep!"

"You do know she shot an elf, right?" Jack asked.

"Oh, I heard. It's one of Serlene's favorite rants." Talisa snorted. "A shame it wasn't her. She's in a desperate need of a lesson in humility, and Serlene should learn the appreciation of silence as well."

Jack laughed. "I can agree with that assessment."

"You shush!" Talisa snapped. "Never speak ill of your previous teachers. No matter how terrible or bothersome they could be, you must still respect the time they've given as instructors."

"But Talisa—" I started.

"But nothing!" she said, now making *me* flinch. "Respect the time that was given. *Always.*"

"Of all the things I should be scolded about, it's about shooting that elf. Even Shadow overlooked it." I frowned.

Talisa rolled her eyes. "It was an accident. Get over it for goddess' sake."

Finishing her tea, Talisa deemed it time for her departure. She glanced at Jack, who hung his head and nodded soon after. Jack explained that it was time for Talisa to speak to his aunt and that he had to pack for the move to Talisa's cottage.

"I wish I could be there to see the old goat cringe." I smiled.

Jack laughed, but quickly stifled it as soon as Talisa shot him a look.

"Do visit, Artemis," Talisa said as she kissed my cheek good-bye. "I want to know all about your weapons training once it starts. Bruises and all."

"Be well until then, Talisa," I said.

I looked at Jack, and it set in: I was really going to miss seeing him on a daily basis. I tried to reassure him during a farewell hug. "You're going to be just fine. I'll visit soon, I promise."

"You better," Jack replied. "I'll haunt you for the rest of your days if you don't."

I slapped the back of his head, and he shrugged in mock innocence. As they left, I cleaned up and decided to visit the one friend I now had left in Ellewynth.

⌒

Lady Clarayne dismissed her servant some time after Shadow's visit. She didn't want the girl around once Lords Celstian and Destrius arrived at the hall—the girl was already bothersome, and the last thing Lady

Clarayne wanted was for the rest of the city to learn about the full-bloods squatting within the Woodland Realm.

Lady Clarayne heard the hall doors slam and felt tense. Lord Destrius was known for making a ruckus whenever he was around, and he made even more of a scene when angered. Oddly enough, it was perhaps the first time Lady Clarayne shared his sentiments.

"Honestly, Destrius, do you have to be so loud all the time?" a male voice scolded. "I'm sure Clarayne has a perfectly good explanation for summoning us back to the hall."

"I was perfectly fine sitting at home with my wife, Celstian!" Lord Destrius snapped. "Willow be damned, we've *just* returned! Avilyne's hell! Official business could wait until the morning for all I care."

Lady Clarayne rubbed her temples as her office door flung open. She glanced at the two Elders who stepped inside; Lord Celstian was the eldest of the three, but no one outside of the elven race would be able to make the distinction. His silvery blond hair hung past his shoulders, and he wore dark green robes that complemented his blue eyes.

Beside him stood Lord Destrius, the youngest of the trio. Lord Destrius was well known for his fiery temper, and while it worried most of the people in the Woodland Realm, he had proved himself worthy of the Elder status time and time again during times of war.

He stood at the door with an angered disposition; his dark blond hair was pulled away from his face, and he wore dark brown robes. His green eyes flared at Lady Clarayne.

"What is just *so* important that it couldn't wait until the morning, Clarayne?" Lord Destrius demanded. "As I recall, it was *you* who said you'd deal with the daily affairs while Celstian and I enjoyed our moment of peace."

"Yes, I'm aware of that, Destrius," Lady Clarayne began. "However, there is a very important matter that requires a discussion. And no, it couldn't wait until the morrow."

Lord Celstian made his way to one of the chairs opposite Lady Clarayne and sat down. His brow furrowed.

Lord Destrius huffed as he sat in the remaining chair. "Explain yourself, then."

Lady Clarayne rubbed her temples once more. "When we returned, we learned of odd disturbances occurring within the realm. They reached almost as close as Talisa's cottage."

"And we sent a messenger to Talisa to investigate," Lord Celstian stated. "Has she already done so?"

"Shadow was the one who went to investigate," Lady Clarayne explained.

"Soleil burn me," Lord Destrius muttered. "The boy takes after you, Clarayne. He doesn't know how to enjoy his spare time. He needs a woman."

"Shadow wanted to enjoy his freedom as much as the rest of us, Destrius," Lady Clarayne scolded, as she ignored the last comment. "I don't understand why he was the one who investigated instead of Talisa, but nonetheless, he arrived today with a brief report."

"And?" Lord Celstian inquired. "Judging from the urgency of your summons, it seems as if you believe we're entering a new battle."

"We very well may be." Lady Clarayne took a deep breath before continuing. "Full-bloods have been found responsible for these deaths."

The room went cold as the lords both shut their eyes and hung their heads.

"What do those damned corpses want with us now?" Lord Destrius hissed.

"Do we even know from which city or territory these particular full-bloods came from?" Lord Celstian inquired.

"Blackwen City, according to Shadow."

"And it just keeps getting better, doesn't it?" Lord Destrius roared, now rising from his chair. "We should have destroyed that city ages ago! We *had* that chance, and you two let it slip!"

"Destrius, you are well aware of why we couldn't do that then. You also know why we will not do so now," Lord Celstian reminded him. "We all well know how Arlina Ravenwing is. She hasn't ventured within the realm for nearly twenty-one years. We remember what happened then, yes? There can only be one reason why she's returned here now."

"Yes, Celstian, she could have learned that we have the dhampir brat living in our city," Lord Destrius answered. "I told you both when

Talisa first brought Tamina's hellspawn here that the *vampyra* would be the death of us."

"And *I* also reminded you that while we do have warring relations with the vampiric races, Artemis' mother helped our people countless times. Tamina did so to create an alliance between us and the Dark Fortress. She would have been the Mistress had she still lived today," Lady Clarayne reminded him, failing to hold back her anger. "To have ordered Talisa to abandon Artemis would have been equivalent to spitting on Tamina's grave and forgetting all that she had done for us."

"Where is Shadow now, Clarayne?" Lord Celstian asked.

Lady Clarayne was thankful for Lord Celstian's interjection. "He's either at home or out for a ride. Our meeting did not end on a happy note."

"I wouldn't have expected it to, seeing how he cares for the dhampir," Lord Celstian said. "I propose we bring him here tomorrow to restate his report to myself and Destrius. Afterward, we can decide how to proceed."

"I'd rather hand over the brat to Arlina while we still can. Then the bitch will stay away from our realm for another twenty years or so," Destrius grumbled.

Lady Clarayne glared at Lord Destrius as she reached for a blank sheet of parchment. "I'll have a message sent to Shadow, and he'll repeat to you what he has already said to me. I agree with Celstian on the matter of listening to the report and then deciding once you two fully understand what lies before us."

"You're too damn soft, Clarayne," Lord Destrius berated her. "Perhaps it's time you stepped down."

"Not all consider it a weakness, Destrius," Lady Clarayne snapped. "And the ones who will decide whether or not I continue as Elder of this realm are the goddesses themselves."

Once I reached Shadow's house, I heard the sounds of arrows striking wood. Whenever I heard that, it usually meant one thing.

He was angry. *Very* angry.

Walking over, I found him—Shadow's hair was bound with a brown ribbon that matched his tunic. His black breeches had patches of dirt along the sides; he must have practiced his swordsmanship earlier.

This didn't bode well at all.

"Shadow?" I called out, wincing as the last arrow he released sank deep into the wooden target.

He didn't respond. Shadow reached for another arrow, notched it along the bow, and released it within seconds. The arrow landed inches away from the previous one, also deep.

Despite the tension I felt, I walked over and grabbed his shoulder as gently as I could. He jumped and twisted my wrist as he grabbed it. I tried not to snap at him as he turned around and realized it was me. He quickly released it, and I rubbed my wrist while ignoring the red finger marks that then formed.

"Artemis, I'm so sorry!" Shadow took my wrist and inspected it. "I...I wasn't myself."

"So I've noticed," I teased.

Shadow shook his head and threw down his bow.

"What happened to you? The last time you were this upset, it was before you told me you were leaving for the war in Fieros Mountains."

"It's worse than that," Shadow explained, while still keeping an eye on my wrist. "Much worse."

"My wrist is fine, you just took me by surprise." I hid it behind my back. I sat on the grass, far from the arrows and the target. "Are you leaving again?"

Shadow sat beside me, looking to the sky. "No, I'm not leaving."

"Then what's going on?"

Shadow rubbed the back of his neck while thinking hard. He glanced at me, and half-smiled. "I can't tell you just yet."

"Meaning you want me to forget about it and not ask you again."

"No." Shadow fell back and moved his arms to cushion his head on the earth. "I will tell you when the time comes. Promise me something though, Artemis."

"Name it."

"There may be a time where I'll come to you and tell you to pack only what is necessary for a trip outside of Ellewynth. When it does come, I don't want you asking questions. You have to trust in me to explain everything when it is safe enough to."

I stared at him. "Is something going to happen to the city?"

"Maybe, maybe not," Shadow answered. "Promise me, Artemis."

"I promise," I said, now looking away.

I was worried. What did he know?

Shadow took a deep breath, and I could feel him watching me. "What brings you here? Talisa was supposed to visit you today. I know how much you wanted to see her."

"She already did," I replied. "And she took Jack away. His training starts tonight."

"Ah." Shadow softly laughed. "A word of advice, my dear…it's better to visit them after at least a week. Talisa tends to put her apprentices through hell and back within their first week."

"Do you think Jack will make it?"

"Well…" Shadow mused. "I could see him lasting a few years. I'll give it two."

"That's awfully generous of you."

"Is it? I thought I was being realistic," Shadow said, shooting me a curious glance.

"I thought *one* year would be considered realistic," I replied. "You're being too nice."

"I'm *always* nice, my dear." Shadow grinned.

"Will that be true even during my weapons training?"

"There's only one way to find out." Shadow stood up and helped me up to my feet. Walking toward the target, he picked up his bow and held it out for me to take. "Why don't we see, hmm?"

It took every fiber of my being not to groan aloud. Memories of past archery lessons flooded my mind; I tried to reassure myself that things would be *much* better this time around, especially since it was just the two of us.

I grasped the bow, felt satisfied with the balance of it in my grip, and took my stance while awaiting Shadow's instructions.

6

Blackwen City, home of the largest full-blood population in all of Arrygn, loomed over the Meristl Plains. Built mostly of steel and iron mined from the hills surrounding the plains, the city was eventually nicknamed the "Dark Fortress." The city itself was in a constant state of darkness, a product of vampire magery. It made it difficult for enemies because they could not strike the city in the daylight hours, for none existed there.

Passing through the gates, Netira acknowledged the guards with a casual nod. Setting foot on the paved slate streets, Netira deeply breathed in the cool air and then surveyed her surroundings.

She loved her home, despite the laws against dhampirs. It pained her to continue watching it fall further into a state of chaos. Blackwen City had been peaceful once long ago; its residents kept to themselves and were of a decent nature. Nowadays, her people prided themselves on thievery, dishonor, and unchecked bloodlust. The leader, or "Mistress," of Blackwen City, Arlina, ruled as a tyrant would: those who opposed her met their end in unspeakable ways. Netira knew those of the Ravenwing clan who were no longer of this world were twisting in their graves because of such changes and behavior. She missed her mentor, Tamina Ravenwing, greatly. Arlina would pay for that as well…someday.

Netira made her way to City Tower, the home of the Mistress and the center of Blackwen's operations. Netira needed to speak with Arlina concerning the scouts she'd sent out; as the city's Second, Netira should have been informed as well as consulted concerning the action, as the purpose of her station was to advise and co-command.

The Mistress was hiding something, and she was going to find out the cause for all the secrecy.

Entering the tower, Netira first stared at the lengthy spiral staircase. Scowling, she began to climb it soon after. Numerous doors, as well as traps, lined the walls along the staircase. She wished she could fly rather than walk up the wretched stairs, but not only would that reveal her true identity, she could also set off those horrific traps hidden within City Tower. Arlina had a perverse sense of humor, especially when it came to her guests.

Netira stopped as soon as she saw the steel door engraved with protective runes. Shaking her head, she climbed several more stairs before cursing at herself and returning to the door. Hesitations aside, Netira pushed it open and stepped inside the chamber.

Torchlight illuminated the chamber, revealing stacks of parchment along the walls and thick tomes that had seen better days.

Netira walked toward the black wood desk placed near the windowsill; she sat on it and leafed through the stack of parchment nearest to her. She smiled to herself as she learned they contained spells translated from the old tomes.

"You've been busy these past few days," Netira mused aloud, returning the parchment sheets to where she found them.

"I needed to do *something* in your absence," a soft, deep voice replied from behind. "It's not easy, you know…covering for someone the others believe you despise."

Netira turned and looked upon the source of the voice: a tall male with lengthy black hair and deep violet eyes. He was wearing a black tunic with black breeches—a common style for the citizens of Blackwen City. He sported several silver rings on his left hand, each with small runes along the bands, and he had a large silver cross earring hanging from his right earlobe. He smiled as he grasped Netira's hand, rubbing it gently.

Netira's smile widened. "I missed you too, Karesu."

She stood up to embrace him. Karesu pulled away after the hug, just enough to steal a kiss from her. When he didn't break it, she did. Karesu chuckled as he caressed her cheek.

"Ah yes, I've forgotten. Not here," he said. "You do realize Arlina can't break into the chamber right? She still needs to be granted permission to enter."

"Still playing with fire, I see," Netira teased.

Karesu kissed her once more. "It is a fun element, my love. It is perfect for describing one's passion as well."

"Speaking of passion, have you noticed anything different with the Mistress lately?" Netira asked as she let go of Karesu. She returned to her seat atop the corner of the table.

"And there is the dirt thrown atop the flame." Karesu frowned while folding his arms. "Her erratic behavior hasn't changed as of late. Why? What did you discover in that little outing of yours?"

"I followed those two scouts to the Woodland Realm," Netira answered. "Bad enough that she dismissed my inquiries about them, but to send them there of all places…"

"As far as I know, she has no interest in the elves," Karesu explained. "I'm not even sure if the whole council knows—"

"The entire council doesn't know shit! Not even the devout Vashti! Arlina *does* have an interest in the elves," Netira insisted. "She sent those miscreants to eavesdrop on their local gossip! What does that tell you?"

"Our Mistress is probably deciding to add more enemies to her extermination list. Or perhaps she's looking for a new stock of blood to supply those goddessforsaken taverns of hers—I don't know. Arlina does rather enjoy the whole tyrannical-bitch ploy…" Karesu paced back and forth, stopping as soon as a realization set in. "Netira…do you remember the last time she ventured to the Woodland Realm?"

"Of course I do," Netira replied. "Nearly twenty-one years ago. She claimed it was to hunt down traitors, but you and I both know that wasn't the truth. She discovered blood relatives living within that realm and eliminated them. She…she killed Tamina."

"What if Arlina somehow missed another blood kin?"

Netira's brow furrowed. "I don't believe that."

"Netira…it makes sense." Netira shot him a skeptical look, and he sighed. "Bear with me a moment. Arlina firmly believes she is the last of the Ravenwing bloodline. She figures she is an example of a 'pure-blood' within our race—"

"*Your* race," Netira corrected.

"*Our*," Karesu stressed, now grabbing her hand.

"Go on with the point you're trying to make," Netira warned.

Karesu shook his head and continued, "Well, Arlina has her goddess complex as you and I both well know." Netira snorted, and Karesu suppressed a laugh. "Anyone of her bloodline considered tainted or not compliant with her point of view is immediately executed by her hand. That, and she doesn't want any opposition to the throne of Blackwen City. If she's returning to the Woodland Realm, she's missed something...or someone."

Netira's finally let herself believe. "Another Ravenwing alive...please let it be a woman. Only a Ravenwing woman can hold the throne of Blackwen."

"If it is another Ravenwing woman, we can only pray to Avilyne that she survives Arlina." Karesu flinched when Netira slammed her clenched fist atop the table. "Netira..."

"This has to stop!" she cried. "It just...it has to stop. There'll be nothing left of Blackwen City if she keeps this up."

Karesu held her; the gesture was welcome. "Neither of us is in a position to oppose Arlina. We knew this, too, when we first made the pact to join her under false pretenses. It is not yet time, my love. If she were to learn the truth of your heritage..."

"She won't learn of it," Netira insisted while trying to calm down. "I must go speak with the Mistress. Arlina will want to know why I left without informing her."

Karesu released her. Netira headed to the door and pulled it open. She didn't want Karesu to see the fear that riddled her the moment he brought up his own fear of discovery.

"Netira?" Karesu called, which made her stop from leaving the chamber. "You left your charm behind."

"I know." Netira frowned as she saw him pull out a small silver ring with a curved rune engraved within the band. "I was in a rush."

He handed it over to her, and she felt his gaze follow her as she moved to the chamber door. Netira stopped once again, sensing a question from him.

"What is it?" she asked as she faced him.

"What…whatever did happen to those scouts?"

Netira tapped her fingers along the doorframe, now looking away.

"Yes, I thought as much," she heard him say. "This is a part of the game I hoped for us to avoid."

The chamber of the Mistress of Blackwen was located at the very top of City Tower, along with the audience chamber; the chambers provided the benefit of overseeing the entire city, as if it were a nest. Appropriate, considering the name of the Mistress line, the Ravenwing. A throne of carved black marble sat in the center of the audience chamber; torches jutted from the walls, positioned between large onyx statues of the past Mistresses of Blackwen City. A statue of the current Mistress was missing; the honor only came once she passed into the next life and was deemed as a worthy ruler by the new Mistress.

Sitting comfortably on the throne with one leg crossed over the other, Arlina yawned. Her short red hair curved along the sides of her pale neck; her gray eyes were frigid and struck fear in her people. She donned a sleeveless red tunic and tight black breeches, along with calf-high leather boots with sharp, thin heels. Poking from the top of her boots were the onyx-jeweled hilts of her prized weapons, the sai. Only the Ravenwing women carried such weapons.

Bored, she clicked her heels against the marble floor, and a couple of servants rushed inside. Arlina could see they were nervous, and she reveled in it; the idea of kindness revolted her.

Kindness made one weak, and she was anything but.

"W-What do you desire, my Mistress?" the first servant spoke while doing his best to avoid making eye contact. The last servant who had done so while asking her desire had lost his head…slowly.

"I hunger in my boredom," Arlina said, her voice masked with a deadly sweetness. "Bring me a flask of the latest import."

The servants rushed out of the chamber and soon returned with a jeweled, silver flask filled with blood—the scent was intoxicating to her. Snatching it from the servant's hands, Arlina took a sip. She immediately spat it out, and her face contorted in disgust.

Fuming, she flung the flask, and the contents spilled all over the first servant.

"You *dare* to bring me this filth?"

"N-No, my Mistress!" the blood-soaked servant answered, kneeling before her.

"At the moment, this is the freshest source of blood we have to offer, my Mistress," the other servant said while hungrily eying her companion.

"Imbeciles! That's what you both are!"

"Apologies, Mistress!" the servants cried in unison as they fell to the floor on their knees and avoided eye contact with Arlina.

"Take that shit away from me, and do not return until you can provide me with fresh blood! Understand? Fresh as in minutes after the slaughter!" Arlina demanded. "Useless fools!"

The servants spewed apologies when they ran out, and she scowled. She sighed after finally regaining her calm. It upset her knowing that there were such lowly full-bloods living in her city. Arlina wanted to dispose of them, but if she did then there wouldn't be any servants left to abuse for her own amusement. No highborn full-blood would be caught doing a servant's work. Although…

Oh, the decisions a leader had to make!

Arlina broke out of her train of thought as she heard several loud knocks. Doubtful that the source of the knocking came from the idiots she bothered to call servants, Arlina realized it might have been someone of importance.

It would be refreshing, of course, to have someone with intellect in the chamber with her.

Ordering her visitor to enter, Arlina saw it was one of her prized scouts, Latos.

Latos approached the throne and kneeled. Hearing the order to rise, Latos did so and kept his head low. His bright red hair was short and spiked, and he wore tight black clothing beneath his black cloak.

Removing the cloak, Latos raised his dark brown eyes to meet Arlina's. He did not keep the gaze for long.

She liked that.

"Netira has returned to the city, Mistress," Latos reported, his voice deep and scratchy.

"Has she now?" Arlina smirked. "Tell me, where did she go and what did she do?"

"She followed the trail of the scouts you sent away two moonturns ago...the ones you sent to the Woodland Realm," Latos answered.

"Of course she did!" Arlina pounded a fist on her black marble throne. "I told her the matter of their departure didn't concern her, and what does she do? She runs off to sate her damned curiosity! What good is it to be Mistress if no one follows orders?"

"Netira did more than disrespect you, Mistress," Latos continued. "She killed them. My two best scouts, wasted..."

"She did *what?*" Arlina rose from her throne, enraged. "The nerve of the bitch!"

"Their deaths are a shame, as they were such excellent scouts, but I can assure you it was not in vain, my Mistress," Latos said. "They may not have known what to listen to, but *I* knew what you desired. And it appears that your suspicions were correct. There is one of your bloodline hidden in the realm of the forest elves. The very last one, my Mistress."

Arlina's eyes widened as she sat back down. "So those wretched dreams were true..."

"Pardon?"

"It is nothing," Arlina answered as she straightened her posture on the throne. The damned thing proved to be uncomfortable on certain occasions. "This is good. It gives me a better reason to attack Ellewynth. Those woodland elves have defied me for far too long. I can finally rid myself of them."

"If I may...?" Latos began. Arlina narrowed her gaze, but allowed him to finish the thought. "Why attack the city outright when we can simply use the fodder for our amusement?"

"Interesting," Arlina mused. "You may continue."

"By now, the Elders of Ellewynth must have noticed the kills by our scouts. I have no doubt that they sent their own scouts to investigate," Latos explained. "They'll learn that our city was behind it; this is inevitable."

"I'm growing impatient, Latos," Arlina grumbled. "Get to the point."

"Netira has grown tiresome, has she not?" Latos smiled, revealing his elongated fangs. "And she killed my poor, poor scouts. Why not pin the blame for the other deaths on her as well? Instead of killing her for disobedience, send her to the elves for their own punishment. They'll see it as a sign of good faith and that you are trying to make amends. Their guard will be down, which will be advantageous for us. When they least expect it,"—he clapped his hands together— "strike at the city and find the blood survivor. Hang the corpse for all to see, as a reminder to our enemies of why they should continue to fear you."

"Devious," Arlina said. "I find myself liking this notion, yet I feel there is more you're not telling me. What other dark thoughts are swirling in that mind of yours, Latos?"

"I have other reasons why I prefer to be rid of Netira," Latos answered. "After all, she is not one of us."

"What do you mean she is not one of us?" Arlina's voice grew louder. "She is a vampire like the rest of us."

"I have no doubt that she is a vampire," Latos said. "*Half,* anyways."

Arlina's blood rushed to her face. Infuriated, she took a sai from her boot and threw it. The sai narrowly missed Latos' head. "*Explain.*"

"Her true nature was revealed when she found the scouts…wings and all. She also mentioned something about forgetting a charm," Latos reported, ignoring the fact that he narrowly avoided a sai to the head. "Sacrificing her to the elves would help correct the embarrassment of her being your Second. No one else need know the truth, save perhaps the council."

"Indeed." Arlina seethed. "Now leave. I have much to think about."

"And what of the traitor in the meantime?"

"Tell her she is to remain within the city until I decide to grant her an audience," Arlina replied. "I don't want her to have any inkling that we know. I want to…to have some fun with this."

"Your will is my life." Latos bowed and exited the chamber.

Arlina tried to regain her composure as she went to retrieve her sai. Lifting it from the ground, she stared at the blade. Sliding it back into her boot, Arlina chuckled.

"First, I'll be rid of you, darling Netira," Arlina said. "Then, I'll get my hands on you, dear little Artemis."

My arms were shaking from the strain. I winced as I felt muscles contort in ways I never imagined they could.

Numerous arrows were embedded in the wooden target; Shadow's were near or in the center of it. The majority of my arrows rested well outside the testing markers; only three were within them.

The pain I felt outweighed my embarrassment.

"One more shot," Shadow instructed. He too was tired. "After that, we can rest for the day."

"I don't think I'll be able to manage one more shot, Shadow."

"In battle, there is little time for rest, Artemis," Shadow scolded. "Shall I remind you of the sieges I've experienced?"

I shuddered. "No. Goddesses, no."

Resigned, I raised the bow. I tried to remember Shadow's instructions: spot your target, raise your bow and arrow while pulling the arrow and string close to your face, aim, and then release.

Aerios blow me. It was easier said than done.

I felt the breeze pick up, and I groaned. Wind was another factor I had to take into account. Concentrating, I released the arrow. To my shock, it landed well within the testing markers; not quite near the center, but still within a decent area nonetheless.

"Now *there's* a shot!" Shadow grinned. "You may relax, my dear."

"Kiare be praised." I breathed, dropping the bow. I tried to regain sensation within my now numb arms.

"Get used to it, Artemis." Shadow laughed. "We start again tomorrow morning."

"Tomorrow morning?" I exclaimed, and I pouted. "Shadow..."

"It was either tomorrow morning or us resuming this later tonight," he explained. My mouth shut. "Yes, I thought as much. Nothing wrong with building a little muscle in those scrawny arms of yours."

"They're *not* scrawny! I resent that!" I folded my sore arms. "Were your lessons anything like this at all?"

"Oh, hardly," Shadow replied. "You're getting off easy. I had multiple sessions in the morning alone, followed by several in the evening. Sleep did not exist in my vocabulary then. Don't ask how many teachers I had."

"Unbelievable."

"I can't complain. I was one of the 'chosen.'" Shadow shrugged. "Each lesson served me well. I made the rank of Master Archer before my century mark. Most elves take *far* longer to reach that feat."

I stared at him in awe. I'd heard the stories before, but he still amazed me. Shadow cleared his throat to break me out of my train of thought.

"Sorry. I realize it could be worse...I could be Jack right now."

"Even *I* cannot compete with Talisa in terms of teaching methods. I can be harsh when necessary, but it pales in comparison to Talisa's level." Shadow shook his head.

He started to say more but stopped when something behind me grabbed his attention.

A young elf stepped into view, bearing a letter in his hand. I knew it was of great importance, as the green tree wax seal of the Elders was easy to see even from here.

"Master Shadow," the elf addressed him, bowing. "I bear a letter from Lady Clarayne."

Shadow's eyes widened, and he quickly recomposed himself. It was common knowledge that he was close to Lady Clarayne. I knew she and her husband had cared for him as a child; they were known for doing that for many of the young orphan elves. I felt there was a resemblance between the two, but the others thought I was crazy to assume they were related.

Perhaps they were right. I wouldn't think Lady Clarayne would ship off her own blood relative to war, after all. Well, she would protest at least…right?

Taking the letter, he dismissed the elf, and we received a parting bow. Opening it, Shadow silently read the letter and cursed once he finished.

"Shadow?"

"The Elders demand an audience with me tomorrow."

Demand? "Do you know when?"

"No." Shadow narrowed his gaze at me. "Don't even think it means you won't have any lessons tomorrow, my dear."

I sheepishly smiled. "I wouldn't dare dream of it."

Shadow laughed as he crumbled the letter in his hand. Ignoring my shock, Shadow went to pick up the archery equipment.

"You should return home," he suggested. "I'll come for you tomorrow."

Nodding, I left.

Before I got far, the feeling of something evil coming rose again. Whatever it was, I hoped Shadow wouldn't be there for it. He'd been through enough already.

7

Jack followed behind Talisa with a smug expression that hadn't changed since the visit to his aunt. He'd been disowned, of course, and he'd expected it. It didn't bother him at all, and nothing would ever top the moment when Talisa had roasted the damned woman alive. Jack never felt sorry for her during Talisa's scolding.

"Wipe that look off your face, Jack," Talisa ordered. "The time for enjoying your aunt's fear of me ended the moment we left Ellewynth's borders."

Jack's expression went blank. "Sorry."

"No apologies!" Talisa snapped. "There are very few instances where one must apologize, and this is not one of them."

"When are those instances that I should then?" Jack asked. Talisa halted, turned, and smacked the back of Jack's head. "Hey!"

"No back-sass." Talisa walked once more. "I won't tolerate sarcasm until after the first year of my apprenticeship. *If* you even survive that long…"

Jack inwardly groaned. "How do you know it wasn't a legitimate question?"

Talisa smacked him again. He mentally braced himself, as he knew the torture was coming, no matter how many times he told himself it'd be well worth the pain.

Packing hadn't taken Jack very long; he took only a few elven robes and stuffed them in a box with books he snatched from the library.

Artemis used to scold him for such deeds, and Jack happily ignored her whenever she did. Stealing them was the only way he'd be able to read the books before being tossed out by the librarian. He cringed at the memory of the old horse face chasing him with her cane.

He should have stolen *that* too.

Talisa broke the silence. "I have quite the collection of books at the cottage. You didn't have to bring your own."

"I wouldn't dare leave these behind," Jack explained. "These books hold the contents that interest me most about magic and people of magic."

"Do they now?" Talisa asked, curious. "Give me an example then."

"Well…there is one thing I've been reading about for several years now," Jack began. He stopped walking and looked through the tree branches to see the sky. "But it seems more like a myth than anything else."

"Didn't anyone warn you that I'm impatient?" Talisa faced him while narrowing her gaze. "Get to the point."

"Yes, I was warned." Jack sighed. "Elementals, the vessels of the goddesses. Do they really exist?"

Talisa smacked the back of his head yet again. Before Jack could retort, she gave him a stare that shut him up. "Get used to that, especially when you ask stupid questions."

"But—"

"But nothing!" Talisa yelled. "Elementals are as real as you and I. They're only considered a myth because several centuries ago they chose to seclude themselves from the rest of the world. And I certainly don't blame them."

"Really? Why though? They can teach others so much about magic!" Jack flinched as he saw Talisa's hand rise again, and grew relieved when she only moved it to fix her hat.

"Indeed they can." Talisa was saddened. "You have to remember that not all share the value of learning that you have, Jack. Elementals are direct links to the goddesses. If a goddess chose to walk among us, she could easily inhabit an elemental. Can you imagine what would happen if an elemental was kidnapped? By wizards, of all people? Can you imagine the pain one could inflict on them if they refused to become slaves?"

"They left to avoid being taken advantage of…" Jack realized. He was sad, yet he understood. "Seclusion can be stifling, though."

Talisa chuckled. "Yes, she said the same thing…"

"She?" Jack raised an eyebrow. "You actually know one?"

"Perhaps," Talisa answered. "Perhaps not. You'll have to earn the right to know the many secrets I keep."

Yeah right, Jack thought.

"Now let's dispense with the chatter. I want you to study your surroundings, because after tonight, you're on your own when it comes to finding my cottage." Talisa smiled.

Jack sighed again, doing what he was told.

Talisa surprised Jack that day with the gift of freedom until the rise of the full moon; he was told to cherish the spare time he had left in his life.

He spent the time settling in his new room, which had formerly been Artemis'. The next time he saw her, it would take a lot of self-control to not laugh in her face; "girly" was the last thing he had *ever* expected Artemis to be.

Seeing the full moon in the sky from the window, Jack frowned and shut the book lying across his lap. He stared at his reflection in the mirror and heard Artemis' voice in his head, telling him to fix his messy hair. Jack chuckled while running a hand through his dark hair.

"Yeah, I miss bothering you too."

"Talking to yourself already?" Jack jumped at the sudden sound of Talisa's voice in the doorway. "I haven't even done anything to you yet."

"Is this yet another thing I have to get used to?" Jack asked, trying to calm his nerves. "You appearing out of nowhere?"

"Perhaps." Talisa inspected the room. "Perhaps not. Master anticipation and maybe I'll decide to ease up on you."

I doubt that somehow, Jack thought.

"Maybe I'll even teach you how to sneak up on others." Talisa winked. Taking another glance at Jack, she frowned. "On second thought, perhaps not."

And there's the Talisa I expected, Jack frowned.

"Well, shall we begin?" Talisa asked as she flashed him a sickly sweet smile.

"Yes, let's," Jack answered as he flinched from the glare he received for using sarcasm.

Jack followed Talisa away from the cottage for what seemed like an eternity, but he didn't dare complain. He also kept silent throughout the trek; Jack was surveying the area in case he had an opportunity to sneak out and explore on his own. Since Talisa knew an elemental, Jack was convinced she wasn't far away from the cottage. He would find her, even if it took the entirety of his apprenticeship.

Jack nearly bumped into Talisa after she stopped without warning. There would have been painful repercussions if he had, he just knew it.

"Welcome." She held out her arms as if to present something of value.

Jack was confused. They stood in a quiet grove of ash trees; there weren't any odd patterns or other magical sensations to note.

"It's just a grove." Jack wrinkled his brow.

Talisa smacked him. "Not everything is as it seems!"

"You know, I won't be much of an apprentice if I suffer from occasional head trauma," Jack warned.

"Interesting that you feel that way," Talisa answered as her smile grew in a slow stretch, "because if I wanted to you to suffer from head trauma, you *would.*"

Rubbing the back of his head, Jack bit his tongue. Observing the grove, he tried to see what was hidden. He grew more confused once he noticed her odd expression. It wasn't until after a moment that he realized he was being tested.

"Oh goddesses," Jack muttered. As he cleared his throat, he looked around once more. "I have to show you the way to whatever you wanted me to see."

"Very good!" Talisa clapped her hands. "Kiare be praised! You're not as hopeless as I thought. Apprentices in the past took several hours at the most before realizing *they* were the ones who had to open the pathway."

Jack bent to the ground while trying to still his nerves. He remembered reading about the veils of the Woodland Realm and figured he had to find one. The veils of the realm were usually a special grove of trees that were able to lead one to a new area hidden from enemies. The Elders of Ellewynth would evacuate the people to these veils, and only Talisa could lift or vanish the entrance.

Or so he thought, until now. Jack never imagined *he* would be able to do such a thing. He shook his head and tried to get "impossible" out of his mind.

Taking a handful of earth in his palm, he shut his eyes and rid his mind of distractions. Afterward, Jack opened his consciousness to feel any sensation of magic within the dirt. Feeling a slight tingle along his fingertips, he released the earth and stood up. With the remnants of the dirt on his hand, Jack held it out toward the trees in front of him.

"One of you causes the veil to fall," Jack whispered. "But which one?"

Moving his open palm across the trees, Jack felt a soft pull of energy farther ahead. He heard Talisa follow him, and Jack stopped in front of one particularly large ash tree. He ran his hand along the rough bark, and felt the same sensation as when he had held onto the earth.

"I will admit I'm rather impressed you found the gate," Talisa said. "But the real question here is, can you open it?"

That's one damn good question, Jack thought. *I don't even know where to begin.*

It was often said that elves could hear the voices of the forest. Jack, however, was not like the other elves. He was different, and he'd always known it. Jack never liked being different, but he also never made the effort to test whether or not he too could hear the forest. Now he wished he had.

Shutting his eyes once more, Jack listened to the pulse of the tree's life beneath his palm.

Water.

Jack stumbled away from the tree after hearing the word.

"What is it?" Talisa asked, while trying her best not to laugh.

"Th-The t-t-tree! It spoke!" Jack cried. "YEOW!"

Folding her arms after the smack, Talisa shook her head. "For someone with so much promise, you truly are dense! Of course the tree spoke. *All* trees can, Jack. People nowadays are just too stubborn to stop and listen to them for a change. A shame, really…"

"Well, it wants water," Jack replied, rubbing his head.

"Of course it does." Talisa ran a loving hand along the bark. "But as you can see, neither you nor I have any. How will you solve this part of the puzzle?"

Jack huffed. "I have trouble manifesting the elements. Well, I have trouble controlling them."

"When you limit yourself, you are heading down the path of defeat," Talisa berated him. "Think, just as you did when you grasped the earth in your hand."

Jack blinked. "I don't have to. You just helped me find a solution."

"I did?" Talisa asked, puzzled.

Jack dropped to his knees and started to dig a hole before the tree. He kept digging until he felt moist soil.

"I learned this trick a few years ago," Jack explained. "I can't create water on my own yet, but I have been able to summon water from deep within the ground. Never really knew how it happened, but I can't complain since it works."

Jack beamed as soon as he saw water fill into the hole. Moments later, enough water rose to cover the exposed roots. Jack felt another pull of energy from the tree, and he touched the bark again.

Well done, elf mage. You may enter the Grove of Kiare's Mirror.

The scenery changed before his eyes—there was no longer a grove of ash trees, but a small clearing surrounded by large oak trees. In the center of the clearing was a large rock wall with a well, constructed of multi-colored pebbles that were arranged to display a pattern of rolling ocean waves.

Jack felt Talisa push his jaw shut. He hadn't realized it was hanging in the first place.

"It's rude to gawk," Talisa said while walking toward the well. "It seems I'll have to instruct you in manners as well."

"B-But…"

Jack couldn't finish his sentence. He was in awe of the sacred ground he now stood upon.

"You know of this place." Talisa smiled. "Good. You'll become more familiar with it during your apprenticeship."

"Talisa, this is sacred ground. *Kiare's* sacred ground," Jack noted. "How is this possible?"

"You know the color of my robes indicate that I am a vassal of Kiare. Long ago, I was appointed the guardian of the Grove of Kiare's Mirror," Talisa explained. Her nails tapped along the edge of the well. "I have always brought my apprentices here, to test their heart as well as their spirit. If they successfully open the gateway and see into the mirror without being overcome by greed for power, then they are worthy of my tutelage."

"What happens if they fail?"

"Are you certain you wish to know?" she asked.

Jack gulped and shook his head.

"Never ask the questions you do not want the answers to," Talisa instructed.

Fair enough, Jack thought. "How did you earn the right to become the guardian?"

"When you serve the realm for as long as I have, even the goddesses learn to appreciate you," Talisa answered. "No, I will not reveal my true age to you. Get that question out of your mind." She paused a moment. "All I will say is that I am one of the oldest living servants of the water goddess. She saved me from a future of darkness. I walk the pathways of this world for as long as she desires.

"Kiare wanted someone who would not be corrupted by the power of the mirror. She wanted someone who would use the mirror in a time of need, like war, and she granted me the privilege of weeding out the overzealous bastards from the ones who genuinely wish for my tutelage. It is important to her that my legacy continues in others, for the sake of the Woodland Realm and Arrygn as a whole. The mirror is also used in determining who should join the ranks of the Elders in each elven realm."

Goddesses, what have I gotten myself into? Jack thought. "So my next test comes from the mirror. What am I supposed to see?"

"The mirror shows the viewer one of many possible futures," Talisa explained.

"Hence why it must only be used in a time of need," Jack said, now understanding what would happen if one took advantage of the mirror's power.

"Yes." Talisa moved aside and motioned for Jack to look into the mirror. "A warning, however—"

"Not everything I see will be pleasant," Jack cut her off. He peered into the water. "Yes, I understand that part well enough."

Jack grazed the surface of the water mirror with a finger, and it responded with a glow.

Tribute.

Jack was startled when he heard the word in his mind, though he should have expected it after his event with the trees. He looked at Talisa, and she tightened her lips. He was on his own again.

He tapped his fingers along the surface, and the glow brightened along his fingertips. An idea for a tribute came to him.

"I don't suppose you have anything sharp on you?" Jack asked.

Talisa's brow furrowed. "For what?"

"It would be helpful right now if you did."

Talisa shook her head, and Jack sighed. He wasn't one for carrying knives, but he made a mental note to start doing so.

He soon found a few small rocks and struck one with the other. A few sharp pieces fell to the ground after a several strikes, and Jack picked one up to inspect it. Satisfied, he returned to the well and held a finger above the water mirror. He made a clean cut in the tip of his index finger, and a few drops of blood fell into the surface, dispersing in swirls.

Accepted.

Jack dropped the rock shards to the ground, and he pressed his finger against his palm to staunch the bleeding. As he looked into the mirror, he saw images beginning to form. He didn't even notice Talisa move closer to the well, curious for what was to come.

Before the images were fully formed, the voice of the mirror spoke once more to Jack:

You will see what no other has seen before. Beware the repercussions, elf mage. It could alter the age of peace Arrygn has long been promised.

"Wait, wh——" Jack said.

The images formed and silenced him. Jack saw a woman running in parts of the forest he did not recognize. As he studied the woman, he felt his stomach drop—she had long, dark brown hair, pale skin, and wore dark clothing. Her right shoulder was caked with dried blood.

Artemis? Jack asked himself. *What happened to you? What are you doing?*

He saw her stop and reach into her boots for a weapon he did not recognize. They were thin blades the length of his forearm with curved prongs extending from the extensively onyx and garnet jeweled hilt; definitely something that Artemis would have.

Another woman came into view, stalking Artemis from behind. She had short red hair and cold, gray eyes. The woman had black clothes that clung tightly to her body, a lengthy black coat, and boots that made Jack cringe, especially at the sight of the heels. She too carried weapons like Artemis', only the jewels in the hilt were all onyx.

Jack's nerves worsened as he realized the woman looked as if she was related to Artemis.

The woman lunged after Artemis and missed as Artemis sidestepped.

"You're still sloppy, Arlina," Artemis said, her weapons raised.

Jack frowned, noticing her eyes as well as the voice difference. The eyes were violet, not hazel. And the voice...the voice was much older and so soft. Artemis' voice was soft only when she spoke to Shadow.

You're not Artemis, Jack realized. *You're the other side of the mirror—her mother.*

The woman named Arlina snarled as she pointed the sharp, thin blade in Artemis' mother's direction.

"Your time is ending, Tamina!" Arlina spat. "You and your half-breed brat are all that's left in my way before I can claim my right as Mistress of Blackwen City."

"Killing off the Ravenwing clan doesn't give you the right to be leader, Arlina," Tamina said, disgusted. "It only makes you a common animal. Even pigs have more honor than you do."

"They have more honor than *you*, dear sister," Arlina answered, equally disgusted. "You brought a diluted bitch into the world after mating with that human." Arlina dramatically shuddered. "I wouldn't enjoy the kill as much as I could if she were a full-blood."

"Watch your tongue," Tamina threatened, her irises shifting to red. "You won't find Artemis. Even when you think you have, just remember that not everything is as it seems."

She was Talisa's friend all right, Jack smiled.

"Spare me the drivel." Arlina rolled her eyes as she ran after Tamina with raised weapons. Her gray eyes made the shift to red as well. "Tonight, you die."

Oh, that's original, Jack mocked. The two began to fight, and another thought came to him. *Wait a minute, the mirror is supposed to show me one of many possible futures. Artemis' mother is dead. She is dead, right?*

Then he remembered the mirror's words—*you will see what no other has seen before.* Jack felt his stomach churn.

He knew what the mirror planned to show him.

Jack watched as Tamina dodged Arlina's strikes with a fluid grace, almost as if she were dancing. You could tell she spent time with the elves with the way she moved. The dance went on for some time before Tamina's weapon hit her mark. Arlina backed away as she clutched her shoulder. Crimson blood dripped from her claw-like fingertips.

"Do you yield?" Tamina asked while twirling the weapon to rid it of Arlina's blood.

Arlina glared at her sister, and she spat saliva, which landed on Tamina's feet.

Tamina sighed. "You are a fool, sister. I truly wish it didn't have to come to this."

Despite the shoulder injury, Arlina dashed after Tamina and resumed her barrage of attacks. Tamina dodged them with more ease, and struck at Arlina's other shoulder. The odd weapon went much farther in than the previous strike, and the blade now protruded from the other side of her sister's body.

Jack cringed, rubbing his own shoulder.

Arlina retreated once more, and she fell to her knees while clutching the other shoulder and Tamina's weapon. Tamina twirled her free weapon and walked toward her sister. Her face showed no signs of remorse; Jack wondered if Artemis would be the same if she were to fight.

Returning his focus to the scene, Jack noticed Arlina's hand slipping inside her jacket. Tamina continued to advance and did not seem to notice the gesture as he had.

Tamina stood before Arlina and grabbed the hair from the back of her head, forcing her to look Tamina in the eyes.

"You can answer for your crimes to Avilyne herself," Tamina whispered. "Let the goddess of death cast her judgment once I send you to the pathways."

"Not before I send you there first," Arlina declared with a smug expression.

Before Tamina could deliver the killing blow, Jack was startled by a loud blast. He heard Talisa gasp beside him.

Tamina's face twisted in pained horror, and Arlina grinned. Tamina's waist moistened with her blood, and Jack felt himself shake. He stared at the weapon in Arlina's hand and recognized it to be a flintlock pistol.

I thought only sailors and merchants used those, Jack thought. *What is a* vampire *doing using one?*

"Didn't think I'd confront you without a trick up my sleeve, did you, sister?" Arlina mocked.

"I knew you were dishonorable," Tamina started, as she coughed up blood and glared at Arlina, "but to rely on *that*…how far you've fallen, Arlina."

Arlina grabbed Tamina by the back of her head.

"This," Arlina said, while waving the flintlock pistol, "you should thank your human husband for."

Tears welled up in Tamina's eyes. "Gavin?"

Arlina noticed Tamina was growing weaker the longer the gunshot wound bled out. Arlina violently shook Tamina's head to keep her awake.

"Stay with me for just a little longer, you pitiful excuse of a Ravenwing woman," Arlina whispered. "You should hear this before meeting the goddess of death."

Tamina shut her eyes. She cried out when Arlina shoved the flintlock pistol into her wound.

"Before your lovely husband told me where you ran off to, we both agreed that I was the better choice to carry out your demise. He gave me this wonderful gift,"—Arlina dangled the pistol in Tamina's face— "and in return I allowed him a...safe...return to the city of his birth. The catch, however,"—Arlina raised the flintlock pistol to Tamina's forehead— "was that I had to shoot you once, just once, as if it came from him. Pretty diabolical for a human, wouldn't you say? He would have made a hell of a vampire, you know, but I didn't feel like soiling my lips with his filthy blood. After all, we both know where he's been."

Tamina spat her blood in Arlina's face and received a smack from the butt of the pistol in return. Arlina wiped the blood away, and Jack felt his hands curl into fists.

"The first shot was from him, sister. This one," Arlina began in glee, while pushing the pistol against Tamina's forehead, "is from me."

Tamina didn't dare look away from Arlina; her stare was defiant.

"I'll see you soon." Tamina smiled while streaks of blood dripped from her lips.

The vision ended at the sound of the blast.

Jack fell on his back, horrified. He glanced at Talisa, who moved a great deal away from the well. Her face was streaked with tears.

"My dear friend..." Talisa whispered. "Willow be damned. I'm so sorry."

"Why did the mirror show me that?" Jack snapped as he stood up. "Why did it show me the past?"

Talisa could not look at him. "I do not know."

"You're the guardian!" Jack yelled. "You *should* know!"

Talisa slapped the back of his head, and Jack yelped. The slap was much harder than the ones before. He knew he was heading into dangerous territory, but he wasn't going to back down.

Not now.

"Idiot, this never happened before!" Talisa cried as she wiped her tears away. The effort was futile, as she continued to sob. "Never in my time as guardian have I seen the mirror show the past to another before. It has to be because of what you are."

"What in Avilyne's hell does that mean?" Jack demanded. "I'm *just* an elf!"

He didn't want to mention to Talisa that he had continually been called an elf mage—the being he feared most—throughout the test.

"No. No, you're not." Talisa looked at the well. "You are an elf mage, particularly of the old mage bloodline of this realm. It is why you have darker features, why you can use magic with ease and oftentimes without control, and it is why you found the gate as quickly as you did. Shadow suspected it after seeing you as you are now as well as hearing Artemis' stories about you. After this little event, I can very well say that I agree you are one."

Jack was furious. "*That* is why my aunt couldn't stand the sight of me and why no one speaks of my parents? Because they all knew?" *No wonder the old goat abused me whenever she could...she thought if she belittled me enough, I wouldn't dare think myself powerful enough to end her.*

"Yes," Talisa admitted. "The last known elf mage caused the first war between us and the dragons. He betrayed us and hoped Ellewynth would be destroyed. This particular mage bloodline is volatile...you need my help if you want to stay as your jester self. As you've learned in Artemis' case, the elves do not forgive past indiscretions."

Jack wanted to find something and smash it. He wanted to wreak havoc. However, something inside him held him back.

"Why did the mirror show me the death of Artemis' mother?" Jack asked, softening his tone.

"I don't know."

Jack realized she truly didn't. "Something is going to happen soon.... isn't it, Talisa?"

"Yes," Talisa replied. She looked at the well once more. "If it showed you that event, of all things, then the only explanation for what's coming is a ripple effect."

Willow be damned.

"Artemis doesn't know the truth, does she?" Jack inquired.

"No."

"Are you going to tell her?" He was infuriated when she shook her head. "What about Shadow? I'm sure he knows the truth as well."

"He won't do it either."

"But he loves her!" Jack yelled. "That's all the more reason why he *should* tell her!"

"It would seem the task of telling this part of the tale has been appointed to you," Talisa said.

Jack froze. "But…"

"Things happen for a reason," Talisa said. "If my theory of the ripple effect is true, then Artemis will learn of it all soon enough. Arlina could very well realize her niece is still alive, and she could come after her."

"And what are *we* going to do should that happen?" Jack asked.

Talisa stayed silent.

Days had passed since the events at the Grove of Kiare's Mirror. Jack had not slept well since seeing the vision from the mirror. He knew what would happen if Artemis learned the truth, and he wondered how Talisa would react when he joined Artemis in her eventual journey to Blackwen City, Arlina's home. He'd lose his apprenticeship; there was no doubt about it. But if it meant losing it in favor of helping his best friend, then Jack would have no regrets doing so.

Jack left the cottage once he saw the streaks of dawn flow into his room, and he tried to stay awake for his daily walk. He groaned whenever he had to, for it was mandatory to take the walk at such an ungodly hour. There were times where he tried to get out of the walks, and Talisa responded by throwing a bucket of ice water at him. As punishment for trying to barter for more time to rest, Jack had to travel in the soaked clothing.

Talisa wanted a report of everything Jack noticed on his walk: how the trees looked and whether they spoke to him or not, if there were more veils in the forest and whether he attempted to disperse them, and so on. Jack did what was asked of him and silenced his grumblings because the walks also proved to be a means of searching for the elemental. He was careful to not ask Talisa any more questions about elementals, for she would surely disembowel him if she knew he was looking for her.

He decided to follow a different path this time; if he had to suffer being awake at this hour of the morning, he might as well make the most of it and explore other paths from the cottage. Jack was grateful he wasn't soaked this morning.

Strolling as slowly as possible, Jack attempted to focus on the voices of the forest. He felt small tinges of energy here and there, and he couldn't help but grin. Several days ago, it all would have frightened him. Now, he enjoyed feeling the life of the forest around him. It calmed Jack.

I wonder if this is a way of turning me into a "proper" elf, considering I'm anything but one, Jack mused. *Artemis can't know about this. She'll never let me hear the end of it.*

His pointed ear twitched as he heard a soft sound of spraying water. Jack could smell the moisture in the air, and he felt his lips curl into a smirk. There was no sign of a waterfall anywhere, and Jack knew he had stumbled on the location of another veil of the forest.

Taking a different approach than the one he used to find the gate to the Grove of Kiare's Mirror, Jack sat on the earth cross-legged and rested his hands on his lap. While shutting his eyes, Jack focused on the sounds and scent of the waterfall. He felt several bursts of energy respond to him and tried to concentrate on the location of their source. The energy bursts pulsed into his mind until one pulled him.

Opening his eyes, Jack followed the pull of the energy and found himself in another grove of ash trees.

"Seriously, what is this?" Jack laughed. "Sooner or later I'm going to suspect that *all* ash tree groves are hidden gates."

Moving his palm along the bark of the closest tree, he backed away as he felt a large burst of energy—more than the gate from the days before.

Jack couldn't hide his excitement.

Either this is another area of sacred ground, Jack thought, *or something very strong is hiding behind the veil. Even better if it's both.*

Returning his palm to the bark, Jack listened for the tree to speak to him. To his dismay, the tree didn't speak.

"Did I offend you earlier?" Jack asked. "If I did, you have my…" He struggled for the proper words. "Sincerest? Yes! Sincerest! My *sincerest* apologies."

Still no word from the tree.

Sighing, Jack moved on to check the other trees of the grove and was met with continued silence. "If I have to get on my knees to show you how sorry I am for offending you, I will do so…"

After the silence and lack of energy, Jack rubbed the back of his neck and kneeled before the trees. He went as far as having his forehead reach the ground.

"Please accept my apology, oh humble…tree," Jack said while scowling for the lack of better terms. "I am wrong to judge where the forest hides its veils. Ash tree groves are *wonderful* places to have a secret retreat."

"The trees were more amused at your words than offended," a voice said from behind Jack, startling him. There was gentle laughter when Jack stumbled as he tried to rise from the ground. "You're rather unusual for an elf."

Once Jack rose, he found himself in the company of a young woman. She was a tad shorter than him, and she had short blond ringlets framing her small, fair-skinned face. The woman wore a flowing brown dress, and Jack saw she was barefoot.

She smiled at him, but he was captivated by the calming light blue eyes that gazed at him. Jack felt as if he could stand there all day and be content just staring into her eyes. He also felt a strange sensation in his chest and rubbed it.

He realized he was being rude. "I'm sorry, my lady. I was just startled because I didn't expect to run into company at this hour."

"Well I'm not of noble blood, so there's no need to address me as such," she said, her voice sweet and pleasant. "And as for the part concerning company…well, *I* tend to take a stroll through these parts often, and much earlier than you."

"I have to applaud your eagerness for rising at a time that I never could, even if I wanted to." Jack chuckled. "And it was proper to address you as such."

She raised an eyebrow. "You don't strike me as the proper type."

"No, I'm not normally." Jack bowed his head and held out his hand. "I'm Jack."

"Callypso." She took Jack's hand and shook it lightly. Jack felt a soothing energy emanate from her hand, like a gentle breeze. "Why were you trying to get past the veil?"

"Well…" Jack's face flushed. "It's part of my apprenticeship. Should I stumble upon such things, I'm to try and get past the, erm, locks."

"Ah. You're Talisa's new pet then," Callypso said. "You're not the first to have tried this particular gate."

"I wouldn't call it that, no," Jack snorted. "And I'm sorry?"

"It's quite all right. And nonetheless, you belong to Talisa until your apprenticeship is over," Callypso insisted while walking past Jack. "You are gifted; there is no doubt about it. You still have quite a bit to learn though."

"What makes you say that?" Jack asked, watching the skirts of her dress sway with the wind.

Where did all this wind come from? He couldn't remember encountering any on his previous crack-of-dawn walks.

Callypso stopped before the tree Jack was apologizing to and rested her hand on the bark of the trunk. He felt that same large burst of energy emanate from her. There was more to her than her pleasing appearance!

"You have to learn when a veil is a gateway to sacred ground, to safe houses," she explained, "and when a veil is a gateway to one's home."

Jack felt his stomach drop; he had been trying to break into someone's home. *That* was why the trees wouldn't let him through. Only if he was invited by the one who created that particular veil would the trees let him through. That's how it worked.

"I'm so sorry…" Jack apologized. "I have *much* to learn still."

Callypso laughed, and Jack felt the wind from earlier pick up again. He liked her laugh.

"It really is all right! And if it's any consolation, I don't think you're like the elf mages of old," Callypso replied. Jack stiffened at the mention of his bloodline. "You shouldn't fear your heritage, Jack. There are great benefits to being an elf mage. One of which you'll learn soon enough."

"Who are you?" Jack whispered.

"I think I've kept you from your stroll long enough." Callypso looked upon the tree and sighed. "It would be wise to keep our meeting between us. Is that understood?"

"Y-Yes," Jack said, cursing at himself for allowing nerves to interfere with his speech.

"Good." She winked before disappearing.

Jack realized she passed through the veil. How did she do it so easily? Better yet, *why* did she have a home beyond a veil?

"Callypso," Jack mused. "What a beautiful name."

Leaving the grove, Jack felt something odd within his chest again. He couldn't explain the sensation, and yet he felt as if there was something tying itself along his heart.

"Soleil burn me." Jack gulped as he realized what it could have been. "Shadow...I need to talk to Shadow. I need to talk to him *now.*"

8

Arlina fumed as she paced around the audience chamber. She felt humiliated as well as embarrassed for not realizing Netira's dhampir heritage.

How had she missed it? How had Netira masked the truth so well for all these years of being her Second?

That traitorous bitch had help, that's how! Arlina thought. *But who would be foolish enough to help her?*

Arlina first thought of her mage, Karesu, because of Latos' mention of a charm, but then she dismissed the idea. He and Netira despised one another; it was evident in every council meeting. It amused her at times, seeing their disgust toward one another. Arlina had to practically force them to work together on past missions.

But she couldn't believe anything she saw anymore, not after Latos' report. No one was above suspicion now.

She sighed as she slouched on her black marble throne. As she crossed her legs, the glint of the onyx-jeweled hilt of her sai caught her eye. Grasping it, Arlina twirled the weapon along her long, pale fingers and tried to think.

She thought of Latos' proposal of sending Netira to the elves as a scapegoat; she found herself considering it. The death Arlina wanted to hand Netira personally wouldn't quell the anger she held, no. She thought of handing Netira over to Vashti, who was well known for her...creative...methods of torture, but that wouldn't satisfy her either. Disposing the dhampir by handing her over to the Elders of the Woodland Realm would give her such amusement.

Her thoughts shifted to Artemis. Knowing the two friends her wretched sister kept, Arlina was sure they wouldn't have told Artemis the truth of her origins and of her mother's death. Arlina wanted to vomit at their idea of protection...the fools.

I'll still attack that damn city, Arlina decided, *simply for housing that half-breed bitch. And then those damned dreams can finally stop.*

Arlina called for a servant and demanded parchment and ink. It was time to start another game with the Woodland Realm Elders, as well as remedy the issue of the known traitor.

Netira's eyes snapped open as she felt a presence outside of her home. She heard the distinct rustling sound of parchment sliding beneath the door, and the presence disappeared once the parchment stopped halfway across the main room. Netira grew wary and went to move from her bed, only just remembering the pale, muscled arm that was draped across her waist.

The moment she moved, the figure beside her stirred and opened a tired violet eye.

"Go back to sleep, love," she whispered, caressing Karesu's face.

"I felt the presence as well." Karesu groaned while stretching, the shared blanket falling to his bare waist. "What do you suppose Arlina wants with you?"

"I don't know," Netira replied as she grasped a blanket that had fallen to the ground during their earlier festivities and draped it across her naked, lithe body. She retrieved the parchment and tore through the crimson crossed-sai wax seal.

She felt Karesu standing behind her, and Netira moved the letter closer for him to inspect.

Netira,

I require your presence in my chamber at noon-time this day. It's been brought to my attention that we have a traitor in our midst, and I desire to consult with you on how to proceed on the matter. It is imperative that you return, for I also desire to reconcile our relationship after such dark tidings.

Arlina Ravenwing, Mistress of Blackwen City

"Would you think less of me if I called her a lying bitch?" Netira growled.

Karesu chuckled as he wrapped his arms around her waist, while slowly tracing her neck with his lips. "Would you think less of me if I agreed?"

"Hardly." Netira smiled as she leaned deeper into his embrace. "Maybe in the sight of others, I would pretend to."

"There will be a day when I will dispose of the pretenses we hold in public, Netira," Karesu replied as he gently nipped the curve of her throat. She loved whenever he did that, for it made her body tingle with need. "And what a day it will be."

"Indeed it will." Netira gasped as he repeated the gesture. She had to move away, or she would never make the meeting with that damned woman. "Who do you think she suspects *now?*"

"Soleil burn me if I knew." Karesu shrugged. He faked a sad expression. "But noon-time draws near, my love, and you should take advantage of Arlina's good graces while you still can. Much to my dismay, mind you."

"We'll play again when I return." Netira stole a kiss and winked when she pulled away. "Be careful when you leave."

"I'll slip out the usual way, don't worry," Karesu answered. He handed her the silver band carved with his special runes. "Don't forget the charm this time either. Otherwise, I'll have to tattoo the runes onto your skin as I did my fire rune."

Netira's grin widened. "Is that a promise?"

Netira stood before the doors to the Mistress' chamber. She knew there was more to the message than Arlina had written, and it unnerved her. If Karesu noticed, she was thankful that he kept quiet about it.

Had Arlina discovered the truth about her? Netira shook her head. She couldn't have. Netira was certain she wasn't followed, and the scout that *had* known the truth of her heritage, she'd disposed of.

Arlina granted her entry after she knocked a handful of times. Walking inside, Netira narrowed her eyes at the sight of Latos beside the Mistress. His smug countenance bothered her, that damn bootlicker. What use was *he* of all people in discussing what Arlina desired to do to this traitor of hers?

"Ah, Netira!" Arlina greeted her as she shifted in her throne. "I am pleased to see you, and early as well!"

"I do as you will, Mistress," Netira replied as she knelt, put off by the tone Arlina used. She was being nice. *Too* nice.

"As you should." Arlina nodded to Latos. "You remember Latos, do you not?"

"Regrettably," Netira answered, not caring if her tone angered the Mistress.

Latos laughed. "I can't say I'm pleased to see you either, former Second of Blackwen City."

Netira felt her stomach drop. "Former?"

How could that be? Avilyne's hell, she was always so careful! Charm and all!

"Oh, Latos! You've gone and spoiled everything now," Arlina huffed. "I had hoped to enjoy the suspense further…"

"Mistress, I ask an explanation for my sudden dismissal from my position," Netira asked while trying to steady herself.

It infuriated her to stoop so low to the woman.

"Your little outing for starters!" Arlina berated her. "How dare you meddle into affairs that do not concern you! How dare you disobey me!"

"I did so only for the sake of the city, Mistress. The scouts you sent were careless and brought unnecessary attention to our kind!" Netira pleaded. "There's only so much war we can wage and survive to tell the tale."

"Spare the Mistress your nonsense, Netira!" Latos seethed.

"Be silent, snake," Netira retorted, trying her damndest to still her hand.

"Both of you shut up!" Arlina yelled, which silenced them both.

Arlina cast her now red eyes on Netira. "For so many years, Netira, I have trusted you and your counsel. I chose you as my Second because you were ruthless in your rise in power, but loyal enough to stay your hand per my desire. Never did I imagine that you would disobey me as gravely as you have." Arlina grasped a sai from her boot, and Netira knew what was coming. "Aerios blow you, *half-breed*."

Arlina leaped after Netira, and Netira barely managed to block the sai with the sword she drew from the sheath along the curve of her hip. Ignoring Latos' curses, Netira shoved off Arlina, but then found her sword hooked in the curved prongs of the sai. Arlina removed the sword from Netira's grasp with a swing and dashed after her again.

Willow be damned, Netira cursed. *I have no choice now. The pretenses are over.*

Dodging the swings of both sai, Netira removed the silver ring charm and flung off her coat. Fully stretched from her back were two large, black, bat-like wings. Her now silver irises watched as Arlina's face contorted with disgust.

"*Abomination,*" Arlina spat, resuming her barrage of attacks.

Netira jumped back as she spread her wings and then flew above Arlina. She landed next to her sword and met resistance—Latos. He wouldn't release his foot from on top of the blade, no matter how hard she pulled on the hilt. Dhampirs were supposed to be stronger than full-bloods, yes, but Netira was in a disadvantage—she had not fed this day. She cursed.

"Forget about me?" he taunted, as the irises of his eyes shifted to red.

"Now how could I forget about you?" Netira grinned as she released her sword hilt and grabbed his neck. "No doubt it was you who discovered the truth and reported it to Arlina. Bottom-feeders like you never last long around here. There were others before you who scrambled to the Mistress and met their own vicious ends when their usefulness ran out. Ask Vashti about it sometime, should I send her to Avilyne's hell with you."

"Until then, dhampir bitch," Latos grumbled, while struggling beneath her grip, "you should worry about your own miserable life."

A loud blast echoed within the chamber, and Netira released Latos as she howled.

She backed away while grasping her now bloodied waist. The bullet shot from Arlina's infamous flintlock pistol had missed her vital points, but it still caused an agonizing pain Netira had never felt before.

When she fell to the ground, she heard Arlina cackle.

"The few bad things about this toy are the occasional misfires and how the shot tends to stray a bit from its intended path," Arlina said, strolling to Netira. "Even so, I'm fortunate for such things. I had no intention of killing you. That would be too easy."

Netira retched up her own blood, and then tried to staunch the bleeding from her waist. "Why do I find that hard to believe?"

"Because,"—Arlina kicked Netira's waist—"I have plans for you, traitor."

"Plans that involve you traveling," Latos added, while licking his lips at the sight of Netira's blood along the chamber floor. "You see, there are others who would prefer to punish you themselves."

Enduring another blow to the waist, Netira tightly shut her eyes. She refused to ask the question that lingered in her mind.

"Before I tell you of your fate, dear Netira, there is something I'm just *dying* to know," Arlina mocked as she grasped Netira by her hair and dragged her onto her knees. "Who helped you all this time? Who masked your true nature from me?!"

Netira flashed Arlina a thin-lipped grin. "You're better off killing me than thinking I will tell you."

"It wouldn't be wise to further upset me," Arlina hissed.

"Learn to be disappointed."

Latos kicked Netira before Arlina could retaliate, and she scowled at herself for whimpering. The pain was unbearable, and she would sooner face Avilyne in hell than continue listening to the two snarling above her.

"Latos, prepare yourself and a few others for travel. I have already sent a letter to Netira's future hosts," Arlina instructed, returning to her throne.

Netira felt herself viciously hoisted from the ground, and she was dragged toward the chamber doors. Before their exit, Netira heard Arlina speak. "Enjoy your time in Ellewynth. And when you arrive, be sure to inform my niece that I'll be seeing her soon."

Netira was too shocked to throw an insult at Arlina. She knew the destination of her exile well enough—Ellewynth was the grand elven city of the Woodland Realm. She was going to be blamed for the death of those poor elves, the ones those scouts had brutalized.

And…did Arlina say "niece"?

Tamina's baby survived, Netira thought before succumbing to unconsciousness. *There truly is another Ravenwing woman in Arrygn…Kiare be praised.*

⌒〜

The dreams of Mother were more frequent after that first one. The worst of them was where I watched her battle with a woman who looked like she could have been a blood relative.

She had cold gray eyes that chilled me each time I saw them. I couldn't hear a word they said, let alone the clashing of the odd weapons they wielded. Each time the dream ended, however, I could hear a loud bang that sent me screaming as I awoke.

Shadow noticed my lack of sleep during our weapons training. He kept asking if I was all right and tried to have me talk about my troubles in the hopes I would sleep better. I didn't have the heart to tell him that my own mother was the one haunting my dreams and that there was another woman who now did the same.

On the times I started to gather enough courage to tell him the truth about the dreams, something or someone got in the way. Perhaps it wasn't time to learn the truth about my mother's death just yet.

I didn't know what tortured me more.

Poor Shadow had his own share of troubles lately. The meeting with the Elders left him in a mood that frightened even me, and I didn't dare ask what happened. He would only glance at me with a half smile when he was caught in the mood, and he would continue instructing me in our lessons. I thought it was fair, considering I couldn't tell him the details of my own issues.

I sat outside by our training ground and yawned as Shadow set up some new archery targets. He caught the yawn and laughed at my sudden look of guilt.

"It's not as if it's early in the day, Artemis," he teased.

"It doesn't matter what time of the day it is," I grumbled. "I'm exhausted either way."

"Still haven't been sleeping well?"

"No."

"Do you wish to speak of the dreams?"

Yes, I thought as I noted Shadow's look of concern.

I sighed when I couldn't speak of it. "No."

"Fair enough," Shadow answered, thankfully unoffended.

"What's that?" I inquired, not only happy to change the subject but also curious about the sealed letter resting beside his bow.

"Our dear Jack has written to us." Shadow grinned as he unraveled the letter. "I hope Talisa isn't torturing him too much."

"He can handle it." I laughed as I moved closer to read Jack's words.

Dear Shadow (and Artemis, for the goddesses know you're there too),

I hope the weapons training is going well and that Artemis isn't complaining too much. Since Talisa hasn't mentioned anyone being shot or killed lately, I assume she's finally learned to aim. (I only jest. Please don't kill me, Artemis. I actually don't know that much of what goes on outside of the cottage.)

The apprenticeship has its ups and downs. For the life of me, I cannot sleep past dawn anymore. I will admit, though, that I'm rather starting to enjoy these walks I'm forced to take. Talisa might make a proper elf out of me by the time my apprenticeship ends! (I can hear you both laughing. Stop it.)

I don't have much free time so I'll just get right to the point. While the question I'm about to ask is directed to Shadow, I have no doubt that you, dear Artemis, will find out about this anyways. So my question is this: is it possible to feel the string to someone when you can attest to feeling it to another? Or am I mistaken and bound to only one of them?

Answer me soon. Willow be damned, it's giving me headaches. And I can't afford any more head-slaps from Talisa.

Jack

"The string?" I asked, confused. "What's he talking about?"

"He's referring to the feeling an elf gets when they find their life-mate," Shadow explained. "We refer to the feeling as a string because that's exactly what it feels like when we're around that particular person."

"Hmm." I took the letter and reread the last part. "He's obviously talking about Lilith, but who's the other one? He's found *another* girl so quickly? How's that even possible? Does Talisa know about this?"

"I don't know what's going on, but as far as I know, the string only happens for one person," Shadow answered. "We'll just have to plan a visit sooner than expected and see who this mystery woman is that he's become attached to."

"Indeed!" My curiosity grew when I glanced at him. "Have *you* ever felt the string before?"

Shadow stiffened, and I noticed how he forced himself to relax. "I have not."

"Willow be damned! Shadow, you're an awful liar!" I fell back laughing, even though I felt a small knot form in my chest. "Tell me, what's her name? Do I know her? When and where did you meet this lucky woman? Is she from this realm?"

"Artemis, there is no one," Shadow insisted. "It is not unusual for an elf my age to have not felt the string. Yet, anyways."

"But it *is* unusual that you haven't even been with a woman yet either," I said while remembering Jack's words the day Shadow returned home.

"For a moment there you sounded like Clarayne..." Shadow muttered.

"As in Lady Clarayne?"

"Yes, and she scolds me about that, *very* often." Shadow noted my inquiring glance. "That should not surprise you. We are close."

"I know," I said. "Even so…" I stared at the clouds and asked the question I'd asked myself for a long time. "Shadow, what are you really waiting for?"

Shadow let out a deep breath. "I'm not so sure anymore."

"Would you tell the woman how you feel?" I asked. "When you finally find her, of course?"

Shadow ignored the tease in my final question. "I'd like to say yes, but it is easier said than done."

"I think you should," I said, somehow noticing the bit of jealousy in my voice.

"You've never mentioned anyone either, my dear," Shadow said. "What are *you* waiting for?"

My confusion to end, I thought. *To understand if what I feel is true, and not just a passing emotion. And if it is, why do I fear it so much?*

You don't want him to see the monster, another thought answered. I shoved it away.

"I don't know either," I finally answered. "I always hear how women want to be swept off their feet, like they need to be rescued, but that's not what I want."

"What do you want?"

I faced him. I could see curiosity in those green eyes of his. I could see the hint of a smile in the curve of his lips. I realized it then. I denied being in love with Shadow because I didn't want him to know the monster I could be. Sure, the dhampir could have come out whenever Jack slept over, but the thought of Jack encountering my other form was less horrifying to me than Shadow seeing it. I did not want a wedge to grow between us because of it.

"I want to love a man who would love me in return," I answered. "There would be no fear between us. If he loved my soul more than my appearance, if he loved my faults rather than my perfections…I would be happy."

Now if only I would stop being so afraid…

"I pray there'll be one who will fulfill those wishes," Shadow said. "I pray he'll be good to you."

I noticed the minor prickle in his tone with the final comment. Before I could say anything, Shadow stood up and grabbed his bow. "I think we've lain around long enough, my dear. Let's get back to your lessons, shall we?"

～⌒

Karesu made his way to the audience chamber and froze as the scent of blood grew stronger with each step he took. Worse, he knew well enough whom the blood belonged to—Netira.

He was surprised when one of Arlina's servants came to his study and relayed a request for his audience. His fear rose when he realized Arlina had learned of Netira's true heritage. Karesu might suffer the same fate, since he was the one who helped mask Netira's dhampir heritage. He doubted it, though, since he knew Netira would rather die than hand him over to the Mistress.

While it seemed futile, he prayed nonetheless to the goddesses, Avilyne specifically, that somehow she was still alive. The laws against dhampirs had always been strict in Blackwen City, but under Arlina's tyranny, they practically spelled genocide.

Karesu entered the chamber and was struck by the amount of servants within. There was a large group of them on their knees, scraping away the dried blood along the floor.

"An ugly matter, mage Karesu," Arlina said, now standing beside him. "A hazard for any Mistress, sadly."

"What happened here?" Karesu inquired, now looking away from the blood. "Or should I look the other way and pretend this doesn't exist?"

"Just dealing with traitors." Arlina shrugged nonchalantly. She led him to the council room. "I'll explain in due time."

Like hell you will, Karesu thought. "What do you require of me, Mistress?"

Arlina pointed to the large sheets of old parchment lying across the marble table. Karesu identified them as maps, particularly of the elven realms. "The elves? What of them?"

"Only the elves of the Woodland Realm interest me. Tell me what you know of their land."

Karesu took one of the maps and ran a long, pale finger along the vast forest of the realm. "The forest of the realm is special…it is the only known forest in Arrygn that has veils or gateways into sacred ground, as well as having hidden shelters. In dire times of war, the Elders residing in the city of Ellewynth will force those unable to fight to hide within the veils."

"Can these veils hide those who aren't of elven blood or of the realm itself? Are there such rules?"

Of course you wouldn't directly ask me if the veils can hide a surviving blood kin of yours, Karesu internally scowled. "It is possible. I would think only those of magical capacity can control the veils, and therefore choose who may enter them. The question would be better directed to the witch of the elves and Kiare's longtime vassal, Talisa. It's been said that she and any who pass her apprenticeship can lead those they wish into the veils of the forest."

"Talisa," Arlina snarled. "A name I haven't heard in ages."

Karesu knew why. Talisa was a dear friend to the sister Arlina murdered years ago. He studied the Mistress, and he was amazed to see her shudder.

Arlina glanced at Karesu. "Do you think you would be able to lift a veil if you came across one? You are a vampire mage. You have great power of your own."

"I can try, but I wouldn't be quick to hope," Karesu explained. "My specialty lies in runes and charms. The forest might not accept my sort of magic. After all, I am of the undead. What thrives on life cannot be accepting of death."

"I suppose that's better than 'no.'" Arlina studied the map and poked the marker for Ellewynth. "Ellewynth's forces have no doubt improved since the last time I dealt with them. Tell me what you know concerning the woodland soldiers stationed there."

"Other than that they're just returning from their second war with the dragons of Fieros Mountains?" Karesu rubbed his cross earring. "The elven forces are tired. They would not expect another call to arms so soon."

"Go on," Arlina ordered.

"Ellewynth itself has not been attacked for nearly a century, as I recall. Not since their first war with the dragons. You've dealt with the soldiers bred from there in less time than that, yes?" Arlina nodded. "While the forces have indeed improved, I doubt the physical defenses have. The elves are a stubborn bunch, and are slow to learn when it comes to sieges. The confidence was always in the soldiers keeping the enemy as far away from the city as possible. No doubt the veils in which they hide the refugees are far enough from Ellewynth that they can fall prey to hunting parties, should you choose such an action." Karesu paused as he watched Arlina absorb the knowledge. "To put it bluntly, why the desire for war with the woodland elves again?"

He noted how Arlina took a moment to think, as if she were carefully choosing her words. "They harbored a traitor to my noble bloodline for nearly twenty-one years. I choose to strike now before they can think of her as a weapon against the Dark Fortress. I want those damned elves to remember who they dare to stand against."

"I assume that I shall be one of the leaders in your strike party."

"You assume correctly."

"And what of your Second?" Karesu asked, no longer using discretion about Netira. "Is she to accompany me and anyone else you designate to lead?"

"Netira is…" Arlina's face contorted into anger, and that was answer enough for Karesu. She pulled out the silver ring charm he'd made for his love, and left it atop the map. "The blood you saw earlier…it belonged to her. She is considered a traitor to Blackwen City."

"Traitor?" Karesu did his best to mask his true reaction. His fear subsided for a moment; Arlina said "is," not "was." "Why does that not surprise me? What has she done?"

"A dhampir in our midst, and not one of us had caught it," Arlina hissed. She sensed Karesu's unspoken inquiry, and she actually indulged him. "It's no matter now, as she is now suffering from a fate worse than death."

Karesu suppressed a sigh of relief, despite the horror he now felt.

She is *alive…for now.*

"I take it she's undergoing the usual torture reserved for her kind?"

"No. I sent her with a small scouting party to Ellewynth. The elves have their own reasons why they wish her dead."

The death of the elves by the scouts, Karesu realized. *She'll be blamed for it. Avilyne's hell!*

"If she still lives by the time we are to attack the city, how do you wish for us to proceed? Take her back and kill her in Blackwen City, or shall we just dispose of her there?"

"Do what you wish. I have no further desire to stain my hands of her filthy half-breed blood." Arlina turned away just before Karesu's face darkened. "Start preparing the strike party. Make sure to leave enough soldiers to defend the city. Once Latos returns, you two will begin the move on Ellewynth. Return tomorrow for discussion on other things I desire for you to carry out."

Karesu bowed his head, as was customary, and he left the audience chamber. He returned to his study and searched for his sword. Now was a good time for a hunt; he couldn't afford for word to spread that he was angered after a meeting with Arlina. Even the fools on the council would piece together his true feelings concerning Netira should they learn of his anger after learning what Arlina did with her.

"Whatever they do to you, Netira, hold onto life," Karesu prayed. "Hold on for when I arrive and take you away from there, my love."

~⌒~

Lady Clarayne sat in her candlelit study and continued to work on the affairs of the city. Lords Celstian and Destrius were in their respective offices as well, a result after their disastrous meeting with Shadow.

Lady Clarayne deeply sighed. She wished the meeting had ended on a lighter note. Lord Destrius had to commission new furniture to be made.

Shadow had arrived as requested and repeated the report he had given to Lady Clarayne. He begged once more that if the event came, they would not give up Artemis to Arlina. Lord Celstian was sympathetic, but not enough to grant his wish. Lord Destrius went ballistic and went as far as calling Shadow a moronic fool for even considering Artemis worth protecting.

The verbal jousting between the two still made Lady Clarayne shake. It was a miracle Shadow didn't physically harm Lord Destrius, no matter how many pieces of furniture the Elder chucked at him. She wouldn't have minded, but she knew it would have been unthinkable. It wouldn't matter if it was in self-defense; Lady Clarayne wouldn't have been able to protect her nephew if he struck an Elder. The laws of the Woodland Realm sometimes irritated her.

Lady Clarayne looked from her desk when she heard a soft knock echo from the doorframe, and she granted entry to the visitor. Lord Celstian entered, holding a small teapot.

"I thought you could use some," Lord Celstian greeted her.

"It is appreciated. Thank you, Celstian," Lady Clarayne said, retrieving two small cups.

Lord Celstian poured what Lady Clarayne noted to be lemongrass tea, and he sat in the chair across from her desk. He sighed in contentment as he took a sip. "It would seem that the return home has been nothing like we imagined."

"Indeed," Lady Clarayne agreed, now sipping her own tea. "I didn't expect the threat of war to return to us for another few years. I prayed for that much of a reprieve, despite knowing how impossible it would have been."

"Have you heard from Shadow since our last, ah, gathering?"

Lady Clarayne lowered her gaze. "I have not. I don't expect we shall hear from him for some time."

"You blame yourself."

"Yes." Lady Clarayne traced the rim of her teacup with her long forefinger. "I love my nephew dearly. He is the last living reminder of my brother, may the goddesses watch over him. It hurts me to watch his heart fall into despair. I knew he cared for Artemis, but I hadn't realized just how much until this recent war. When we hand Artemis to Arlina, whenever that may be, Shadow will be lost to us as well. I'm not sure if I can accept that."

"He can take care of himself, Clarayne," Lord Celstian explained. "He's proven that time and time again. Shadow can protect the girl while he continues his duty to the realm. I've no doubt that he will."

"It still feels despicable to me. We took her in because her mother served the realm, and now we're throwing her back to the monsters in order to save ourselves."

"Sometimes one must do a little evil in order to achieve a greater good." Lord Celstian noted the dark look from Lady Clarayne. "I will admit I feel a little vile as well."

"I sense there's more stirring in the darkness than we originally believed."

"And what will you do if it is so?"

Lady Clarayne frowned. "I'm not sure anymore." She stood up and wandered toward the windowsill. "Both my body and spirit are still taxed from dealing with the dragons. And perhaps we're not supposed to be involved in what's to come."

"We're just supporting pieces of the game now, you think?"

Lady Clarayne glanced at Lord Celstian and chuckled. "I think I'm just speaking nonsense. We've had a long day today with this cursed paperwork, after all."

Lord Celstian laughed and was about to comment until the door slammed open; Lord Destrius stomped into the quarters. As usual, he was irate. Lady Clarayne noticed he held an opened and nearly crumpled letter at his side.

"Destrius, what has gotten you into a twist now?" Lord Celstian asked, preventing Lady Clarayne from snapping about the mistreatment of her door.

"Spare me the jests, Celstian." Lord Destrius threw the crumpled letter atop the desk. "What do you make of *that?*"

Lady Clarayne picked up the letter and stiffened as she read it.

"Clarayne? What is it?" Lord Celstian inquired.

"The letter is from Arlina," Lady Clarayne explained, nearly choking on the words.

"Let me see it."

Lady Clarayne handed the letter over to him.

Greetings to the Elders of Ellewynth,
The Lords Celstian and Destrius, and the Lady Clarayne,

I understand that my letter may not be well received since our cities have not always been amicable. However, I promise you that there is no trickery about. I only wish to right a few wrongs that were recently committed.

It has come to my attention that your realm has been experiencing "odd" deaths, and I am saddened to say that one of my own was responsible for the murders. I was livid when I discovered it and am deeply embarrassed that this occurred. After much consideration of the punishment to be dealt, I decided that the right to punish such unacceptable behavior rightfully belongs in your hands, and in a few days time a small scouting party will arrive at your borders to hand over the culprit. Her name is Netira, and she was formerly the Second of Blackwen City. Do with her what you must. She has already suffered for her crimes to the Dark Fortress.

I do not expect forgiveness or gratitude, again because of our relations and actions from the past, but I do hope we can get past this horrible incident.

Sincerely,
Mistress Arlina Ravenwing of Blackwen City

"What do you make of it?" Lord Celstian asked.

"I sense a trap," Lady Clarayne replied.

"As do I. However," Lord Destrius started as he snatched the letter from Lord Celstian, "if she is sending the one responsible for the deaths, then I will forgive the arrogance of that woman…for a time, anyways."

"We should have Shadow in the receiving party when their scouts arrive," Lord Celstian suggested. "He was the one who discovered this, after all. He could probably identify this Netira and help put our suspicions at ease."

"Ask him yourself," Lord Destrius snapped. "I have no desire for seeing that bastard again anytime soon."

Lady Clarayne opened her mouth to yell at him, but Lord Celstian stood up and grabbed her arm.

"Don't," he whispered to her. He glanced at Lord Destrius. "We will be on guard. Only time will tell whether we will encounter more treachery, or whether we encounter the real truth of the matter."

9

I didn't see Mother or the other woman with the cold gray eyes this time. There was a small scouting party moving through parts of Arrygn that were unknown to me; I counted four scouts, and they were escorting one woman in a small caged carriage. Even with the cloaks with odd symbols stitched within the hems, I could tell they were full-bloods.

The woman in the cage, however…she wasn't one of them. She may have looked like a full-blood, but she did not feel like them.

She felt…she felt like me. A dhampir.

The scouts didn't notice my presence. They continued to follow the lead of the tall male with short and spiked red hair. His black eyes were nearly as frigid as the gray-eyed woman from the previous dreams, but he did not seem as dangerous. He bade the others to march on as he strolled to the side of the cage. The woman within glared at him, and he responded with a laugh.

"Enjoying the view, Netira?" he asked, as he dangled a small wineskin in front of the bars.

I could smell the blood release into the air as he removed the wooden cap and sipped it.

The woman he called Netira eyed the wineskin hungrily. Even so, she did not move to reach for it.

"Come now. Surely you want some sustenance after receiving such wounds?" The man said while he flashed a sadistic smile. "A simple plea is all I need from you, dhampir."

It was true then.

"I wouldn't trust anything that comes from you, Latos." Netira shifted farther away from the bars.

That's when I noticed her wounds. She had dried bloodstains along her waist, as well as her arms and chest. She was brutalized, but not so much that she couldn't function.

Latos reached through the cage to grab Netira's neck and forced her face against the bars. He shoved the wineskin into her mouth and forced her to swallow the blood. Netira managed to break free and tried to spit out the force-fed blood.

Latos laughed as he hid the wineskin in his cloak.

"Why would I have a need to poison you?" Latos feigned innocence. "As much as I enjoy your agony, I need you to live long enough to arrive at the city."

"Once you leave me to the elves, Latos," Netira began, "I'd suggest you learn to look over your shoulder at all times. I just might appear and give you what you deserve."

"Spare me, you filthy dhampir bitch." Latos left her.

I walked beside the cage and saw Netira's face darken. She had refused the blood even though she desperately needed it. Was she like me? Did she hate her heritage enough to suppress it? I wondered what was going through her mind, and I also wondered why the full-bloods were sending her to the elves.

Wait. Was Netira coming to Ellewynth?

She will help you when it is time.

The voice startled me. It sounded like my own, but not quite.

"Mother?" I called.

She will show you the way.

I woke up when I felt a gentle caress along my cheek. When I sat up, I sighed; no one was in my room.

I fought off a chill as I hugged my knees to my chest. This dream differed greatly from the earlier ones. The voice…it had to have been Tamina. Mother obviously thought Netira was of some importance… but for what? And why?

She will show you the way.

"Show me the way to where?" I asked aloud. "What are you trying to start, Mother?"

There was no reply. Not even an echo within my mind.

"What is coming?" I demanded. "What are you trying to lead me to?"

She will help you when it is time.

"Time for *what*?" I cried, getting tired of all the dreams and hidden messages.

It was silent again, and I cursed in my broken Elvish.

I saw it was dawn when I glanced at the window. I needed to talk to Shadow.

After I put on warmer clothing, I grabbed a cloak and headed outside. A walk to clear my mind would help before going to see him.

Arlina awoke from her slumber as she reflexively jumped up from bed. She grumbled once she realized the blankets clung to her due to sweat. The dreams were getting worse; Arlina wondered if she would ever slumber again without seeing the face of her wretched sister.

Tamina is dead. She is *dead*.

No one could survive a bullet to the head, not even a full-blood...right?

"I've killed thousands, and of all the faces that come to haunt me, it had to be *yours!*" Arlina spat. "Willow damn you, Tamina. Stay in Avilyne's hell, where you belong!"

I have a promise to keep.

Arlina felt horror seep into her body once she heard the words.

That couldn't have been Tamina. Tamina is dead! *Dead!*

Oh, but it is me, *sister...after all, I did* say I would see you soon.

Arlina saw an ethereal figure form in front of her bed, and she refused to admit fear even when the figure transformed into the dead body of Tamina. Her long brown hair fell past her shoulders, and her dark clothes were stained with her own blood. Her violet eyes were cold.

Tamina smirked at her sister. Arlina's gaze wouldn't leave from the bullet hole in Tamina's forehead.

"Avilyne's hell," Arlina whispered. "A specter?"

More or less, Tamina answered, as she hovered toward the windowsill. *But it's of no importance.*

"You're the one causing the dreams!" Arlina accused. Tamina nodded, disinterested. "Why? Why now?"

Your time is running out, sister. Tamina tapped the other bullet hole within her waist. *Fate has decided it's time to collect after all the chaos you've caused. You must now pay the price. Avilyne has a special hellhole just for you.*

"Aerios blow you. You speak nonsense."

The goddess of death has a special place reserved for you, sister. I've seen it. Tamina saw the glare and laughed. *Don't give me that. You brought this upon yourself. Not even you are immune to the repercussions.*

"Leave me be!"

So be it. Allow me the pleasure of a few parting words. And you should not take my words lightly, Arlina.

"Just say your damned words, and get the hell out of my bedchambers."

Tamina shrugged. She floated beside Arlina and grinned when the Mistress of Blackwen shuddered after her ghostly hand passed through her real one.

Attack Ellewynth if you so desire. You won't accomplish the goal you're really after when you do. As I've said, you won't locate Artemis. She'll find you. She'll be the last thing you'll see before your soul is claimed by our patron goddess.

After the last of Tamina's words, Arlina watched her sister dissipate. Arlina cursed herself when she felt the beads of sweat drip from her chin to her chest.

She was the Mistress of Blackwen City—she did not know fear. She *was* fear, and neither she nor anyone else was going to forget that.

"If Avilyne wants me in her little hellhole, she'll have to come and put me there herself," Arlina snapped. She looked at the spot where Tamina had hovered, as if she were still there. "I'll drag that daughter of yours with me, you bitch!"

Shadow leaned against the balcony railing, watching the sunrise. He hadn't slept well; he'd seen a face he hadn't looked upon for so long.

The death of Tamina had hit hard for both him and Talisa. The three fought alongside one another in the service of the Woodland Realm for numerous years; the heir to the throne of Blackwen City had hoped her service would help build a positive relationship between the Dark Fortress and the woodland elves. Tamina had ended her service, however, once she met Gavin, Artemis' father.

Shadow never liked the man.

He knew Gavin's true nature from the moment they met, but for Tamina's sake, he kept silent on the matter. Talisa shared Shadow's sentiments, but she made them well known. Tamina nearly severed her friendship with Talisa because of it, which made Shadow more afraid of voicing his opinions of the man. The situation grew worse when Tamina decided it was best to hide her full-blood heritage from Gavin, especially since he was rather vocal concerning his hatred of the undead. As understandable as it was that she had kept silent, Shadow and Talisa knew it would ultimately be disastrous to keep her heritage a secret from the human.

And then Artemis was born.

After the tragedy of Tamina's death, Talisa begged the Elders to keep Artemis within the Woodland Realm. She was born there, and should have had its protection. Shadow remembered that fated day well, for it was only a few days after Lord Destrius joined the Elder ranks. Shadow first began to despise him then, for Destrius wanted to execute Artemis just because of her heritage. If it weren't for Aunt Clarayne and Lord Celstian, Artemis wouldn't have made it through her first year, let alone her twenty-first.

Shadow never met Artemis until she was six; he was dealing with yet another wave of rebel full-bloods from Tamina's city at the time, and he had to stop by Talisa's cottage for her special medicinal herbs. It was an odd yet fun memory. He never imagined a dhampir loving to climb trees more than an elf child. Artemis always had a way of surprising him, even in her bleakest of moods.

The complications with Artemis came after she moved into Ellewynth, where Shadow saw her regularly. He felt the sensation of the string when he first met her in Talisa's cottage, high up in that tree surrounded by apples, and he cursed himself for it. Talisa knew of it, and told him numerous times that it was nothing to be ashamed about. She would even give him rational explanations concerning the situation, specifically stating that guardians sometimes fall for their charges, and vice versa.

"I fell in love with mine," she said to him then.

Even with that knowledge, it did not make Shadow feel any better. The more time he spent with Artemis, the deeper he fell. He thought she would be awkward with him should he attempt to court her now. It would have hurt him deeply to lose the friendship they shared.

It was at that moment that he remembered the dream.

In his dream, Shadow was riding Azrael. He was fleeing Ellewynth, and he felt something reach out and force him to a stop. Shadow was shocked to find Tamina standing beside Azrael, casually stroking her mane as if it were just a normal thing to do.

Stop being so ashamed, she scolded him. *Artemis needs you now more than ever.*

Shadow tried to explain everything, and Tamina shut him up by laughing. She called him an overthinking fool, and she told him he had to be her daughter's rock. She said he belonged at her side. Something was coming, and he was a vital key in what was now unfolding.

No more running away, Shadow. Eventually, you will have to step into the light. Your fate is intertwined with hers, and it will never unravel no matter how much you pray for it to. Accept it.

He couldn't stop thinking about Tamina's words. Shadow had no doubt something was stirring in the world. He just didn't know how he could help, let alone understand his part within this new game.

"You're playing a dangerous game yet again, Tamina." He stared toward the rising sun. "When will you learn?"

Talisa wandered through the forest when dawn came. She ordered Jack to skip the mandated morning walk for the day and to lock himself in her library studying the pasts of the known elf mage bloodlines. It wasn't something she had wanted to do so soon, but after the dream she'd had, Talisa needed Jack to be ready.

Avilyne's hell, *she* needed to be ready.

Hearing the sound of the waterfall, Talisa placed her palm along an ash tree and felt the energy respond with a soft thrum. She wasn't granted entry to the veil, which meant that the one she was looking for wasn't within.

"Where is she?" Talisa asked.

She has yet to return from her stroll. My apologies, witch of the elves.

"No need for apologies, ancient one. I'll just have to find her through other means." Talisa smiled as she rubbed the bark. "Return to your slumber."

She left the ash tree grove and continued her walk. She thought about the dream once more and fought the urge to cry.

After seeing how her dear friend died due to Jack's encounter with Kiare's Mirror, Talisa shouldn't have been surprised to see Tamina again so soon. In the dream, Tamina had been sitting in Talisa's herb garden, just as she used to when she still lived. Before Talisa could say a word, Tamina stood up and hugged her.

I have a favor to ask of you, my dearest friend. There'll be another time for questions, I promise, she said, sensing the onslaught of inquiries Talisa wanted to ask. *Send your elemental to find my weapons. Artemis will need them soon. The elemental is the only one who can retrieve them.*

Talisa asked what was going on. She spoke about the ripple effect she had mentioned before to Jack, and Tamina only frowned.

The game is on, Talisa. Artemis will have need of you, and she will require the elf mage as well. He may not be ready now, but he will be a valuable asset to her nonetheless. Make sure your elemental finds my sai. Without them, Artemis won't stand a chance against her.

Talisa awoke before she could ask Tamina any more questions.

"I suppose it was inevitable that this should come to pass," Talisa muttered. "I just hope you know what you're doing, Tamina."

Jack was desperate to fall back asleep, but his body decided to rebel against the need. He was on edge; he had felt some strange presence in the cottage earlier. Talisa forced him to stay inside today, which meant that she felt something as well. Jack wasn't brave enough to ask her what the presence was.

He had no desire for a head-slap or being splashed with ice water so early in the day.

Jack tried to follow his teacher's suggestion of studying the previous elf mages, but he couldn't focus. His mind drifted to Callypso, and he cursed himself. Jack knew there was more to her than her appealing visage, but he couldn't pinpoint what it was. A part of him felt that the answer was slapping him in the face and he was just too dense to notice.

However, he did notice the letter that Talisa had thrown at his lap before she left. It was from Shadow, and Jack couldn't bring himself to open it. Each time he made the move to do so, the fear of the soldier's words restrained him.

"Oh, just open it already, you idiot!" Jack hissed as he snatched up the letter and tore through the green wax seal.

Hello Jack,

Artemis sends her love (and threats). We were both quite amused that you may be a "proper elf" when you return to us! Artemis bet you would last a week at most before you return to your old self.

Now onto that little dilemma of yours. As far as I know, the string occurs for one person only. There is a difference between the string and simple lust, you know. (I know you're glaring at this point. You should stop before you get another one of those headaches you complain so much about.) Whoever this new woman is, she must certainly be something in order for you to forget all about Lily. I'm afraid I can't really be of much help to you, Jack. If you feel the string for two women, I hope you realize you can only choose one. All I can tell you is to choose wisely.

Artemis and I plan to visit you and Talisa sometime soon. You can introduce us to your mystery woman then. Maybe you'll even receive our blessings.

Shadow

"Soleil burn me, why do the both of you enjoy tormenting me?" Jack whined. "I'm not lusting, damn you! This is a damned conspiracy!"

He could imagine the looks he'd receive from both Shadow and Artemis if they heard his response. Artemis would glare and call him an idiot, while Shadow would simply shake his head and flash that sarcastic smile of his.

Shadow had no right to judge; he had his own problems, like denying his feelings for Artemis. Artemis was in the same predicament, even if she wouldn't acknowledge being in one. Jack would much rather be in his current trouble than in theirs. When the day came for those two to come together, the victory would be his. He would make sure to never let them hear the end of it either—the physical abuse they would hand him would be well worth it.

He tossed the letter aside and was startled by the knocks on the front door. Jack grabbed the small curved knife he had grown accustomed to carrying after his first night of the apprenticeship, and tucked it away in his tunic sleeve.

"Who is here at this hour?" Jack grumbled, knowing that Talisa would have walked in with or without announcing herself.

Reaching the door, he felt a soothing energy he recognized instantly. Jack opened the door and somehow managed to suppress a stupid grin when he saw her.

Callypso stood outside the door, her light blue eyes still hypnotic to him. She wore a flowy peach dress this time and was still barefoot.

"Hello, Jack," she greeted him, with a soft smile. "I have to admit I didn't expect to see you here. Aren't you supposed to be on your walk?"

Jack rubbed the back of his neck and tried to still his nerves. "Sadly, Talisa confined me to the cottage."

"That is a shame, as it's such a nice morning for a stroll," Callypso replied, as a small wind lifted the blond curls that framed her face.

Jack grew mesmerized at the sight; she was such a beauty.

Then he realized he was being rude and quickly moved aside so that she could enter.

"Why don't you come inside? I'm afraid Talisa isn't around, but perhaps you'd like some tea until she comes back? Unless you're in a hurry, of course." Jack scowled at himself for babbling like a youngling.

"I'm in no hurry." Callypso stepped inside. When she wasn't looking, Jack took the knife out of his tunic sleeve and hid it in the closest bookcase. "I would love some tea."

She let him lead her into the kitchen, even though Jack surmised that she'd been in Talisa's cottage before. Callypso settled into one of Talisa's cushioned chairs and studied the room.

"Nothing much has changed since I was here last..." she observed.

"If you don't mind my asking," Jack began, "how long ago was that? Better yet, how exactly do you know Talisa?"

"Let's just say I've known her for far too long." Callypso smiled. She crossed her legs while folding her arms. "I'm partial to vanilla hazelnut, if you don't mind."

"I don't," Jack answered. "I see you're still favoring the cryptic approach."

"I do enjoy a good mystery."

"Please don't tell me you were once an apprentice to Talisa."

"Goddesses, no!" Callypso chuckled. "I value my friendship with Talisa far too much to discard it by accepting an apprenticeship."

Jack stood up to retrieve the teapot, and then he returned to hand her a small teacup. "You are something else, though."

"Oh?"

"I can't figure it out yet, but you're definitely more than you're letting on."

"If you hadn't realized that by now, you wouldn't be much of an apprentice." Callypso laughed at Jack's sullen look. "I meant no disrespect, Jack."

"No, it's fine."

"Why did Talisa venture out of the cottage so early? It's not something she normally does until much later in the day."

"I didn't ask." Jack was going to mention the odd presence he felt earlier, but decided that he too, would be cryptic. "Something was bothering her. She looked as if she didn't want to be disturbed."

"Probably a wise move on your part." Callypso sighed. "I wonder if..." She noted Jack's look of interest and waved him off. "It's nothing. I'm just musing aloud."

"I could be of some help. I muse aloud all the time." Jack grinned.

"I wondered if she's out looking for me. Something...something strange has been in the air lately, and I wanted to talk to her about it," Callypso explained as her face darkened.

So she felt something too. "That has been a recurring theme lately."

"Tell me, what do you know about spirits? Particularly of those who long ago passed from this world?"

"Spirits of the deceased either linger or disappear into the hands of the goddess of death, Avilyne," Jack replied while tapping the armrest. "Those who linger do so because their souls refuse to move on."

"That's not always the case," Callypso said. "Spirits that linger have enough strength left over to have personal vendettas carried out for them. It always starts with dreams, and then strange events follow soon after."

Who are you, Callypso? "You've been sensing a lingering spirit lately?"

"I can feel the spirit in the winds." She shuddered. "I'm not sure what to make of it."

Talisa said to me that a ripple effect was coming after we saw Tamina's death in Kiare's Mirror, Jack thought. *Is Tamina the spirit she's referring to? Did we feel Artemis' mother this morning?*

"Jack?"

"Sorry, I was thinking of something." Jack blinked. Callypso raised an eyebrow, and he shrugged in response. "It's nothing, really."

"You know something."

"As do you."

"Ah, now I see what you're trying to do. I tell you why you feel there's more to me than meets the eye, and then you'll explain what you know about my suspicions."

"Something like that."

Callypso rose from her chair and left her teacup beside the teapot. She smirked as she walked toward the front door. Jack followed and watched her wander into the open forest, looking to the sky.

"I'm afraid I just can't tell you, elf mage," she sighed. "You'll have to work harder at learning my truth. I suspect you have an idea, and I can see that you do not trust the thought. You should learn to pay more attention to your instinct. It might save your life one day."

Before Jack could speak, she disappeared. A gentle wind blew through his hair and his clothes.

He wished Talisa was around for a head-slap. He'd even take the ice water.

"It's you," he said aloud. "You're an elemental. You've been here before my very eyes."

Another realization set in—he felt the string for an *elemental*. Jack looked to the sky as if he was watching the goddesses. "This torture is for all the nights at the tavern, isn't it? Soleil burn me. What a mess I've gotten myself into."

Talisa found herself before the gateway to the Grove of Kiare's Mirror. She hadn't meant to come here, and she doubted the one she was looking for was within besides. There was no need for Kiare's vassal to be here; Talisa had enough of the grove it after seeing Tamina's death.

"I didn't expect to find you here," a voice said from behind her. "That seems to be the theme of the day—surprise."

Talisa smiled when she saw the curly, blond-haired woman wearing a flowing peach dress. "Callypso. Just the one I was looking for."

"I thought as much, since you weren't home." Callypso chuckled.

"You went to the cottage?" Talisa raised an eyebrow. "Willow be damned, you've met Jack. I apologize already if he gave any offense."

"No apologies necessary, since I've met him before, Talisa," Callypso replied. She laughed at Talisa's stricken expression. "The blame lies with me. I told him it would be in his best interests to stay silent on the matter."

"He has a fascination with elementals, Cally," Talisa explained. "He probably realizes by now that you are one. You'll never know peace again."

"I wouldn't count on it." Callypso sighed. "He has so much potential, but he is rather dense. Our dear Jack fears his instinct. He has doubted himself for too long, and it's hindering his abilities to grow."

"Don't get me started on the boy." Talisa rubbed her temples. "Let's get down to it, shall we? You went to the cottage for a reason. Is there something amiss?"

Callypso nodded as she fixed her skirts and sat against a tree trunk. "I've been sensing a lingering spirit in the wind. The energy trail this spirit left behind has been disturbing to me."

"Oh?" Talisa realized Callypso spoke of Tamina's recent visit. She fixed her robes as she sat against a tree opposite the elemental.

Callypso wrinkled her nose. "I sense some of it on you as we speak. Have you had an odd dream or encounter lately?"

"Yes," Talisa admitted. "It's what I wanted to speak to you about. You're feeling the energy of a dear friend who was murdered a little over two decades ago."

"That explains why the energy trail is so strong." Callypso rested her chin in her hand. "What did it want?"

"*She* asked me to send you to find her weapons," Talisa answered. Callypso grew confused. "Tamina was a vampire, a full-blood from Blackwen City. She fought alongside Shadow of Ellewynth and me for many years in service to the realm. She was a master of the sai. The weapons and skills are only passed down to the women of her bloodline, the Ravenwing."

"That part I know," Callypso said. "How did she die?"

"By Arlina's hand."

Callypso froze. "As in Arlina, the current Mistress of Blackwen City?"

"Indeed."

"They were sisters, yes?" Talisa nodded, and Callypso frowned. "It would appear that Tamina desires revenge. You're now a piece in the game that she created. It would seem that I will be joining in as well, whether I wish to or not."

"She only asked for you to find her weapons, Cally. That would be your only service."

"And who will be the one to wield them should I choose to retrieve them?"

Talisa pursed her lips. "Artemis, Tamina's only daughter and the last living kin to Arlina."

"The little dhampir who used to run rampant around your cottage?" Callypso asked. Talisa nodded again. "No. Absolutely not. I loved that little girl. I will not put her in harm's way."

"I won't deny that I am uneasy about this as well," Talisa said, "but it must be done."

"Why must *I* be the one to find these weapons of Tamina's?"

"You're an elemental," Talisa answered. "You have also lived in this forest long enough to know where things are hidden. Tamina wants you to find her sai and then hand them to Artemis once the time is right. It's better if you just return them to me. I do not think Tamina will mind that."

"Avilyne's hell." Callypso rubbed her temples, seeming as if she was having an internal debate.

Talisa rarely saw her this way. "What troubles you, old friend?"

"I will look for the sai and retrieve them," she answered, after a moment of silence. Before Talisa could express her gratitude, Callypso raised a hand to silence her. "I will do so under the condition that I cleanse them. I worry, Talisa. Spirits that linger for as long as Tamina has...they've lost themselves. They lose all sense of sanity and focus on the one thing that keeps them here in our world, which oftentimes is anger. If she returns again, and I have no doubt that she will, please be cautious. She will not be the same Tamina you were once so fond of."

Callypso disappeared into the wind before Talisa could respond. Talisa found she couldn't say a word even if she wished to.

Her friend was right, and it hurt her to think that Tamina could be someone else now.

〜◦

As soon as I stepped outside of Ellewynth's borders, I felt some sense of peace return to me. I'd always wanted to venture away from the city, but I was never able to take the extra step into the open forest...not since Shadow and Talisa first left for the war.

I lowered my hood and relaxed as I felt the cool breeze brush against my cheeks. It felt as if I were living back at Talisa's cottage, where I was free to roam around and safe from any disturbances.

I heard the snort of a horse, and I was surprised to find one standing behind me. The horse's white coat glistened in the rays of the sunlight, and the golden eyes flashed with a sense of amusement. I held up a hand and was about to stroke the bridge of the horse's nose, but I hesitated and kept my distance. The horse huffed as it pushed its head beneath my palm.

I felt feminine energy from the touch, and I beamed; the horse was a mare.

"You are beautiful," I said as I enjoyed the feel of her soft coat. "You'll have to forgive my hesitation earlier. The last time I pet a horse... well, he panicked and nearly knocked my head off."

The mare shook her head, as if in embarrassment. I decided I liked her.

"No need for apologies. Horses don't usually like me because of what I am. They think I come to feed on them. Lucky for you, I actually hate horse blood. I only drink fox blood," I babbled, now rubbing her neck. "If it was possible, I wouldn't even drink it."

The mare butted my shoulder with her head, and I laughed instead of feeling shocked. "I can understand that emotion well enough. Shadow, an elf soldier in the city, thinks it's foolish for me to avoid it too."

"It's as I said before…you have to accept your nature, my dear." I saw Shadow walking toward us, and the mare trotted beside him. "And as for horses, they tend to reflect the nature of their caretaker. Azrael here is in a class all of her own."

"Azrael is *your* horse? It's no wonder why she isn't afraid of me."

Azrael returned to my side and dipped her head for me to rub once more. Shadow folded his arms with a smile.

"Regardless of her rider, Azrael judges others for herself," Shadow explained. "She is not like the other horses. For that, I let her roam as free as she desires. Azrael also chooses her own company."

"I can see that." Azrael didn't attempt to move away from me; I could feel her contentment with the attention I was giving her. "What are you doing out here? And so early, I might add?"

"I felt a stroll might help with the mood I've been in lately. I was going to take Azrael along, but it appears she's perfectly happy being pampered by you."

"I'm enjoying the fact that something isn't running away from me at first glance." I grinned. "Does your mood have to do with the Elders, or is there something else adding to it?"

"Something else," Shadow replied. "I am more curious, however, as to why *you're* out here."

I looked away.

"The dreams are getting worse, aren't they?"

I opened my mouth to say yes, but no sound came out. I then nodded, since my speech failed me.

"Mine are haunting as well," Shadow said. "The something else I was referring to earlier…I saw someone I hadn't seen for a very long time. That same someone just so happens to be dead."

My eyes widened, and then he knew.

"All this time…you've been seeing your mother."

"It's been unpleasant," I answered. "It hasn't only been her."

"Who else have you been seeing?"

"Other vampires." I thought of the gray-eyed woman who always fought Mother in the dreams. "There was a full-blood woman who was always fighting against Tamina. She…she looked as if she were my kin."

I saw Shadow stiffen at the mention of the woman. "Describe her a bit more."

"She had such cold gray eyes. It's the most memorable thing about her," I said. "I don't know anything more than that. And each time she and Mother fought, there was no sound."

"Odd."

"I know." I moved to sit comfortably on the ground, and without skipping a beat, Azrael joined me. Shadow followed and sat across from us. "Who is she?"

"I have an idea of who she may be. But…" he paused as he rubbed his temples. "Artemis, if it is who I think it is…she's very dangerous. It wouldn't surprise me if you meet her soon."

"You're evading the question, Shadow. Who is she?"

He didn't answer.

"Is this part of the explanation you'll give me when you feel it's safe to?"

"Unfortunately." Shadow nodded. "I don't want to jump to conclusions just yet. I want to be able to have enough of my own questions answered before saying anything else."

"I suppose that's fair enough."

"You mentioned vampires before, which implies that you saw more than just your mother and the woman she fought. Who else did you see?"

"I saw a small scouting party…also full-bloods."

"What were they doing?"

"They were escorting a caged carriage. A female dhampir was inside of it." I remembered Netira's hatred for Latos, and how Mother said she would be the one to show me the way to wherever I was supposed to go. "She's supposed to be someone important for something that's to occur."

"Where are we supposed to find her if it turns out to be true?"

"I'm not so sure." I studied the forest and frowned. "I didn't recognize the part of the forest they were in, but the dhampir mentioned something about the scouts taking her to the elves. I don't know to which elven land specifically."

"Only the Woodland Realm and the Oceanic Realm have forests within their borders," Shadow explained. "I suppose we'll just see what happens in time, hmm?"

I nodded, while still remembering Netira and the shape she was in. "What's coming, Shadow?"

"I can't say for certain," he answered. The three of us stood and started to walk back toward Ellewynth. "I think it'll be an event that will change everything we know. I'd rather be prepared than to be caught unawares."

10

Netira stirred in her cage as the sunlight warmed her face. There was a benefit to being a dhampir, since she rather enjoyed a good sunrise.

Her escorts were hidden beneath heavy and dark cloaks with small runes stitched at the hems. It was Karesu's handiwork; it was part of his duty to Blackwen City as a mage to find efficient ways for full-bloods to maneuver within the daylight hours. The cloaks were preferred more by the scouts and a score of Arlina's stealthier warriors, but of course, it wasn't enough to satisfy them.

Netira realized they weren't moving once she awoke. She moved closer to the bars of the cage, wincing with each gesture, and noticed the scouts were taking cover in a small cave. She could hear their conversation as well as some other noise and understood they were feeding. Netira could smell deer blood, and she salivated. Her wounds weren't fully healed yet, even with Latos' stunt of force-feeding her.

She didn't trust him. He would have poisoned her for his own amusement and then reported to Arlina that she had committed suicide before reaching Ellewynth. She would expect nothing less from such scum.

Retreating to the farthest corner of the cage, she tried to recall how long they'd been on the road. Her sense of time was altered due to her injuries from both Arlina and Latos, but she remembered just enough to know that they'd been away from the Dark Fortress for at least a week.

Netira didn't recognize the part of the forest they were in, which led her to believe they were either on a less known route or they were closer to Ellewynth than she originally thought.

Her chances of survival grew slimmer the closer she came to the woodland elves. Unless she was able to locate or even encounter Artemis upon her arrival…Netira couldn't allow herself to hope.

"Forgive me, my love," Netira said quietly. She rubbed her chest as she thought of her vampire mage. She couldn't even call on the power of the fire rune he tattooed onto her skin, between the pointer and middle finger; it sapped so much of her energy with each use, and she would have been a fool to use the rune in her current condition. She didn't even fully recover from the time she called on the rune to burn the bodies of the scouts and the elf. "I was suspicious, but not enough to protect myself from this."

"Praying, are we?" she heard Latos mock her. Netira glared at him the moment she laid eyes on him. "Come now. Why would the sacred sisters listen to a filthy half-breed?"

"They'll listen to anyone over you," she spat. "At least I had a legitimate reason for my deceit. You? They'll jump on any kind of opportunity for someone to send you to a special circle of hell Avilyne holds for your sort."

"Who will be the one sending me there, I wonder?"

"Me."

Latos snorted before letting out a belly laugh. He frowned when he noted her serious gaze. "I'd like to see you try it."

"Be careful what you wish for," Netira answered. She turned away, signaling she was done speaking with him.

She heard Latos swear at her while he returned to the others in the cave.

Netira sighed and moved a hand over the gunshot wound in her waist. It was healing slower than she expected, which made her wonder what ammunition Arlina used with that damned flintlock pistol of hers. It didn't help that she was shot twice by it in so short a time either.

"Blessed sisters of Eolande," Netira prayed, "be merciful and guide me to Artemis upon my arrival. Let me live long enough to carry out

Latos' murder. Let me live long enough to see my city return to the glory it once held."

⟋◯

Callypso rode the wind for days after Talisa's request of finding the sai of Tamina Ravenwing. The more she roamed, the more she felt the energy trail of something *different* from the forest; it seemed the weapons were calling to her, drawing her to them. The energy was so dark…not only did it worry her, but it also made her ill.

Tamina was thorough, however. She made sure only those she wanted to find her sai would do so.

It made Callypso all the more uneasy. Her experiences with lingering spirits always ended in tragedy. She prayed to the goddesses that this one would be different, especially for Talisa's sake. She couldn't blame her friend for wanting to believe an old face of the past wasn't scheming something sinister, but she hoped Talisa would also listen to reason.

While retrieving the weapons was the only true part she had to play in this game, Callypso knew that she would have to participate more than she desired to. She would be the only one able to sense Tamina's presence and energy trail among those who would eventually travel to Blackwen City and carry out Tamina's revenge. Well, the elf mage would also be able to sense Tamina if he embraced *all* of his power. His resistance against his true instinct hindered his growth as a being of magic.

What a tragic waste, Callypso thought.

Having ditched the flowy dresses she normally wore for a lightly colored tunic and breeches, Callypso moved through the forest with a different kind of ease. She even donned dark leather calf-high boots, much to her distaste. They were to better cover her tracks, as well as to act as a shield for stray malevolent energy that would have been able to seep into her otherwise. She used the same reasoning for her hands, which were gloved in soft, brown leather. Whatever taints the sai may have held after all these years, Callypso wasn't going to give her elemental body the chance to absorb them.

Callypso felt the pull of the weapons strengthen, and she halted. She could feel the cold wind of death linger in the air, and she saw patches of the earth redden as if they were stained with blood.

Callypso had arrived at the resting place of Tamina Ravenwing of Blackwen City, the once heir to the throne of the Dark Fortress.

"I know you are here, specter of the past," Callypso called out, while avoiding the gurgling red patches of earth nearing her feet. "Reveal yourself, and show me the location of your prized sai."

There was no reply, but she did feel Tamina's spirit energy rise in the area. Callypso huffed, noting that she should have expected the specter's silence. Tamina knew Callypso didn't trust her, did she not? Why would she make the retrieval of the sai easy for her?

Callypso studied the red earth patches, and with hesitation, laid a gloved hand over one. She was bombarded with overwhelming emotions of betrayal and hatred, and she thanked the goddesses she'd had enough sense to wear the gloves. Without them, the emotions would have consumed and incapacitated her. She now understood why the sai were left behind; Arlina must have had her share of mishaps in the attempt to retrieve them.

It must have infuriated that dark woman to not be able to bring back a trophy of her greatest kill. Callypso couldn't help but smile in satisfaction at the thought.

The elemental looked around in case Tamina decided to appear in a visible form. She was nowhere to be found, and Callypso returned to the dirt to dig. The gloves were quickly soaked, and Callypso grew sickened at the metallic scent of blood.

"I do pity you, Tamina." Callypso stared at her soaked gloves. "You never had proper funeral rites. If you had, your blood wouldn't stain the earth the way it does now."

You've seen this before, elemental. You've lost loved ones to the chilled hands of murder.

Callypso looked ahead at the now visible ethereal form of Tamina. The woman wasn't what she expected at all; Tamina was hauntingly beautiful. Her brown hair cascaded loose past her shoulders, and she wore a sleeveless black dress that trailed far from her bare feet. Her skin was paler than any vampire Callypso had encountered before—it was the true sign of death. Tamina's violet eyes were stern on the elemental.

"Yes," Callypso finally answered. She returned to the digging. "I've watched children murdered before my eyes…all for the pursuit of power."

That's why I chose you, Callypso, Tamina said, drifting closer to the hole Callypso was digging into. *Not only are you a wind elemental, but you are also one who could move through the dark web of murder and safely retrieve what was lost.*

"This isn't fair to Artemis," Callypso snapped. "What you're planning will destroy her. Do you not care for her? She is your daughter!"

Tamina looked away as her hands clenched into fists.

Do not make the mistake of thinking I do not love my daughter. She is my heart, the fiber of my being…and my sister wants her dead. I won't have her going into this fight unarmed.

"Don't make the mistake of thinking I don't know who may have reminded Arlina of Artemis' existence." Callypso glared. "Lingering spirits such as you stay for only one reason: revenge. You started a dangerous game, the end result of which may be Artemis' blood on *your* hands. Is that what you truly want? Why bother going through the effort of hiding her away, only to lead her back to the one who would slaughter her for pure amusement?"

It would be wise for you to choose your words carefully, elemental.

"And it would be wise for *you* to learn that I do not fear idle threats."

Callypso stopped digging as soon as she felt her hands brush against something solid. When she looked down, she saw the bony remains of the specter before her. She spotted two thin blades the length of her forearm, with curved prongs extending from a remarkably jeweled hilt. Picking them up, she rubbed the earthy remains away from the embedded garnet and onyx. They were oddly dull for such rare jewels. "I will have to purify them before Talisa hands them over to Artemis."

You will do no such thing.

"If Artemis is to wield them, I want to make sure she's the only one doing so." Callypso watched Tamina. "I cared for her when she was a child in Talisa's cottage. She helped return joy to my heart. I will not let you destroy her. If she were to learn the truth about all this, you would be lucky if she still wished to fight on your behalf. Artemis views you as a fallen angel, you know." Tamina looked away. "I swear it now…I won't let you taint her soul."

Tamina stood up and drifted away from Callypso. She then turned to face her and smiled.

Do what you must. Just know that the sai aren't the only way I can make my presence known on the battlefield, elemental. I'd worry more about your own soul rather than my daughter's. Your kind is so frail…I'd hate to see something terrible happen to such a "sacred" being.

II

"Soleil burn me," said an irritated female voice, which drew Shadow's attention. "I was just getting used to being home and not having to report to the Elders on a moment's notice. Remind me why we are doing this again?"

"Because we're soldiers of Ellewynth, Serlene," Shadow stated. His annoyance at his companion grew by the second. "Talisa is busy with her own agenda, so naturally, the Elders thought of you to accompany me."

The elf he called Serlene scowled, and then focused on riding her dark brown mare. Serlene looked similar to her younger sister, Lily, only her blue eyes were cold instead of innocent, and her blond hair was always tightly pulled into a plaited bun. She was considered short by elven standards, but was still taller than the average human or vampire.

Shadow disliked her. Even so, he respected her enough as a combatant on the battlefield…as long as she wasn't stationed as an archer. Serlene may have been an archery instructor, but her emotions ruled her. She was better with the sword despite her protests of using it.

Lord Celstian had earlier summoned both Shadow and Serlene to the Hall of Elders and ordered them to meet with the full-blood escorts from Blackwen City. Serlene had been briefed about the situation, and Shadow sensed a trap by Arlina. Not that they would listen to him, of course. Lord Destrius was not much help either; he was furious that

Talisa had dismissed their orders to accompany Shadow because she had returned to her position as an instructor.

"Another one of your bright ideas, this teaching business," Lord Destrius said then to Shadow.

It must have been by Willow's hand that Shadow kept his silence. As for Aunt Clarayne, she couldn't hide her sadness each time she glanced at him. Shadow pretended to ignore her whenever it happened. He'd apologize to her one day.

Maybe.

"Are you even listening to me, Shadow?" Serlene demanded, still in a foul mood.

Shadow reined Azrael to a halt and faced the woman. "The more you whine and scowl, the easier it is for enemies to find and ambush us. Either you lower your voice, or I will do it for you. You really must learn to appreciate the beauty silence has to offer us."

Serlene glared at him, but eventually nodded. Satisfied, Shadow nudged Azrael to a trot. Serlene followed quietly behind him, but to his dismay, the silence didn't last for long.

"You're acquainted with Jack," Serlene stated. At least she kept her voice low. "I suppose it was inevitable, seeing as how you keep the company of the *vampyra*."

"*She* has a name, Serlene. I suggest you use it," Shadow corrected. He sighed as he tried to regain a calm composure. "But yes, I am acquainted with Jack. What of it?"

"Lily speaks of him often," Serlene said. Shadow tried to imagine what would happen if her frown became permanent. The disfigurement just might suit her. "I think she even cares for him."

Shadow smiled as he kept his gaze on the path ahead. "Would that be a terrible thing, Serlene, for Lily and Jack to join lives with one another?"

"Absolutely! He looks very much like the last damned elf mage that sent us to war with the dragons. And now he's being trained by Talisa of all people! Goddesses protect us if that imbecile insults someone who would then take it out on our realm." Serlene made a swift hand motion from her forehead to her chest, a common gesture in respect to the goddesses.

"It means nothing, Serlene," Shadow insisted. "Similarities in appearance don't necessarily mean similarities in actions. Jack has great potential to bring some good into the world."

"As well as some evil."

"Everyone has the choice to do good or evil in Arrygn," Shadow explained. "Take yourself for example, Serlene. You were not 'chosen' as I was. Instructors feared your anger and rash mindset would cause more harm than aid. Yet here you are, a soldier of Ellewynth despite it all. Take care of your own demons before you judge the ones of others."

Serlene's lips tightened, and Shadow was grateful that she finally shut up. Suddenly, he heard something that did not belong to the forest and pulled Azrael to a quick stop.

"What's wrong?" she asked.

Shadow held up a hand to silence her and pointed to the left a moment later.

"They're near," he whispered. "I can hear the carriage."

Serlene gripped the hilt of her sword, and Shadow did the same. Shadow saw dark forms shifting through the moonlight of the open forest and counted four scouts, each wearing dark, heavy cloaks. He noticed the strange runes stitched into the hems of the cloth, and thought it had to be the work of a mage. How else could they have traveled so quickly if not within the daylight hours?

"Where's the carriage?" Serlene inquired.

Shadow wondered that as well, but only gave a shrug. "We're dealing with full-bloods, Serlene. They plan to toy with us before handing over their prisoner. It is their way."

The scouting party stopped several feet away from Shadow and Serlene. Shadow saw that Serlene tightened her grip on the reins due to her mare's nerves. Azrael was the opposite; Shadow had to steady her before she trampled the vampires.

"Easy, old friend," he murmured, rubbing her neck. "Not tonight."

The leader of the scouting party came closer to him and Azrael, and Shadow heard the figure take a deep sniff. The hood lowered and revealed a man with short red hair, spiked. His fangs elongated as he grinned.

He addressed the others: "It would appear that we are in the presence of the famous Shadow of Ellewynth."

"This is him?" One of the scouts snorted. "I've seen human men more dangerous than him."

The leader sniffed in Serlene's direction and frowned. "Not much of a grunt, famous Shadow. She's rather weak, even for the elvenkind."

"I could say the same of the one who stands before me," Shadow replied, before Serlene could spit out a retort. The leader laughed and crossed his arms. "Where is the prisoner your Mistress spoke of?"

The man kept silent, which irritated Serlene. Shadow wished Talisa were here with him instead. If the full-bloods didn't kill Serlene, Shadow would most likely cripple her himself.

"Why bother hiding the carriage you're keeping the captive in? I'm sure you're aware our hearing is as great as yours, full-blood," Serlene snapped.

"Simplicity bores me." The leader yawned. "As do you."

Shadow moved Azrael in front of Serlene's mare as a reminder that he was the one in charge. He pitied the woman's students, Artemis especially. It was no wonder she hadn't learned a thing.

"Whom does Arlina send to entertain us?" Shadow asked, now playing the game.

The full-blood bowed mockingly and continued to smirk. "I am Latos, Shadow of Ellewynth."

"Latos." Shadow crossed his arms. "Arlina must not think very highly of you, full-blood. If she had, you'd have a title following your name. You can't be more than a simple servant looking for a boot to lick."

Latos frowned while the rest of the full-bloods laughed. Serlene was smug herself.

"I wouldn't be so sharp with my words, elf," Latos growled. "The forest may be your home, but it could easily turn on you as well. I could remind you why you should fear the dark."

"Enough, Latos. Get this prisoner detail over with. We must return to the Mistress as quickly as possible," one of the cloaked figures barked.

Shadow stared at the group behind Latos and felt an odd shiver run through his spine. Something about that statement made Shadow wonder about his earlier sense of a trap.

Latos snapped at the others, and they all disappeared into the shadows. Moments later, a small, barred carriage came into view. It stopped several feet in front of Shadow and Serlene, and Shadow barely contained his shock as he recognized the one trapped inside. Her shoulder-length red hair was tangled with dried, dark blood patches, her face was covered with dirt and more blood, and her dark brown eyes showed just how much pain she was in.

He gazed at Netira, the one who wanted to save her city from Arlina's tyranny.

"Do with her what you will," Latos said. "We have no use for traitorous bitches."

"If you're expecting praise from us, I'm afraid you won't receive it. Return to your Dark Fortress and we needn't have a reason to meet again," Shadow said, while motioning for Serlene to take the carriage.

Serlene released the horses that pulled the carriage and attached the ropes to her mare. The scouts, save Latos, dashed into the darkness, and all heard the pained terror of the released horses.

Shadow and Latos watched one another, and the full-blood was the first to leave.

"We will meet again, famous Shadow," Latos promised. "One does not insult a full-blood and live for long."

Serlene snorted after Latos disappeared.

"He is rather pathetic, no?"

"Now is not the time for that." Shadow replied.

"And her?" Serlene motioned to the carriage. "She looks as if she hasn't fed during her trip. There's no point in presenting her to the Elders if she is close to walking the pathways to Avilyne."

Shadow watched Netira, and she stared at him in confusion. She couldn't understand why he watched her with such recognition.

"She will make the rest of the trip." Shadow looked away from the dhampir. "We'll scrounge something up just to hold her over."

Everyone knew of the prisoner that Shadow and Serlene brought in. The elves were in a jolly mood because of it. They felt safe again. Shadow's mood, however, had worsened since his return. I tried to hide his weapons whenever he returned from the Hall of the Elders, but that method backfired each time; he'd either find them before our lesson could start, or he'd produce another weapon he owned that I had no knowledge of. After that, Shadow would curse Lord Destrius under his breath.

Hearing the insults and then being met with a feigned innocence afterward was actually quite amusing.

"Careful there, Shadow." I laughed. "One of Lord Destrius' little spies will catch wind of your negativity and squeal."

Shadow didn't join in the laughter. "I will never understand how the goddesses chose that man to be an Elder."

"They're not even questioning her?" I asked. "I hear Lord Destrius keeps pushing for her immediate execution."

"No, they're not questioning her." Shadow tapped his bow and frowned. "The dhampir is innocent of the crime. My word alone, however, won't help her."

"Why not?"

"I kept her out of my report to the Elders, remember?"

I sighed.

Shadow had explained to me before how he left Netira out of his report, feeling it was unnecessary to explain there may have been a possible mutiny in the future of Blackwen City. Just the mention of the Dark Fortress promised nightmares.

When he came back from escorting the prisoner to the Elders, he told me of the whole ordeal. My dream had been a reality, and it frightened me. I wanted to see Netira. Shadow didn't think it was a good idea, but he didn't understand my need to see her. If it meant sneaking into the Hall of the Elders on my own, I'd do it.

I could see Jack's proud and smug face at the thought of it.

Even with my often guilty conscience, I had to do it. Netira was a key to whatever event that was to come, and I wanted to find out why.

"Artemis?"

I felt a sharp jab in my side—Shadow's bow.

"That hurt," I grumbled.

"No daydreaming during archery lessons," Shadow scolded. "Your enemies will take full advantage of your lackadaisical attitude."

"I wasn't daydreaming."

"Yes, that could be true..." Shadow mused. "After all, you did have this scowl stuck on your face for some time. Not much of a fantasy in that daydream, hmm?"

"One day, Shadow." I hit his shoulder and then took aim at the wooden target several feet away from us. "One day, your sharp comments are going to catch up to you, and I will be there to laugh at you."

"Until then, my dear, you'll have to learn the art of focusing. My so-called sharp comments will mean nothing to you once you do."

I released the arrow, and it landed inches away from the center. Shadow nodded his approval and handed over another arrow to be notched and shot. I tried to conceal my groan.

I hated archery. Willow damn the soul who created it.

Netira preferred the barred carriage for a prison than the one the elves stuck her in. At least the carriage had a light source. Her current cell was dark, damp, and highly uncomfortable. The only source of light was the torches that lined the walls.

The Elders were under the impression that she was a full-blood, despite her proclamations of being a dhampir. She was too weak to show her true form, which condemned her further in their eyes. The only one who seemed to believe her tale was the male elf who had helped escort her to Ellewynth—the one they called Shadow.

Netira had heard tales of the famed Shadow of Ellewynth for as long as she could remember. He was what full-bloods considered a "worthy kill" due to his skill on the battlefield. Whoever could kill him would win eternal glory in Blackwen City. The matter was silenced, however, whenever Arlina was around. Netira believed Arlina had encountered the elf in past excursions, hence the immense hatred for the man. It must have been embarrassing for the Mistress, to have slaughtered as many elves as she had, but not Shadow.

The sudden scent of blood invaded Netira's nostrils, which led her astray from her train of thought. An armored elf entered her line of sight, carrying a large gourd. Netira smelled animal blood and sniffed harder to determine which kind. She smiled when she discovered it was the blood of a deer—a personal favorite of hers.

The elf kept his silence as he left the gourd in front of the bars. Once he exited the prison hall, Netira crawled to grasp the gourd and gulped its contents. Leaning against the cold stone wall, she wiped the excess blood from her lips and felt her wounds tingle.

The wounds from Arlina's flintlock pistol were still in the process of healing—the duration of the healing was unusual, even for a dhampir. There was something odd about the ammunition Arlina used for the pistol, and Netira prayed to never to cross paths with the blasted weapon again. Feeling the wound re-knit itself a little bit more, she relaxed and let out a sigh.

Netira's thoughts shifted to Artemis, the surviving kin of Arlina. She wondered if the girl would seek her out, seeing as the news of her imprisonment would be the latest gossip in the city. Netira wondered if Artemis even knew the truth of her bloodline.

Artemis Ravenwing, alive…there was hope for her city yet.

"She *must* know something…" Netira said aloud. "I doubt the elves would let her forget such a thing."

Artemis knows nothing of her true heritage, a soft voice spoke, startling Netira.

A woman came into view, and Netira felt her jaw drop.

The woman who stood before her had long brown hair that hung loosely past her shoulders, and she wore a sleeveless black dress that trailed along the narrow hallway of Netira's prison. She was barefoot, and was also paler than any being Netira had encountered. Her violet eyes were cold—the same sort that Arlina's gray eyes exuded.

You seem confused, child of Blackwen, the woman said, gliding toward the bars.

"You just…" Netira sputtered. "It can't be. You can't be her."

Whom do you speak of?

Netira failed to restrain a shudder. "You were murdered long ago…you once watched over me before I went into the service of Blackwen's Mistress."

Say it, Netira. I know you want to.

"It all makes sense now," Netira said as tears filled her eyes. "It makes sense why Arlina suddenly knows of Artemis and will stop at nothing until she is dead. You…you fed her paranoia!" The woman said nothing, and Netira forced herself to look into the chilly violet eyes of the specter before her. "You're sacrificing your own daughter's peace just to exact your revenge, Tamina?"

Tamina chuckled, but it wasn't the soft laughter Netira remembered. She was far more like her sister now than Netira wanted to admit.

You're not the first to accuse me of using Artemis.

"It's not an accusation, Tamina. It's the *truth*." Netira felt her heart drop further the longer she stared at her mentor. "A lingering specter for more than twenty years…you are not the Tamina I once knew. I would be foolish to believe otherwise."

Tamina drifted through the bars and knelt beside Netira. She grinned, which chilled the dhampir.

My dear girl…you know nothing.

"You speak as if I know nothing of heartbreak and betrayal, but I know plenty of it, Tamina!" Netira snapped. "I would *never* sacrifice the one I love for my own means of revenge."

Tamina laughed at her as she drifted away from the cell. Tamina's form was gone, but Netira knew her former mentor was still there. She could still feel the dark energy the specter exuded.

One day you'll understand, Netira, she heard Tamina say, *and you'll find yourself doing the same. You won't love that mage forever.*

Once nightfall came, I grabbed the darkest cloak I had and securely fastened it. It was time to see Netira. I knew Shadow was only trying to protect me when he tried to dissuade me, but sometimes I wished he didn't feel such a need to.

I left home and walked the slated paths of Ellewynth. I passed by the tavern, Willow's Garden, and thought of Jack. Drunken nitwit or not, I did miss him. I hoped Talisa wasn't pushing Jack too hard in his apprenticeship.

I eventually found my way to the Hall of the Elders. I saw candlelight in one of the offices and took a deep breath. I hoped the candlelight belonged to Lady Clarayne, as she was the only Elder to ever acknowledge my presence and smile rather than sneer or cower at me. I'd have to apologize to her one day for the future break in.

There were two soldiers stationed at the side entrance of the hall, where the paths led to the prison cells below. I walked to a set of trees that stretched over them and climbed one as quietly as possible. I could have flown up there, but I had no desire to attract attention. That, and I never truly practiced using my wings. Not consciously, anyway.

Jack once told me an old tale he had read about concerning dhampirs and their wings. Granted, it was in one of his mythology books, but I could never get the story out of my head. A full-blood woman beloved to Avilyne fell in love with a human. She had a child, a girl born with bat-like wings. It was the first time a union ever occurred, and the child could not be controlled. The vampiric blood did not meld well with the human sort, and the wings were thought to be a curse. A vassal of Avilyne beseeched the goddess of death on behalf of the full-blood woman, and Avilyne was angered with the mother. Avilyne had explained to her that the wings were not a curse but merely an asset for her favorite creature. The goddess of death then decided to spare the mother further grief, so she made it so that a dhampir could hide their wings. The price, however, was that it would be painful to do so.

As if I didn't already have enough reasons to curse my dhampir heritage.

I watched the two soldiers and realized one of them was asleep on his feet.

Perfect.

I snapped a few twigs and threw them toward the front of the hall. The sleeping soldier jumped at the sound.

"What was that?" he asked as he grasped his sword hilt.

The other one grumbled. "Just some squirrel running along the rooftop."

"Sounded like twigs to me," the first soldier argued. "How long was I asleep?"

"Long enough to start snoring in five-minute intervals," his comrade answered. "How does your wife manage to sleep beside you with that infernal noise?"

"Aerios blow you."

I chided myself for thinking a few twigs would move them away from their post. Suddenly, I heard someone else walk up to them, and I groaned when I saw it was Shadow. I cursed my ill luck.

"Shadow! What brings you here this time of night?" the previously sleeping soldier asked, while taking care to seem more alert.

"I have some questions to ask of the vampire," Shadow replied. He paused a moment. "Though it would appear that I'm not the only one who carries this wish."

I saw him look up in my direction, and I couldn't hide my guilt. The guards took note of me and nearly fell over with shock.

"How long was the *vampyra* there?" one of them cried.

I truly despised that word. Shadow hated it just as much.

"*Artemis* has been there for only a few minutes," Shadow corrected. "Come down from that tree before you hurt yourself, my dear."

I climbed down and removed the hood. There was no end to my guilt after Shadow shot me an irritated glance. Cue Jack scolding me for feeling that way.

"I'm sorry," I whispered.

Shadow didn't answer and faced the guards. "Let us through."

"Are you sure it's a good idea for the *vam*—"

"*Artemis*," Shadow and I simultaneously snapped.

"Are you sure it's a good idea for her to see the she-vamp down there?" the soldier asked, growing more nervous the longer Shadow glared at him.

"I won't repeat myself," Shadow said.

The two quickly moved away, and I followed Shadow into the hall and down the dark pathways.

"Are you really that angry with me?" I asked.

Shadow stopped but did not turn around to face me. "Not entirely."

"I had to, Shadow," I pleaded. "I needed answers."

"I know," he sighed. "I had hoped you would have waited a little while longer."

"Why *are* you seeing her this late in the night?"

"I wasn't lying when I said I had my own questions that needed answers," Shadow explained, finally facing me. "You'll be learning a lot of truths tonight, Artemis. *Many* truths. You will hate both me and Talisa for some time because of them."

I felt my brow crinkle in confusion. "Hate you and Talisa?"

"Yes."

Willow be damned...how much did they keep from me?

"Shadow, I can't ever hate you or her."

"It's too early for you to say, Artemis." Shadow started walking the pathway again.

I decided to keep quiet, and we stopped at an archway lit by torches. Taking one, Shadow then pointed to the right. Peering over his shoulder, I saw the cell and its lone occupant.

Netira looked far better now than she had in my dream, but I could tell she was still in a lot of pain. A large gourd was lying on its side along the bars, and I could smell from where I stood that it once contained deer blood. The scent aroused the hunger of the dhampir within me, and I clenched my fists while attempting to push the sensation away.

It would not claim me. Not now.

Shadow and I stood side by side in front of the bars, and Netira's gaze fixed on me. It must have taken some effort for her to stand, but she managed well enough and walked closer to us. She sniffed the air and then sighed with relief.

"It *is* you," Netira said. "You look like your mother, Artemis Ravenwing."

Ravenwing. I've heard the name connected to mine before, but I never had the urge to question why. I only ever wanted to know what happened to Mother…anything else concerning my vampire heritage, I happily ignored.

"How…how do you know who I am?" I asked. "And how did you know my mother?"

Netira looked to Shadow. "She really knows nothing?"

"Not everything," Shadow replied. I felt him tense beside me, which did not help my nerves. "Why did she send you to us? What is she planning?"

"Who are you two talking about?" I inquired, confused. "And I'm still waiting for my answers from you, Netira."

"You're aware of my name," Netira said, retreating to a corner of her cell. "Then we're all playing into her hands. Kiare be praised."

I gripped the bars as my annoyance rose from her last bit of sarcasm. "Answer me. What is going on?"

"We're all pawns in a game of revenge, daughter of Tamina Ravenwing," Netira answered. "It would appear I'm just another piece to help protect the 'queen' of the game, so to speak. Assuming, of course, your Elders don't execute me first for a crime I didn't commit."

"So it is true?" Shadow moved forward. "Arlina is aware of Artemis' existence here in Ellewynth?"

"So it would seem." Netira crossed her arms.

"Arlina?" I knew that name too. It was cursed more than my own by the elves. "Who is she?"

"She is the Mistress of Blackwen City, Artemis," Shadow reminded me. "Of the Dark Fortress."

"And she was Tamina's little sister," Netira added. "That makes her your aunt, your blood relative. You're the last of the once great Ravenwing clan."

I froze.

The dreams of my mother fighting the unknown woman with the cold, dark eyes flashed before me, and I felt something in my mind click.

"Artemis?" Shadow rested his hand on my shoulder.

"Arlina wouldn't happen to have short, cropped red hair and cold gray eyes…would she, Netira?" I felt my body shake.

"She would." Netira nodded, now returning to her spot before us. She looked deep into my eyes. "You've been haunted in your slumber. It's worse than I thought."

"My mother was murdered by her own sister?" I tried to keep my voice steady.

"Avilyne's hell, Shadow." Netira looked at him in disbelief. "You're a pitiful excuse for a guardian if you didn't even bother to warn her of all this! She is the only other Ravenwing woman who lives!"

"He's *not* my guardian. He hasn't been for many years." I glared at him. "Why didn't you ever tell me?"

Shadow tensed more. "I only wanted to protect you."

I felt the tears form and fought to keep them from falling. I backed away from Shadow and Netira.

"Artemis, have you been seeing your mother outside of your dreams?" Netira asked.

"No, why?"

"I have a feeling you will soon," she explained. "To answer your question earlier, I knew your mother when I was a child. She watched over me, particularly because I am like you…a dhampir. We're not accepted in Blackwen City, so she helped me hide my true heritage so that I could stay."

"You pretended to be a full-blood just so you could stay in that despicable city?" I snapped.

"It wasn't always such a dark place, Artemis," Netira said. Realizing I was planning to keep my opinions of Blackwen City to myself, she continued on. "I was framed for the murders of the elves of this realm. It was a perfect plan for Arlina, as she had also discovered the truth about me. Arlina knows you are here, Artemis. She wants to finish the task she began long ago, which was to murder all living kin so that she can be the only true Mistress of Blackwen City."

"I am of Blackwen City…" I spat, while tasting foulness the moment the statement left my lips. "A child of Blackwen."

"Your bloodline ties you to the Dark Fortress, yes." Netira sighed. "You have a legitimate claim to the throne…the only true claim. Only Ravenwing women can hold the throne, and you are the only other one left in Arrygn. Tamina was supposed to inherit it as soon as your grandmother chose, but Arlina…she took fate into her own hands."

"I don't want it." I gripped the bars in anger. "If it's a fight Arlina wishes for, however, then I welcome it."

Netira laughed. "I admire your fire, Artemis. I'll promise to remember you after Arlina slaughters you."

"That will not happen," Shadow swore.

"Oh?" Netira arched an eyebrow at him, amused. "You know Arlina well enough. I know there's history there. It *will* happen, elf. You didn't warn her, so I can only assume Artemis is ill-prepared to meet her in combat."

"Is that why she sent you?" Shadow asked.

"As I said before, it appears I was brought here to assist you as well as her," Netira answered, now irritated. "Whatever that dear specter of ours is planning, I'm now thrown into the mix."

Who in Avilyne's hell was this specter they referred to?

Shadow rubbed his brow, as if feeling a headache coming on.

"This queen you spoke of earlier?" I asked. "Is it me?"

"Yes," Netira answered. She shot a pitying glance. "I'm sorry, Artemis."

"I don't want your apologies," I growled. "Mother said you would be the one to show me the way. Where is she referring to?"

Shadow shut his eyes as Netira sighed.

"It would appear that your mother wishes for me to show you the way to Blackwen City. I can bring you there without Arlina's knowledge, since I once spent much of my time on the streets," Netira said. "The choice is yours whether you wish to or not. You will encounter Arlina sooner or later."

"She is coming here." Shadow's hands clenched into fists. "Arlina will strike Ellewynth."

"I'm not sure when, but yes…" Netira looked away. "She will."

"Then it would seem that the only option left is for me to spring you loose," I mumbled.

"What was that?" Shadow asked.

"Nothing," I dismissed him.

"That was certainly something, Artemis," Netira said, obviously curious.

"Maybe I'll consider telling you about it on another visit," I said as I took my leave.

After the visit to Netira's cell, Shadow watched Artemis stomp away from him without saying so much as a single word. It was expected, given that he *had* kept all those secrets from her.

He was angry at himself; he should have made Artemis go home when he found her in the tree. *He* should have been the one to tell her the truth, not Netira. Shadow knew that whenever Artemis decided she would speak to him again, he would have to explain everything.

The part about the string he felt for her, however...that he would not reveal.

Shadow reached his home but decided to keep on walking. Once he set foot in the open forest, he whistled a familiar tune and heard Azrael answer him. She trotted toward him within moments, and she rested her head on his shoulder once she saw his sadness. Shadow stroked her mane while his free hand clenched into a fist.

"I should have told her sooner," he said, continuing the self-blame.

Azrael butted into Shadow's shoulder, as if scolding him.

"But it is my fault," he insisted. "I'm letting my...concerns...for her get in the way."

"Oh, so you're *finally* admitting it?"

Shadow was startled at the sudden sight of Talisa. She laughed as he scowled at her.

"Avilyne's hell, Talisa!" he snapped. "Must you insist on doing that?"

Talisa frowned as she removed her signature dark blue pointed hat. She was wearing a white tunic and dark blue breeches that hid under calf-high, dark leather boots. She only wore such clothing when traveling, which piqued Shadow's curiosity. Talisa's lengthy black hair was surprisingly plaited into a tight bun, with a few wisps of the white streaks lying freely along the sides of her face.

"Shadow, I look forward to the day you admit to Artemis that you love her. I really do." Talisa dramatically sighed. "Until then…"

"Why are you here when you now have an apprentice?" Shadow demanded.

"Just because things between you and Artemis have temporarily gone sour doesn't mean you have to be a sourpuss to me!" Talisa berated him. Shadow kept silent, mostly out of irritation. "Oh fine, you stubborn fool. I was looking for you."

"Really now."

"I'll overlook that bit of sarcasm, elf," Talisa warned. She then sighed. "Things have been, ah, strange."

"Get to the point, Talisa." Shadow rubbed his brow. "I'm not in the mood tonight."

"Just to let you know, I really dislike it when sourpuss Shadow is out and about," Talisa scolded. She rolled her eyes after Shadow glared at her. "Fine, fine. I've…I've been seeing Tamina."

Shadow focused on Azrael when he felt her shake at the mention of Tamina's name.

"She's been visiting us all."

"What's that supposed to mean?" Talisa asked. Shadow glanced at her, and she then understood. "Willow be damned. She visited Artemis."

"In a manner of speaking," Shadow replied. "Artemis now knows the truth about Tamina as well as her noble bloodline."

"What?"

Azrael dipped her head at the sudden scream, flicking her ears as if she were in pain.

"Apologies, Azrael," Talisa said. Her focus returned to Shadow. "*You* were the one who made it clear that we had to keep silent on the matter around Artemis! How did this happen?"

"When push comes to shove, you push back," Shadow answered. "For some time, Tamina has been visiting Artemis through dreams, showing her fighting a woman who we well know and thoroughly hate. She's been seeing the very precursor to her mother's death."

"Goddesses..." Talisa gasped. "She really knows everything, then? Throne and all?"

"Yes."

"Wonderful. Callypso might be right after all..."

"Callypso? Your elemental friend?"

"Yes. Tamina wanted me to send her to her gravesite," Talisa explained. "She wanted Callypso to find and obtain her sai."

Shadow's eyes widened. "Another player in the game..."

Talisa shot him a confused stare. "What are you talking about? Who else is involved?"

"This game Tamina is stringing us along in," Shadow answered. "And the other person is a dhampir named Netira. She is the former Second of Blackwen City, and now a prisoner of Ellewynth."

"As in the same Netira who is responsible for the death of those elves?" Talisa asked.

"She's innocent, Talisa," Shadow stressed. "The ones who were responsible met their end by her hands. Arlina punished her with a harsh version of exile."

"As expected from that usurper. How strange that Arlina did not know about the girl's heritage..." Talisa mused. "What doesn't make sense right now is why Tamina would send the dhampir to us."

"Think about it, Talisa. You've just told me that Tamina sent Callypso to find her sai, which I would assume she would want to be used by Artemis. Netira may be exiled from her birthplace, but that only means that her purpose is...?" Shadow stopped, hoping Talisa would understand his point. He relaxed a bit when he watched her expression shift.

"She's the way into the Dark Fortress."

Shadow nodded. "I think Artemis intends to spring Netira free and have her guide the way to Blackwen City."

"But Artemis barely knows the woman!"

"It won't stop her." Shadow frowned. "She needs time to think, though. All of this did come at once."

"You can't let her go. She'll be killed, even with Tamina's sai at her disposal."

"She won't go alone with Netira." Shadow took a deep breath. "She may hate me at the moment, but I plan on making things right between us again."

"So you'll accompany her, should she make the decision to leave."

"Yes, I will."

"And what if Arlina comes and attacks Ellewynth? You are a soldier. You have your duties to the realm. You know what happens if you abandon them."

Shadow mounted Azrael and stared ahead into the open forest.

"She *will* come and attack Ellewynth. And my priority will be Artemis' safety. Ellewynth...Ellewynth will have to rely on others to defend her. If I am branded a deserter, so be it."

"You can't mean that." Talisa was horrified. "I won't let you go with her."

"I mean every word," Shadow said. "I already know you'll come with us. Jack will follow along because he's your apprentice, and Callypso will come because she'll worry about your well-being."

"Callypso will *not* go with us," Talisa snapped. "She's already treading on dangerous ground, living the way she is right now."

"Oh, I think she'll come along." Shadow smiled as he saw Talisa covering her mouth after her words. "I know you, old friend. As for Callypso, the fact that she's an elemental will not stop her from joining us."

Talisa sighed in defeat. "When did things become so disastrous?"

Azrael snorted at her, which made Shadow laugh.

"Indeed, Azrael. Nothing ever goes the way we plan."

"You truly are a gift, wise one." Talisa patted Azrael's neck. Azrael nudged Talisa as a way of saying thank you. "You're certain of this." Shadow nodded, and she sighed once more. "I'll go to Artemis. I can handle a peeved dhampir, after all."

"Best of luck to you."

"Shadow…promise me you won't do anything stupid tonight."

Shadow didn't answer as he rode off.

I sat on my windowsill, staring at the night sky. My eyes itched and puffed after crying for so long. As upset as I was with Shadow, I understood why he'd kept the secrets. If I were him, I'd probably have done the same.

It still hurt, nonetheless.

And Netira…there was something about her that piqued my curiosity. I'd never met another dhampir before, and I was intrigued, despite her being from Blackwen City. She hid her heritage too, but after meeting her, she did not seem to share the struggles I had.

Avilyne's hell, the Dark Fortress. I hated that half my blood traced back to that place, not to mention that I had legitimate ties to its throne. I didn't want it, but it did not matter. Arlina was coming to Ellewynth, and she would most likely burn the place down after killing me. There was no way I could fight her, not with the low level of skill I possessed. If I could free Netira and leave Ellewynth, I could prolong my encounter with my aunt. I could learn how to fight from Netira during our journey, even if it was just a matter of defending myself from Arlina.

I had to try.

Before I could free Netira, I would have to speak to Shadow. It would only be fair to our friendship for me to say my farewells to him. Once I left Ellewynth, I wouldn't ever see him or the others again. The thought pained me, but it would be the right thing to do.

No one should have to suffer anymore because of who I was.

"Artemis?" I heard a female voice call from below. I saw Talisa standing in front of my door.

"Talisa?" I said, confused at her presence. "What are you doing here in Ellewynth? Where's Jack?"

"I wouldn't worry about him," she answered. She beckoned for me to move. "Why don't you come down and join me for a moonlight stroll?"

"I mean no offense, but I would prefer not to leave my home tonight."

Talisa crossed her arms. "Let's try this again. Why don't you come down and join me for a moonlight stroll?"

I noted the tone she used, which meant she was here for important matters rather than a casual visit. I nodded.

I didn't bother to change out of my nightgown, and I especially ignored the need to bind my hair. I took a cloak from my trunk and wrapped it around my shoulders. Once I stepped outside, Talisa flashed me a satisfied smile and linked my arm with hers.

"I've heard you and Shadow are not speaking. Or should I say, *you're* not speaking to him," she began, while leading the stroll.

I groaned. "Temporarily. I've…I've learned a lot of things tonight."

"Yes, I know," Talisa said. "I take part of the blame for keeping the truth from you about your mother, Arlina, and your noble bloodline. Shadow and I thought it would be better to give you a clean slate, so to speak. Don't be too hard on him."

"I understand," I answered. "But these are the truths I needed to know."

"Would anything have changed?" Talisa asked. "Sometimes a lie can do some good, Artemis. You would have loathed yourself more than usual if you learned the truth of who you were while you were still a child."

I changed the subject. "Talisa, why are you in Ellewynth? Shouldn't you be at your cottage instructing Jack?"

"Normally, yes." Talisa snorted. "I had some matters to discuss with Shadow. Once I found him, I learned of your events in the Hall of the Elders. I thought perhaps you'd like to talk."

"There's nothing left to talk about." I frowned. "Netira needs to be freed, and I must go to Blackwen City."

"You plan on fighting Arlina then? You can barely fight as is."

"I'm well aware of that."

"Are you so eager to throw your life away, Artemis?"

"No," I snapped. I took a deep breath as we continued our walk. "I think it's time things are done on *my* terms. Not Arlina's, not Shadow's, and certainly not my mother's."

"Shadow mentioned you've been seeing Tamina through dreams."

"Dreams, visions, call them what you will." I glanced at Talisa, who continued to watch me with concern. "I now understand that she's been trying to tell me that her own sister murdered her and that Arlina is coming after me. Escaping Ellewynth and journeying to Blackwen City will give me enough time to prepare for her."

Talisa groaned. "If only it were so simple."

"You think there's more?"

"I *know* there's more." Talisa frowned. "I'm sure you think so too. I know you're a stubborn one, but you can't be that dense!"

"That's awfully comforting, Talisa."

"I call it as I see it, dear one, and you've known it since you were a child." Talisa stopped and took my face in her hands. I could now see the tears in her eyes. "Don't go to Blackwen City. Trust Shadow and me to protect you here, as we always have. Please, dear one. You've always feared your dhampir heritage, especially because you believed it would make you kill people. You will be killing people willingly if you go on this journey."

I grasped her hands and brought them down. I didn't let go of them, and I looked right into her eyes with tears of my own. She was right about the killing part…it was going to take some time for me to accept that.

"I'm sorry, Talisa. I love you both, but this is something I need to do. Arlina will come for me. I want to make sure that when she does find me, I can put up a fight and end it all."

"You'll leave us and put your trust in some dhampir you barely know?" I could hear the pain in her voice, and it was breaking my heart.

"Yes," I said after a moment of silence.

Talisa was in disbelief. "I won't let you do it. Shadow won't let you do it."

"I'm going to Blackwen City whether you like it or not, Talisa," I stressed. "The only other option left is for you to join me, and it's not an option I'd prefer."

"And whether I go with you or not is something *you* have no control over, Artemis," Talisa snapped. "And what about Shadow? Don't you care enough about him to maybe change your mind and let him help?"

I sighed and turned away.

"I do care about him…but Shadow has done enough for me already."

12

Karesu walked into the morning light, squinting at the view of the forest ahead. He did not wear the rune cloaks the scouts and soldiers donned; he was simply adorned with a black tunic with billowing sleeves and black breeches. He twisted the silver band that rested on his middle finger while feeling the curved engraved runes along his fingertips. With the charm, he welcomed the sunlight. Netira had helped him gain an appreciation for the daylight hours since its creation.

The ring had been a tedious project, one that Arlina constantly praised him for once he was met with success. What the Mistress didn't know was that someone else had begun the project ages ago; Karesu only added a few more tricks of his own. He was in the process of making one for Arlina, only she demanded it be a bracelet rather than a ring. And of course, she ignored his warnings that the construction of the bracelet would take longer. Karesu had the idea of adding other runes along with the protective ones for sunlight, but thought it was safer not to. He still had to serve the damned woman until he could find Netira in Ellewynth and escape.

Karesu remembered how Netira wanted to save their city. He recalled how he swore to help her do so. The dream was the only thing letting them sleep at night, considering all the dark things they had done in Arlina's name. That dream of saving the Dark Fortress was lost now. He was certain he could hide himself and Netira from Arlina, even if it meant isolation from the rest of Arrygn. Karesu knew he wouldn't regret such a notion. He found himself enjoying the idea of solitude with Netira.

Ignoring the rest of the brood, he strolled around the camp and felt for any source of magic nearby. The forest of the Woodland Realm had its own deep, ancient magic, and it always fascinated Karesu. Had the circumstances been different, Karesu would have been delighted to stay and study the energy sensations the forest produced. The veils were the most intriguing aspect of the realm, and he made a mental note to apologize to the forest one day for the forceful violation he would have to commit.

While on his walk, he passed by Arlina's tent. Karesu could feel the malice from where he stood, and out of sheer morbid curiosity, he thought to see the Mistress. Before he could announce himself, Arlina herself stepped out. Wearing one of the protective runes cloaks Karesu first created, she eyed him with caution.

"What are you doing here, mage?" she asked, her tone cold.

"I was curious to see if you needed my assistance," he replied, amused at Arlina's squinting. It appeared she hadn't slept well again. "After all, we grow closer to the forest."

"If I want your assistance, you'll know it," Arlina snapped.

Karesu watched Arlina gaze at the forest, and he couldn't mistake her shudder at the sight.

It took some self-control for him not to smile at her misery.

"Mistress, are you well?" he inquired, taking care to sound concerned.

Arlina quickly shifted in his direction with visible annoyance. "Of course I am well. What kind of ridiculous question is that?"

"You were shaking," Karesu answered, while desperately trying to hide a smirk.

"It was the wind moving my cloak!" Arlina barked. "I *do not* shake."

"Very well, then." Karesu started to take his leave. He then stopped. "Oh, I almost forgot. You do not mind if I take some time along the borderlands, of course?"

"What in Avilyne's hell for?"

"You wanted me to discover the veils and their locations," Karesu reminded her. "I'll need some time in the borderlands. Alone."

"Do what you want." Arlina waved him away. "Get out of my sight."

Making sure to bow, he walked away from Arlina. He returned to his tent and made sure to arm himself with his sword, which had unique, swirling calligraphy etched into the blade. Unlike the runes he created and worked with, the calligraphy was of something much older; there was great power in this sword, which he hadn't been able to unlock. While Karesu hadn't any knowledge of what or where the calligraphy was from, he had kept it hidden from Arlina and done endless research back in Blackwen City. Karesu could find neither what the calligraphy meant nor why it felt so much like a part of his magic. He'd always held the feeling that even without the proper knowledge it would prove useful one day—besides its obvious use.

He sheathed the longsword and took a deep breath. Karesu was ready to venture into the borderlands of the Woodland Realm.

Callypso sat cross-legged on the earth, staring at the pair of sai that lay a far distance from her. Ever since she'd retrieved them, Callypso felt the need to wear gloves and boots more and more. She didn't want Tamina's lingering energy within the weapons seeping into her spirit and tainting it. The conversation she'd had with the specter disturbed her enough.

Narrowing her gaze at the favored weapons of the Ravenwing women, Callypso recalled the growing number of failures she'd had in the effort to purify them. She had gone as far as taking them to the Grove of Kiare's Mirror, hoping the water goddess would take pity on her and send some answers.

To her dismay, that failed too. Tamina's will was far too strong, and it worried the elemental. She snatched up one of the blades and looked closely at the hilt embedded with garnet and onyx.

"Odd..." Callypso said.

The jewels were dull and remained so after Callypso rubbed them with a gloved finger. There was no shine to them, no luminosity.

It puzzled her.

Taking the other sai and hiding the weapons in a dark handkerchief, Callypso stood up and followed the path to Talisa's cottage. It had been some time since she last saw the witch, and she figured Talisa might have been annoyed that she hadn't returned to her with the weapons. Riding the wind, Callypso arrived at the cottage before the night set in.

Before she knocked on the small oak door, it opened. Callypso found herself face to face with the elf mage, Jack. His startled expression made her chuckle. His actions toward her in general were amusing.

"Hello, Jack," she greeted him.

"C-Callypso!" he said, still catching his breath. "What brings you here at this hour?"

"I was in need of Talisa." She crossed her arms. "Where were *you* planning on going?"

Jack straightened his posture and moved a few wayward brown strands of hair behind his pointed ears. "I was just going to sit out here for a bit. I needed a break from the homework Talisa left for me."

"Homework?" Callypso frowned. "She's not home?"

"She hasn't been for some time," Jack explained. "Something came up in Ellewynth, and she stayed behind. I don't know when she'll be back."

"Do you know what's going on?"

Jack snorted. "Like Talisa would tell me anything outside of what's 'necessary' in my apprenticeship."

"That is true, yes."

Callypso had hoped she could leave Tamina's sai with Talisa and then return home. She especially wanted to return to her more comfortable garb. The soft leather gloves and calf-high boots stifled her connection to the earth and the forest.

It was something Callypso hated.

She walked over to a little bench by Talisa's herb garden, and Jack joined her. She noticed him staring at the handkerchief she held, and

Callypso thought hard about whether or not to inform him of Tamina's sai. Her thoughts halted once she noticed the dark look on Jack's face.

"Jack?" she asked. "What's wrong?"

"There's something not quite right in that handkerchief you're carrying," he answered, while slowly moving away from her on the bench.

"Oh?"

Callypso was intrigued. Could Jack really feel the taint of the weapons? Was he finally learning to trust his intuition?

"That's why you're here to see Talisa," Jack said. "Whatever is hidden in that thing, you're afraid of it...so afraid that you don't even want it to touch your bare skin."

Callypso raised an eyebrow. "And why would that be?"

Jack smirked. "Last time I checked, elementals tend to cover up more when they're near something with malevolent energy. They're more likely to absorb it if they don't."

"I'm impressed." Callypso patted Jack's shoulder. "You've finally figured out my secret."

"You once told me I had to learn to trust my instinct. That's when I listened to the little voice in my head." Jack smiled. Crossing his arms, he returned his gaze to the handkerchief. "So what mischief did you bring here?"

"I'm not sure you'd really want to know."

"Callypso, I've been stuck in that cottage by myself for some time now," Jack answered while rubbing the back of his neck. "I welcome anything different."

Callypso burst out laughing. Someday, he will regret saying such things.

"How knowledgeable are you of weaponry?" she asked, laying the handkerchief in her lap.

"Depends." Jack shrugged. "I'm not fond of swords. I know a little bit about smaller weapons, especially of the throwing kind."

"Oddly enough, I can see you armed with throwing knives. Remind me to keep to your good side," Callypso teased. "Have you ever heard of the sai?"

Jack grew puzzled. "Sai?"

"I'll take that as a no." Callypso shut her eyes for a moment. "They are unique weapons used in the Dark Fortress, Blackwen City. Only one particular bloodline, the Ravenwing, wields them."

Callypso noted the dark look returning on Jack's face, and it actually scared her. She saw his hands clench into fists and wondered if he too knew the truth of what was to come.

"Are they thin blades, forearm length, with curved prongs extending from a jeweled hilt, by any chance?" Jack inquired.

Callypso felt herself shake. "How did you know that?"

"Because I've seen them before," Jack said, no longer facing her. "I've heard the Ravenwing name before as well. It's...it's not an event I can forget, no matter how hard I've tried."

Callypso felt sorry for him. She almost asked how and where this happened, but thought to spare him from further torment.

She found she didn't like seeing him so disturbed.

"You're aware of what's going on? Of what's to come?"

"If what's to come is my friend, Artemis, learning the truth and going to Blackwen City to avenge the murder of her mother, then yes, I'm aware," Jack replied, massaging his temples. "You have Tamina's sai then. Because you mentioned lingering spirits the last time you visited, I can only assume you meant her. You were sent to fetch them."

"Yes."

"And the longer a spirit lingers, the longer their anger changes and consumes them and their loved ones. Any article of theirs that was left behind at their grave site carries their taint, hence your extensive coverings."

"Yes, and I'm supposed to give these to Artemis." Callypso sighed.

"Can't you purify them?"

"That's the thing, Jack. I've tried." Callypso threw the handkerchief to the ground, which exposed the sai. She couldn't stop herself from flinching at the sight of them. "Tamina's spirit is just too strong. I can't get rid of the connection she shares with her weapons. I don't know what they'll do to Artemis, but I know it'll be *very* malevolent. I don't like it."

"Leave them with me."

Callypso nearly choked when Jack said the words.

"What?"

"You are still learning your gifts, Jack," Callypso reminded him. "What could you possibly do that I couldn't?"

"You're uncomfortable around them, and I know how elementals prefer to be connected to the natural world," Jack explained. "I may not be able to do much, but at least I can help give you some temporary peace."

Sweet of you, Callypso thought. *Foolish, but sweet. Perhaps he* can *be of some help considering how focused he seems now...*

Callypso picked up the sai and wrapped them once more in the handkerchief. Handing them to Jack, she smiled.

"I wish you luck," she said. "You don't have much time."

13

Several days had passed since the event at Netira's cell. Shadow had yet to see Artemis.

He couldn't blame her for her anger.

He stood in front of the Hall of the Elders and crossed his arms. A cool breeze picked up, and he ignored the loose dark blond strands that waved across his vision. Shadow felt it important to visit his aunt one last time. He knew Artemis was going to free Netira somehow soon, and she would have the dhampir lead her to that goddessforsaken city.

Whether she wanted it or not, he was going to leave Ellewynth behind and aid her.

Once inside the hall, Shadow was shocked when he saw his aunt sitting behind her desk. It appeared she hadn't slept in days—her normally serene face was now creased with stress, and her plaited hair was half undone. Her ivory dress looked shabby, and Shadow realized Lady Clarayne hadn't left her office for some time.

He didn't envy her position.

"My dear nephew," Lady Clarayne greeted him, her voice hoarse. "What brings you here at this hour?"

Shadow moved beside her. "When were you home last, Aunt Clarayne?"

"It matters not, Shadow," she answered. "I thought after the last few meetings we've had, you wouldn't be returning here at all. Not directly to my office, anyways."

Shadow's gaze lowered. "I've come to apologize."

"For what?" Lady Clarayne chuckled. "For being true to your feelings? For standing up to Destrius? You needn't apologize for such things."

"Nonetheless, I feel that I must apologize for that and more." Shadow backed away and returned to his spot in front of her desk. "I know it hasn't been easy for you, especially with Lord Destrius' hatred for me. I've…I've come to—"

"I know what you're doing," Lady Clarayne interrupted. "You won't have to apologize for that either, Shadow. You're doing what you feel is right. I do not fault you for it."

"You realize it'll mean I can never return home to Ellewynth again, once Arlina attacks and my disappearance is noticed," Shadow whispered. "I would be branded as a traitor…a deserter."

"Sometimes one has to do a little evil in order to accomplish a greater good." Lady Clarayne stood from her chair and embraced him. "You will always be my blood, Shadow. Whatever you choose to do, I will support you. You should know this by now."

Shadow felt the tears well up in his eyes and shook his head. "You will have to be the one to condemn me for desertion."

"The unfortunate aspect of politics." Lady Clarayne stepped back. "Things will return to normal once the issue of Arlina is taken care of. I won't leave you to rot."

"I very much doubt that." Shadow rubbed his brow. "Normalcy, I meant…not the part of you leaving me to rot."

"You're certain Arlina will attack Ellewynth?"

"Yes. Netira confirmed it."

Lady Clarayne sighed heavily. "Goddesses help us all."

"Lord Celstian will listen to you. Have him lead Ellewynth's people to the veils as soon as possible," Shadow pleaded. "I will be gone before then."

"Does Artemis know you're planning to follow her?"

"I'm not sure," Shadow admitted, "but it matters not."

Lady Clarayne stroked her nephew's cheek. "I hope she realizes how much of a prize you are."

"Aunt Clarayne…"

"Never be ashamed for what you feel in your heart. Not everyone is lucky enough to know what love is, no matter how brief it may be."

Shadow looked away. "I wouldn't forgive myself if I let her leave without the help she needs."

"I know, dear one." Lady Clarayne gestured to the door. "Go to her."

"I'll miss you, Aunt Clarayne," Shadow said before he left. *I hope you can forgive me one day.*

Karesu ignored the brood that surrounded him as they continued into the depths of the Woodland Realm. He did, however, keep a close watch on the Mistress. Arlina looked sickly as she marched beside him, and she was quick to snap at anyone who offered to help her. The vampire mage even noticed the deep scratches along her forearms.

He wondered what could possibly drive her to such a state. Wouldn't Arlina be excited for the upcoming slaughter of her enemies and blood relative? Why the scratches?

Karesu shook the thought from his mind and focused on the world around him. The veils were well-guarded; they wouldn't reveal themselves to him, and he couldn't pinpoint the source of their energy fast enough to locate them. An ancient defense, the veils were. It was no wonder the elves managed to flourish despite their numerous wars.

"Stop!"

The order came abruptly from Arlina, and the company came to a halt. Arlina fell to one knee, grasping her chest. Karesu knelt beside her and tried to keep her steady.

"Mistress, are you all right?" Karesu asked.

"No…" Arlina's normally cold gray eyes were filled with fear as well as pain. "Rest…we must rest."

"Mistress, we've stopped so many times already. We'll never reach Ellewynth at this pace," a voice behind them whined.

Karesu groaned, for it belonged to Latos. The smug bastard was a thorn in Karesu's side, and he longed to rip the man's head off. Well, he thought to burn him first, and then he'd dismember the leech. "Should the rest of us continue while you stay behind for a spell?"

Arlina used Karesu for balance as she snapped up and smacked Latos across the face with the back of her hand. The scent of his blood permeated the air, and the others began to hiss with delight. Karesu, too, couldn't help but enjoy the moment.

"How dare you act as if you're my Second?" Arlina seethed. "We *will* get to Ellewynth soon enough. For now, make camp! Anyone who desires to do otherwise, speak now. I beg you to."

No one answered her as they all moved to make camp. Arlina shoved past Latos, and Karesu followed after her. Arlina slipped behind a large tree far from the sight of others and fell to her knees, once again grasping her chest.

"Mistress?" Karesu knelt beside her.

"Karesu, there's something in this goddessforsaken forest that's doing this to me." Arlina shook. Karesu noticed how she was scratching her arms, how she didn't even flinch when she raked over the scabs and drew blood, and he understood then that the Mistress was losing her sense of reality. "She's doing this to me...that wretched specter..."

She? "Mistress, what are you speaking of?" Karesu asked, genuinely puzzled. There wasn't any magic he knew of in the forest that could cause the symptoms he now saw Arlina exhibiting. Paranoia was usually a self-inflicted disease. "Who is this 'she' you're referring to?"

"No one," she growled. "Mind your own business."

"Mistress, let me help you." Karesu tried to assist her to stand from the ground. "If this continues, you won't be in any condition to fight. I know that's the *last* thing you want."

"I need the cordial, Karesu," Arlina demanded. "I don't care of the side effects you spewed at me; I need to rest. I need...rest..."

Arlina fainted into Karesu's arms. He reminded himself to burn the clothes he now wore, just to rid them of the woman's essence. A shame really, for he rather favored this current attire.

Once he laid her on the ground, he reached into the purple velvet pouch that hung beside the sword on his hip. He pulled out a tiny vial of a viscous white liquid. It was milked from a particular root that grew in the outskirts of Blackwen City, and Karesu had learned long ago that it contained powerful properties. The root contained a liquid that could help heal physical ailments while putting the person into a comatose state. But some never woke up from taking the cordial Karesu managed to make of the mysterious root, and those who had experienced symptoms such as extreme hallucinations and psychotic outbreaks.

In essence, the side-effects made a full-blood more dangerous than they already were. Researching the root through the texts proved useless, as there was no mention of it.

"Well, I couldn't care less if you woke up or not," Karesu began as he pulled the rubber plug from the vial. "You're already psychotic. But since I still have need of you, and you're one stubborn bitch when it comes to meeting with Avilyne…"

He pushed apart Arlina's lips with his fingers and slipped a few drops of the cordial down her throat. Her body shook violently for several seconds, and she then stilled. That was a normal reaction when one drank the cordial. He knew the Mistress would wake from it; Arlina had far too many agendas to fulfill before submitting to such a death.

A scout found them and informed Karesu that the Mistress' tent was set up. After being sworn to discretion concerning the Mistress of Blackwen, the scout helped Karesu haul Arlina from the ground and carried her to the tent.

I awoke in a pile of clothing I had loosed from my trunks in an effort to pack. I smelled the fox blood before seeing myself covered in it. My back ached as it never had before…I must have flown for some time.

My control had slipped more than I thought. How was I going to face Arlina if I couldn't even contain the dark side of my heritage?

I grabbed all the bloodstained clothes I'd slept on and rushed to toss them into the fireplace in the main room. I slipped out of the ones I wore once I was in the washroom, and I ignored the inflamed reds of my skin as I scrubbed the fox blood from my body. My vision blurred more the longer the process took; the monster was winning.

It was a good thing I was leaving Ellewynth. Perhaps that was the true reason I wanted to escape in the first place. Wouldn't it be simpler to let Arlina rid Arrygn of another monster?

No, a part of me answered. *You must fight. You must live.*

I crawled out of the washtub and curled into a ball. I didn't want to die, but neither did I want to live in fear.

Images of the dream where Mother and Arlina fought flashed into my mind. I sat up and clenched my hands into fists.

This fight isn't just about you, I thought. *It's about Mother too.*

I had to fight Arlina...for Mother's sake. Perhaps the sudden moment of courage would stay with me for the rest of my days.

I forced myself off the ground and threw on a clean tunic and breeches. The material clung to my still wet and reddened skin, and I did not bother to brush my hair. It waved whether it was soaked or not, so it did not matter. I stared at the last set of bloodstained clothes and gingerly picked them up.

Once I reached the fireplace, I hesitated to throw away the bundle in my hands. I couldn't tear my gaze from the scarlet blotches in the fabric.

"You are a monster," I whispered. "You always will be."

The knocks that echoed into the room startled me; I dropped the bundle on my bare feet.

Who was here at this hour? Avilyne's hell...did I leave a visible trail of fox corpses behind?

Against my better judgment, I opened the door, and I stood face to face with Shadow. He looked exhausted, with his hair loose and glazed green eyes. He became more alert when he saw my inflamed skin color and tear-stained face. Shadow reached out to touch me, but I pulled back. It was then that he noticed the bloodied clothes I'd dropped beside the fireplace.

"Avilyne's hell," Shadow whispered. His focus returned to me. "Another blackout."

I nodded. "I'm losing myself."

"We can work through this," he said, as he stepped forward once more.

I took another step away from him. "There's no working through this."

"Artemis—"

"Stop it!" I cried. "Shadow, I am a *vampyra*. I kill animals with no memory of it! Sooner or later, it could be you, or Jack, or Talisa! Why do you keep my company knowing that one day I could kill you?"

Shadow shut the door behind him. He took off his cloak, and he went to pick up the bundle of clothes. He shut his eyes a moment after he tossed them into the fire. When he eventually opened them, Shadow walked toward me. He grabbed my arm before I could back away.

"Look at me," Shadow said, his tone gentle. When I didn't, he lightly grasped my chin and forced me to gaze at him. "You are a dhampir. You are a child of both the light and the dark. You kill foxes, and you will kill people one day." His grasp grew firm when I tried to look away. "Monsters…they have no remorse. They enjoy stealing lives. They enjoy inflicting pain. You are not tainted, Artemis. There *is* a safer and easier way to live with this."

"But—"

"Artemis, I am a soldier," Shadow interrupted. "You keep my company when you're more than aware of what I am capable of. I've been killing since long before you were born. Those faces haunt me every night I close my eyes. What haunts me more are the faces of those who could have been saved. If I did not serve in the wars, those who *were* saved would not be here today. We do what we must, my dear. You are *not* lost, do you hear me? None of us would let that happen." He wiped a tear of mine away. "No one is without a trouble. I do not keep your company merely because you are Tamina's daughter. I do so because I enjoy it. I do not linger around hearts filled with darkness…I keep to those filled with light."

I pulled him into a tight hug. "I'm sorry."

"You're apologizing because…?"

"I just am."

Shadow sighed. "Don't give up. Fight the despair. You must make peace with who you are. Only then will there be control."

"It's hard to when there are other things that plague my mind."

I felt him wince. "In truth, that is why I'm here."

"I'm glad you are," I admitted. I let go of him and sat in front of the fireplace. He did the same. "We need to talk about what happened. All of it."

"I should have explained things a long time ago," Shadow sighed. "I just thought you deserved—"

"A clean slate. I know." I cracked the first smile I'd had in days. It wasn't a true smile, but it was enough to show Shadow that I had stopped being angry at him. "I have so many questions to ask, and I don't know where to begin."

"You don't have to ask them all tonight, Artemis."

"But I'm..."

Leaving, I finished in my mind. I stopped myself from saying it aloud.

"Leaving?" Shadow said, as if reading my mind.

He had a knack for doing that sometimes.

"I'm not leaving," I corrected.

"You're a terrible liar," Shadow said. "You forget that I know you. I also know that you're going to break Netira out of prison and have her lead you to the Dark Fortress."

I shut my eyes. "I am."

"And just how do you plan on breaking her out of the Hall of the Elders?" Shadow inquired. "You failed to sneak in the last time we were there."

"I haven't figured it out yet."

"You were going to leave without even saying so much as good-bye to Talisa or myself?" Shadow's voice rose.

"I was going to! Somehow, I would have!" I snapped. "This isn't easy for me, Shadow. You don't have someone out there who wants you dead because of a blood tie and the right to a throne. I don't want to set foot in that damned city, and yet I have no choice! Either I let Arlina find me here and get killed, or I meet her there and..."

Shadow frowned. "And get killed?"

"I'm trying to delay it by leaving before she gets here."

"Did you see the state Netira was in when she first arrived in Ellewynth? How do you think she came to it?" Shadow said. "Netira has been fighting *much* longer than you have. Even if Netira helped you control the dhampir and prepare for a fight against Arlina, it still wouldn't be enough."

"I have to do *something*, Shadow."

"Yes, but you also must realize that you will have to take more than one life in this journey of yours. Arlina will throw her underlings at you. They will not show you any mercy." Shadow folded his arms when I couldn't spit out a retort. "Forgot about that, didn't you?"

"I tried not to think about it."

Shadow shook his head. "Artemis, you do not have to be on your own."

"If you're implying that you're coming with me, I don't want you to."

"It's not your choice whether I go or not!" Shadow yelled. He rubbed his brow while trying to calm down. "I swore to your mother once that I would always watch over you. Even if I hadn't, I would *still* watch over you. I've already told you why."

I was silent.

"I'm not letting you leave without me, Artemis. I'm not letting you march into that evil city with only Netira at your side."

"Shadow…"

"Willow be damned." He chuckled to himself. "How the roles have reversed…"

"Shadow, I can't have you leave your home," I pleaded. "They'll need you to help defend the city once Arlina attacks. You are a soldier of Ellewynth. Duty *demands* that you stay."

"I've already made my decision," Shadow declared. "You need me more than Ellewynth does."

I froze. "You'd be named a deserter. After all you've done for the realm…you can't possibly want that for yourself."

"I'm not changing my mind." He grinned. "I'm rather stubborn, remember?"

"Aren't we all?" I sighed as I gave him a small hug. "Thank you, Shadow. I know this isn't easy for you."

"It never is." He glanced at the practice sword lying close to the fireplace. "I don't suppose you've been practicing during our silence, hmm?"

I could not hide the guilt, which made him laugh. "I'm a pitiful student. We established this a long time ago."

"Not pitiful," Shadow said, grasping the hilt of the practice sword. "Just lazy."

"Fair enough." Shadow then smirked at me, and I grew wary. "What?"

"Someone needs to catch up on her weapons training." He stood up. "Come."

"No." I gulped. "Right now? Seriously?"

"Oh, I'm *very* serious," Shadow said. "Even more so now, with what's to come. I've found that practicing with the sword helps relieve stress, which you're in great need of."

Defeated, I snatched the practice sword from him and slipped into a cloak.

"So be it." I frowned as I punched his arm.

Shadow only winked as we ventured into the moonlight and headed toward his home.

Jack confined himself to his study and stared at the sai. The very feel of the weapons made his skin crawl.

How was Artemis supposed to safely wield them if they couldn't be purified? What would happen to her once she had them? He feared that even when informed of the malevolent aura of the weapons, Artemis would still choose to fight with them.

She was female after all. *All* women are stubborn.

He picked one of them up and grew confused as he glanced at the embedded onyx and garnet within the hilt. As far as he knew, jewels were supposed to shine, sparkle, or whatever else others would say about them. The jewels in the hilt were dull. When Jack rubbed them with a damp cloth, they were unchanged.

Tapping his temples, Jack refused to admit defeat. There was a reason the jewels were like that, and he was going to find out why…even if it took him all night.

"If Talisa were here, she'd be giving you a head-slap and berating you for missing something so obvious," Jack grumbled, while running his hand through his long, messy dark brown hair. "Think!"

Jack tapped each jewel hard with a fingertip, and he sighed when there was no response. He wracked his brain over and over again and realized he just wasn't going to figure it out. Feeling frustrated, he flung the sai in his hand across the room. His eyes widened when he saw the jewels flash within seconds of it landing in the wall.

"What the…?" He walked across the study to retrieve the weapon. The jewels in the hilt were still dull, but there was something different this time around; they now had a minimal shine to them. It was a subtle difference from before, and Jack knew that throwing it triggered something within the jewels.

Once he pulled the sai from the wall, he wondered what Talisa would do to him should she discover the hole. He shuddered at the possibilities.

I only threw it, Jack thought, as he stared at the sai in his grasp. "How did that…?"

It was done in anger, elf mage.

Jack froze when he heard the soft female voice in response to his question. He'd heard that voice before; it was the voice of the woman he'd seen murdered in the vision at the Grove of Kiare's Mirror.

Jack turned around and fell hard to the ground, shocked. There was a tall woman standing before him, colored with the palette of death itself. Her deep violet eyes showed amusement as they studied him. Her long brown hair spilled over her bare shoulders and arms; the woman wore only a billowing, sleeveless, black dress with a train extending far from her bare feet.

Jack knew he was in the presence of Artemis' mother, Tamina.

"You-you're Tamina," Jack managed to say as he tried hard to stand back up. "Willow be damned. Artemis really does look like you."

Of course she does. Daughters tend to be the mirror image of their mothers, Tamina said, gliding to the table where the other sai rested.

Jack gulped when he saw her hand passing through both the sai and the table, and he noted her look of annoyance.

"Why are you here?" Jack asked, trying to be cautious of his tone.

Tamina smiled at him, and he flinched, as it was the same one Artemis would flash on occasion.

I felt my weapons being used. I was merely curious as to who was doing so. You have an interesting energy, elf mage...very interesting energy.

"How can you tell that?" Jack finally got to his feet. He made sure to keep his distance from her. "My energy, that is."

Talisa has been in Ellewynth for some time now, has she not?

"Yes..."

So you're not overworked then. Tamina huffed, while folding her arms. *How is it possible that my daughter is best friends with an imbecile?*

"I resent that," Jack grumbled. "I'm doing what any other person would do when they don't understand something, and that's asking a question. *You're* the rude one who won't even answer me."

You have a feisty spirit. Good. Tamina walked over to the open door of the study and gestured for Jack to follow. *You want to understand the mystery of the jewels within my sai? Then be a good boy and follow.*

Jack found himself following Tamina to Talisa's library, and she spun around with a grin. He couldn't decide whether to feel afraid or annoyed.

"So...what am I looking for in here?"

Have you learned anything about dragons yet, elf mage?

"Nothing more than I'd already read about," Jack frowned.

He hoped she would get to the point soon.

Such a promising prospect you are, Jack. You should really be more inquisitive.

"What in Avilyne's hell do the dragons have to do with your sai?"

They were the first to introduce jewels to Arrygn and embed them into weapons for their champions. I suggest you pay closer attention to all the histories of the dragons within Arrygn. You'll find your answers there.

Tamina glided past him, but Jack couldn't let the specter leave without getting more answers.

"You're the reason Callypso couldn't purify the sai."

Tamina stopped and shifted her head ever so slightly, indicating that he had her attention.

Jack felt himself gulp involuntarily and knew there was no backing away now.

"You've been a lingering spirit for a little over twenty years. They're your link to the living world, are they not? If they are purified, you'll disappear."

Foolish boy, Tamina walked closer to him. Jack shuddered as he felt a chill along his neck. *While it is true that I am the reason the elemental couldn't purify the sai, it is not true that I would disappear should they be purified.*

"Then why won't you let Callypso purify them?" Jack asked, while doing his best not to be intimidated by the spirit.

That is none of your concern.

"And what of Artemis?" Jack felt his anger rise. He'd grown up with Artemis and knew her sorrow for her deceased mother. "Your sai could put her in more danger than that sadistic sister of yours. Don't you care enough about her that you'd help rather than endanger her further?"

The forces that are in play are bigger than you could ever imagine, elf mage. I know you'll accompany my daughter when the time comes. Do her and the rest of your companions a favor and stick to the more important matter at hand, which is making yourself useful. Read about the dragons and their jewels. You'll understand the sai better once you do, and you'll be able to help Artemis do so as well.

Jack watched Tamina walk away again, and he felt his face heat up.

"You're no concerned mother!" Jack spat. "You're only a pathetic form of energy taking up the world's space, driven solely by revenge. Stay away from Artemis, specter! If she were to learn that you would even go as far as sacrificing her for your own agenda, she wouldn't think twice about abandoning the cause to avenge you."

The smirk Tamina flashed at him made Jack's insides churn. How was this the same woman Shadow and Talisa revered?

I'd choose my words more carefully in the future, Jack, Tamina warned. *Someday you'll have to pay for them.*

Tamina disappeared before his eyes. Jack nervously ran his hands through his hair again. He should have known better than to let his anger speak for him.

"Damn specter…" Jack muttered, now annoyed rather than angry. "Let's see if you were really trying to help me or not."

Jack wandered around the library shelves, keeping an eye out for any books that specifically mentioned the history of Arrygn's dragons. Jack paced around, but stopped short when one book's spine caught his glance: *The Winged Jewels of the Sky.*

Snatching the book from the shelf, Jack settled himself on the floor and leafed through the pages. He stopped once he found a chapter about dragon jewels and started to read:

The first noted war the dragons of Arrygn had was with the walking dead, or what are now commonly referred to as vampires. More specifically, they warred with the "full-bloods" of what is now Blackwen City, as well as other vampiric territories (several of which no longer exist). The vampires wanted to snatch the territories the dragons had seized during their own campaigns.

While the victory rested with the dragons, they were impressed with a female warrior of the Ravenwing clan, the bloodline in control of Blackwen's throne. The Queen of the Fire Dragons herself ordered that she be gifted with her own jewels, so that they could be melded with the precious weapons of the Ravenwing, the sai. The warrior's bloodline was bestowed enough jewels to gift many future generations so that they too could have jeweled sai.

Jack nearly choked.

The name of Ravenwing had returned again. He had not realized that bloodline stemmed from Blackwen City alone. Willow be damned, it was the only bloodline to rule the city's throne! Artemis was a noblewoman!

He wondered how he was going to explain all of this to Artemis on top of seeing her mother's murder in Kiare's Mirror and then seeing the specter in person.

After a gulp, he continued on:

Since then, it has become customary for dragons of each realm to bestow jewels or jeweled weapons not only to their champions at the conclusion of war, but to the opposing warriors who impressed them. The jewels themselves are known to be useful in battle, as they are capable of containing the wielder's essence within them and of healing the warrior whenever necessary (dragons originally created jewels to be used as a healing tool). If the wielder is to pass from this world, their essence might still be contained within the jewels of their weapons. They must not be passed to another for use without purification. Unspeakable horrors can occur if the weapon isn't purified.

Dragon jewels are dangerous if not handled properly. They must be handled with the utmost care.

"Yes, I'm well aware of that, thank you!" Jack snapped. "Soleil burn me! Artemis is from a noble bloodline that just so happens to have dragon jewels embedded in their weapons."

Getting up, he slipped the book under his arm and pondered.

"The jewels of Tamina's sai reacted when I threw them in anger." Jack paced the library. "It is obvious her essence is still within the jewels. But why react to anger?"

After pacing some more, Jack stopped and groaned. He put down *The Winged Jewels of the Sky*, and gave himself a slap to the back of the head.

"Moron!" he yelled. "Tamina is a lingering spirit! She has *changed*, and that means the essence within the jewels has done so as well! She's an angry spirit! *Of course* the sai would respond to another's anger."

Snatching the book again, he made his way to his study and grabbed a cloak.

"I need to find Callypso. Maybe this can help in the damned sai's purification," Jack said, finding himself feeling happier at the mention of the elemental's name.

Talisa yawned as she walked into the study of Lady Clarayne. She sighed while rubbing her gray eyes. Talisa had been staying in the guest chambers of the Hall of the Elders since the night she spoke to both Shadow and Artemis. To her dismay, she was still clothed in her blue silk nightgown; her escort didn't give her the chance to change into something more appropriate.

She was, however, able to grab her pointed blue hat. While her hair was gathered in a messy braid, the hat could help cover the mess at the crown of her head.

Talisa yawned once more and watched Lady Clarayne turn to face her. Talisa couldn't help but feel pity for the woman; it appeared she hadn't slept much either.

"Forgive me for waking you at this unspeakable hour, Talisa," Lady Clarayne began. "I assure you, I wouldn't have done so without good reason."

Talisa inclined her head as her greeting and chuckled. "It matters not the time, my lady. What do you require of me?"

"I need you to lower the veils," Lady Clarayne ordered.

That request woke Talisa.

"You believe Arlina will attack Ellewynth."

"I'm following the instinct of a loved one."

"Have you spoken to the vampire about Arlina?" Talisa asked. "Have you even spoken to Lord Celstian about this request?"

Talisa didn't bother to include Lord Destrius; she knew better.

Lady Clarayne shook her head. "No need to. There would be no debate concerning the safety of the people in the city. Start gathering those unable to wield a weapon—"

"A child can easily wield a weapon," Talisa muttered. She clamped a hand over her mouth when she realized Lady Clarayne had heard her. "Apologies!"

"It's fine, Talisa." Lady Clarayne smiled. "I want you to take those we do not wish to fight to the open forest, and hide them past the veils."

"Very well." Talisa tipped the brim of her hat and smirked. "And what if your people decide to curse me for interrupting their slumber?"

Lady Clarayne laughed. "Then I trust you'll remind them of the pains you put your apprentices through."

Talisa rolled her eyes, but nonetheless smiled. "That'll work."

14

Arlina kicked through the frail wooden door of the cottage and was surprised at the disarray of broken glass and furniture within. She found herself pouting; someone had destroyed her sister's home before she could.

Ordering her scouts to stand watch outside, she went inside to investigate. It was hard not to make her presence known to anyone who might have remained in the home, as Arlina couldn't avoid stepping on the sea of glass shards.

Still taking in the sight before her, she caught a familiar human scent. It grew stronger the closer she moved to what was once a bedroom. She gripped a sai hidden within her boot while she slowly pushed the half-hinged door. Arlina pursed her lips at the sight of a human male sitting cross-legged in the center of the room. His back was to her; his shoulder-length black hair was in a crazed mess that mirrored the state of the cottage, and she noticed his tunic and vest sported claw-like tears.

Arlina couldn't help but smirk, as she then understood what happened.

"Gavin," she called, taking a firmer grip on the onyx-jeweled hilt of her sai.

The man she called Gavin didn't respond. Arlina decided to move in front of him, and when she noticed a flintlock pistol in his right hand, she knew to keep her distance. The hazel eyes that peered at her through strands of stringy black hair were dark and angry; Arlina found it enticing.

"What do you want, you hateful full-blood bitch?" Gavin demanded as he stood.

He was much taller than Arlina, and he was of a burly build. Arlina thought he was wasted as a human. He was wasted even more once he made it a habit to bed her sister.

"Hello to you as well, my bastard of a brother-in-law," Arlina replied, folding her arms and pointing her sai outward. "Where is my dear sister, and where did she take that little brat?"

"They're gone." Gavin looked away while tapping the barrel of the flintlock pistol. "Gone before I could kill them."

Arlina raised a brow and didn't bother to hide her amusement with him anymore. "Yes, and the tears in your clothing aren't any indication that you tried."

"Shut up, you corpse hag!" Gavin seethed.

Arlina shrugged. "As far as I was concerned, you were so madly in love with my sister." She began to pace around him, taking pleasure in his rising anger. "You were overjoyed at the birth of a daughter. The dishonorable merchant was suddenly living a life of legitimacy. What a laughable concept!"

"As far as I'm concerned, my daughter never lived. That hellspawn monster that masquerades in her body destroyed her soul the second it was born!" Gavin cried, as tears welled in his eyes.

He glared at Arlina as she began to laugh hysterically.

"Oh, my apologies!" she said, now hugging her waist. "I'm just surprised, really. How is it that a well-known merchant such as yourself—wait, let me rephrase that. How is it that a well-known smuggler such as yourself never encountered a dhampir child before? You've had dealings with vampires before!"

"I fail to see the humor in this, Arlina."

"You'll forgive me if I see the humor in the fact that you had no notion you were bedding a corpse all this time! Did you honestly believe that the look of hunger on dear Tamina's face was that of lust? She wanted to eat you, you pathetic waste of a human!" Arlina exclaimed, while her laughter continued.

She stopped laughing when Gavin held the flintlock pistol inches from her face. Arlina sighed and tapped her sai with a clawed finger. "What? You're going to shoot me now?"

Gavin narrowed his gaze at her. "If I know Tamina well enough, she is heading toward Ellewynth. She's going to that bastard elf, Shadow, and that crone stuck in a maiden's body, Talisa. What you choose to do with that information is up to you."

"My, my!" Arlina gave an exaggerated gasp. "I actually expected to be shot in the face, and here you are being generous!"

"You are truly annoying, Arlina," Gavin cursed.

"You know, when that kind of generosity is given to me, the person usually expects something in return," Arlina mused. "What is your price?"

Gavin loosened the grip on the pistol and let it swing with the hilt facing her so she could grasp it. "I want to return to my home city without being hunted by your lapdogs. I want nothing to do with this life anymore…I want it behind me."

"And?" Arlina asked, gesturing toward the pistol.

Gavin handed it over to her and then made his way to leave. Stopping at the half-hinged door, he turned. "When you find her, make sure she knows exactly *what she's done to me."*

Arlina's eyes snapped open, and she felt sharp pains in her chest. Even with the agony, she felt herself chuckling.

"So-called death serum…to think a cordial of all things could have ended me. Hah!"

She reached for the jacket that was neatly folded beside her cot. Slipping into the sleek, warm leather of her long jacket, she felt the opening flap of her tent with her fingertips. She smiled when she felt the crispness of the night.

She was greeted by the scouts and warriors of her city when she stepped out, and Arlina scoffed to show her acknowledgement of them.

She was hoping to find the location of Karesu's tent. Arlina wanted to find him and requisition more of the cordial he made for personal use. Not only was she refreshed, but she also didn't feel the soul-sucking energies of both the forest and her specter sister. The scratches on her arms were gone as well.

Arlina recalled the memory she'd relived while under the influence of the milky root cordial. Gavin was both a face and a name she hadn't seen or heard since the night she disposed of Tamina. Arlina couldn't help but grin; it was *such* a fond memory.

What happened afterward was an even sweeter memory that she wished she'd relived in the comatose state as well.

"Mistress. You're awake."

Arlina recognized the voice of the mage and watched him step out of the tent closest to her.

"Of course I'm awake." She glared at him. "Did you think I would fall prey to the hazards of the cordial like the common scum that live on the streets of the Dark Fortress? No."

"I meant no disrespect." Karesu bowed his head. "I'm only surprised, as the cordial had you in its grasp for only several days. Those who've woken from it didn't do so until at least a month's passing."

Arlina felt amazed. Several days?

It felt as if she'd had one night's rest.

"What has been going on since my, ah, slumber, if you will?"

"I've sent several scouts to keep an eye on Ellewynth, as we are only a night's march away," Karesu explained while tying his hair back with a silver ribbon. She noted his agitation by the constant breeze of the forest. "If you're wondering about Latos, do not worry. He has kept his silence, especially since I took temporary command."

Arlina noted the enjoyment in Karesu's normally stoic violet eyes. She thought he could become a worthy Second.

"And what news of Ellewynth do we have?" Arlina asked.

"There has been some strange activity as of late. One scout spotted some groups leaving the city in what they believed to be in a 'discreet' fashion," Karesu answered. "One scout claimed that the one leading them is Talisa herself."

"Talisa?" Arlina tapped her chin and thought for a moment. "They're being hidden away in the veils then."

"Do you think Netira could have told them? Even so, why would the Elders have listened? They despise vampires."

"She could have. But if I remember correctly, Clarayne is still one of the Elders of Ellewynth. She would have heeded Netira's words, if that traitor said any. Clarayne could also have suspected this from my letter, and is taking what she believes to be necessary precautions," Arlina grumbled. "We'll have to make them pay, Karesu."

"How should we do so, my Mistress?"

"Normally, I would have dispatched Latos and several others to intercept those traveling and cause some chaos." Arlina dramatically sighed. "I think the honor now belongs to you, mage."

Karesu inclined his head. "So shall it be done."

She watched Karesu step back inside the tent, and Arlina motioned for another scout to join her.

"Mistress?" the scout inquired.

"Have the others prepare for battle. Karesu will need you and one other to accompany him and take care of those running to the veils. *I* want to march straight to Ellewynth," Arlina ordered.

Her anticipation for the blood of her enemies rose. She *loved* that feeling.

"As you command, my Mistress."

Talisa was ferrying the elves deemed unfit to serve Ellewynth to the veils of the open forest for what felt like an eternity. Some refused her order to flee the city, but they changed their minds the moment she dragged them out of their homes by their pointed ears with her sharp nails.

Clearly, there were those who had no idea what her past apprentices had been through. Talisa wondered how that was even possible, since the elves were infamous for gossip. Then again, the elves were also infamous for looking the other way on certain matters.

To Talisa's surprise, the children were more cooperative than the adults. They enjoyed the idea of walking to the open forest; it was something that was rare for them, as they were never allowed to venture there unescorted. A child was one of the most precious treasures to the elves, especially when childhood was so short-lived in their culture.

While ignoring the grumbling of many, Talisa moved past the group and was amazed to find Serlene's sister, Lily. Lily was wearing a simple white robe, and she held a child's hand in each of her own. She was maintaining a smile, but Talisa could sense the anger within her.

"Hello, Lily," Talisa greeted her as she began to walk beside her.

"Talisa," Lily slightly bowed her head. "How do you fare?"

"Oh, don't start with the pleasantries. It's far too late in the night for it." Talisa frowned. "Or too early in the morning, if you prefer."

Lily chuckled. "Both are truth."

Talisa urged the children Lily held to move forward, and she noted Lily's now sad demeanor. "What troubles you?"

"It's..." Lily began, with a sigh, "it's not fair. I should be back in the city with Serlene and the others. I'm a capable bow-hand, and I know Ellewynth will need all of her soldiers."

"But that's just it," Talisa said. "You are not a soldier. Not yet."

"Shadow was officially a soldier when he was only three decades old. I'm nearly the same age, and my own sister was my instructor," Lily fumed. "Why can't I do the same?"

"For starters, your sister is a mediocre archery instructor at best," Talisa explained. "And second, Shadow had *the* archery instructor since he was able to lift a bow. It was also fortunate that he had the skills necessary for war before they were even taught to him. He was also one of the 'chosen'. They train a great deal more than those who aren't picked, as you well know."

"Even though I wasn't picked to join the 'chosen', you can't deny that I have skill with the bow."

Talisa sighed. The girl was worse than Jack.

"Yes, you have skill, Lily...but you are not *there* yet." She rubbed Lily's shoulder in an effort to comfort her. "I promise that you will be of use to the realm in a war one day. Right now, it seems you're more useful in keeping the children happy."

Lily shrugged as she smiled. "I suppose so."

"There's that smile." Talisa winked. "Why do I still sense some uneasiness?"

"Well..." Lily rubbed her nose and avoided eye contact. "I was also wondering how Jack is."

"*Jack?*" Talisa failed to hide her amusement. "Why?"

"He is a friend." Lily flushed. "Serlene never approved, but..."

Ah, I know why. Serlene can see that you love him, Talisa thought, *even if you're unsure of it yourself.*

"She never approved of Artemis either," Lily continued, breaking Talisa's train of thought. "Artemis has such a sweet soul. I wish others could see it."

"People fear those different from them," Talisa reminded her. "And she's a dhampir. The hatred the elves carry for any with vampiric blood runs too deep."

"But Shadow cares for Artemis!" Lily pointed out.

"Yes, because he was a dear friend to her mother and feels the need to continue being her guardian."

Lily crossed her arms, and her brow furrowed. "Here I thought it was because he loves her. I thought Artemis loved him as well, but she scolded me for saying so. I've seen how they look at one another! How could they deny it?"

Talisa burst out laughing. "Oh, Lily…that is one matter I dare not meddle in."

"Somehow I doubt that."

"Oh, fine." Talisa shrugged. "For now, I dare not meddle in it. It's not fun when they're moody about it."

Lily chuckled and was about to say something, until she came to a sudden stop.

"What is it?" Talisa asked. "We're not at the veils yet."

Lily didn't say a word as the rest of the group stopped. One of the children who ran ahead screamed. Talisa and Lily ran to where the child stopped, and Lily choked on a sob.

The child had found the mangled corpse of an elf. Talisa saw the elf's throat torn out, and its chest was ripped apart. She inhaled sharply.

"How could this have—"

"Lily, lead the others back to Ellewynth," Talisa cut Lily off. "And be quick about it. The paths to the veils are no longer safe."

"But—"

"You will do as I command, as a good soldier would, and you will make sure no harm comes to the children and your fellow elves!" Talisa barked. "*Go.*"

Lily ordered the group to turn back, and Talisa felt some of her calm return once the group was out of sight. Returning to the body of the elf, Talisa knelt beside it to examine it further. She spotted multiple puncture marks all over the corpse, and before she could study the odd wounds in the remains of the neck and shoulder, Talisa felt cold steel rest beneath her chin.

A single arm restrained her and crushed her chest from behind, and she silently cursed herself for allowing someone to capture her with such ease.

"You're losing your touch, witch," a male voice said.

She did not recognize him. Talisa could, however, sense an odd power within him…it wasn't quite like Jack's, but it was similar enough.

"I should have known the corpse was a trick to have me stay and send the others away." Talisa frowned. "Tell me true: Do you enjoy being a worthless lapdog to that bitch Mistress of yours?"

The grip of her captor tightened, and the sword was getting uncomfortably close to her throat.

"Tell *me* true," the voice mocked, "do you enjoy knowing that even *you* can be wrong?"

Talisa chuckled. "If you're not one of Arlina's whelps, then why hold me at sword point?"

"Because you are Talisa, the great witch of the elves and Kiare's vassal," he answered, now removing the sword and turning her around.

She saw her captor and took in the black clothing along with his long black hair, bound with a silver ribbon. He wore a large, silver, cross-shaped earring on his right earlobe, and Talisa noted the dark look in his deep violet eyes. "You have someone dear to me held prisoner in Ellewynth. You're going to lead me to her, and I would think twice about trying to lead me astray."

Someone dear? Talisa thought, puzzled.

"Why?" Talisa inquired, now noticing the silver rings the man wore on his left hand. Her initial judgment of him was correct. "Judging from the runes on those rings of yours, I'd say you're a mage. You wouldn't even break a sweat bringing down the prison bars."

"The bars, no. I wouldn't," he said. "I have no desire, however, to bring any unwanted attention to myself. You will take me into the city as discreetly as possible. Once I get Netira and am guaranteed a safe escape, I will spare you your life, Talisa."

Talisa raised an eyebrow. "Amazing."

The man frowned. "What?"

"You'll have to forgive me if you honestly think that I believe all of this." Talisa laughed. "You're obviously well trained by your Mistress. I'm sure Arlina got impatient that the Elders haven't disposed of Netira and decided to send you to finish the job. Lies are all you full-bloods know."

The mage took her by surprise again and held her tightly against his chest. His sword rested beneath her chin once more. "It would be in your best interests not to anger me, witch. Now *move*."

After the training Shadow decided to spring on me, I was too tired and bruised to return home that very moment. Shadow, of course, offered for me to stay the night. Even with my grumbling of it all being his fault in the first place, I accepted.

I made my way to one of the spare rooms that I had often slept in before Shadow left for the war. Falling face first onto the bed, I felt my legs throb and ache. Even with the extra strength I had from the fox blood, I was in pain. I didn't bother to get up and massage my legs. My mind changed, however, the moment one leg caught a cramp, and I snapped up to relieve myself of it. I stopped when I noticed Shadow standing in the doorway, clearly amused.

"Don't even start, Shadow," I warned, as I winced from the cramp.

"Wouldn't even dream of it," Shadow replied, trying hard to stifle his laughter. "There are easier ways, you know."

"For relieving leg cramps?" I rubbed my leg again. "This usually works for me."

"I understand you have a tendency for being masochistic, but there are simpler ways of getting rid of them," Shadow explained. "Granted, I wouldn't be as entertained—"

"Oh, just stop and tell me already!" I snapped.

"Lie down," Shadow ordered, walking to the bed. "Lift up the leg that hurts."

I did what I was told, and he gently took my cramped leg. He slowly moved it around, and once he angled it a certain way, I felt the cramp lessen.

"Wow," I managed to say after the relief from the ache.

"Feeling better now?" Shadow flashed a smug grin.

"Yes, thank you." He let go and stepped back. "Learned that from the fighting days?"

Shadow ran a hand through his loose dark blond hair; I knew he was tired, but he still seemed as alert as he was when we started the lessons. "Yes. When you run and fight as much as I have, you learn how to remedy such things."

"Don't you ever tire of it?" I asked, folding my arms.

Shadow nodded.

"And yet, you still wish to continue fighting."

"I will never stop fighting for those I care about," Shadow answered. He stiffened after he said that. Before I could ask what was wrong, he waved me off. "Someone has to make sure you know what you're doing out there."

I chuckled. "Fair enough."

"You should rest." Shadow made his way to the doorway. "I'll wake you for breakfast."

"Are you implying that we won't have a morning training session?" I asked, feeling hopeful.

"I never said that." Shadow grinned. "Sleep, Artemis."

15

A rlina took in the sight of Ellewynth. She always wanted to destroy this city, this so-called gem of the Woodland Realm. Her sister brought shame on the Ravenwing name by serving the Elders of this realm; Arlina would restore its pride by burning it down. Ravenwing women do *not* serve.

"Mistress." Latos appeared by Arlina's side. "The elven guards have been disposed of. I have stationed some of our soldiers by the gates should more come out."

"Well done," Arlina praised him. "Unload the barrels and place them against the gates."

"Yes, my Mistress," Latos bowed before disappearing.

The gates of Ellewynth were made of stone; in their first war with the dragons, the elves lost their barricade in a fiery blaze. Arlina would do the same, only with gunpowder and silver bullets she used for her flintlock pistol. She brought enough barrels of them to destroy Ellewynth twice over.

Arlina walked toward a barrel and was pleased to see a trail of gunpowder link from one barrel to another. She instructed her soldiers to place silver bullets within the gunpowder trail; she was going to make sure that Ellewynth wouldn't survive to see another morning.

Her impatience grew when she saw her soldiers lining the farthest parts of the gates with barrels and she yelled for them to place the rest in front of the stone where she stood.

"Make sure a trail extends to where I am," Arlina ordered as she took several steps away from the gate.

"It is too bad that the mage is out terrorizing elves by the veils," Latos said as he returned to Arlina's side. "He could have set the city on fire for us."

"I did not want to drain his magic," Arlina said. She took out her flint-lock pistol. "If you value your skin, I would suggest you move back now."

Latos moved quickly, and Arlina grinned as her finger moved to the pistol's trigger.

~_~

After some time walking through the open forest, Karesu settled for tying Talisa's wrists with a silver rope he'd made to prevent one's magical abilities from being used. Even so, he kept out his sword; the very one with the strange calligraphy etched into the blade. Karesu held it inches away from Talisa's back, nudging her occasionally when she stopped without reason.

"How much longer is it to Ellewynth?" Karesu asked, narrowing his gaze at the back of Talisa's head.

He knew the witch would take any opportunity to toy with him, despite being held at sword point.

Talisa snorted. "We still have quite a walk left to go, vampire mage. I suggest you keep your impatience to yourself."

Karesu moved the point of his sword to the curve of her spine and poked it. "I warned you earlier, witch, that it is unwise to anger me."

"Yes, yes." Talisa dramatically sighed. "I've heard you _several_ times already." She faced him. "How does Arlina stomach you?"

"The question you should be asking is how I stomach her," Karesu grumbled. He noted Talisa's puzzled expression. "What?"

"You truly meant that."

Karesu rolled his eyes. "Of course I did."

"Who are you, mage?" Talisa asked. He sensed genuine curiosity from her. "Really?"

"It matters not," he answered. "Move."

Ignoring Talisa's frown, he forced her to continue walking.

"If you insist on being boring and repetitive, I'll just have to find a different way to entertain myself." Talisa grinned widely. "You won't say anything about yourself, but maybe I know a lot more about you than you think."

It was Karesu's turn to frown.

"I'll listen only if you promise to shut up afterward."

"How rude!" Talisa pouted. She flinched when he raised his sword. "Anyways, it's obvious you're a full-blood from Blackwen City. Several of us were aware of Arlina's coming, so you're definitely one of her whelps. However, you've shown that you dislike her. She may be a master of deceit, but she does not realize that her own mage has been playing her. You've been playing her for so long that she hasn't realized her precious mage fell for a dhampir during his schemes. Am I doing well?" Karesu didn't bother to answer, which made Talisa chuckle. "I must be. Silence speaks volumes, you know."

Karesu poked her with his blade, but Talisa only smiled at him.

"So now we move on to Netira. I've heard it on good authority that she was formerly the Second of Blackwen City. My source also mentioned that she was sent here to be blamed for the death of those elves, just because Arlina was angry with her. I'm certain your Mistress must have been furious that her most trusted advisor was something *less* than her—"

"*Enough*," Karesu growled, with his sword cutting into the back of Talisa's robe. He only broke the skin as a fair warning. "Enough. Don't presume to think you know what it's like."

Talisa shivered at the cold steel's touch. "But I *do* know."

Karesu shut his eyes and counted silently to regain his calm. "What exactly do you know, witch of the elves?"

"I know that you're not the only man in this world who loves a dhampir and hides it," Talisa explained. Karesu couldn't hide his shock at her statement. "And now, I'm thinking you didn't kill that elf I found before you captured me. You must have come out here with scouts. Seeing as how you're the only one I've encountered out here, I can only assume you've relieved them of their living privileges."

She's a clever one, this witch, Karesu thought. "And what if I did?" Karesu asked aloud. "I've still captured you. Perhaps I'm just as evil as they are."

"Perhaps you are," Talisa said, continuing to walk. "Unbind my hands, and I'll take you to Netira."

"I think not."

"Your choice, mage." Talisa shrugged. "Once you make your escape with her and I happen to run across you again…be it several minutes after or years from now, be assured that I will kill you."

Karesu had to laugh. "Is it to satisfy your wounded pride?"

"No one captures me and lives long enough to tell the tale."

Karesu didn't have a reply. He thought if the circumstances had been different, he could have been friends with the witch. Until then, Netira's safety was his main priority.

Karesu realized they were close to the outskirts of Ellewynth, and frowned.

"You said we had much farther to go."

"I lied." Talisa snorted. "You should have expected that. Even my own apprentice would have."

Before Karesu could respond, they were both startled at the sudden explosion of fire coming from the outskirts of the elven city. There were mixed screams of fear, confusion, and battle cries. Karesu recognized the calls from his fellow full-bloods.

Fire engulfed the stone gate of Ellewynth, the only gate by the common path of the realm. The flames licked at the tree trunks surrounding the city and charred the branches and leaves. Smaller trees within the outskirts were swallowed up by a vermillion blaze, and their embers set fire to other nearby vegetation.

Arlina had gone ahead to the city without him. He found himself livid; he should have known that she would do this.

Aerios blow you, Arlina, Karesu thought.

He noticed Talisa, who had a horrified expression on her face. Looking back to the spreading waves of fire, he grabbed Talisa's hands and cut the silver rope.

"What? What are you doi—"

"Go help your elves," Karesu cut her off as he sheathed his sword. "Discretion went out the window the moment that bitch set Ellewynth on fire."

Talisa studied him for a moment. "I still stand by my word, vampire mage. Don't think this sudden act of kindness will spare you."

Karesu grinned at the witch, which confused her. "I welcome the challenge."

Before she could reply, Karesu left her behind and rushed toward the city.

⤳

Arlina was enamored with the chaos that surrounded her. She enjoyed the sight of the flames, and the slow-burning death of the elves brought her a depraved sense of joy.

Sai drawn, she began to search for her niece. It shouldn't have been hard, as daughters tended to be the mirror image of their mothers. She grabbed an elf and twisted them into a headlock. Arlina held the tip of a sai inches away from the elf's eye.

"Amuse me, my pointy-eared cattle," Arlina demanded. "Where is the one called Artemis?"

"Find the *vampyra* yourself, full-blood bitch," the elf spat, struggling vainly to break free from her grip.

Arlina shook her head. "Tsk, tsk, tsk."

She shoved the sai into the elf's eye and twisted it for good measure. Once she felt the body go limp in her grasp, she dropped the corpse and licked the blade of her sai clean. "My, my. It's true what they say about the elves...the longer you let them live, the better their blood tastes. Perhaps this shall finally change my mind about the old vintages."

Arlina looked around and only saw elves and her soldiers fighting one another. There was no sign of Artemis.

Not yet.

The blast woke me up.

When I ran to the window, I was horrified to see the fire that now surrounded Ellewynth. I was even more frightened when I saw unarmed elves being attacked by speeding shadows. The bells above the Hall of the Elders rang—the songs reserved for danger. It could only mean one thing: Arlina was here.

Avilyne's hell, I didn't get out of the city in time.

"Artemis!" I saw Shadow standing in the doorway, sword in hand. "We need to go."

"We're too late," I said, still shocked.

Shadow grabbed my arm and pulled me with him. "I can still get you out of the city."

"What about you?" I asked, confused.

"Don't worry about me."

When we came outside, Shadow whistled a sweet tune. He did so while watching the open forest and didn't notice a full-blood running toward us.

The full-blood stopped the moment he saw me; his eyes widened.

"You're dead," he gasped. "It can't be."

The full-blood's head fell off after I was blinded by a flash of Shadow's sword. I felt myself take a sharp breath when I saw the head roll across the earth.

"This is what you will be dealing with, Artemis," Shadow explained as I watched the blood drip along the blade of his sword. "The dhampir would not have hesitated."

I heard a horse's neigh, and I saw Azrael trot closer to us. Shadow grabbed my waist, hoisted me atop her, and whispered a few words in Elvish in her ear.

I realized he wasn't coming along. "Shadow?"

"She will take you to Talisa's cottage," he explained, now looking at me. "Azrael is too fast for any of the full-bloods to chase after. The rare ones who can catch up with her, she'll trample. You will be safe."

"Come with me," I pleaded.

Shadow gave me a sad smile. "I can't. I have to get to Netira before Arlina does." He took my hand and squeezed it. "You worry too much. I'll see you before the dawn, I promise."

"But—"

Shadow pushed Azrael off, and I watched him rush back to Ellewynth.

Please be safe, I thought while holding onto Azrael's neck.

"Mistress!" a voice called along the screams.

Arlina saw that it was one of her scouts. She slashed through an elf's throat with a sai and licked the blood. "What is it?"

"There is a woman who looks like your sister, Tamina!" the scout cried. "She tried to escape to the open forest, but our soldiers forced her back into the city. I regret to inform you that we could not contain her. Shall I send reinforcements to aid in her capture?"

"She will be heading towards the gates..." Arlina murmured. She then shook her head. "I will take care of it myself. Find Latos and tell him to report to me should he come across this Tamina look-a-like."

We could not make a clean escape from Shadow's home to the open forest. As soon as we drew close to it, a large group of heavily-armored full-blood soldiers cornered us. Even with Azrael's unnatural speed, she would not have made it past them unscathed. We had no choice but to ride into the city and make for the gates.

I prayed the gates still stood. This inferno grew by the second.

I felt my jaw and back ache after smelling the blood of both the elves and vampires. I could not let the dhampir run free, not even in the danger I was in.

Azrael neighed as I saw the gates come into view. Not all of it was destroyed, thank the goddesses. I felt a sliver of hope the closer we rode toward them, but it switched into panic the moment I saw a figure stand by the opening in the gates we hoped to pass. It was a woman with short, red hair, and I felt a knot form in my chest once I saw the same cold, gray eyes that haunted my dreams. The irises shifted to red, and her fanged grin widened as she raised a strange looking pistol toward us. Azrael whinnied and tried to turn away quickly, but we fell to the ground, hard.

I coughed as I felt pain flare on the side of my body I landed on, and my vision was blurred once I opened my eyes. My senses sharpened as I smelled blood—my own. I could feel the slickness of it once I moved my hand to my head.

"At last, we meet," a dark voice said as I heard footsteps move closer to me.

It was hard to focus on the moving figure, but I didn't need to see clearly to know that it was *her*. The voice matched her coldness.

"Arlina." I coughed as I tried to get up.

I cried out once I felt a sharp kick to my stomach. Arlina cackled above me, and I felt myself being rolled over so I could face her. She placed her foot on my chest to pin me down. The sharp heel of her boot pricked my skin through the tunic.

"Artemis." She hissed. "Avilyne's hell, you are the spitting image of my poor, poor sister. Perhaps I should free you from that curse now."

"Better to look like her than you, murderer!" I spat.

I grabbed her ankle and rolled my body so she would fall. She did so, and I started to run away once I got my bearings. My head throbbed with each step. I was forced to a stop once I heard a loud blast, and I felt the air of some projectile close to my cheek. A burn prickled my skin soon after, and I turned around to see Arlina's face twist into annoyance.

"Only a burn, eh?" Arlina sighed dramatically. "It seems the goddesses wish for me to toy with you before you die. So be it."

I could not find a weapon nearby, and I knew then that I messed up by not taking one while riding through the city. I felt the monster within try to claw its way out of the cage I forced it into, but I still refused to set it free. I would rather die as Artemis, consciousness retained, than Artemis, the *vampyra* who slaughtered both friend and foe.

Arlina dropped the pistol as she rushed after me. I settled for a half-charred branch for a weapon and ran towards her. She knocked the branch out of my hands and struck me hard across the face. The pain in my head tripled and my vision blurred more. Arlina gripped my throat and shoved me against a tree trunk.

"Pathetic," she growled. "I wouldn't enjoy choking the life from you, as weak as you are. Your disgrace of a mother put up more of a fight!"

My jaw ached and I felt my eye teeth elongate. I could not feel the wings on my back, and with what little strength I had left, I used to cage the monster within. I kicked at Arlina's waist, but she swatted my leg away with her free hand.

"Ah, there she is." Arlina grinned. "Perhaps there is a Ravenwing woman in there after all. We are a feisty bunch, after all. You're still so helpless though…how disappointing."

"Enough of this," I coughed as I let go of her of arm and reached for her face.

Arlina moved her head aside as I expected she would, and I used the distraction to kick at her leg. A strange weapon fell from her boot when I did so, and I took the brief moment to shove her away so that I could grab the weapon. I realized it was one half of the weapons she used to fight Mother with, the ones with the thin blades with curved prongs and extensively jeweled hilts. Before I could grasp it, I felt Arlina's claw-like nails grip my arm. I winced as they cut into my skin and drew blood.

"A tricky little bitch, you are!" Arlina cursed as she threw me against the tree. "I wonder what part of you should I tear apart first?"

I spat out the blood that filled my mouth. "Come near me again, and it'll be *you* who loses something."

"Is that so?" Arlina laughed. "In that case, let's see how well you try to tear a limb from me while I rip out your heart. Unless you shift into your dhampir form, you'll never stand a chance against me."

"I can kill you without shifting," I assured her. I forced myself to stand and tried hard to hold the fighting stance Shadow taught me. "Come and take my heart, murderer…if you can."

Arlina growled as she rushed at me. Before she could lay a hand on me, a white blur rammed into her—Azrael. I watched the ruler of Blackwen City curse Shadow's mare as she struggled to stand, and Azrael let out a harsh neigh. I knew what she was trying to tell me and I ran to mount her. Another blast echoed when the mare began to run, and we both fell to the ground again. Azrael cried as she tried to stand, and that was when I saw the flower of blood on her rear leg.

"Damn you, Shadow's pet!" Arlina yelled. "You're just like your master! That infernal elf meddled in affairs that did not concern him either!"

"Meddling is more *my* specialty than his," a voice corrected.

Talisa came into view. I was never so relieved to see her. I was confused when I saw her wearing a nightgown and stopped myself from asking her questions.

She moved in front of Azrael and me, and I saw bloody cuts and cloth tears along her back. What happened to her?

"*You*," Arlina spat.

"Time hasn't been kind to you, hateful bitch," Talisa said. "I didn't think it was possible for full-bloods to develop wrinkles. Oh wait. Those are just your veins popping. I didn't think that was possible for corpses either! You must really be under so much stress!"

"And I see you're still as miserable as ever, crone," Arlina retorted. "Still wandering Arrygn, cursed to be Kiare's pawn until she sees fit to release you from the chains of life. It must be tiring, seeing all the ones you love waste away as the centuries continue to pass."

"I will not watch this one waste away," Talisa swore as she gestured toward me. "You cannot have her, Arlina."

"Try and stop me, witch!" Arlina cried as she rushed after Talisa.

The two grappled with one another, and Talisa barely managed to shove off Arlina.

"How badly is Azrael hurt?" Talisa asked as she blocked Arlina from attacking me.

"She can't run!" I answered.

Talisa swore loudly and fell after the Mistress of Blackwen punched her in the jaw.

"Once I'm through with you, crone, I'll kill Artemis and that damned horse!" Arlina yelled.

Talisa cupped her jaw and faced me. "Touch the tree beside you, Artemis! Do it now!"

There was a veil this close to the city gates? How?

"I won't leave without you, Talisa!" I argued.

"No one is leaving here!" Arlina screamed as she ran toward Azrael and me.

Moments before Arlina could reach us, Azrael bucked at me and I hit the tree beside us. I groaned when I felt a sharper pain in my head this time, and I waited a moment before forcing myself up from the ground. When I had, I realized I was in a new environment. I saw Talisa's cottage close by.

A snort drew my attention, and I saw that Azrael was here too. It was then that I noticed strands of hair from her tail were in my hand; she was able to come because I held onto her.

Before I could apologize, I felt light-headed. My legs buckled beneath me.

"Avilyne's hell..." I coughed before slipping unconscious.

Arlina froze once she saw Artemis and the mare disappear. Her niece was in her grasp and that witch let the dhampir brat slip through her fingers!

"Better luck next time, Arlina," Talisa smiled. Her chin was red from the earlier punch the Mistress of Blackwen dealt her. "You'll never catch her. Not while I and Shadow are around to protect her."

"I will kill all of you if it is the last thing I do!" Arlina swore.

Arlina gripped her sai. The cries of those calling her name stopped her from attacking that damned crone. She spotted Latos and several other soldiers running towards her. Latos joined her side, his jaw and other parts of his body covered in congealed blood. The soldiers flanked in between Arlina and the witch. Talisa merely glared at them.

"Why are you here?" Arlina hissed.

"I did not spot the Tamina look-a-like, but I did find the Hall of the Elders," Latos reported. "I thought perhaps she would be hiding there."

You're too late, imbecile, Arlina thought. She suddenly found herself smiling. Artemis slipped away, yes, but there was one more person in this wretched realm worth killing.

"Well done," Arlina replied. "Take me there at once." She glanced at Talisa and waved. "Catch me if you can, crone! I have a meeting with a certain rose."

16

Karesu raced through Ellewynth to locate the jail that held Netira prisoner. When attacked by an elf soldier, he held back any killing strikes and simply incapacitated them so that he would not be followed. When encountered by his fellow full-bloods, Karesu came up with the excuse that he had an urgent message for the Mistress.

The full-bloods of Blackwen had always been confused at Karesu's "code" of fighting; he would always meet an opponent head on. He may have pretended to be a despicable person, but Karesu still valued the ideal of the "honorable warrior." If it weren't for him being a mage, Karesu was sure Arlina would have disposed of him because he gave too much respect to those he met in battle.

As Karesu ran, he wasn't sure what worried him more—finding the prison yet being too late to save Netira, or encountering Arlina and being forced to hunt his love with her. In the end, he decided his ultimate objective was to find the prison and figure it all out from there. To do that, however, he would have to locate an Elder.

In the elven society, the Elders were the ones who had complete control over the prison. Karesu scowled as he thought he should have kept that bothersome witch hostage. Surely Talisa would have saved him the time and effort of locating the prison.

As soon as the thought crossed his mind, an arrow grazed his right ear. As his fingers brushed his cross charm earring, he was relieved to find it still intact. Another arrow shot past the now torn sleeve of Karesu's tunic, and when he found the tree that concealed the archer, he leaped and knocked down his attacker. When they both reached the ground, he was horrified that the archer was nothing more than a youngling.

She stared at him with angry blue eyes, her long blond hair now filthy with dirt and scrunched leaves.

"Do your worst, vampire!" she spat. "I do not fear death!"

Karesu sighed and got off of the girl. He stretched out a hand to help her up, and she stared at him with confusion.

"Do you wish to keep to the ground?" Karesu asked, kneeling on one leg while still holding out a helping hand.

"You're trying to trick me," the girl said. "If I let you pull me up, you'll slip that fancy sword of yours into my belly and drain me of my blood."

"I thought you did not fear death."

"I don't!"

Karesu rubbed his temples. "Just how old are you? Why are you fighting?"

"I'm defending my home like any other elf of Ellewynth!" she snapped, pushing herself from the ground while keeping her distance from him. "I'm older than you think. I'm as old as Shadow of Ellewynth when he first became a soldier. You know of him, I know you do."

"You may be trained, but you're no soldier, girl," Karesu replied. "Don't go chasing the fame that will curse instead of enrich you. Go run to the veils while you still can. Ellewynth has fallen. There's nothing more you can do."

"I can still fight!" she yelled, pointing to the tear in his sleeve.

Karesu chuckled. "I don't think your intention was to rip my clothing."

The girl flushed and went to charge him. He sighed and was about to side-step away from her swinging bow, until he saw one of his full-blood comrades run toward the girl from behind. Karesu saw the girl's eyes widen as he moved his sword forward. She fell to the ground to avoid his swing, and she was startled at the sound of Karesu's blade parrying the other full-blood's short sword.

"What treachery is this, mage?" the full-blood spat, his fangs fully elongated and his face and clothing covered in elven blood.

"It's none of your concern," Karesu answered. He looked at the girl after shoving off the full-blood. "Run."

"What are you trying to pull?" she said, evidently shaking.

"I already told you! You're just a youngling," Karesu explained. "It is not yet your time."

"Arlina will hear of this!" the full-blood threatened, as he pressed forward for another attack.

Karesu pushed off the full-blood once more and parried multiple sword strikes. With a sweeping arc of his blade, the full-blood's head rolled to the ground. The elf girl shut her eyes while covering her mouth. The calligraphy suddenly brightened, and then it dimmed once the blood disappeared off his blade. Karesu knelt beside the girl.

"Now you see that if I wanted you dead, you would have been," he explained. "Run while you still can."

"But…why?"

"I…I'm not the same as them," Karesu said, remembering his conversation with Talisa. "Perhaps you will be willing to trade some information with me in exchange?"

"I don't trust you, full-blood," the elf girl growled. She then sighed. "But for saving my life, I might feel a little generous."

"Where is your prison?"

The girl was confused. "What for?"

"I need to save someone I love before my kind gets to her first."

The girl was silent and looked away. "Love?"

"Yes. It's imperative that I find her. Can you tell me where your prison is?" Karesu begged.

The girl stood up and grabbed her bow, notching another arrow. Karesu's grip on his sword tightened, but she shot the arrow in the western direction. Confused, he noticed her preparing to dash away.

"Looks like I missed," she said, with a hint of sarcasm.

Raising an eyebrow, he realized she had given him a direction in which to find the prison.

"Will I know what it looks like?" Karesu asked.

She nodded. "You're bound to find an Elder in that direction. One of them is sure to be guarding the prison."

He watched her dash away before he could thank her, and he smiled when he saw her run in the direction away from the fighting. Running west, he took a deep breath and prayed.

Arlina stood before the Hall of the Elders and frowned as she stared at the carvings and other intricate woodwork. She very much wanted to destroy the building and see who would call it "pretty" afterward.

"*This* is the Hall of the Elders, Latos?" she said, unimpressed.

"Yes, Mistress," Latos answered. He licked what was left of the congealed elf blood from his chin. "We'll burn it once your business with there is done."

Burning it wouldn't be enough, Arlina thought as she kicked the door down to enter.

The scent of tea wafted through the hall, and Arlina scowled. The damn elves and their obsession with tea! She never understood the need to consume watered-down leaves.

It was disgusting.

She spied the three main doors, and she grinned when she saw the door with the silver rose. "This one is Clarayne's."

"I would have assumed so, since she *is* The Rose," Latos muttered.

He yelped when Arlina smacked the side of his head with the onyx-jeweled hilt of her sai.

"When I want your commentary, I will ask you for it," Arlina berated him, as she walked closer to the door. "Stand guard outside of the hall. I do not want any interruptions from that witch or pitiful elves thinking to pull off a rescue attempt."

Latos bowed his head while still rubbing it, and vanished from the hall. Arlina pressed a hand against the wood and felt excited when she noted the Elder's presence on the other side. She tapped her nails along the door, and when she felt the Elder startle at the sound, Arlina kicked through the door and held out her arms as if expecting an embrace.

"Lady Clarayne!" Arlina mocked her with a bow. "What an *honor* it is to see you again! The Rose herself! Kiare be praised."

"Spare me, Arlina." Lady Clarayne's hand gripped the hilt of her curved blade. "I knew you would come here. How could you pass up such a glorious opportunity, Mistress of Blackwen?"

"I'm touched!" Arlina put a hand over her heart. "Truly, Clarayne. Here I thought you'd forgotten all about little ol' me."

"Even when you're sent to the abyss, I will *never* forget you," Lady Clarayne hissed, pointing her sword at Arlina.

"Still sour after all these years?" Arlina sighed. She began to pace the room while twirling both her sai. "He was only a husband, you know. They *can* be replaced. It happens all the time! I'm sure there were plenty of other men who were willing to take his place." Clarayne's face darkened, and Arlina pretended to be shocked. "What? You mean to tell me after all these years you haven't taken another man to your bed? That is a dreary thing, to deprive yourself of some fun."

"Be silent," Lady Clarayne demanded, her control of her patience diminishing.

"I'm sure your dead darling wouldn't mind. After all, don't they always say to live on, just for them? The whole 'live for each moment' speech?" Arlina chuckled. "Oh wait…he didn't say any of that. What *did* he say before I broke through his ribs to rip out his still-beating heart? Oh, yes! I remember now."

"Don't you dare, you bitch!" Lady Clarayne yelled.

"He said, 'I will always love you, my rose.' He said, 'We will be reunited in Willow's Grove once more.' Do you have *any* idea how hard it is to keep down the bile after witnessing such a sickening moment?" Arlina taunted. She enjoyed the growing anger she felt from the Elder. "I've heard better lines spewed from drunkards."

Lady Clarayne shut her eyes and took a deep breath. She then began to laugh, which confused Arlina.

"Goddesses, am I witnessing the first crack of the lady's sanity?" Arlina frowned, while folding her arms.

"I pity you, Arlina, truly," Lady Clarayne said, mocking Arlina by using the same gesture of holding her hand over her heart. "Destroying the joys of others, just to gain as much power as possible. Even vampires cannot live forever, let alone in solitude, Arlina. Were you so jealous of your sister because she had things you could never have? The promise of a throne? Love? A child?"

"Only weaklings allow themselves to be tied down by such useless anchors," Arlina scoffed. "I rather like power. I can do whatever I want, however I want. Why would I want to ruin that with an annoying, attention-seeking child and an overbearing husband? After seeing *your* husband, I knew right then and there I had made the right choice of taking the path I did."

"You're despicable."

"You've known this for ages, Clarayne. Why should now be any different?" Arlina reminded her as she jumped past the desk and backed Lady Clarayne against the wall. Her sai created sparks along Lady Clarayne's sword.

"I will not go easily, Arlina," Lady Clarayne growled, shoving Arlina off.

"There's no fun in an easy kill!" Arlina beamed. "How I've waited for this moment..."

Shadow ran as fast as he could to the Hall of the Elders. It was taking him longer than he thought, for there was a full-blood at every corner and Shadow was too well-known for them to ignore. He fought his way through each one, and Shadow stopped himself from running off once he saw a familiar face doing battle with a full-blood.

Her pointed blue hat was missing, and he wasn't sure if he should laugh or be horrified at the sight of her fighting in her nightgown. Talisa caught sight of him and glared.

"Don't you dare judge me, Shadow!" Talisa snapped while catching a full-blood by the throat. She tossed him into the flames of what was once a cluster of oak trees. "Shut it!"

Shadow moved to strike down a full-blood who attempted to sneak up on her, and he then succumbed to laughter. "Do I really want to know, Talisa?"

"You stupid elf!" she fumed as she stole a sword from one full-blood and killed it. "I am the *last* person you want to toy with right now!"

He grinned after he disposed of a full-blood who leaped at him from above. "You're amusing when you're annoyed, did you know that?"

"I would smack you right now if the circumstances were different," Talisa grumbled, while rubbing her hands along her bloodied and dirt-stained nightgown. "This was my favorite, too…"

"I'm sure you could find a spell that would fix that, Talisa."

"Enjoy all of this now while you still can. You still have *many* favors left to do." Talisa glared.

"And you call *me* a killjoy." Shadow sighed.

"My good mood ended the moment Ellewynth caught fire." Talisa huffed.

"I sent Artemis to your cottage. She is with Azrael."

"*I* sent them to my cottage," Talisa corrected him. "Arlina nearly succeeded in killing them both."

Shadow froze. "No…"

"She *is* safe, I swear it. They both took my personal veil," Talisa explained. "Kiare will reprimand me for letting that happen, but I am willing to suffer the consequences. They're both hurt, but they will be fine. Jack will know what to do with them."

Shadow clenched his fist. He was angry. Arlina found Artemis and he wasn't there to protect her. And Azrael hurt as well? It took a lot to stop himself from abandoning Netira's rescue just to go find them. They were in great need of the Blackwen City dhampir.

They realized they had a reprieve from attacking full-bloods, and Shadow took the opportunity to catch his breath. He then noticed small tears in the back of Talisa's nightgown, as well as many cuts that were recently made by a sword tip. "What happened? What did you do?"

She cursed when she saw him staring at the cuts. "We're not the only ones looking to spring Netira from her prison. She has a full-blood lover."

"Oh goddesses," Shadow answered, as he ran a bloodied hand through his hair. "And you think this lover of hers will get to her before us? I doubt he'll be able to succeed."

"Shadow, he's not the common idiot full-blood from Blackwen City! He's a *mage*. A damned vampire mage!"

Something clicked in his mind. He'd had suspicions that a mage was serving in Blackwen City, not only because of the strange runes that were etched in the cloaks of the full-bloods, but also because of how Netira was able to briefly control the element of fire. He didn't expect a *vampire* mage, let alone him being Netira's lover.

"Avilyne's hell!" Shadow swore. "We need to get to Netira before he does."

"And how do you propose we handle the mage should we encounter him, Shadow?" Talisa snapped. "I'm sure he's part of Arlina's council as well. That means he has a hell of a lot more resources than we will after this battle. He will hunt us down until he gets Netira back."

"He gave you those cuts, huh?" Shadow asked. Talisa nodded. "So… why did he do so rather than kill you?"

Talisa sighed. "He let me go to help save Ellewynth. A lot of good that did…that bastard…"

"Let's ignore the fact that he actually captured you and you're still recovering from wounded pride," Shadow said, ignoring another glare from the witch. "This full-blood's a mage, yes. He's also in love. That can work to our advantage, Talisa."

"Speaking from personal experience, Shadow?" Talisa winked.

Shadow glared at her. "We must get to the hall before he does. If we do meet the mage, I'll handle it."

"I swore I would kill him, you know," Talisa spoke as they ran. "We must also reach the hall before Arlina does. She already had a head-start. That damned woman sicked her soldiers on me before I could stop her."

Shadow cursed. Arlina would certainly go after his aunt considering their history. And now that Artemis escaped her…

"Run faster, Talisa!" Shadow ordered as he quickened his pace.

The wooden hall came into sight, and there wasn't a soul to be found. The fire had not yet reached the building, which led Shadow to hope that they made it before the Mistress of Blackwen.

Shadow walked to the steps and stopped once he caught a glint to his right. He rolled over and spotted a knife in the ground where he stood before. Shadow waved Talisa off before she could speak.

"Go! If my aunt is still inside, get her out safely. I will get Netira once I'm done here. Move!"

Talisa nodded and disappeared into the hall as a full-blood appeared before Shadow. He recognized him from the time when he and Serlene had gone out to the open forest to claim Netira.

Shadow was face to face with Latos.

"Famous Shadow." Latos grinned. "We meet again."

"Bootlicker," Shadow responded. He took his fighting stance. "The only title you'll ever receive in this lifetime, it seems."

"You've insulted me once and still live," Latos reminded him, while letting his tongue run over his elongated eye teeth. "A mistake I will not repeat."

"Talking never got one anywhere," Shadow said, raising his sword. "Only actions did."

Latos disappeared and reappeared beside Shadow, the same knife Shadow had missed now back in Latos' hand. Shadow raised his sword to block the thrust Latos intended for his shoulder, and he angled his blade enough to create an opening to Latos' chest. Before Shadow could land a punch, Latos disappeared again. He was too fast for Shadow to catch as he sliced through Shadow's sleeve, making a deep cut within his arm.

Taking a step back to admire the blood seeping through Shadow's sleeve, Latos smiled.

"Your blood smells delectable, famous Shadow," Latos taunted, his irises completely red. "But I can't end this just yet. I need to add a little more...spice...to get your blood just the way I want it."

"I thought you'd have been used to disappointment by now," Shadow said, ignoring his bleeding arm. "Perhaps you're as old as I am. I have more titles than you'll ever have. It's a shame really..."

Latos disappeared again, and Shadow raised his blade over his chest, parrying the knife that suddenly appeared inches from the uninjured arm. The full-blood resorted to making the same move as before, and Shadow shifted his weight and heard Latos curse; he knew he'd drawn the vampire's blood.

Latos held a hand to his now cut shoulder and glared at Shadow.

"I never fall for the same trick twice, you see," Shadow explained, taking a stance once more.

"You *let* me cut you, elf!" Latos spat. "You did it so you would know how I attack! You tricky bastard…"

"Well, well." Shadow smirked. "Perhaps there's some hope for you in Arlina's ranks after all."

Shadow rushed Latos, and he could feel the full-blood's fear at the display of his speed. The glyphs along Shadow's blade glowed whenever it made contact with the vampire's skin, and as Latos moved to strike, Shadow created an arc with his sword that traced along Latos' chest. Latos screamed, and Shadow knew the full-blood felt he was burning alive with that strike. Shadow's mysterious blade always had that effect on vampires, though he never knew why.

"What have you done to me, elf?" Latos bellowed in fury. "What sorcery is this? You're no elf mage!"

"It's an old trick that I don't need to have magical abilities to use," Shadow explained. "In case you hadn't noticed, I'm in a hurry. I didn't want you to forget our encounter, however."

Now appearing behind Latos, he slammed the back of the full-blood's skull with the hilt of his sword. He smiled as he watched the vampire fall unconscious. "Until the next time we meet, bootlicker. I promise I won't be so merciful then."

17

I felt something pat my cheek. The feeling continued as the pressure of it increased.

"Avilyne's hell, please don't be dead."

Jack's voice.

I forced my eyes open, and I saw Jack's face. Relief had spread on his face.

"Hey there," I coughed.

"Thank the goddesses," Jack praised. He hoisted me from the ground and carried me inside of Talisa's cottage. "What happened? How did you get here? How did you get those wounds?"

I remembered the mare. "Azrael...she is hurt. Tend to her first, Jack! I'll be fine."

"Keep your stubborn self,"—Jack gently put me down on the bed that once belonged to me— "on this bed while I go do that. From the looks of your head and the grimace you made when I picked you up, you have a concussion."

"I'm all right," I assured him.

"Like hell you are," he frowned. He wagged a finger at me. "Stay here. I'll be back after I tend to your horse. And stay awake! If I have to throw ice water on you, I will!"

He left before I could scold him about being bossy. My vision blurred as I tried to focus on the ceiling, and I fought the urge to shut my eyes.

The moment I did close them, I saw Arlina. She was pointing that pistol at me. I screamed as I heard the blast, and I was immediately splashed with ice water. An arm held me down when I tried to leap away.

"Sucks to be on the other end of these things, hmm?" I heard Jack say.

"What was that for?" I barked.

"You went to sleep, woman!" he yelled. "I was gone for a while and everything!"

"No, you weren't!" I glared. "I *just* shut my eyes!"

"You have a concussion!" Jack shook his head. "You can die from this, Artemis. You have to stay awake. I refuse to lose my best friend."

I sighed. "You almost did tonight."

Jack froze. "What in Avilyne's hell is going on?"

"Ellewynth…" Tears formed in my eyes. "We were attacked."

"*What?*" He ran a hand through the mess of dark brown hair and shuddered. "How?"

"Full-bloods from Blackwen City."

"Oh goddesses…this is happening sooner than I expected."

"What? What do you know?" I asked, confused. "*How* do you know whatever it is you know?"

"I should be over there…" Jack started to pace. "I can't leave her behind like this…"

"Jack?"

He rubbed his head. "I can't leave you here alone. You'll fall asleep if I go."

"Tell me what you know," I demanded. "I'll stay awake if you do."

He bit his lip and crossed his arms. "Fine. You will tell me exactly what happened in Ellewynth as well as other things you know and then I will tell you what I know."

"Deal." I shifted myself on the bed and was met with a glare. "What? You're the one who changed my bed!"

"It stopped being yours once I moved in here," Jack said. "Got any better ideas of where to lie down?"

"Outside," I answered. "The grass has more cushioning than this!" I grumbled at my wet clothes. "Can I at least change?"

"Being cold will help keep you awake."

"When did you become so evil?"

"I'm Talisa's apprentice. Enough said."

He cleaned the blood off of my arm and head, and then he patched me up. Jack carried me outside afterwards and placed his cloak beneath my head as a pillow. At least the stars were a better alternative to the ceiling. I was able to study Jack as he sat beside me. He'd lost weight since I last saw him, but his legs were a different story.

Talisa was working him with these hikes!

"What?" He asked once he caught my stare.

"I didn't think it was possible for you to gain some muscle on these," I smiled as I pointed to his legs. "You really enjoy those hikes, hmm?"

"Some days," he winked. "And I wouldn't tease if I were you. You may have such a rough exterior, dhampir, but deep down inside is a little girl who, on occasion, *likes* being one. Your room here is proof enough."

"And here I thought I missed you," I grumbled. My gaze returned to the stars. "How is Azrael?"

"Sleeping," Jack answered. "She actually let me touch her this time. The mare was rather protective of you when I first knelt beside you. Injured or not, she was ready to knock my head off."

"Azrael is Shadow's horse."

"It's no wonder then," Jack chuckled. He then sighed. "Tell me about the attack, Artemis."

"It burns." I felt the tears again. "The city, I mean." I took a deep breath. "The Mistress of Blackwen, Arlina…she is my aunt. I am a child of Blackwen." The anger returned after I said it. "I am tied to its throne."

"Unfortunately, I knew about that." Jack raised his hands defensively when I shot him an accusing look. "Let me explain."

He did so. Jack recalled how he saw Mother's murder in a training exercise Talisa gave him. He told me about how he was an elf mage, particularly of the old bloodline in the Woodland Realm. Jack was upset when he finished his tale.

"You're nothing like those bastards," I assured him.

"Artemis, I am *related* to them!" He snapped. Jack shut his eyes and calmed himself. "Apologies. Considering you're going through the same situation, I shouldn't be yelling at you."

"They're not trying to kill you at least."

"I don't think they actually know I exist, or if they're even still alive for that matter," Jack replied.

I felt his apprehension and changed the subject. "Jack...tell me about my mother's death."

Jack flinched. "It was horrible, Artemis. No one should have been through that."

"What did Arlina do to her?"

"Why must you know?"

"Because I just have to!" I replied.

Arlina almost killed me in Ellewynth. My moments of defiance when she belittled me were the only thing that kept my fear from being visibile to her. I knew Arlina was capable of so much more than she showed in the city, and I needed to know everything I could about her.

"Artemis...you're going to go to the Dark Fortress, aren't you?"

"Yes," I answered. "I will have to end this one way or another. I can't let her haunt me forever. Even if I die over there, at least there'll be an end to the suffering."

"Don't ever say that," Jack snapped. "Even if there were more miserable moments than happy ones, dhampir blackouts and all, your life is still worth something."

I blinked. "Being out here has done you some good, Jack. A long time ago, you would never have said such a thing."

Jack blushed. "Well...there are things worth living for."

"Like friends," I said.

"And love," he added.

Jack quickly covered his mouth as I flashed a wolfish grin.

"Yes, love is certainly the one thing worth living for." I patted his leg as he flushed with embarrassment. "And yes, I did read that letter you first sent to Shadow. Who is this mystery woman, Jack? Who is she to make you forget about Lilith so quickly?"

"She is someone I can never have." He buried his face in his hands. "Of all people to feel the damned string to, it's a woman impossible to be with!"

"Have some more faith in yourself. No one's ever out of reach. You know this."

"When you meet her, you'll understand."

"I think you're just being unreasonable."

"Unreasonable?" Jack shook his head. "Unreasonable. I can tell you what's unreasonable. How you ignore your feelings for Shadow. *That's* unreasonable."

"You don't understand, Jack," I said defensively.

"Goddesses, you're thick in the head!" Jack frowned. "Tell me right now that you're not worried about him. Tell me you're not thinking of him right now, praying that he arrives at the cottage in one piece. Deny it to me, Artemis. For the past eight years that I've known you, all you've ever done is talk about your time with him. I dare you to deny it."

I sighed, because I couldn't. There was just that one factor that Jack continued to forget about: the little to no control of the monster inside of me.

"You *really* don't understand."

"Artemis, one day you'll stop lying to yourself about it."

"One of these days, that sharp tongue of yours is going to cost you," I warned.

Lady Clarayne spat the blood that filled her mouth after Arlina dealt a punch to the side of her face. Arlina was still the fierce warrior she had been the last time the two fought. Lady Clarayne, however, was feeling the fatigue of recent events catch up with her the longer the fight dragged out.

It was not how she imagined the end would be, but she chuckled to herself. Nothing ever went the way one planned, especially when you were both a warrior and an Elder.

She watched as Arlina circled her, and Lady Clarayne held the sword closer to her chest.

"I guess it's true what they say about old age," Arlina said with a mock sigh. "How disappointing. I expected more from you, Clarayne."

"The life of a leader is a tiring ordeal, Arlina," Lady Clarayne said, keeping her eyes on the Mistress of Blackwen. "Something you've never learned, obviously."

Arlina disappeared and flashed beside Lady Clarayne, her sai inches from the Elder's throat. She slipped her blade in front of the sai just before the steel could sink into her flesh, and she tried to break free from the sudden vice grip Arlina applied. Lady Clarayne felt one of the sai push through the back of her shoulder, and she gritted her teeth as the pain traveled down her arm.

"Why do you continue to resist me, Clarayne?" Arlina whispered into her ear. "Can't you see that I'm trying to do you a favor? Don't you *want* to be reunited with your husband?"

Lady Clarayne felt the cloth along her arm cling to her skin as the blood from her shoulder soaked into the material. "Only on my own terms."

Lady Clarayne forced her body to push backward, and she shoved Arlina into one of the bookcases. Stunned, Arlina lost her grip on the sai embedded in Lady Clarayne's shoulder, and the Elder took the brief opening to pull it out. Dropping the sai to the ground, Lady Clarayne looked to where Arlina had been and found she was gone. She ignored the urge to grip her bleeding shoulder, and instead shut her eyes to heighten her sense of sound. Lady Clarayne knew Arlina was still in the room; it wasn't like Arlina to leave a battle unfinished.

Sensing something behind her, Lady Clarayne opened her eyes and swung her sword, only to be met with resistance from the remaining sai. The irises in Arlina's eyes were an intense crimson—the sign of true bloodlust in a full-blood. The resistance didn't last long, as Lady Clarayne felt her shoulder buckle under the pressure. The Elder found herself falling to the ground as Arlina pushed her enough to make her lose her footing.

"You have truly disappointed me, Elder." Arlina tsked as she gripped the sword Lady Clarayne had dropped. She couldn't remember letting go of the hilt. "It's rude to excite someone only to crush their hopes soon after. I do hope your comrades prove to be more of a challenge than you have this night."

Lady Clarayne only glared. She didn't want her last words to be hateful, even if the woman deserved it.

Before Arlina could swing the sword, the door to the office splintered. Lady Clarayne felt relief once she saw Talisa standing where the door once had. Arlina hissed and ignored the fact that she had a helpless Elder on the ground.

"You again." Arlina spat.

"Did you really think those fools of yours were going to stop me?" Talisa raised a palm, and Lady Clarayne knew that Arlina could feel the power of the magic Kiare bestowed on her from where she stood. "Step away from Lady Clarayne, and I will consider letting you flee."

"It's a shame. Even with all the power at your disposal, you're still so weak." Arlina laughed. "Mercy is a wasted sentiment, Talisa. It's what separates me from the rest of you soft saps. I know to eliminate all those who oppose me, without remorse."

"Someday, you will understand and appreciate the notion of mercy," Talisa said, her palm still raised. It faintly glowed blue. "I won't ask you again, Arlina."

Arlina raised her arms in defeat and sighed. Lady Clarayne was puzzled; what was the Mistress of Blackwen City plotting?

"I suppose I could let your precious Lady Elder live another day," Arlina decided, folding her arms and moving away from Lady Clarayne. "I don't take too kindly to being ordered around though, witch. You've already stole the true prize from me, and we all know I could care less for respecting my elders."

Arlina rushed toward Talisa; they both fell to the ground and grappled with one another. Lady Clarayne couldn't mistake the smell of burnt flesh as Talisa's hands glowed a bright blue against Arlina's skin. Kiare's power of water represented life; of course it would harm a being who survived on consuming life. Arlina hissed in pain, and Talisa yelped when the Mistress of Blackwen gripped her messy braid, pulled her head back, and sank her elongated eye teeth into the witch's flesh.

Lady Clarayne tried to move, but her shoulder flared and her legs refused to obey. Talisa kicked Arlina off and immediately put a hand to her now bloodied neck.

"You taste like the goddess you serve, witch," Arlina said, wiping her lips. "Salty…watered-down…useless."

"I'm sure Avilyne has her own ideas of how you'd taste once you end up in her hell," Talisa said through gritted teeth. "I'm sure Kiare would let me join her in watching Avilyne do so."

Arlina moved to grab Talisa again, but she shifted her movement at the last moment as a beam from the ceiling of the office fell. Flames began to engulf the woodwork and the room. Talisa moved to Lady Clarayne's side as Arlina cackled.

"While I prefer to deliver the killing blow myself, the idea of you two burning alive is so much more appealing." Arlina moved away from the two. "If you do live, Talisa, I do hope we get to play again."

Talisa glared as Arlina disappeared, and Lady Clarayne coughed as the heat and smoke began to overwhelm her.

"Can you move, my lady?" Talisa asked, careful not to move the injured shoulder as she helped pick her up.

Lady Clarayne coughed and weakly nodded. "What of Shadow? And Artemis?"

"Artemis is safe in my cottage. Shadow—" Talisa coughed and looked away from the Elder. "Shadow is safe as well."

Lady Clarayne knew the statement was false, but was grateful that Talisa thought to soften the blow. She knew her nephew. His honor would have kept him here to aid Ellewynth…and his honor would have him flee to be beside Artemis soon after.

It was going to break her heart to name him a deserter, even though he had stayed behind to fight. The others would not see it as valor; they would call him a traitor because of his running away with Artemis.

The blast woke Netira from her slumber on the prison cell floor. She could smell the blood of both the elves and full-bloods as well as the scent of fire in the air. She swore under her breath. Arlina was here, and Netira was still stuck in this damned cell.

Her time had run out.

She gripped the bars in haste and pulled. Netira cursed as she felt the wounds Arlina had dealt her open up. She'd never fully healed from the fight, and that one particular Elder made sure she barely fed during her imprisonment.

She contemplated killing this Lord Destrius more times than she imagined killing Arlina. Netira failed to see how a man so insufferable had risen to the rank of Elder; the sacred sisters had an odd sense of humor.

Once she was fully standing, Netira smelled more of the inferno from the blast she'd heard. It was strange to her that Arlina resorted to fire, though she quickly dismissed the notion, realizing fire caused more suffering than Arlina could ever hope to deal to the Woodland Realm elves herself.

Netira cursed again.

She pulled at the bars once more and felt defeated when they refused to budge. If she were at full strength, they would have moved.

"I've been walking a thin line since the beginning of my existence, and it grew thinner the day I became Blackwen's Second," Netira snapped. "And now my luck runs out while being imprisoned of all things! Aerios blow you!" She pulled at the bars and sighed in resignation. "Goddesses."

"They don't answer to the likes of you, *vampyra*," a male voice snapped, drawing Netira's attention to the entrance of the prison hall.

Vampyra was an Elvish curse aimed toward her kind, so she knew she wasn't dealing with Arlina or another full-blood from her city.

"Your city burns," Netira said as she squinted her eyes to see the identity of her visitor. "And yet you're here, keeping *me* of all people company. You might want to rethink your morals, elf."

She felt a strong hand clamp tightly around her throat, and Netira saw that she stood face to face with Lord Destrius. Her hatred for him continued to grow.

"Your kind should have been exterminated ages ago," Lord Destrius spat, his grip on her throat tightening. "Clarayne and Celstian are fools to believe in mercy. I told them this would happen. I told them that if we kept that stupid *vampyra* brat in our city, your Mistress would wreak havoc on us."

"Whether…Artemis was living…in your city or not, Arlina…would have attacked Ellewynth…anyway," Netira squeaked. She grabbed Lord Destrius' outstretched arm and tried to break his grip. "Killing…me… will achieve…nothing."

"Oh, but it *will* achieve something, *vampyra*." Lord Destrius smirked. "Personal satisfaction. My city has been destroyed thanks to your Mistress. I can now go and return the favor. I won't rest until I destroy every last bit of your precious Dark Fortress. Blackwen City has reached the end of its existence. A pity you won't get to see it burn."

Arrogant prick, Netira thought as she continued to fight the Elder's grip on her throat.

She felt the pressure prevailing over her, and she averted her eyes so that the last thing she would see before death claimed her wasn't the intense hatred that seethed in the green eyes of Lord Destrius.

What she did see when she looked away from the Elder stunned her—Karesu was standing in the doorway. It couldn't have been possible, of course, for Arlina had surely made him her Second and had him watch over the city in her absence.

Netira felt tears fill her eyes. When the figure of Karesu moved closer, Netira realized he wasn't a hallucination due to the lack of oxygen; he was *here*. Lord Destrius sensed something was amiss, and he threw Netira down as he drew his sword to parry the attack Karesu dealt. When Lord Destrius saw the runes within the jewelry as well as the calligraphy-etched blade Karesu carried, he swore.

"A vampire mage," Lord Destrius said, stunned. "There *is* such a thing."

Karesu narrowed his gaze at him. He kept his hold on the sword hilt, pushing Lord Destrius away little by little. "Release your prisoner, Elder of Ellewynth."

"Or what? You'll murder me?" Lord Destrius scoffed. "You can try, but you'll end up just like her sooner or later…a permanent corpse."

Netira forced herself off the ground as she rubbed her throat. She could still feel the remnant pressure of the Elder's fingers along her skin, and she shuddered. Karesu's gaze met hers, and she blinked back tears.

"I will get you out of here," he swore.

"If Arlina finds you here…" Netira managed to say, coughing as the intake of air pained her.

"I don't give a damn about that infernal woman. I *will* get you out of here," Karesu declared, now looking at Lord Destrius. "Release her, and I will spare you your life. You have my word."

"The word of a full-blood means nothing to me," Lord Destrius said, beginning his attack. "You're in love with her, aren't you, mage? I thought love was a foreign concept to a vampire."

Karesu kept his silence as he continued to clash blades with Lord Destrius. Netira gripped the bars and pulled yet again, desperate to be freed. The Elder was indeed formidable and evenly matched with her love, something Netira was not used to seeing.

Lord Destrius forced Karesu's back against the bars, making Netira jump at the loud thump his body made. The Elder's blade was close to Karesu's throat; only Karesu's sword kept the other steel away from cutting it. Karesu kneed Lord Destrius just above his groin, and he rolled away to avoid the wide trajectory of the Elder's curved sword. He looked up at Netira and ran to the bars.

Netira felt heat emanate from the spots where Karesu laid his hands, and she backed away. The bars started to melt, but not fast enough, as Karesu rolled away once more to dodge an angry barrage of strikes from Lord Destrius. Frustrated, Netira kicked at the bars, but they still wouldn't budge.

"There are those that would call you admirable for trying to pull off a rescue attempt, mage," Lord Destrius said, suddenly backing off. "And there are those that would call you a fool, for you're only prolonging the inevitable. The two of you will still meet your death out there even if you somehow manage to slip past me, which isn't very likely. I was made an Elder of Ellewynth for my war prowess. I will *not* be bested by the likes of you."

Both Netira and Karesu sighed.

"You're not very original, Elder of Ellewynth." Karesu raised his sword and adjusted his stance. "I do hope someone else is in charge of your paperwork. It'd be a shame to be the laughingstock among the elven Elders of the other realms."

Lord Destrius growled as he charged Karesu, and the sparks from the blades continued to fly. The attacks were faster and even more calculated than before; Netira saw Karesu struggle to keep his normally smooth footing. The bars still weren't weak enough for Netira to break through, and she felt her panic rise. She froze when she saw a successful leg sweep by Lord Destrius, and Karesu landed hard on his back.

"You disappoint me, mage," Lord Destrius said, circling Karesu. "I expected a better fight from you. I expected to be attacked with magic. I guess the whore isn't worth that much trouble, hmm?"

"Elf prick!" Netira snapped, feeling her dhampir nature rise. The wings from her back extended, but she was not strong enough to maintain the form; it pained her to hold it.

"A dhampir?" Lord Destrius spoke in disbelief. "You actually gave us the truth?"

"Hard to believe that a *vampyra* is capable of such a thing, huh, you bastard?" Netira hissed, her eye teeth fully elongated and her irises silver.

Karesu took advantage of the distraction by rushing after the Elder, only to fail; his waist met the tip of Lord Destrius' sword. Netira gasped when she saw Karesu's shirt cling to him with his blood. The Elder smirked and pushed the sword farther into him; Karesu's cry of pain shattered Netira, and she cried out as she pulled on the bars. They barely shifted, and she knew she would never get out in time to aid him. Karesu's violet eyes shifted to a deep red, and he cried out once more when Lord Destrius removed the sword from his body. Karesu coughed, and his chin was speckled with his own blood; Lord Destrius watched him with glee.

"How should your final death be dealt, mage?" Lord Destrius inquired. He directly kicked Karesu's wound, and Netira looked away, tears streaming down her cheeks. "Shall I be just and give you a quick beheading? Or shall I savor the moment and throw you into the flames which you cast upon my city?" He grabbed Netira by the throat again and forced her to look into his eyes. "What do *you* think, dhampir? Should I be merciful and spare you the sight of my final stroke? Or should I kill you now and enjoy more of his screams?"

"How about neither, you bastard?"

Netira knew the voice, as did Lord Destrius.

Before the Elder could turn to face the newcomer, there was a loud thud on the back of the Elder's head. Netira could feel air returning to her body once more, and she coughed as the air pained her throat. As Lord Destrius' body slumped, Netira met the angry and annoyed stare of the famous Shadow of Ellewynth. He too was covered in splotches of blood, and his green eyes averted to Karesu's slumped form. Netira grew frightened, as she felt Shadow would kill the man.

Shadow bade Netira to move back, and he kicked at the burned bars of her prison cell. After a few series of stomps, the bars fell. Netira rushed to Karesu's side and propped his body against her chest. She held his head in her arms and kissed him. Even with the pain, Karesu returned the kiss as passionately as he normally would.

"Karesu, you dangerous fool," she said as she broke away, her hands now moving to his wound.

"I thought that was why you chose me." Karesu moved his head to fit in the crook of her neck and inhaled her scent. He placed a soft kiss beneath her chin. "You kissed me in front of someone. Does this mean…?"

"Yes, yes it does."

"You must be the vampire mage that managed to kidnap Talisa and still lived to tell the tale," Shadow interrupted, while extending a hand to Karesu.

Karesu eyed his hand warily, but took it. "And you are Shadow of Ellewynth, one of the most feared elves in existence."

"Guilty." Shadow grinned as he helped pull Karesu to his feet.

Netira held the other side of Karesu and was relieved that Shadow wasn't going to kill him.

"You attacked an Elder." Karesu motioned toward the incapacitated Lord Destrius. "*Your* Elder, and from behind no less. How honorable of you, Shadow."

Shadow frowned. "There's nothing honorable about that prick."

"I feel we could be good friends, elf." Netira smiled, as she shared the same sentiment. "I am saddened he did not meet death, however."

"His time will come," Shadow reassured her as he led them to the stairway. "The more important thing right now is getting you both out of here. I will take you to Talisa's cottage."

"It is appreciated, but unnecessary." Karesu winced. "Netira and I must get as far from your realm as we can, as quickly as possible. Arlina must not know this happened."

"I'm aware of that, mage," Shadow sympathized, "but you are both in *my* hands now. You do not have the strength to fight me off, let alone argue with me."

Netira felt her heart begin to break; she was a pawn in a game created by her old mentor, and she still had to aid Artemis Ravenwing. Karesu had no knowledge of this, and she knew he would not take it well once he did. He might want to run away and start anew, but she had to keep up the fight to save their home.

"I fear *we* may not be good friends, Shadow of Ellewynth," Karesu said, angered. "Netira and I have a need to disappear. We can fend for ourselves."

"Karesu, we must go to Talisa's cottage," Netira interjected, trying to ease the rising tension between the men. "There is something I must tell you, but only after you get treated and gain some rest."

"Netira—"

"My love, listen to me!" Netira begged. Karesu's eyes were back to violet, and they were filled with sadness as they focused on her. "We *will* have the chance to live together as we often dreamed of, and it *will* be in Blackwen City. But it must wait just a little while longer. There is something of great importance that I must do, and I will not carry it out until I know that you are well and safe. You would do the same if it was me in your shoes, and don't you dare attempt to deny it."

Karesu's sigh of resignation told her that she had won the argument, and Shadow chuckled.

"Now that that's settled, shall we focus on getting the both of you out of here?" Shadow suggested. "We've already lost a lot of time. Arlina could be in the hall."

"What?" Karesu and Netira snapped in unison.

"Talisa warned me about that possibility. I was lucky to have missed her when I came in, but we may not be so lucky now. Now do you understand my urgency?" Shadow explained.

"Avilyne's hell…" Karesu swore.

Netira smiled. "It's things like *that* that made me choose you."

"I do not mean to be rude, but I would save such banter for later," Shadow said, urging the two to move faster.

As the trio walked up the stairs, they were overwhelmed by the heat of the flames as the hall began to crumble around them. Netira let go of Karesu and tried to find a clear path, and she was surprised when she saw Shadow push through, regardless of the debris. It still surprised her to see him guard Karesu; there was a lot more to this elf than others gave him credit for.

She respected Shadow all the more.

Netira was relieved once the three escaped from the hall. Her relief switched to horror, however, as she saw what was once a beautiful city now reduced to a dark site of ashes and corpses. It was a fate Blackwen City now shared, as she knew the elves would retaliate.

"Netira, you'll have to take charge of Karesu," Shadow instructed as he grabbed his sword and defended the two from the oncoming onslaughts of the full-bloods.

When the full-bloods noticed whom Shadow was protecting, their fury intensified.

"Traitors!" one of them spat, while lunging after Netira and Karesu.

"The Mistress will hear of this, mage!" another cursed, running with a sword raised.

Netira reached for Karesu's sword and learned there wasn't a need to, as Shadow blocked any of the strikes thrown their way. She noted his left arm wavering a bit with each swing, and she then noticed his arm was wounded.

"Karesu, can you still manage to fight?" Netira asked, fearing Shadow might not be able to keep up the protection.

"I can try, but I would only slow you two down." Karesu coughed. He moved a hand to the wound Lord Destrius had dealt him. "The most I could do is shield, and it wouldn't last very long. I need to feed, and soon."

"Willow be damned." Netira frowned while taking hold of Karesu's sword. "Save what strength you have left then. Getting to Talisa's cottage will take a lot of it."

"We still have to get out of Ellewynth first, my love," Karesu reminded her, wincing as she moved him so she could block a strike.

"Avilyne's hell!" Shadow swore as he continued to fight off full-bloods. "We do not have time for this!"

Netira swore as well, as she continued to fight the others off alongside Shadow. She knew Karesu could last some time without blood despite his desperation for it, but she didn't want to push what little luck they had left. When had Shadow disposed of the last of the full-blood wave, he helped hold Karesu again and apologized when he forced them to a run.

"If there was ever a time for Talisa to appear, now would be fantastic," Shadow muttered.

"Perhaps not." Karesu grimaced. "She swore she would kill me on sight. I have no desire to meet her in this condition."

"Talisa has more honor than that, mage," Shadow explained. "She'll let you recover first, *then* she'll kill you. She at least gives her opponents a fighting chance."

"She will do no such thing if she wants my cooperation," Netira snapped.

Shadow chuckled. "I'll let you two handle that. Your lover did kidnap her after all."

"Lover?"

The three froze as soon as they heard the harsh female voice. Netira noticed Shadow's visage shift to one of hatred; it was a voice he must have not have heard in a long time, and for good reason.

It's all over, Netira thought as they all turned to face the Mistress of Blackwen herself.

Arlina was covered in soot and blood, and she focused on Netira.

"So you still live, traitor," Arlina said, while resting a hand on her hip. "And the company you keep…how *interesting*."

Karesu returned the glare Arlina sent his way. Arlina then looked over at Shadow and grinned. Netira could feel the chill coming from Shadow's gaze from where she stood.

"I'm surprised you even came to Ellewynth at all, Arlina," Shadow began as he moved in front of Netira and Karesu. "You always struck me as someone who didn't like to get her hands dirty."

"How I would still love to cut off that sarcastic tongue of yours, elf," Arlina replied. "I'd rather tear apart the half-breed brat instead. You and Talisa won't be able to protect her forever. Perhaps I'll let you live just to watch me strangle her. I bet you would enjoy it, Shadow."

Shadow's grip on his sword tightened, and Netira prayed he would maintain his calm. "You're welcome to try. Perhaps I'll be able to watch her strange the life from you instead. I know I would enjoy that."

"I doubt that, seeing how pitiful she was when we met. I would have killed her along with your damned mare had Talisa not interfered. All is not lost, however!" Arlina grinned. "Your precious home is destroyed. Your Elders will retaliate, and if my niece is anything like my despicable sister, the guilt of that alone will bring her out of hiding. So I'll ask you once and only once. Where did Talisa send Artemis?"

"She is safe from you, Arlina," Shadow answered. "You can burn all of Arrygn and she would still escape you."

"Hide her all you want, Shadow. I *will* find her," Arlina threatened. She looked upon Karesu once more. "Why, Karesu, you've broken my little black heart! I can't let that go unpunished. Such a waste, as you *are* Blackwen City's only vampire mage."

"I'd rather let the mage gift die with me than to continue serving you," Karesu snapped.

"Perhaps you will soon enough. Someone's beaten me to the kill, I see," Arlina said as she eyed his wound. "How will you live with yourself now, dear Netira? He doesn't have much time, you know. The only way Karesu will survive is if he feeds…and you conveniently have someone here who can provide a full meal for him."

Netira frowned. "No."

"Shadow's a strapping young man. His blood would provide enough strength to save your precious mage lover. And that wound of his is quite deep...are you willing to save him at the cost of your protector?"

"I will do no such thing," Karesu declared, his irises back to crimson.

"Even if it meant my sparing both your lives?" Arlina proposed, while tapping a long finger on the sai that rested along her folded arms. "Do you desire your freedom? You've fought so hard already...you might as well accept my offer and grant me this one little show of Shadow's death."

"They're not fooled, Arlina," Shadow said. "You've never been one for keeping your word."

"Suit yourselves." Arlina shrugged. "Can't fault me for an attempt at entertainment, now can you?"

Before any could answer, Arlina and Shadow crossed blades. Netira could feel Karesu beginning to fade.

"Just hold on a bit longer, Karesu," Netira pleaded, while doing her best to keep him standing.

"I'm too stubborn to die, Netira." Karesu cast a weak smile. "I have much left to do before I leave this world."

Netira half-smiled and held tightly onto his sword in case Arlina chose to attack her as well. Arlina had her hands full, however, as Shadow continued to be a formidable opponent. The Mistress of Blackwen cursed as Shadow managed to shove her over, and she took several steps back to catch her breath.

"Tired, are we?" Shadow inquired, his sword still raised.

"From killing an Elder? Never," Arlina replied.

Netira watched the color drain from Shadow's face.

"You lie."

"Do I now?" Arlina asked while circling him. "Why does it matter to you? The good soldier of Ellewynth failed to carry out his sworn duty to the realm and her people. You chose to aid vampires instead of your own leaders."

Netira knew Shadow's patience was thinning, but she was also amazed the man didn't cut Arlina down after saying such things.

"I don't believe you," Shadow said.

"You're welcome to believe what you wish," Arlina said. "I'm tired of talking."

Instead of going after Shadow, Arlina disappeared and reappeared behind Netira and Karesu. Before Netira could defend them against her, Karesu shoved her out of the way; she stumbled into Shadow. Arlina was shocked to see Karesu blocking her sai with his bare hands, his palms covered with his own blood.

"Well, well," Arlina scowled. "There's still some fight left in you yet."

Karesu ignored her and faced Shadow and Netira. She felt her body shaking as she realized what he was about to do.

"Karesu…" Netira wavered.

"Shadow," Karesu called. "I only know you by reputation, and that includes your sense of honor."

"Karesu, please…" Netira said, as she felt the tears form.

"This was not what I intended, Netira. It's as you said before—we will have to wait just a little while longer before we can live together in peace…even if means abandoning Blackwen City to do it, I will do so without regret," Karesu explained.

Netira felt her chest grow heavy.

"Shadow, flee and watch over her. Keep her safe. Carry out whatever it is that must be done."

"No! I'm not leaving you here!" Netira cried, as she felt Shadow restrain her. "I won't leave you! Willow damn you, don't do this!"

Karesu only smiled. "I love you, Netira. We *will* see each other again, I promise you this."

"Aerios blow you, Shadow! Let me go!"

Netira struggled to free herself from the elf's grasp, but he was far stronger than she at the moment.

"Go! Now!" Karesu yelled, as he shoved down Arlina.

Netira felt Shadow hoist her from the ground, but she couldn't tear her gaze away from Arlina overpowering Karesu. She heard Shadow apologize countless times to her as they continued to run farther from the fiery remnants of Ellewynth. Her only reply was a piercing scream that echoed throughout the forest.

It did not even come close to the sound of her heart breaking.

18

Jack and I continued to stay outside of Talisa's cottage, even with the minor spat from earlier. I told him my end of the tale, had another argument about my memory concerning the veil I took to get here, and the silence returned when I refused to speak more about Arlina. He would sharply poke me, however, whenever I would shut my eyes.

Jack was right. It sucked being on the other end of these things. I wasn't even drunk.

"You know I'm not one for prolonged periods of silence…right, Artemis?" Jack said.

"I'm still processing everything you've told me, Jack," I answered.

It wasn't a complete lie, as it did disturb me to know that my mother's presence affected my best friend as well. I knew there was more that Jack didn't tell me, but I was grateful for it at the moment.

"I understand this, but you also have to realize that I have been by myself in this place for some time now," Jack whined. "Silence drives me insane."

"Your lady friend hasn't been keeping you company?" I teased.

Jack coughed a bit, and I patted his leg. "I suppose this is payback, isn't it?"

"Oh, I wouldn't call it that." I grinned. "I would call it being the dutiful best friend."

"Lies!" He glared.

"All right, maybe there's a *little* payback," I admitted. I tried to prop myself up from the ground, but stopped when my head felt heavy. I sighed and returned to my original position with Jack's cloak as my pillow. "Can you at least tell me her name? What does she look like? I need *something*, Jack."

"No names. Not yet." Jack ran a hand through his messy dark brown hair. "She's a bit shorter than I. She's got the most captivating blue eyes I've ever seen...I could lose myself in them and never feel the need to escape. And just the way the wind picks up those blond ringlets of hers..." Jack noticed my look and narrowed his gaze. "What evil thoughts are you thinking of now, woman?"

"Nothing evil at all. I thought when you were a complete idiot in front of Lilith you were just a fool in love," I explained. "I see now that what you feel for Lilith is infatuation. The way you speak about this lady friend of yours...Jack, you *glow*."

He cleared his throat and folded his arms. "As I said before...it's complicated."

"It's only complicated because you're making it so."

"If only that were true..." Jack rubbed the back of his neck. "Artemis, I can't have her. She's an el—"

I held up a hand when I heard footsteps. I forced myself to stand and recognized the person to whom the footsteps belonged to. "Oh goddesses..."

"Is that...?" Jack began, as we both watched Talisa carrying an elf woman on her back. They were battered, bloodied, and covered in soot. Jack had to catch them both as Talisa nearly collapsed on the ground. "Talisa? Avilyne's hell! Artemis, get over here and help me—it's Lady Clarayne!"

I helped Jack pry Lady Clarayne's unconscious body from Talisa's back, and we laid them both carefully on the ground. "What happened?"

Talisa coughed as she took a few deep breaths. "Ellewynth burns still. Willow protect the ones who managed to escape." She took another deep breath. "I couldn't get them all to the veils in time."

"Did you use the veil you sent Azrael and me through?" I asked.

"Wait a minute." Jack glanced at his teacher. "You really sent them through your personal veil? I thought no one but you could pass through it."

"I broke that rule. I'll pay for that consequence soon enough." Talisa coughed. "Don't you dare feel guilty about it, Artemis. I was not going to let Arlina have you."

"What about Lords Celstian and Destrius?" Jack asked before I could speak. I let him get away with the interruption and watched him inspect both the women's wounds.

Lady Clarayne was still breathing, thank the goddesses. She was, however, unresponsive to Jack's touch. Talisa would have none of it herself.

"Help me up, will you?" Talisa snapped, beating Jack's hands away from her ruined nightgown and her wounds. "I'm fine! Just a few scrapes and burns, and a hell of a lot of fatigue. Satisfied?"

Jack and I couldn't help but chuckle despite ourselves as we helped her sit up. Good ol' Talisa.

"Lord Celstian is safely hidden in the veils. Lord Destrius, the stubborn bastard, chose to stay back and fight. Shadow and I managed to reach the Hall of the Elders in time for me to find Lady Clarayne—"

"Is Shadow all right?" I interrupted. "Why isn't he here with you?"

"When we separated, he was occupied with a little brawl." She noted my concern. "It wasn't something he couldn't handle. He'll be fine, Artemis. Shadow went to rescue Netira."

"Netira is the dhampir you told me about, Artemis?" Jack asked.

"Yes." I glanced at Lady Clarayne, and felt the overwhelming guilt return. My head was hurting too. "We should patch you both up."

"See to Clarayne," Talisa insisted. "I have to go back."

"You're *not* going back." Jack ordered. He cringed when Talisa glared at him. "All right, fine! But at least let me clean you up a bit?"

I flinched at the sound of the harsh slap Talisa dealt to the back of Jack's head. Now I knew why he whined so much about them in his letters.

I would have too.

"There is no time!" Talisa snapped. "I have to help Shadow retrieve Netira. I have to get them back here before they run into Arlina."

Before either Jack or I could argue with her, a harsh neigh silenced us. A white blur galloped past us, and I was horrified that Azrael ran off despite her injury.

"Azrael, wait!" I yelled, starting to run. Talisa grabbed my arm before I could move any farther, and she shook her head at me. "But Tali—"

"Leave it be, Artemis," Talisa said, defeated. "Azrael left to retrieve her rider. She'll prove to be as useful in bringing them back as my personal veil would, injury or not. You two get your wish after all. Help me get Lady Clarayne inside, will you?"

Shadow felt he and Netira were far enough from the burned city of Ellewynth to safely catch a few breaths. He watched Netira fall to her knees when he released her. When he tried to touch her shoulder, she flailed her arm at him. Shadow took a few steps back and shut his eyes when Netira let out a pained scream. She buried her face in her hands, and she heaved with each sob.

He shared the sentiment, as he knew Arlina was talking about his aunt when she bragged about murdering an Elder.

"May Willow guide you to her grove and into paradise," Shadow prayed as he turned away from Netira.

"Aerios blow you!" Netira snapped. "Don't you dare start your damned rites of passage, elf!"

Shadow faced her and glared. "The only reason I refuse to retaliate that remark is because you need this quick moment to process what your lover has done. And the prayer isn't for him, dhampir. It was for my aunt."

"Your aunt?" Netira asked, confused.

"My aunt was Lady Clarayne. She was more commonly known to you as The Rose of Ellewynth," Shadow explained. Netira gaped. "Arlina came to the hall to kill her. Talisa must have gotten there too late...I don't know. The Mistress of Blackwen wouldn't have said what she said if it wasn't true."

"Oh goddesses..." Netira covered her mouth.

"As I said before, I will let that remark slide. Next time, however, I won't be so forgiving," Shadow warned. He sighed when she looked back in the direction of Ellewynth. "You shouldn't fear for Karesu. Arlina won't kill him."

"He betrayed her. He's as good as dead."

"As have you, and yet here you are." Shadow felt the wound in his arm flare, and he gripped it. "Karesu is leverage. Arlina will kill you herself now since the Elders failed to do so. She knows you will come to Blackwen City to rescue him. And we will."

"Why are you willing to do that, Shadow?" Netira asked, rubbing her now red and puffed eyes.

"Because Artemis will want to." Shadow felt some ease when he thought of her. He thanked the goddesses that Talisa helped her escape Arlina. "It'd be her way of thanking you for the help you'll be giving us."

"It's not considered help when you're an unwilling pawn in a specter's game of revenge." Netira scowled.

"It is if you've stuck to the decision of guiding as well as fighting besides her." Shadow faced Netira. "I cannot say that Karesu will not suffer at the hands of the Mistress of Blackwen, but he will live because his love for you will make him do so. Don't count him out of the game just yet, Netira. Hold onto faith."

Netira half-smiled at him. "Artemis is lucky to have someone like you, elf...even if she hasn't realized that yet."

"She knows," Shadow said, confused.

"No, she does not." Netira stood up and dusted the earth from her legs. "And if she does, she's in denial. As are you."

Shadow inwardly groaned. Now wasn't the time for this.

Netira raised an eyebrow and smirked. "I saw the way you looked at her the night the two of you came into my prison. There's a lot more to your guardianship than you choose to believe."

"We've rested enough." Shadow coughed in the attempt to end the conversation. "We still have some lengths to go before reaching Talisa's cottage."

"As you wish, elf." Netira started to walk, but stopped as soon as she heard a horse's neigh. "What in Avilyne's hell...?"

"Azrael." Shadow sighed with relief.

Even injured, she came back for him. Kiare be praised.

It took some time to clean the wounds Talisa and Lady Clarayne had. Lady Clarayne was still unconscious, but when we settled her into Jack's room, she seemed peaceful enough.

I prayed she had comforting dreams.

Talisa shooed us both away once her treatment had finished. She demanded to be woken up once Shadow returned. I reminded myself to never let Talisa be denied her rest, and I swore to never give her a reason to head-slap me in the future. I still couldn't get the sound of it out of my head from when she hit Jack.

I went outside to sit on the steps. Jack came out as well, only he now had on a traveler's cloak. He also had a cup filled with an odd-scented tea. Jack held it out for me to take.

"Where are *you* going?" I asked, as I took the lukewarm tea.

"I'm going to look for someone," he answered. "Drink it. It'll help your head. Talisa made it before she went to sleep. I'm going to keep needing your help in patching people up."

"You're needed here, Jack," I reminded him, realizing who he was going to search for. "Now's not the time for any of that. You wouldn't even leave me here alone!"

"Talisa will want her here," Jack replied, ignoring my comments. "Once Shadow and Netira arrive, we'll have to discuss what's going to happen next. Better it be sooner rather than later. And you're underestimating that tea. It's a pretty potent elixir, one I was supposed to learn after a couple of years of being Talisa's apprentice. You'll be fine after drinking it."

"You're referring to the discussion concerning my going to Blackwen City and confronting Arlina there," I said while ignoring the tea bit.

"You should have known that we wouldn't let you go by yourself, Artemis," Jack scolded while fastening the clasp along his neckline. He smirked as he pulled the hood up. "*I* sure as hell wasn't going to let you go and have all the fun without me."

I chuckled. "No, I suppose not."

Jack patted my shoulder. "Shadow is fine. He'll be here soon."

"I know."

"I'll return as soon as I can." Jack winked. "In one piece, I promise. I know the pathways here well enough to avoid danger, even though I can handle a few brawls or two."

"Jack, *I* can wield a sword better than you."

"Oh, I know a few more moves since the last time we trained together," Jack said, pretending to be offended. "Be careful when waking Talisa should Shadow return before I do. Bring some sweets to her room. Those tend to keep her calm long enough before she can snap at anyone."

"She wasn't like that when I lived with her…"

"You were lucky to be the daughter of her best friend. You were also lucky you weren't her apprentice," Jack said as he walked away. "You'll find some sweets by the tea cabinets. Sugar cubes would suffice as well. And drink that tea, woman! *All* of it."

I sighed. "Be safe, Jack."

I watched him disappear into the open forest and felt the sadness return. Ellewynth was destroyed. Even if I somehow survived my future encounter with my aunt at the Dark Fortress, I knew I wouldn't be welcomed into Ellewynth once it was rebuilt…not after what Arlina did. There was no room for me here at Talisa's cottage either, with Jack's apprenticeship and all.

"You're getting ahead of yourself there, Artemis," I said aloud, rubbing my forehead. "You act as if you'll even survive your fight with Arlina. She almost killed you in Ellewynth."

I shuddered and then eyed the tea. I sniffed it and coughed. I couldn't discern the contents of it, but I trusted both Jack and Talisa. I took a sip and immediately felt the need to gag. I took a deep breath after I lost the urge to heave, and I pinched my nose.

"Bottoms up," I muttered.

It was easy to gulp the liquid because of its lukewarm temperature, but it was still awful to ingest. I coughed and fought off the feeling to vomit.

I heard footsteps behind me. Before I could turn around and look, I felt a hand gently grasp my shoulder, commanding me to stay. I looked at the person who now sat beside me, Lady Clarayne.

Her green eyes were pained and showed fatigue. She was wearing one of Talisa's nightgowns, as we'd had to dispose of the bloodstained dress she was brought in.

"My lady, you should be inside resting!"

Lady Clarayne shook her head. "My shoulder burns. It's keeping me up."

"Let me look at it. Maybe we missed something."

"Artemis, I'm fine," Lady Clarayne insisted, with a chuckle as well as a cough. "It only means it's healing. You and Jack have given me enough healing cordial for it to start doing so as quickly as it has."

"Well, I'm glad it's healing so fast then."

Lady Clarayne gave me a sad glance. "You and Jack are quite the healers. I have a feeling you two had to learn such gifts on your own... so early..."

"Guilty," I answered as I put the now empty cup aside. "When you're considered an outcast, you come across more injuries than you'd like. And when the healers refuse to acknowledge you, you have to take it upon yourself to learn a thing or two. We had the books...the rest was just up to us to be the willing patients to one another."

"I am sorry your time in Ellewynth was unpleasant. It should not have been," Lady Clarayne apologized, grasping my shoulder once more.

"If anyone should apologize, it is me. Your home is destroyed because of who I am."

"Artemis, do not blame yourself for such a tragedy." Lady Clarayne looked to the sky. "Arlina is a dark soul in a world filled with injustice, bitterness, and hatred. There are many others like her. Someone else would have done the same, simply because of their hatred for us. You were a scapegoat for her to make a move against us...another prize to win for doing something she has wanted to do for ages."

"I can't help but feel guilt all the same."

"I know, child." Lady Clarayne moved her hand away. "I am guilty as well, I confess. We knew an attack from Arlina was possible, and we did not act. I moved too late, and that is just as terrible as looking the other way."

"You knew this would happen?"

"We sensed something would come our way," Lady Clarayne explained. "Shadow especially. He did his best to persuade us not to give you up to Arlina just to spare Ellewynth and other elven lives."

"Goddesses."

It explained all the meetings Shadow held with the Elders and why he was so furious. It also explained the promise he made me make, to be ready to flee with him at a moment's notice, no questions asked.

"I'm afraid I agreed with the idea of handing you over."

"It was for the greater good," I said, after a moment of silence. "If I were in your shoes, I'd have done the same. Once I learned the truth of Arlina and my bloodline tracing back to the throne of Blackwen City, I was ready to leave and face her in the Dark Fortress." The thought petrified me more after encountering her in Ellewynth, but it was something that needed to be done. "As you can imagine, Shadow didn't like the idea."

"That's because he still considers himself your guardian," Lady Clarayne said. "He wouldn't dare give up anyone he cared for without a fight."

"I know." I watched the open forest. "It's what makes him such a great friend."

Lady Clarayne chuckled to herself.

"My lady?" I asked, confused.

"Forgive me."

"I'm not sure if there was something I missed."

"It matters not, dear one." Lady Clarayne looked to the open forest as well, and I felt some courage to ask whether or not she was related to Shadow. She seemed to have sensed that need, because she kept watch of me. "Ask, child."

"Shadow...you and he are blood relatives, aren't you?" I asked.

"What makes you say that?" she asked, amused.

"You two seem so similar, even in appearance," I answered. "I mean, I meant no disrespect by prying. It's a silly question, I shouldn't have asked."

"It's no disrespect at all, Artemis." Lady Clarayne assured me. "He and I are tied by blood. Shadow is my nephew."

"I knew it!" I said, jumping up. "No one believed me, but I knew!"

"You are a clever young lady." Lady Clarayne smiled. "Since Shadow's birth, it was a mutual decision among the family to keep our ties discreet. We knew from the day he came into this world that he was special. We knew he would surpass the others of his generation...the aura he exuded then was so great. Azrael's mystical appearance confirmed what we felt." Lady Clarayne smiled at the memory. "We didn't want the others assuming there was favoritism because his aunt is a respected Elder of the realm."

"It must have been hard though...fighting alongside him in the wars of the past."

"Indeed, but I felt honored as well. He is a skilled warrior, as you well know." Lady Clarayne rubbed her bandaged shoulder and winced a bit. "I'm fine, don't fuss. I should be used to such things in my age."

"My lady...please promise me something once you return to Ellewynth."

"What would that be?"

"Shadow would be declared a deserter once he is found missing after the fire," I said. "Please do something to prevent that. That is his home, his only home. He deserves to have a place there still, no matter what's transpired."

"I of all people know this, Artemis." Lady Clarayne sighed. "Shadow was prepared for the consequences. He spoke to me about them." I gaped, and she patted my back. "He knows I will always be there to support him, even when the others won't once the proclamation is made. I cannot stop what the other Elders will do. *You* can promise me something though."

"What's that?"

Lady Clarayne stood up and smiled. "Should he lose faith at any time during your journey, just remind him to follow his heart. It's what he's done so far, and it would be a shame should he stop doing so."

I stood up as well, and slowly nodded. "I can do that."

"Remember to follow yours as well," she said as she took my chin in her hands. "The truth of the heart is far stronger than that of the mind.

Also…home doesn't necessarily mean where you stretch your roots… oftentimes, it means who is by your side."

Before I could reply, she walked back inside. I held a hand over my heart and felt it pound fiercely against my palm.

~⌇

Jack traced his way to the paths where he would usually encounter Callypso. Occasionally, he would lay a hand along the bark of the trees in the effort to sense her within the veils. But Jack only picked up the refugee elves that Talisa hid before the attack of his home city; he hoped Lily was among them.

I see now that what you feel for Lilith is infatuation. The way you speak about this lady friend of yours…Jack, you glow.

Jack grumbled when he heard Artemis' comment in his mind. She might have been right, she might have been wrong. He knew what he felt for Lily…but he also knew what he felt for Callypso. Jack cursed the string.

Why did it have to be for a woman he couldn't have? Did elementals even love?

Of course they love, Jack thought, *but it can't be in the sense that the rest of us do.*

Jack swore as he felt a headache come along. It was impossible, it would always be impossible, and there's nothing that would change that. The most he could do was enjoy the company she provided.

"Jack? What are you doing out here?" Jack jumped when he heard her voice. "Forgive me. I didn't mean to startle you."

"Oh, don't worry about me!" Jack answered. "I'm all right."

When he saw her, his heart dropped. Her light blue eyes were puffed and her face was red—she had been crying. "Willow be damned, are you all right?"

Callypso shook her head as she rubbed her bare arms. Jack took off his cloak and went to drape it around her shoulders, but she refused it.

"It doesn't matter whether I have a cloak on or not," Callypso explained. "I can still feel the deaths in the wind...through the earth... such senseless murder."

"Then I do not have to tell you about Ellewynth," Jack said, saddened.

"No, you do not." Callypso shut her eyes, and a few tears slid down her cheeks. "All elementals can feel the death of Ellewynth. It's so overwhelming. We can still feel the flames engulf each branch...each twig... each leaf...down through the trunk to the roots of the city. The most any of us has been able to do is to contain the fire within the city boundaries. Once Arlina's horde disappears, we must all return to replant...to rebuild."

"Was it a mistake for me to seek you out?" Jack asked.

"It wasn't a mistake. I know why you've done so." Callypso wiped the tears from her cheeks, despite more of them falling. "It's time."

"Yes..." Jack wished he could hold her in his arms and comfort her. "I felt Talisa would want you there as soon as Shadow returns."

"I'm sure she would," Callypso sighed. "It'll only get worse from now on...you realize this, don't you?"

"We can stop it," Jack insisted. "We can stop Arlina and prevent more unnecessary death."

Callypso sighed as she patted his shoulder. "There will always be death in this world, Jack...just as there will always be villainy. It's a part of life. There is nothing else we can do but be there to help rebuild what has been and will be destroyed."

I hadn't moved from the steps since Lady Clarayne had returned to Talisa's cottage. I couldn't even say how long ago that was. I just knew that I couldn't leave, not while Shadow and Netira were still out there. I also worried for Jack, even though I knew he could very well handle himself. Jack's newfound self-sufficiency was a strange notion to grasp.

As for rest, it was something I would not get this night...or what was left of this night.

I heard a neigh in the distance and felt myself shake; I hoped it was from Azrael. Quick galloping sounds echoed closer to the cottage, and I realized it *was* Azrael. Standing from the steps, I watched the mare slow her pace to a trot; she carried both Shadow and Netira on her back.

Kiare be praised, they were safe.

I couldn't speak a word as they dismounted. Azrael gingerly walked to Talisa's herb garden and rested her injured leg on the earth. I'm sure Jack was going to tend to her again, even though there was no sign of blood on her. Netira only nodded to me; I noticed her eyes were puffed and her face had been streaked with tears. She ran off before I could ask what happened.

"She needs time to be alone," Shadow explained, noting my confusion. "Much has happened this night, for everyone." He saw the bandages on my arm and head, and he immediately pulled me into a tight hug. "I am so sorry, Artemis. I should have went with you. I am glad Talisa stopped Arlina from getting you."

I could feel the dried blood on his tunic and knew he was hurt, and I could smell the wound in his arm.

I didn't care. He was here, and he was safe.

"You did what you had to do," I said. "I'm all right, and Jack helped Azrael. I'm just relieved you're back."

"I told you I would return, my dear," he said softly.

"I know. I knew you would but..."

"I know. You're a worrywart," Shadow chuckled. He gently touched the side of my head. "Concussion?"

"It's been taken care of," I explained while trying not to make a face. That tea was appalling, but it did help. My head felt normal again. "Disgusting tea and all."

"Ah. I know of it."

I wanted to laugh at the grimace he made, but the smell of ash on him stopped me. Ellewynth was gone. Our home...burned.

"Shadow...Ellewynth is..." I glanced at him, and I could see the mixture of pain and anger in his eyes.

"Ellewynth is destroyed. I know. She will be rebuilt. It wasn't the first time, and it won't be the last."

"You won't be able to return."

"I am fine with that, Artemis," Shadow answered. "I more or less sealed my fate once I...well, I struck Lord Destrius."

"You did what?"

"I struck an Elder." Shadow's grin widened. "I will *always* enjoy that moment."

"You're terrible." I laughed.

"I'm allowed such moments." Shadow winced when I moved the piece of his sleeve that stuck to his wound. "I'm fine, my dear."

"It needs to be cleaned, Shadow." I frowned. "This is a deep wound."

"I know that." Shadow returned the expression. "I can feel that much, after all."

"Inside. Now." I pointed toward the cottage. "I trust Netira will stay close by, and we don't have to wake Talisa right now. You can use the time to relax."

Shadow froze. "Talisa is here?"

"Of course." My brow furrowed. "She came some time ago."

"Did she...did she bring anyone with her?"

"She brought Lady Clarayne with her. They were both injured and exhausted," I explained. "Your aunt had a nasty shoulder wound, but she'll recover with time."

Shadow pulled me into another hug. I knew he was crying because I could feel the tears fall into my hair. "Oh, thank the goddesses."

"Shadow, you thought she was dead?" I asked, rubbing his back.

"I'll explain later." Shadow finally registered all I said beforehand. "You called Lady Clarayne my aunt."

I smirked. "Because she *is* your aunt. You do realize I had my suspicions, right?"

"Of course you did," Shadow sarcastically replied. "It isn't common knowledge, Artemis."

"It's not as if I'll tell anyone." I pushed him to walk toward the cottage. "Stop trying to prolong the inevitable, Shadow. I have to patch you up."

"Avilyne's hell, when did you become so controlling?" Shadow laughed.

"I'm not controlling!" I yelled.

Shadow opened the door but refused to enter. "After you, my dear."

I groaned. "Why do I always have to go first?"

"Because I was trained better than that, Artemis." He smirked as he walked ahead. "Since both Talisa and my aunt are asleep in the more comfortable rooms, where do you intend to patch me up?"

"Go to Talisa's library. It's quiet enough there so we won't disturb their rest."

"As you wish."

I crept into my old room where the bandages, cordials, and salves were left behind, and I did my best not to wake Lady Clarayne. I took a quick peek at her shoulder, and as I held a hand close to the bandages, I felt minor heat. It was less than before, which meant Lady Clarayne was speaking the truth about how fast her shoulder was mending. It was a blessing indeed.

I then stopped into the kitchen to grab a bowl for water and a wash-cloth. Once I made it into the library, I found Shadow seated atop a table; he had such a scowl on his face.

I couldn't help but laugh.

"I get the feeling you give the sour look to any who tend to your wounds," I said, placing the supplies beside him.

"It's not something I enjoy."

"Then you should try harder to avoid receiving such things," I teased. "Take off your tunic."

"What?" he coughed.

I was amused at his horrified expression.

"Take off your tunic," I repeated. "Do you really intend for me to just bandage your arm as is? I have to clean off the dried blood that's all over you."

"I can do that myself."

"Shadow, stop acting like a youngling and just take off the tunic," I ordered. "Soleil burn me, you're so stubborn!"

"Just be quick about it," Shadow begged.

He fumbled a bit, and I saw he was taking off what appeared to be a chain along with the tunic. He hid the chain quickly before I could inquire about it.

Once the tunic was off, it took a lot for me not to gasp. They say the price for one's fame in battle is the amount of scars one receives. Shadow had many across his torso. When I moved closer to his arm, I noticed the bigger and longer scars along his back.

I hadn't realized I was actually tracing the line of one with a finger when he let out a small laugh.

"I wouldn't keep doing that, Artemis," Shadow warned. "I'm rather ticklish."

"Shadow…" I began, afraid to ask the question that popped into my mind.

"I wasn't always a patient soldier," he explained, reading my mind. "I was once more careless than I'd care to admit."

"Avilyne's hell," I whispered as I started to wash the blood off his shoulder and arm.

"The scars on the back…they're from a dragon," Shadow continued, now looking at me. "Not from this recent war, but from a previous one with them long ago. It was my first war campaign, and I was determined to prove myself, just like any other soldier of Ellewynth. I accompanied a scouting party to patrol one of the dragon keeps, desperate to show that my archery skills were worthy enough to compete with the veterans. Another scout found us and reported that our encampment was ambushed. We ran as fast as we could to return and aid them.

"I was careless not to observe my surroundings, you see. While I aided the other archers to bring one of the larger dragons down, I was clawed by a much younger dragon. They call the young ones hatchlings, and they are just as dangerous as a grown dragon. If I hadn't been moving as I was shooting, I would not be sitting here with you today. I was lucky the hatchling was too erratic in his attacks to dig his claws deeper than he already had. If I didn't learn the lesson then, I certainly learned it in bed rest."

"Goddesses," I managed to say while moving the washcloth to the wound. Shadow gritted his teeth. "Apologies. I'm trying to do this without causing too much pain. The good news is that it was a clean cut."

"I wasn't worried."

I started applying the salve, and he winced a bit. "Stay still, elf."

"It's cold."

"I never pegged you for someone who whined so much." I chuckled.

"I don't," he replied. Shadow glanced at me after a moment of silence. "It's interesting to see you this way."

"What way is that exactly?" I asked while reaching for the bandages.

"Authoritative," he answered. "I like it."

"Don't get used to it." I began to wrap his arm. "That side of me doesn't come out very often."

"That side of you has to," Shadow urged. "Artemis, I value your naiveté, and more times than I'd like to admit, your sarcasm. Once we set out on this journey, your authoritative side needs to come out. You have to be one with the dhampir as well. There is no room for error."

I sighed. "I know. It's just..."

"You're afraid. I know." Once I finished wrapping his arm, Shadow gestured for me to sit beside him. "Fear *is* useful, Artemis. Once you can master it, you will turn into the fierce warrior that I know you can be."

"Just continue adding the pressure, why don't you?" I frowned.

"I only speak the truth." Shadow grinned. "Now, can you pass me my tunic?"

"No."

"You don't really just expect me to sit here solely wearing breeches, do you?" Shadow asked, horrified.

"I doubt you would fit into any of Jack's clothing, but I can fetch you something so you can cease to be embarrassed." I giggled.

"I am fine wearing the one I came in for now," Shadow insisted, while failing to retrieve his tunic from me.

"That thing is covered in blood and is beyond saving!" I argued. "I have to dispose of it."

"Artemis, please just give it to me," Shadow pleaded.

"Absolutely not," I said as I wrenched the tunic from his grasp. I got up from the table and quickly felt Shadow grab me from behind. "Have you lost your mind, Shadow?"

"Just leave the tunic behind and I swear I will let you dispose of it once you return with a replacement." Shadow bargained.

I stopped struggling and remembered the chain he had tried to hide earlier. "What's on the chain?"

I felt him freeze. "Chain?"

"You were trying your very best to discreetly remove a chain while you were taking off the tunic," I explained. "Why is that?"

"I don't know what you're talking about, Artemis." Shadow muttered. "Give me the tunic, and I will free you. I'll let you find a replacement, and I will wear it without complaint."

"I'm not sure if I want to anymore. This is far too amusing." I grinned. "What's on this chain of yours?"

"Avilyne's hell, woman!" Shadow yelled. "Take the compromise!"

"Just what are you hiding?"

Shadow was about to say something, until the door of the library opened; in walked Jack and a woman shorter than him, with short blond ringlets and light blue eyes. She was wearing a flowy brown dress and was barefoot.

The looks on their faces matched our own.

"Perhaps we should have knocked, hmm?" Jack said, as that stupid smile of his reached from one pointed ear to the other.

Shadow immediately released me, and I gave in and handed over the bloodstained tunic. I folded my arms while shaking my head in disbelief.

"I'd be careful if I were you, Jack." I glared.

"I've heard that one before." Jack frowned. "Welcome back, Shadow. Looks like Artemis took care of you well enough."

"She has indeed," Shadow said, ignoring the snickers from Jack.

I looked closer at the girl who accompanied Jack. There was something about her that seemed familiar. It was when she smiled that I suddenly had the memory of a young woman who played with me in Talisa's garden when I was a child. She looked much different then, but the smile…they were one and the same. The more I watched her, the more I recognized the energy vibes she exuded.

"Cally?" I said, taking a step closer to her. "Callypso, is that you?"

"It has been many a long years, Artemis," she greeted me while nodding "You've grown into a beautiful young woman."

Jack's jaw dropped. "Wait a minute…you two know each other?"

"Yes. And I know Shadow as well, though not as well as either of you," Callypso admitted.

"We knew of one another through Talisa's tales beforehand," Shadow elaborated.

"How do you know Artemis?" Jack asked, dumbfounded. "You never told me you actually met her!"

"She was a child, Jack," Callypso explained. "It was when Artemis still lived here."

"Cally watched over me for a few years before she had to leave." I hugged Callypso and then pulled back to study her. "But you looked so different then!"

"It's the beauty of being an elemental, youngling." Callypso shrugged. "Shifting our appearances has been one of the many ways we've managed to survive this long."

"Oh goddesses…" Jack buried his face in his hands. "Soleil burn me."

Shadow walked up beside him and gave a loud clap to his back. "Why don't you wake Talisa, Jack?"

Jack glared after the grin Shadow flashed him. "I hate you right now."

"I know," Shadow replied as he messed up Jack's hair. "And get me a fresh tunic too, please? Before Artemis tries to rip this one off of me again?"

"I don't know, Shadow…" Jack began, as he started to walk away, "somehow I think you would enjoy that."

Jack slammed the door before Shadow could catch him.

"I will murder him," I heard Shadow mumble.

"What was *that* about?" Callypso asked, confused.

"Nothing," Shadow answered, returning to his seat atop the desk. "In the meantime, why don't you tell us how you've been, Callypso?"

"Of course. There is much that needs to be told," Callypso said, as she and I joined Shadow at the table.

19

Arlina grudgingly feasted on some of the elf corpses the others brought her while she waited for the rest of her scouting party to return to their encampment. Arlina was both ecstatic and furious—ecstatic because she had finally burned down the city she'd wanted to destroy for as long as she'd existed, and furious because in the end, Artemis escaped her.

Willow damn Talisa and Shadow's mare! She was so close to killing the filthy mixed-blood brat! That dhampir even dared to fight back! The effort was pitiful, of course, but it still infuriated Arlina. She was going to rip out Artemis' heart with her bare hands. She was going to stomp on the organ while watching the life fade from the girl's eyes.

Soleil burn them all! Arlina would not let Artemis escape her again. She would not stop until she was the last Ravenwing woman left in Arrygn.

And how could the Elders have kept Netira alive for so long? The mere thought of it disgusted Arlina, and she flung one of the corpses outside of her tent to relieve some of the anger.

"People are so useless these days," Arlina grumbled. "It's heartbreaking."

"Mistress!" a full-blood called as she entered the tent.

Arlina blinked at the girl. "Did I give you permission to enter my tent?"

"N-No, my Mistress!" The girl fell to her knees. "B-Bu-But I bring good news! We have found Latos!"

"Oh. He survived after all."

Arlina found she truly didn't care about the scout. Maybe she should...after all, he had proved to be of *some* use to her. "Where is he now?"

"He is being tended to," the girl reported, careful to look straight at the ground.

Arlina walked over to the girl and took her chin in hand. She made the girl look into her gray eyes, and she smiled.

"Good work," she praised.

Before the girl could give her thanks, Arlina grabbed the girl's neck and snapped it. Arlina watched the body crumple to the ground and sighed. "Someone get in here and clean up this mess! *Now!*"

Several full-bloods burst into her tent and began to remove the corpses. Arlina walked out and ignored the wounded soldiers of her camp. They could take care of themselves; they still had the ability to walk, therefore they could hunt on their own.

Arlina stopped in front of a tent with two guards and smirked. "How is our prisoner?"

"He won't last until the sunrise, Mistress," the first guard reported.

"Did you acquire what I asked of you?"

The other guard pulled out a small violet pouch from his jacket. "As you ordered, Mistress."

"Good." She took the pouch. Opening it, she found a glass vial filled with a viscous, milky liquid. "If you hear any screams...carry on."

"Yes, Mistress," both guards replied as they stepped aside for her to enter.

Once inside, she found herself admiring the work of her lackeys. Strung up by his wrists in the center of the tent was the mage, Karesu. His body was limp against the tree trunk the full-bloods had snatched from the forest, and Arlina wrinkled her nose at the smell of ash.

Halfway to him, she thought twice about moving any closer. When she realized he was genuinely unconscious, she frowned. Whoever it was who dealt such wounds to the man had deprived her of some entertainment.

I can't understand why there are those who hate me enough to spoil such fun.

Annoyed, Arlina smacked Karesu hard across the face. She became cheerful when he awoke.

"Good. You haven't found the pathways to Avilyne just yet."

"I'd rather be in the presence of the goddess of death than in yours," Karesu said, his violet eyes now locked with Arlina's gray ones.

"Spare me," Arlina groaned. "We both know I'm not going to let you die, Karesu. You're far too valuable for me to dispose of."

"Even if you treat me," Karesu began, "I would not aid you. I want no part in your twisted world any longer."

"Well, suck it up, because you have no other choice," Arlina said. She suddenly smiled. "No pun intended."

Karesu coughed, and flecks of blood spotted his lips and chin. Despite her earlier gorge, Arlina felt her bloodlust rise once more. She shook away the feeling by dangling the pouch inches from Karesu's face.

"You intend to feed me the cordial," Karesu stated.

"Yes." Arlina was disappointed when she couldn't detect any trace of fear in his voice. "I know you won't die or encounter the side effects. You are a mage after all…and a stubborn prick to boot."

"Then get it over with," Karesu snapped.

"Uh, uh, uh!" Arlina wagged a finger. "Not so fast! I have some spare time before the sunrise, and I want some information."

Karesu rolled his eyes. "You'll find that you are wasting your time. Torture me all you wish, Arlina."

"Oh, I plan to." Arlina stood close to Karesu's body and grabbed his chin, forcing him to look at her. "To think, I had such high hopes for you to become my Second. Avilyne's hell, you were bedding the half-breed!" Karesu glared at her, and she laughed. "Does that anger you, my calling your precious love a half-breed? It's the truth, mage. What was so exotic about her, anyways? Did you have something against a full-blood woman? Are we too pure for your liking?"

Karesu cursed once Arlina moved his face away and traced the outline of his neck with her lips. Her fangs were elongated, and Arlina chuckled when she felt Karesu trying to wrench away from her.

"I'm sure you enjoyed this when you had Netira wrapped around you, doing what I am now," Arlina whispered into his ear before nicking the lobe with a fang.

"Believe me when I say that I will enjoy watching you die, whether it be by my hand or someone else's," Karesu threatened. "Each...slow... moment of life that slips from you."

"So you say."

He hissed when she bit into his neck. His blood tasted so sweet; she wanted more. "How long have you been sleeping with your precious dhampir wench, mage? How long have you helped her hide from me?"

"Does it anger you, Arlina?" Karesu smirked. "Does it anger you to know that you were bested by your own subordinates of all people?"

Arlina bit into his neck once more, only harsher this time. Snatching his face in her hands, she glared at the violet eyes that showed nothing but hatred toward her.

"I could have given you everything, Karesu," Arlina growled. "Everything. Why betray me?"

"Blackwen City has lived with your taint for far too long," Karesu replied. "It's time someone wiped it away."

"Shut up." Arlina smacked him, and Karesu laughed at her. "I said shut up!"

"What's the matter, Mistress?" Karesu asked. "Is that fear I sense?"

"Silence!" Arlina cried as she gripped his neck.

It would have been so easy and simple to choke the life from him, but she knew she couldn't. She needed the bastard alive for now. "That's better."

"Aerios blow you. Kill me now," Karesu said in between breaths. "Why do you hesitate?"

"Haven't you been listening? You're far too valuable to be disposed of," Arlina replied, releasing him. "For now, at least."

The look on Karesu's face brought a strange joy to Blackwen's Mistress; it was realization mixed with fear and loathing.

"You plan to use me as leverage," Karesu said after a moment of silence. "You intend to lure Netira here. And since Shadow was with her, you intend for him to follow. If they come, then you're certain the one you desire most will too...you want Artemis to come to you."

Arlina yawned. This was getting boring.

"Perhaps." Arlina removed the stopper from the cordial. "Perhaps not."

"You hope that offering a trade to Netira will make it even easier to obtain Artemis. You could kill me now and still make the offer, but you enjoy torture so you'll stay your hand. You always did like killing one's loved one in front of others," Karesu continued. "Netira won't do it. My life isn't as valuable as the other remaining Ravenwing woman in Arrygn."

"Oh, shut up."

She pinned Karesu against the tree trunk and forced the cordial in between his lips. Once she removed the glass vial, Arlina held a firm hand over his mouth. She moved it only when she knew Karesu had swallowed the milky liquid.

Once he fell unconscious, after the brief moment of his body violently shaking, Arlina inspected the vial and noticed she had given him nearly half of it.

"Well, this will prove to be interesting," Arlina said as she pocketed the vial.

Netira rubbed her chest, feeling odd sensations of pain. Karesu was suffering; she knew that much.

She couldn't believe he had sacrificed himself so that she and Shadow could flee. Netira punched the ground; Karesu should have been here with her. He would have been treated, he would have gained some rest, and the two could have run away by now, just like they once dreamed of.

And yet, she couldn't abandon Blackwen City. She and Karesu swore to one another that they would save their home. She couldn't give up now.

There was the matter of Artemis to consider as well, and the part Tamina wanted Netira to play in this game of revenge. She wanted to help Artemis, that much was true…but Netira didn't like the feeling she was getting ever since her dead mentor visited her prison cell. Something very dark was coming, even though the whole point of guiding Artemis to the Dark Fortress was to be rid of the evil.

Goddesses, Netira thought. *I don't like this at all.*

Looking back at the cottage, she wondered how the famed Talisa would receive her. Karesu apparently kidnapped her, which caused Talisa to swear to kill him on sight. Shadow and Artemis wouldn't let that happen, but Netira wasn't sure if she could rely on the two to help her rescue her lover should the time come.

Once I make it to Blackwen City and lead Artemis to Arlina, Netira plotted, *my part will be over. I can rescue Karesu myself.*

It'd be her way of thanking you for the help you'll be giving us.

Netira shook her head to rid her mind of Shadow's earlier statement. When the time came, she would leave them behind to deal with Arlina so that she could free Karesu. She wouldn't regret it.

"Someone should really fetch this Netira woman from outside," Callypso suggested once Jack returned to the library with Talisa, along with a tunic for Shadow.

Talisa stared at Callypso, surprised at her presence here. She then frowned once she noted Shadow's arm. "Shadow, you're bandaged. That means you have been here for some time."

"Artemis felt it prudent to attend to me," Shadow replied, while having a hard time fitting into Jack's clothing.

"Did you now?" Talisa's grin widened at me.

"He needed treatment," I explained. "I was going to wake you when I was finished."

"Well, at least it's still dark outside, so I can believe that," Talisa replied with a shrug. Ignoring the glares from both Shadow and myself,

Talisa focused on Jack. "What are you doing just standing there? Fetch us some tea and snacks! We're going to be up for some time."

"Why do I have to get it?" Jack grumbled.

"Because you're my apprentice and you belong to me until I say otherwise!" Talisa said, while clenching the fingers of her right hand. "Hurry up!"

Jack disappeared while the rest of us tried not to laugh at the display we had just witnessed. I did feel bad for him though. I knew the feeling well enough from my weapons training with Shadow.

"Shadow, be a dear and fetch the Blackwen City dhampir as well." Talisa ordered, as she took a seat at the table.

"Shall I wake Lady Clarayne while I'm at it?" Shadow said, still fumbling with the ill-fitting tunic.

"No. Leave her to rest." Talisa replied. "I will return her to the ruins of Ellewynth myself at dawn. Lords Celstian and Destrius will worry about her if she does not return."

"Thank you, Talisa," Shadow said, as he too, disappeared.

Callypso and I glanced over to her in confusion.

"For keeping her safe," Talisa explained.

"Does he not realize that we all have the knowledge that she and he are tied by blood?" Callypso asked.

Talisa looked at me, horrified. I waved her off. "I already knew, Talisa. Lady Clarayne told me herself."

"Lady Clarayne was awake?" Talisa asked, alarmed.

"Yes," I answered. "She's fine. She was just worried, and she returned to rest quickly enough."

"I finally get some sleep, and I miss *everything*," Talisa whined as she swatted her leg in annoyance.

"Don't pout, Talisa." Callypso laughed. "There will plenty more opportunities for such instances to occur again."

"What instances?" I asked, confused. Callypso and Talisa beamed, and I knew then what they referred to. "Soleil burn me...nothing happened!"

"Artemis, Jack and I walked in to you being restrained by a bare-chested Shadow," Callypso said as her grin widened from ear to ear. "That image speaks volumes."

I buried my face in my hands, and the women practically cackled. "It meant nothing! He refused to let me dispose of that bloodied rag he arrived in."

"You mean to tell me that a bare-chested man grabbed you from behind and you felt *nothing*?" Talisa exclaimed, aghast. "Willow be damned, we have so much work to do with you! That action alone should have excited you somehow!"

"These things take time, Talisa." Callypso dramatically sighed. "You know this well enough."

"I'm an impatient being, Cally!" Talisa pouted. "She needs to learn these things, and fast. No woman should live with such ignorance!"

"I'm still standing here!" I said, my face flushed.

"You're a woman now, Artemis." Talisa sighed. "For your own sake, do something about it."

"I'm *not* talking about this!" I yelled.

Talisa was about to speak until Jack returned with a tray filled with teacups and cookies. He was horrified when he noticed all three of us staring at him.

"Did I interrupt something?" Jack asked, taking care to set the tray on the table as fast as possible.

"Not at all," Callypso answered.

"We're merely discussing how Artemis is ignoring her womanly desires," Talisa said, snatching a few of the cookies.

Jack doubled over in hysterics. I rolled my eyes.

"I give up." I raised my hands in defeat. Jack was choking now. "There is nothing wrong with me!"

"Artemis, don't get me started about that," Jack said, trying to regain his composure as he took a seat. "Talisa, can you fill me in on the details as to why she is doing such a thing?"

"Jack, if you dare to add to this ridiculous conversation any more, I won't hesitate to mention a few things of our own conversations to these ladies," I threatened, as I moved to stand behind him. I gripped his shoulders and gave a few harsh squeezes. "You *know* of what I speak."

Jack froze and cursed in the Elvish tongue. Callypso and Talisa were confused, and I found a small smile of satisfaction forming on my lips.

"You can be evil sometimes, Artemis," Jack whispered.

"You would do well to remember that." I released my grip on him. I took a seat beside Jack and snatched a few cookies myself. "What shall we speak of now as we wait for Shadow and Netira?"

"I'm rather intrigued of these conversations you've just mentioned," Talisa said, resting her chin in her hand. I could feel the irritation from Jack, and Talisa raised an eyebrow at him. "Can't we know *something?*"

"I may be your apprentice," Jack began, while glaring at me, "but there are *some* things that are considered sacred. I expected more from my dear friend here."

"I'm just casually reminding you that I, too, can make your life miserable within seconds." I smiled as I took a bite of a cookie.

"This isn't over," Jack muttered as he picked up a teacup.

"Far from it." I winked.

The library door opened, and Shadow walked inside with Netira. She looked more depressed now than when she first arrived. I could tell she was in physical pain as well. I knew Netira was still suffering from the wounds she had when she first arrived in Ellewynth, but I couldn't tell if she had any new ones.

"Netira, welcome," I greeted her. "Do you require any treatment? You look ill."

Netira waved me off. "It is nothing that can't be cured through cordials and salves, but thank you, Artemis."

"You will need to feed soon, yes?" Callypso said, standing up.

She strode over to her and took one of Netira's hands into her own. Callypso's face darkened, and I could feel Jack tense while we watched. "Goddesses…I'm so sorry."

"What are you?" Netira said, her dark brown eyes now wide with fear mixed with amazement.

"Callypso is an elemental," Talisa answered, catching Netira's attention. Talisa laughed when she noted the apprehension Netira tried to hide. "Ah. I see my reputation precedes me."

"There's also the matter of someone we have in common," Netira answered.

"If you're referring to your mage, then yes, there is a matter," Talisa replied.

"Mage?" I asked.

There was *another* mage involved?

"Yes, we will get to that," Talisa explained. "Sit. All this standing produces more tension that we do not need."

We all gathered around the table and took our seats. Shadow sat beside me, and Jack wiped the grin off his face when Callypso sat beside him. Netira sat at the head of the table, as she was uncomfortable being near both Talisa and Callypso.

"How is there an elemental here?" Netira asked, rubbing the same hand Callypso had grasped earlier.

Callypso chuckled. "My reasons for being here are my own."

"You are of the wind," Netira said, finally allowing herself to relax. "It felt as if there was a calming breeze when you held my hand."

"I was trying to see what you saw in terms of the attack," Callypso explained. "I saw…other things."

"What did you see?" Jack asked.

Netira raised an eyebrow at him. "A dark-haired elf from the Woodland Realm? Interesting."

"We can talk about my lineage later," Jack replied, knowing full well what Netira's implications were.

"I meant no offense, elf," Netira apologized. "I was only voicing my intrigue."

"Stick to Jack." Jack sighed, annoyed at being called "elf."

"Jack then."

"I don't mean to be rude, but I'd like to hear what Callypso saw," Talisa said, irritated.

"Heartbreak," Callypso replied as tears formed.

Netira looked at her hands in her lap, and Shadow sighed.

"I can elaborate on that," Shadow started. "I rescued Netira as well as Karesu from the Hall of the Elders. Karesu is a full-blood from the Dark Fortress. Coincidentally enough, he's a mage."

"And Netira's lover," Talisa added, tapping her fingers along the dark wood of the desk. "Before the rescuing happened, this Karesu both kidnapped me and forced me to show him safe entry into Ellewynth. Before that could occur, Ellewynth burst into flames. The vampire mage was…courteous…to release me so that I could aid the elves."

"And now we know where those cuts on your back came from." Jack sighed. "I never imagined my master in such a situation. You're supposed to be untouchable."

Jack yelped from the head-slap, and Shadow coughed to cover up his laughter. I wasn't sure if I felt sorry for him anymore, seeing how Jack continued to put himself in harm's way.

"Moron," Talisa muttered, as she shook her now reddened hand.

"Where does the part of you attacking Lord Destrius come in, Shadow?" I asked.

"You did what?" Talisa and Jack yelled in unison.

Netira smiled at the memory while Callypso struggled to restrain her own smile.

"When I came to Netira's cell, Lord Destrius was there. He was going to kill her, just as he was going to finish off Karesu." Shadow folded his arms. He somehow managed to fit into Jack's tunic, though his discomfort in it was obvious. "I happily interfered. I already know that I will be considered a deserter once the others return to Ellewynth's ruins and find me missing from duty. I'm fine with that. I just wanted Lord Destrius to have one final fond memory of me."

Talisa burst out laughing. "Avilyne's hell, Shadow! I would have loved to see the look on that man's face."

"You still can, once you help Lady Clarayne return." I smiled.

To be honest, I wanted to see Lord Destrius' expression as well. It was still terrible on Shadow's part to strike an Elder, but the sight would have been grand indeed.

"Yes, that is true. But still!" Talisa wiped a few tears from her face. "Apologies. Continue, Shadow."

His visage darkened. "We encountered Arlina after we escaped the Hall of the Elders, which was already burning down on us."

I felt myself shake at the mention of her name; Jack did the same. I couldn't get rid of the image of her pointing that pistol at me. I rubbed my neck and remembered the feeling of Arlina's grip on it.

Shadow continued to tell the tale of what happened in Ellewynth, and when he spoke of how the vampire mage, Karesu, stayed behind so that Netira and Shadow could escape, I understood Netira's agony then.

A few of us flinched when she pounded the table with her fist. I was about to get up to console her, but Shadow grabbed my hand and shook his head. Talisa had already made her way to Netira and knelt so that they could look directly at one another.

"I know I have my private grudge with Karesu," Talisa began in a calm tone, "but that does not mean that he isn't a good man. Arlina will not kill him. He is still too useful to be disposed of. She *will* use him as leverage against us in an attempt to lure you away. I know what you're thinking, Netira. Don't succumb to it."

"You do *not* know," Netira muttered.

Talisa sighed. "I loved once, Netira. I lost him in the most horrific way possible. Believe me when I say that there is a chance to rescue him, and we shall. Once we reach the Dark Fortress, we will rescue Karesu just as we will aid Artemis."

"Just so you can kill him once he heals?" Netira said, angered. "I won't risk that."

"I trust you will let Karesu deal with his own matters when the time comes." Talisa stood back up. "I give you my word that I will help rescue him from Arlina. He let me go to help the elves, and I can repay the favor by helping him...just this once."

"Talisa will give him the world's largest head-slap, Netira," Jack joked, and then he tried to distance himself from his teacher.

I hesitated at first, but I then found the courage to say what needed to be said.

"I don't expect you to trust us..." I began. "I know you've been dragged into this game of revenge you mentioned when we first met, but you can at least trust Talisa and the rest of us when we say we will aid you. Once all of this is over, you would be free from my mother's desire of vengeance. We will not disturb you and Karesu further."

Netira smiled. "You are your mother, Artemis. You even bargain like her."

"Now that we have that matter settled, we should discuss the actual details of the journey," Callypso said. "We'll need supplies and weapons.

We must map out the most discreet route we can take, and we must figure out what towns and villages are safe to stop in. Arlina will have her spies out there, as she will be desperate to know where Artemis is. We have to be wise."

"You're still bent on coming with us, Callypso?" Talisa asked, wary.

"I told you before, old friend," Callypso replied, "I am coming no matter what. I can be useful to you all since I *am* an elemental. I will be able to sense—"

"All right, all right, you're coming," Talisa cut her off.

"Talisa, I should state the main reason why I'm coming," Callypso said, confused.

"To sense certain danger, yes," Talisa answered, giving her an odd look as if to say, *be silent.*

I frowned. More secrets…I wasn't sure how I felt about it. Secrets had a nasty way of coming back to haunt people, and I didn't want that happening to us on the journey to the Dark Fortress. There was too much at stake already.

"When you return Lady Clarayne to the ruins of Ellewynth," I said to Talisa, "would it be possible for you to check on our homes?"

"Is there something in particular you'd like for me to look for?" Talisa inquired. "It would be rare if anything survived the blaze, Artemis."

"There could have been some trunks of clothing that might have survived," I said. "For Shadow, maybe some of his weapons…it's worth a try, yes?"

"It would have to be discreet, you realize this," Talisa explained. "Once it's discovered that you're gone, they will try to destroy anything of yours that *did* survive. The same will go for you, Shadow."

"There's only one real thing of importance that I am certain survived the fire and would like to be brought back to me," Shadow said, his demeanor weary. "I'm sure you are aware of what I am referring to, Talisa."

Talisa took a moment to think, and then nodded. Callypso went to one of the shelves and retrieved several maps of Arrygn. Jack excused himself to fetch something from his room, and the rest of us huddled closer to the table to inspect the maps.

"I have limited supplies here, but we will need to make a stop in Westyron at some point," Talisa said, pointing to a large city on the map far from the Woodland Realm.

Netira frowned. "Arlina will have scouts stationed there. We cannot risk stopping on that city."

"Westyron is the one stop in this journey that we must take, regardless of the risk," Talisa stressed. "I have contacts in the city, and they know better than to loosen their lips to others."

"Westyron is a human-run city, Talisa," Callypso reminded her. "And there are unscrupulous characters there. How are we going to disguise two dhampirs and two elves there? They are infamous in imprisoning anyone who isn't human."

"It can be done," Shadow said. "There is an inn we can stay in and be assured discretion. I also have a merchant there whose services I require."

"Oh?" I asked. "And what is that?"

"It's weapons related," Shadow answered.

Weapons for *me*. Soleil burn me.

"Speaking of weapons!" We watched Jack walk back in, and he carried a rather large cloth bundle in his arms. "This is for you, Artemis."

"What is that?" I asked, staring at the bundle he held out in front of me.

Callypso distanced herself from us, and Talisa held a hand to her chest. I noted the look of intrigue on Netira's face, as well as the look of concern on Shadow's.

"Just open it, Artemis," Jack said, rubbing his arms as if cold.

Moving the cloth he placed on the table, I stared at what was once hidden. I felt as if all the air escaped my lungs as I recognized the weapons from the dreams...from the nightmares of Mother and Arlina.

"Tamina's sai," Shadow whispered. "You've found them."

"It is the weapon of your bloodline, Artemis Ravenwing," Netira said.

"I've explained this to her," Jack said.

"Netira, can you elaborate?" I asked. "It's better to know as much as possible."

"Full-bloods of Arrygn were once divided into clans. Blackwen City is home to a good number of descendants from these ancient bloodlines, and has been ruled by the women of the Ravenwing clan since the beginning of its existence," Netira explained. "It was said that when a child of their respected clan came of age, they inherited their own set of the weapons their bloodline favored. The women of your line favored the sai, and that tradition was one of the few that survived throughout the ages. Had Tamina been alive, you would have had your own set rather than being forced to use hers."

I picked up one of the sai and admired the embedded garnet and onyx in its hilt. As I rubbed them, I felt strange hints of energy transfer to me.

"What's wrong, Artemis?" Shadow asked, noting my puzzlement.

"They...they feel strange," I answered, while unable to take my eyes off of the gems.

"They haven't been purified," Callypso warned. She still kept her distance. "It seems you did not fare well either, Jack."

"All I've learned is that the dragon jewels within the sai are difficult to purify," Jack explained.

"Is that so?" Callypso replied, her sarcasm apparent.

"Goddesses, just how many more things do you know that you haven't yet told me?" I asked him, now putting down the sai.

"I'm sorry, Artemis." Jack sighed. "Everything has been happening so fast, you know?"

"That goes for all of us, Artemis," Shadow added. "Everything will become clear in time."

"Preferably before we leave!" I yelled.

"One thing at a time, Artemis." Netira yawned while rubbing her eyes. "How secure is your cottage, Talisa?"

"Secure enough to be hidden from Arlina and her scouts," Talisa replied. "For now."

"Then I suggest we all get what rest we can before we continue planning for the trip," Netira suggested. "You will take Lady Clarayne back to Ellewynth and search the houses as Artemis asked. The rest of us can prepare while we await your return. And yes, Artemis, you can use the time then to learn what the rest of us know before we depart. I'd rather you have a clear mind going into this journey instead of being angered at your friends and myself."

"That would be appreciated."

"While Talisa is gone, Shadow, Callypso, and I will figure out our route to Westyron. Once we get there, we can figure out the next safest route to Blackwen City," Netira added. "Talisa, you can look over the plans once you return and have a final input as well. We wouldn't want you to feel left out, after all."

"I suppose I can appreciate that," Talisa said.

"What am I supposed to do?" Jack asked. "You left me out."

"Ah, yes. You." Netira smiled. "Any dark-haired elf from the Woodland Realm I've encountered or learned of in the past has always proven to be a mage. Assuming that you, too, are an elf mage, I trust you will figure out the right books to take with you."

"You want me to haul books with us?" Jack inquired, unimpressed.

"You will have to regardless," Talisa said, patting his back. "Your apprenticeship will not be put on hold because of this."

"And you *love* books, Jack," I reminded him.

"I do love books," Jack whined, "but I can be of more use than just carrying a bunch of them for research purposes!"

"I do not jest when I say that it is an important task, Jack," Shadow said. "You would be of more use to us if you could learn to control your abilities."

"Fine," Jack sighed, defeated. "Fine! I'll look for books when I wake."

"Then it's settled," Netira said, yawning once more. "Let us go rest."

Hearing the others mutter their agreement, I picked up my mother's sai and stared at the jewels again. Jack called them dragon jewels, which meant that they were much more than simple gems. They were known to have magical properties, or so I'd heard.

Callypso grasped my shoulder, and I noted how fearful she was.

"Cally?" I asked. "Is something the matter?"

"A word of caution, Artemis," she warned, eyeing the sai with distaste. "Use these only in desperation. I do not trust these weapons."

"But why?"

Callypso shook her head. "I will explain in due time. Promise me that if they continue to feel…strange…to you, that you will not continue to fight with them."

"Um, I promise."

Callypso frowned. "You will understand what I mean soon enough, youngling."

20

"*Did you not sleep well, my darling?*"

Karesu looked at the woman who shared his violet eyes and shook his head. The woman walked beside him and pulled him into a hug.

"*The spirits again?*" she asked.

Karesu nodded as he pulled away from her. He stared at her long silver hair, and he then noted the amount of jewelry she wore; each piece was engraved with strange runes.

"*Grandmother,*" Karesu began, fumbling with his hands, "*they keep asking me to help them. I want it to stop.*"

"*Karesu, you are gifted,*" she said, running her long fingers through Karesu's hair. "*It is in our bloodline. You are directly descended from one of the ancient clans of the full-bloods. We are the seers. We are the healers. We are the vessels that magic can flow through to maintain balance in the world.*"

He watched her tap the silver owl-shaped pendant that rested on her chest. It was the animal that represented their shared bloodline, much like the raven that the bloodline of the Mistress revered.

"*I don't want this,*" Karesu argued. "*I just want them to go away.*"

His grandmother chuckled. "*When I was your age, my darling, I did not want this gift either.*" She stood up, and pointed to the colorful vials that lined the shelves, as well as the charms that lay across the wooden tables of her apothecary. "*There is a beauty to helping others, dead or alive. To be a mage means to help keep the balance once someone tips it and causes disarray.*"

"Then why don't you help the Mistress and serve Blackwen City in City Tower?" Karesu asked, even though he already knew the answer.

"Because it is not my destiny, child," his grandmother replied. She faced the door of the store, and they both watched other full-bloods pass by. *"My place is here, in this shop. It seems the spirits have taken a particular liking to you, Karesu. I can show you how to keep them at bay. They will still be around, mind you, but they will not be so invasive. Perhaps it will be best…lingering spirits can be troublesome."*

"Lingering spirits?"

"They are those who refuse to walk the pathways to Avilyne to be judged," she explained. *"They are malevolent beings who want revenge. If we mages are not careful, they can possess us and commit unspeakable acts."*

Karesu sucked in a breath. *"I do not want that."*

"I know, my darling. To keep them away, however, you must accept your heritage. You must accept that you are a mage. Your gift means nothing if you ignore it."

Karesu blinked at his grandmother and thought of her words. She believed deeply in the ideal of *"destiny,"* and she never ceased to remind him that he had a great one…but it would be so only if he would take the steps necessary to reach it.

He frowned. Would it really be so terrible to accept a part of him that would always be there? Would it be awful to be just like the woman who loved and cared for him so?

"Karesu?" She was worried about his silence. *"Forgive me if I am pushing this. I know you have the makings to be a great mage of Arrygn, and I would hate to see my only grandson deny his path. If you do not want it, I swear to leave you be from now on. I'll make your charm myself."*

Karesu gave a small smile. *"They say everything happens for a reason, right, Grandmother?"*

"Indeed they do."

"Then…then what can I do to keep the spirits at bay?"

"You're certain you wish to do this yourself?"

Karesu nodded. *"It would be a shame to waste such a willing teacher."*

His grandmother laughed and hugged him. *"Yes, it would."*

She bade him to follow her to the back of the store, and she pointed to the jewelry she wore, the ones with the strange runes. *"I will show you how to make charms. Once you can master their creation, I can then teach you the art of runes and how to manipulate them into silver so that you can ward off anything you so wish."*

"Why do I feel as if there's a catch, Grandmother?" Karesu asked, wary.

"Nothing slips past you, hmm?" His grandmother chuckled. "It is true. There is always a catch when working with magic and obtaining a balance. There is always a price that must be paid, dear one. Nothing can be cast or created without a consequence. The same can be said for life in general. Remember this."

Karesu nodded as he watched her open a rickety old wooden door. He peered inside and was amazed to see the walls covered with yellowed parchment, each containing what seemed to be hundreds of differing runes. He could smell the sharp, metallic scent of silver, and he could feel the heat of the fire that came from the cauldron that burned in a corner of the room. Karesu realized this was his grandmother's study; no one was ever allowed inside.

He felt honored.

"Perhaps your future study will be more glorious than my own, but for now, this will have to do." She gestured for him to sit on the only bench in the room.

"Grandmother..." Karesu began, as he watched the liquid silver in the cauldron bubble. "What exactly is the price to create the charm I want?"

"That is not up to me to tell you," she answered, the fire reflecting into her calm violet eyes. "Only you can know the answer to that. Once you create, cast, and work with the magic within you, the answer will come."

Karesu gulped. "Can my life be considered a price?"

His grandmother folded her arms, hesitant to answer. "Indeed it can. If such a price were asked, Karesu, I pray that it be for good reason. Never allow such a price to be collected if not for the greatest cause of all."

Karesu felt the fear rise within him. What if the charm to ward off the spirits required him to give up his life, or part of it?

He wasn't ready for that.

"Look into the cauldron, Karesu. Grab the tongs that are there beside it. Embrace the heat from the element you love most."

Karesu did as he was instructed, and looked to her for more direction.

"What do you feel?"

"I feel..."

What did he feel? He looked at the tongs and stuck them into the liquefied silver. He began to stir, confused. "I don't know. I don't know what to do."

"You're not listening hard enough, my darling." His grandmother laughed, moving a few wayward silver strands from her face. "Close your eyes if you must, but always listen to the voice within you."

Karesu shut his eyes and tried to listen to this "voice" his grandmother mentioned. He got frustrated when he was met with continued silence, and he forced his eyes open.

His grandmother was amused at his anger.

"Nothing is instantaneous, my darling," she said. "Impatience is the curse of youth."

"Why can't I hear anything?" Karesu asked as he continued to stir with the tongs.

"Another curse of youth." His grandmother sighed as she rubbed her brow. "Child, you must maintain a calm demeanor about you when you work. There is no need to rush anything. You'll only be given sloppy creations in return if you do. Now that would be some cause for frustration!"

He felt his grandmother rub his back, and he shut his eyes once more. Karesu tried to listen, and was startled when he heard an unfamiliar voice.

Blood.

Karesu jumped, and he splashed some of the silver onto the walls and floor.

"F-Forgive me, Grandmother!" Karesu cried, horrified.

His grandmother guffawed. "Oh child, we all jumped when we first heard the voice of the one collecting the price."

"But who was that?"

"No one can say for sure, my darling." His grandmother tapped her chin in contemplation. "Some have said it is the goddesses themselves, speaking as one entity. Others say it is the evil seduction of temptation, but those mages in particular are nothing but superstitious fools."

Karesu regained his calm as he listened to his grandmother go off on a tangent. He looked back to the tongs, and then to his finger.

"What did the voice ask for, Karesu?"

Karesu moved his forefinger to his now elongated fangs and felt the skin give way as he pricked it. He held it over the cauldron, and they both watched as a few drops of his blood fell and swirled within the silver. His grandmother sighed as Karesu frowned.

"Do you have anything I can use to mold the silver in?"

"Of course," his grandmother answered. "Is there anything in particular that calls to you?"

"I just need a mold that I can cut into," Karesu explained.

"Then I shall return in a moment."

She stepped out and returned moments later with a mold she normally used to create her own charms and jewelry. She handed him a thin blade. Karesu knew she watched closely as he sliced an odd shape within the mold. Karesu took the tongs and let the drops of silver slide into the cut mold. He repeated the process until the form he'd cut was filled.

"Now it just has to cool," he said, satisfied.

"I'll admit I have my own moments of impatience," his grandmother said, holding a hand over the mold. Karesu shivered when he felt a chill emanate from her palm.

"But now you have to pay a price for that!" Karesu frowned.

"Not a big one, I promise." She winked. "Now take out your creation. I want to see what it is."

Karesu pulled out a now hardened silver piece that was shaped into a cross. There was a curved point at the tip, and he ignored the wince of his grandmother when he forced it into the soft part of his right ear.

"I'll find out soon enough if this works," he said as he flicked the cross. He flinched at the small sensation of pain from the now pierced earlobe.

"If not, I'll just have to be content in calling you a pirate." His grandmother smiled. "An earring. How interesting!"

"Are you disappointed?"

"Not at all, my darling."

Netira awoke and felt a sharp pain in the soft part of her right ear. She rubbed it with her fingers. She pulled them away and was relieved when she didn't spot any blood. She was confused, though, as to why she felt such a pain.

She glanced around the main room and was satisfied she hadn't woken up any of the others. Taking care to maintain stealth, she took one of the cloaks that was left on the floor and stepped outside.

Netira sat on the steps and looked at the sky, which was only slightly lighter than when she first arrived at the cottage. Rubbing her fingers along her ear once more, the image of Karesu's cross earring came to mind.

"You're suffering," she murmured. "I would give anything to be there so that I could free you from it." Netira tightened the cloak around her while resting her head atop her knees. "I pray to the sacred sisters that they spare you from the worst of it until we get there."

～❯

I was back in Ellewynth, as if Arlina hadn't attacked at all.

I was walking the path to Shadow's house, and I found it strange that there wasn't anyone around—it was so empty.

My footsteps were heavier than usual; when I looked down, I saw the jeweled hilts of Mother's sai sticking out from my boots. I did not remember how they got there, and I pulled them out. I gasped the moment I saw them covered in blood.

As I dropped them, I tried to wipe my bloodstained hands on my cloak. More blood appeared the more I tried to rid myself of it.

"Their lives are yours."

I froze when I heard her. I saw Mother standing with folded, bare, pale arms; her violet eyes were cold, and she wore a black dress with an unusually long trail of cloth. I reached out to her, but she pulled back; Mother had a look of disgust on her face.

"You weren't supposed to run away. You were supposed to keep on fighting her," she said as she picked up the sai. "You could have ended Arlina's madness."

"I'm not strong enough," I answered. "Not yet. And...and the elves..."

"Dead. All dead!" She threw the sai at my feet. "All because of you. All because you are repulsed at your dhampir heritage. You could have saved them!"

"I didn't mean for this to happen!" I cried. "I didn't leave the city in time! The dhampir would have made things worse...I have no control over it!"

"Excuses!" She walked up and slapped me hard. "Unforgivable. You're no daughter of mine. You're no true Ravenwing woman."

I felt my bloodied hands clench into fists as I glared at her.

"You dare say that when one of the reasons I'm going to Blackwen City is to avenge you?"

I grabbed a sai and threw it. It missed her, and it made a loud thud as it impaled the tree trunk behind her.

Mother's reaction was only a grin. "Good. You're releasing your true anger. It's a powerful tool, Artemis. Remember that when you face an opponent, Arlina especially."

She walked away before I could respond. When I looked back at my hands, they were clean of the blood. I found myself walking back to the tree where the sai was. When I pulled it out, the tree trunk began to bleed.

"What in the world?" I dropped the sai. I could not stop the blood flow, not even with both hands.

"Remember," Mother began as she appeared beside the tree, "once you begin to take life, their blood will always stain your hands. You'll have the blood of your loved ones on you as well…no one is immune to the consequences of one's actions."

I realized I wasn't touching a tree trunk anymore, but an actual body. When I recognized the familiar green eyes that stared lifelessly into my own, I screamed.

~⟲

I snapped up from the floor and felt the blanket move with me as it clung to my sweat. I looked at my hands and remembered how much blood had covered them in the dream. Once I saw who that tree had been in the end…

I fought off the urge to scream.

I rushed to the washroom and shut the door, and removed one of the floorboards that hid the underground well. I filled up the bucket that was beside the door and thrust my hands into it.

In reality, they weren't covered in blood, but I couldn't help but feel like I had to keep washing them; I couldn't shake the sensation of it. The harder I rubbed my hands together, the harder it was to keep myself from crying.

It wasn't until I felt hands clasp my own together that I realized I had woken someone. I didn't have to look to know who it was.

Shadow said nothing, and moved the bucket aside. I choked back a sob when I saw real blood on my hands. My nails had somehow shifted to claws, and I had scratched deep into my palms.

Avilyne's hell…I was a mess.

"The dhampir is trying to tell you to stop," he said quietly, while taking one of the washcloths and wrapping it around my hands. Streaks of red surfaced on the cloth.

"I just wanted the feeling to go away," I explained, shaking. "I wanted the sight out of my head."

"I understand it," he said.

"How do you deal with it?"

"The nightmares?"

"The nightmares as well as the fighting." I now felt the pain the claws had created and frowned. "You've been a soldier for most of your life. How do you live each day knowing you have blood on your hands?"

Shadow sighed. "It's as I told you before. Sometimes it haunts me... and sometimes I'm just numb to the feeling because I *have* fought for so long. You will learn how to deal with it all as time goes on."

"I dreamt I had the blood of all the slain elves from Ellewynth on my hands," I revealed. "Dead. All dead." I shuddered as I repeated Mother's words. "Because of me."

"It wasn't your fault, Artemis," Shadow said, his tone sharp. "Arlina would have done this whether you had or hadn't been in Ellewynth."

"But it *is* my fault, Shadow," I growled. "And I'm now taking the rest of you to your own deaths."

"Artemis, you're not leading us into anything. The rest of us are capable of making our own choices, and we've made them."

"I saw Mother as well, Shadow."

He stiffened. "And?"

"It's probably best not to speak of it anymore."

"As you wish." Shadow looked at my hands again. "We're waking up Jack."

"There's no need."

"Yes, there is," he insisted as he folded his arms. "I will stick around to make sure that Jack tends to your hands."

I narrowed my eyes at him. "Is this payback for the tunic bit?"

"Oh, no." Shadow smirked. "I have yet to think of what I can do to you for that."

Aerios blow me.

Talisa cursed as she felt the soreness from the battle in Ellewynth. She glanced at Lady Clarayne and knew the Elder felt worse than she looked. The Elder noticed her glances and waved her off.

"I'm fine, Talisa," Lady Clarayne assured her while adjusting the cloak borrowed from the witch. "Artemis and Jack did their jobs well."

"I know they did." Talisa wrinkled her nose as the smell of ash intensified. They had almost reached the city that once held such beauty in the realm. "You didn't even speak to Shadow."

"On the contrary, Talisa, I did. You were still asleep."

Talisa was shocked. "I'm losing my touch on these things!"

"Don't be so hard on yourself." Lady Clarayne chuckled. "I've kept my stealth."

"Clearly!" Talisa stopped laughing once she saw that the ground beneath her feet was covered with burnt vegetation and soot. "Avilyne's hell. I never imagined I would see this again so soon."

Lady Clarayne sighed. "Neither did I. It was impossible to believe that Ellewynth would always stand, but I hoped I wouldn't have to relive its destruction."

"You were a child at the time," Talisa reminisced.

"And you were then as you are now."

Talisa frowned. "My lady, you know I detest being reminded just how old I *really* am."

Lady Clarayne smiled, even though she knew she shouldn't have mentioned Talisa's "special" situation.

"Forgive me, old friend."

"I've already forgotten." Talisa shrugged. "How did your conversation with your nephew go?"

"He and I had already said our good-byes," Lady Clarayne answered. "This time…this time it was much harder for the both of us. He means to never return."

"Shadow will be called a deserter, I know this…but surely that can be changed after this is all over?"

"He also attacked an Elder, Talisa." Lady Clarayne's lips curled into a wistful smirk, and Talisa knew the Elder enjoyed that fact as well. "That cannot be overlooked. Even if Destrius deserved it, Shadow committed an act that is unforgivable in our culture."

"Sometimes one must do a little evil to achieve a greater good," Talisa recited, trying her best to ignore the crunching sounds of the forest beneath her feet. "Something you would have said in similar matters, if I recall."

"Indeed I would. But Shadow has chosen his path. I cannot change it even if I wanted to."

"He'll return," Talisa said. "You know this."

"Return alive from Blackwen City? Yes, I believe this," Lady Clarayne said.

"Thank the goddesses! You're both safe!"

The women saw Lord Celstian rush toward them, and they realized they had reached what were once the gates of Ellewynth. Talisa noticed the Elder hadn't gotten any rest either, and he embraced Lady Clarayne. He did the same with Talisa, and she couldn't help but laugh.

"My lord, it would take *far* more than a fire to end me." Talisa moved her hands on her hips in a defiant stance. "I think Lady Clarayne should be offended as well!"

"I meant no offense, Talisa," Lord Celstian apologized. "Kiare be praised, I'm just relieved to see the both of you here and safe."

"Where is Destrius?" Lady Clarayne inquired.

Lord Celstian rubbed his brow. "I left him back in the ruins. One of the healers is seeing to what he describes as a never-ending ache in the back of his head."

Talisa burst out laughing. "It's his ego that's really hurting."

"Oh, I've no doubt about it," Lord Celstian replied. "As amusing as it is, that was an inexcusable action your nephew committed, Clarayne. Where is Shadow now? I have not found him."

Lady Clarayne cast her glance to the ground. "He fought for this city and the realm, Celstian. He fought during the attack."

"I know this," Lord Celstian said, stern. "No one will forget all that Shadow has done for us. I know you are aware of where he is, Clarayne.

I beg of you, send for him. His honor will not be questioned should he come back."

Lady Clarayne now watched her fellow Elder. "Shadow has a path he must follow, Celstian. I cannot take him away from it."

"He is a soldier of Ellewynth, Clarayne. Shadow was not released from duty," Lord Celstian sighed. "If you will not send for him, then you condemn him to our laws."

"No." Talisa put an arm around Lady Clarayne's shoulder to console her. "She frees him from them."

"What did you do to your hands?" Jack demanded when he returned to the main room with healing supplies.

"I don't want to talk about it." I frowned at the smug look on Shadow's face. "Enjoy this little victory of yours while you still can, Shadow."

"I'll enjoy my true victory soon enough, Artemis." Shadow winked. "And if you pull that stunt again, I'll personally drag you from your slumber to begin your weapons training session, hands or no hands."

"I'll pay handsomely to see such a sight." Jack laughed. He flinched when he caught my glare. "I'm only curious if you'll attack him the same way you did me back when Serlene taught us."

"We'll find out soon enough, hmm?" I muttered, as Jack rubbed a salve into my palms. I hissed when I felt the flare of stings the moment the salve touched the cuts. "Avilyne's hell!"

"My, my," Shadow snickered. "The healer whines as well."

"Shut up," I snapped.

Jack grinned. "Shadow, you must stay around more often. It's amusing to see Artemis annoyed and being abused instead of me."

"I don't think it matters, Jack," Shadow said. "She'll find ways to abuse you nonetheless. And to her defense, you have a tendency of *asking* for such pain, as evidenced by the amount of head-slaps I have seen Talisa hand you."

"He's a glutton for punishment, aren't you, Jack?" I nudged him. "More so emotionally."

"Once again, Artemis," Jack grumbled, "you are an evil woman."

"Has Netira returned?" I asked, ignoring Jack's glares.

Shadow shook his head. "She hasn't moved from the cottage steps. She'll come in when she's ready to."

"Callypso disappeared as well," Jack sighed.

"She's an elemental, Jack. She'll do that."

"Do you know where she went?" I asked.

"She went with Talisa and Lady Clarayne," Shadow answered. "I don't know if she was going to accompany them to the ruins of Ellewynth, but I know she left nonetheless. She'll return before midday, I'm sure."

"I didn't know Talisa and Lady Clarayne left already." I frowned. "Did you get to speak with your aunt before she left?"

Shadow ran a hand through his hair. "Naturally."

"You'll see her again," I assured him.

"Perhaps."

"Silly girl, don't play so rough next time," Jack said as he finished bandaging my hands. "Whoever it is that you're killing in your dreams, tell them to send in a healer too. I need my beauty sleep, you know."

I narrowed my gaze at him. "If you didn't just wrap my hands, I would hit you."

"Like I haven't heard that before." Jack moved far enough so that I couldn't reach him with a kick either. "Now that I'm awake, I'll be in the library. Disturb me *only* if it means it's time to eat."

He left the room before I could spit out a retort.

"Moron," I cursed.

"You always said he was more of a nuisance when he didn't get any rest," he said as he rubbed the bandaged arm.

"How is it?" I pointed to it.

Shadow stopped touching the bandages. "It burns and itches, but we both know that's a good thing. I just got used to the idea of being free from these damned things…"

"There'll be much more of them on this journey," I said.

"Feeling brave now?"

"I'm a mix of everything right now," I admitted. "I know the dreams will continue too. I don't know what frightens me more."

"It's all normal, Artemis," Shadow insisted. "You encountered Arlina. She tried to kill you. Your mind is just processing everything. If you continue to overthink things…"

"I get it." I stood up. "Do you think Jack will be cross with me if I 'disturb' him again?"

Shadow chuckled. "Maybe. Why do you ask?"

"There was something I wanted to ask him," I replied. "About dragon jewels. Apparently the jewels in Mother's sai were from the dragons."

"I can tell you some about them," Shadow said. "Dragon jewels have more magical properties than ordinary jewels, but I'm sure you already knew that. It is a custom for dragons to gift a set of jewels to their champions after a great battle or war has ended, but they also do so for the warriors who fought and left an impression on them. Depending on how impressed they are with the warrior, they sometimes give enough jewels to hand down for several generations. That was the case with your bloodline, or so your mother once explained."

"So it's as Netira said. If Mother was still alive and I lived with her, I would have had my own sai with its own set of dragon jewels," I said. "You've fought in several wars with the dragons…do *you* have dragon jewels?"

"I do. It's what I asked Talisa to retrieve for me. They are also excellent healing tools, you see. They have a way of catching the essence of their user and can restore their energy, so to speak, in their time of need," Shadow explained. "Tamina would have commissioned for your sai to be made for your sixteenth year. I was told it's when the women of your family always received theirs."

"If that were true of the dragon jewels, then why didn't they heal Mother when she was fighting Arlina?"

Shadow shrugged. "It's not an instantaneous thing, Artemis. Dragon jewels are tricky. They require enough stored energy from their user before they can be used for the task, and it doesn't heal you all at once. It's exactly like a trip to the healers…you get patched up, but you're not whole. You're just healed enough to keep on moving. The jewels are merely an easier way to heal rather than relying on salves and bandages."

"Fair enough," I said. "Netira would know more about the Ravenwing bloodline, wouldn't she?"

"She would be the one to ask, yes," Shadow replied. "The most I know is that the full-bloods of Arrygn disbanded the clans long before I took my first breath. Naturally, there are those who cling to the ancient bloodlines and try to invoke the rights it once brought them."

"Like Arlina."

Shadow nodded. "The one right, if you wish to call it that, which Blackwen City has kept is that a woman of the Ravenwing clan must be the Mistress of the Dark Fortress. Avilyne herself created the decree, Tamina once told me."

"And what if a woman of the Ravenwing clan wanted nothing to do with the throne?" I scowled.

"That's a bridge you must cross someday."

I frowned. "Willow be damned."

"You'll *have* to deal with it sooner or later, Artemis. You're the only other Ravenwing woman left." Shadow chuckled. "Did you have any other questions about the dragon jewels?"

I was grateful for the topic change. "Unfortunately, the other questions I have about them are for both Jack and Callypso."

"I see." Shadow stood up. "Did I help at least?"

"You always do."

"What do you mean Clarayne won't send for Shadow? Get that traitorous prick back here to Ellewynth to face his charges like a man!"

Talisa rubbed her brow as the sound of Lord Destrius' voice brought on a headache. She found herself questioning why the goddesses felt this man would be a great Elder. Perhaps the goddesses were just punishing the Woodland Realm for something she just couldn't figure out yet. Kiare never felt the need to tell her, despite Talisa being the water goddess' vassal. Talisa then thought maybe she *didn't* want to know the answer; it might infuriate her more.

"For goddess' sake, Destrius!" Lord Celstian barked. "Keep your voice down! Those of our people who remain are distraught enough. We must keep a more positive outlook for the sake of the others right now."

"Willow damn you and send you to Avilyne's hell!" Lord Destrius snapped as he kept a hand on his bandaged head. "You *know* striking an Elder is an unforgivable act! Order a hunting party for Shadow, and pay them if they bring him back crippled. I want that smug, insubordinate little—"

The slap echoed throughout the ruins.

Lord Celstian was stunned. Talisa wasn't sure if she should be horrified or grateful, as silence was a golden treasure when it came to Lord Destrius. The urge to laugh was there, but she knew better than to let it escape her lips. Talisa never wanted a similar treatment from the woman who dealt the blow to her fellow Elder.

"Clarayne…you struck me." Lord Destrius held his now reddened cheek. "*You struck me!*"

"So I have," Lady Clarayne replied, angered. "Should I choose to leave the city for a walk, would you send a hunting party after me to answer for the action of one Elder disciplining another? No, I think not, you single-minded bastard."

If Talisa were able to cheer as a sign of victory, she would have done so right then and there.

"Clarayne—" Lord Celstian started.

"Be silent, Celstian!" Lady Clarayne snapped. "This imbecile abused his right as an Elder when he went down to the prison and tried to execute the vampire prisoner. All for his own amusement, Celstian! Destrius would have claimed that it would have been for the good of our people to eliminate another full-blood from Arrygn."

"That's a lie your disrespectful nephew spewed, Clarayne!" Lord Destrius spat. "You conspired with him to help free that *vampyra*, and then you ordered him to attack me! Now you helped the traitor escape. Does that please you, Clarayne? Does it please you to know that you're responsible for the exile of your precious Shadow?"

"*Silence!*" Lord Celstian bellowed as he stepped between Lady Clarayne and Lord Destrius. "Leash your wounded ego, Destrius! I will not tolerate any more of your ridiculous outbursts!"

Talisa smiled; thank the goddesses *someone* was taking control of the situation at hand.

Lady Clarayne was about to speak, but Lord Celstian's glare silenced her. "And as for you, Clarayne! No, I do not believe you were involved with any of the conspiracies Destrius conjured. I cannot say the same for Shadow, however, as he is not even here to defend himself. He struck an Elder and helped a prisoner escape. Shadow fought for Ellewynth and the Woodland Realm as duty commanded, but it does not change the fact that he ran. I will send out a hunting party to find him. If Shadow returns with them willingly, then I will overlook the fact that he fled the city. If not, then I have no choice but to declare him a deserter. Should any of us run into Shadow again, it will mean his death."

Lady Clarayne's face twisted in horror. "You cannot mean that."

"My lord, you should think this through," Talisa pleaded.

"My decision is final," Lord Celstian stressed. "Forgive me, Clarayne, but it must be done."

Lord Destrius huffed and stomped away. Lady Clarayne looked to the ground as she fell to her knees.

"My lady!" Talisa rushed to her side.

"Talisa…" Lady Clarayne shook. "Fetch whatever you have need of from the ruins and return to your cottage. Warn Shadow and the others. I fear you'll have more than full-bloods to worry about on your journey to the Dark Fortress."

"Shadow will not kill any of the kindred," Talisa reassured her. "His honor will not allow it."

"I know this…but if I know Destrius as well as I do, he *will* make sure there is an executioner among the hunting party." Tears formed in her eyes. "I would never forgive myself if Shadow were caught unawares by this."

21

I went to the library and found Jack. I noted the book he had stashed under his arm: *The Winged Jewels of the Sky*. It was an old and large tome, and it certainly interested me.

"Taking that book along for the journey?" I asked.

"Of course!" Jack beamed. "It has a lot of information about dragon jewels too. So, is it time for food yet?"

"No," I answered. He frowned. "I wanted to ask you about something."

"That tone of yours has never meant pleasant conversations," Jack said.

"These are dark tidings." I looked at the rest of Talisa's books and frowned. "You and Callypso mentioned something before about purifying the sai. Why is there a need to do so? And why did Callypso seem so afraid of being near them?"

Jack took a deep breath as he put down *The Winged Jewels of the Sky*. "Are you sure that's something you really want to know about, Artemis?"

"I'll only obsess more if you don't tell me, remember?"

Jack bit his lip and sighed. "You might want to take a seat."

"All right." I did as he suggested. "I'm sitting. Spill."

"Have you…" Jack cleared his throat. "Have you ever heard of lingering spirits before?"

"No, I can't say I have."

"Goddesses, I wish Callypso was here right now." Jack nervously laughed. "She's more of an expert on them than I am."

"You just miss her," I teased. "But continue please."

"There are occasions where, after one meets their death, particularly by violent means, the soul does not always take the pathways to Avilyne's realm. They tend to stay behind," Jack explained. "The longer a spirit lingers in Arrygn, the greater their need for revenge. The imbalance in the world they create is just as great. Are you with me so far?"

"Yes."

"Some lingering spirits are stronger than others," Jack continued. "The longer they stay in our world and avoid Avilyne's judgment, the more the madness consumes them. Should they encounter a loved one, they would not recognize the spirit at all; their original personality would be gone. Some have tried to remedy the situation by purifying the gravesites, giving a reburial, and so on."

"What does my sai have to do with a lingering spirit?"

"Your mother is a lingering spirit," Jack answered. "Most of us have encountered her in the waking world. You've only seen and spoken with her through dreams. I'm not sure why this is. When I met her in this very library…Soleil burn me." Jack shuddered. "Artemis, she's not the Tamina we've heard so much about. She was not the same person I saw in the vision that day."

"Goddesses…"

"Your mother is not a typical lingering spirit either, and that is the main reason Callypso is accompanying us to Blackwen City," Jack said. "Callypso would be able to sense her before the rest of us would. We all fear what Tamina could be capable of. She orchestrated this journey for you to undertake, which I fear will lead you to your death if you're not careful. I don't know how she means to benefit from it other than you taking down Arlina, but neither do I want to give your mother the chance to lead you astray."

"She is the real reason why all of you are coming with me."

"Yes and no, Artemis," Jack said. "Even if Tamina hadn't orchestrated the event, we all would have gone with you. We care too much."

"Does Callypso think my mother's spirit is connected to the sai even in death?" I asked, now remembering Callypso's words of caution.

Jack nodded. "I agree with her. I tried purifying them myself and failed miserably. When dragon jewels are given from one person to another, you're supposed to purify them so that they don't have any essence of the previous owner left."

"Why has it been so difficult?" I asked.

"Again, Tamina is not your typical lingering spirit. She's been wandering Arrygn for as long as you and I have been alive, Artemis." Jack rubbed his forehead. "You *must* be careful when you fight with them."

"I felt a strange energy sensation when I held them," I recalled. "Is that how they're supposed to feel?"

"I've never had dragon jewels before, so I cannot tell you." Jack shrugged, apologetic. "When I held onto them, I felt nothing. Despite my being a mage, I don't have a strong connection with the jewels and the sai as you do. Callypso fears to be near them because she is an elemental. Anything with negative or dark energy could easily consume her. I don't know how they'll affect you, but a word to the wise either way: don't fight in anger."

I had a flashback to the dream of Mother and how she said it was good that I was finally releasing my anger.

Avilyne's hell.

"Artemis?" Jack snapped me back to reality. "You look ill. Are you all right?"

"I'm fine," I dismissed him. "I need to grab some air."

"Artemis, what's wrong?"

"Nothing, Jack." I flashed a quick smile. "I just need a refresher. Perhaps I could convince Netira to rejoin us."

Arlina hated the daylight hours. Absolutely *despised* them. She never understood what was so wonderful about the sunlight.

If it weren't for the traitor mage's trinkets, Arlina would have burned to ash. If it were up to her, all of Arrygn would have been covered in eternal darkness, just like her precious Dark Fortress. Arlina appreciated the moonlight from time to time as well; she couldn't deny that. But the daylight hours…if only it were possible to obliterate the sun!

No one would miss it. She'd be doing them all a favor.

She looked back to her resting place; Arlina never tired of the sight of a chained Karesu. He twitched now and then, still under the influence of the cordial. Arlina wondered what the mage dreamed of. Perhaps he was reliving memories as she had when she took the cordial to escape the energies of both her wretched specter sister and the forest of the Woodland Realm.

She grinned as she recalled the memory of Gavin. His despair was so *delicious*. It was a shame she wasn't under the cordial long enough to relive another memory that involved the human merchant.

Now *that* was delicious.

Arlina walked toward Karesu's sleeping form, but stopped once she sensed another presence within the tent. She could not hide her horror when she spotted her sister sitting in the chair she had been in seconds ago.

Tamina smiled at her, her forehead still bloodied by the flintlock pistol that was used to murder her.

"What do *you* want?" Arlina hissed. "I just got used to the idea of you being gone for good."

Is that so? Tamina chuckled as she took a lock of her dark brown hair into her fingers and twisted it. *Get used to my presence, sister. I'm not going anywhere for a very long time.*

"Say what you wish, then leave me be, specter," Arlina snapped. "I have my own matters to attend to."

Still licking your wounded pride from the betrayal of your Second as well as your mage? Tamina asked, crossing her legs to get comfortable. *Or perhaps you are still cross at the fact that you failed to kill Artemis? Pitiful, dear sister, pitiful.*

"Leave me be, damn you!" Arlina yelled. "Get out!"

Tsk, tsk, tsk. If you expect others to know their manners, you must lead by example. Tamina smirked as she stared at the mage. *Keeping the mage alive was smart, I'll give you that. You'd best hope he awakes from the cordial, considering the amount you gave him. It'd be both a shame and waste, should he expire.*

"Make your point known and get out, Tamina."

You're no fun. I am needed elsewhere, so I'll comply with your desires this time. She flashed a grin. *If I were you, I wouldn't rush home to Blackwen. I would stop in Westyron.*

"Westyron?" Arlina said, confused. "Why in Avilyne's hell would I go *there* of all places?"

Because I know how you just love to toy with your enemies before you dispose of them.

Tamina then disappeared, and Arlina frowned.

Westyron? The mostly human-run city of trade and despicable commerce? True, she had once favored the place, but she soon began to hate it once she met the man who controlled the city. *Once* controlled the city, rather.

Arlina found herself liking the suggestion. Would Gavin be there now? Was Tamina offering up the man to be killed just as he did her? Or was there a greater prize in Westyron than Tamina was letting on?

"Fine, sister," Arlina decided. "I'll play your little game, just this once."

———

I stepped outside and found Netira had moved from the cottage steps to the bench in the herb garden where Azrael was grazing. She looked terrible; she must not have gotten any rest.

"You didn't sleep well," she said, echoing my thoughts. I sat beside her. "What in the world have you done to your hands?"

"I don't think any of us have slept, really," I replied while flexing my hands to stretch the tightness of the bandages. "As for my hands...let's just say everyone's entitled to their odd moments."

Netira nodded with understanding. "I once almost rubbed my hands raw after my first kill. I couldn't get the sensation of blood off of my hands no matter how clean they were."

"I've only hunted animals," I said. "Foxes. Oftentimes it was done against my will."

"What you will be hunting now is no different from animals, Artemis. Arlina is the worst of them all," Netira explained. "You deny your dhampir nature the freedom it deserves. Are you ashamed of what you are?"

"Yes."

"I was once too." Netira laughed. "I couldn't understand why I was born a dhampir instead of a full-blood. Like you, I never knew my parents. I was living in the streets of the Dark Fortress, hiding whenever the patrols of the Mistress were about."

"How did you become Arlina's Second?"

"I had to do many things I'm not proud of, Artemis," Netira explained. "It's what happens when you fight for survival. I was found one day by your mother. She took me in and mentored me. Tamina helped find charms and cordials for me to take to hide my heritage from the others of Blackwen City. When she left, I was so angry. She never even said good-bye."

"How long ago was this?" I asked, hoping the inquiry didn't seem rude.

"I'm much older than you think," Netira answered. "We'll just leave it at that when it comes to my age. If you must know a few more facts, then I will reveal that it is true I served the Mistress, your grandmother, for many years before Arlina usurped the throne."

"You could have escaped Arlina's rule."

Netira shook her head. "I love the city more than you could ever know. I've done horrible things in Arlina's service, as has Karesu, but it was a cover so that we could find a way to restore Blackwen City to its former glory. Karesu and I dreamed to love one another out in the open and to live in peace. Just because I grew up in harsh circumstances doesn't mean that the future generations of the Dark Fortress should as well."

She would make a great leader, I thought. *Better than I would.*

"And my mother?"

"I thought nothing more of her after she left," Netira explained. "I felt she abandoned me. Once I heard of her murder, I mourned."

I remembered what Jack told me in the library. "Her spirit visited you, yes?"

Netira blinked, stunned. "So you've figured it out."

"Not exactly," I answered. "Pulled out of my denial is more like it."

"It happens to even the best of us, Artemis," Netira said. "She did visit me. Only once, when I was still in that wretched prison cell."

"She'll return again," I said. "Will you promise to tell me when she comes to you again?"

"As you wish." Netira watched Azrael and sighed. "I feel there is more you wish to ask of me."

"I wanted to ask you about the Ravenwing bloodline, but perhaps you can tell me of it when we're on the journey instead." I took a deep breath. "As you pointed out earlier, I am ashamed of my dhampir nature. I've suppressed it for as long as I can, and I know it's not the wisest of choices. I've paid for it with my diminishing control. I've never met another dhampir before, so I was wondering if maybe..."

"You'd like me to show you how to be a true dhampir?" Netira asked. I nodded. She ran a pale hand through her shoulder-length red hair. "There's no such thing as a proper dhampir, Artemis. However...I will show you how to control the hunger that comes once you unleash your true self."

"There's one more favor."

"Which is?"

"I have no knowledge of the sai. Would you spar with me?" I begged. "Shadow's been teaching me how to fight, but I feel you know more about fighting with the sai than he does."

"More so from the receiving end of the attacks," Netira grumbled. "I'll do what I can."

"Thank you." I stood up from the bench. "And Netira...don't give up hope."

She was confused. "Huh? Why do you say that?"

"I think it's something you needed to hear," I answered. "It's an important thing to hold onto at a time like this."

Callypso was on the path to the cottage when she found what she needed: her own set of dragon jewels. Only Talisa knew that Callypso was once a warrior, in the days when elementals freely roamed Arrygn. She was saddened when she realized the time was before Talisa became Kiare's vassal.

The elemental only had a few curved daggers left in peak condition. She hoped that she could accompany Shadow to this blacksmith of his in Westyron, and she would have the master create a blade with the dragon jewels she earned long ago. Callypso knew she would spill as much blood as the rest of the group on this journey.

She only hoped that Artemis would not succumb to the strange power of her mother's sai.

Irritated that she would have to wear the calf-high leather boots as well as the thick leather gloves from here on out, Callypso reminded herself that it could be worse.

She could have still been in hiding with the rest of her kind, after all.

Well, well, a familiar voice greeted her. *The elemental thinks to return to the path of the warrior.*

Callypso saw the specter, Tamina, in the same black gown that trailed far behind her. Her long brown hair was now in a braid that lay across her bare, pale shoulder.

"What brings you to haunting me now, Tamina?" Callypso asked as she walked past her.

I thought to ask how the purification of my sai was going, Tamina began, *but it seems that both you and the elf mage failed. I warned you that you wouldn't be able to do it.*

"You don't seem like the gloating type, Tamina," Callypso said. "Then again, you *aren't* really Tamina Ravenwing. You're just an angry shell of what she once was."

You still believe that I'm a mere lingering spirit who lost her mind after all these years wandering Arrygn? You naive girl. I thought you were much smarter than this.

"Considering you've come to torment me in particular instead of your daughter,"—Callypso tried to keep calm— "I can only assume you have a message for me. Speak it, then, so that I can return to Talisa's cottage in peace."

I would be careful with that tone, if I were you, Tamina warned. *Those boots and gloves of yours will not protect you from me forever, elemental.*

"I do not cower from threats, specter." Callypso glared. "Speak your message."

If you attempt to separate my daughter from the sai, you will face grave consequences, Tamina explained. *The same consequences will happen should you or the idiot elf mage try to purify them again.*

"You cannot return from the grave, Tamina," Callypso stated. "I will not stop any attempts to purify those weapons."

You'll kill Artemis before she even gets the chance to strike Arlina down.

Tamina disappeared, and Callypso felt the words hit her heart. Somehow, she knew Tamina was telling the truth. Callypso rubbed her chest and looked to the sky.

"I know you all are watching!" Callypso yelled. "Don't you dare let a lingering spirit succeed in creating the greatest imbalance Arrygn will ever know."

<hr>

Callypso didn't return to the cottage until midday, and Talisa didn't return until the early settling of night. The others strategized on what routes to take to Westyron and Blackwen City, as well as what veils were considered safe enough to hide behind now that Talisa had informed us of Lord Celstian's decree of Shadow's eventual status as deserter. Shadow seemed indifferent when Talisa told us what had taken place in the ruins of Ellewynth, but I knew he was suffering inside.

Talisa did manage to find the pouch of dragon jewels Shadow had mentioned to her, but that was the only success she had. She didn't have much time to explore the ruins since she felt it prudent to warn the rest of us about the elven hunting party.

I hated politics. I understood the need for it, but I still hated it.

I hid myself away in my old room and searched for any article of clothing of mine that Jack could have missed once he moved in. If met with success, I prayed they would still fit.

Frowning because Jack had taken over every aspect of my room, I heard a strange noise outside the window; I saw Jack suddenly stumble onto the ground while walking. Leaning out of the window, I watched Azrael stand beside him and nudge his back with a hoof.

"Jack?" I called out. "What mischief have you gotten yourself into now?"

Jack's head slowly moved and searched for the source of my voice. I tried not to chuckle when his earth-covered face finally spotted mine.

"I'm not drunk this time, I swear it!" Jack insisted.

I burst out laughing. "For once, I believe you. Your words aren't slurred, and I'm sure Talisa would have your head on a spike if she found out you'd been drinking."

Jack used Azrael to hoist him from the ground. She snorted into his face, causing some of the dirt to fly off. He swept away more of the earth from his clothes and then found the cause for his stumble: an outstretched tree root.

"Talisa's garden is conspiring to end me," Jack sighed. "Who or what isn't, nowadays?"

"Consider it some sick sense of flattery, Jack," I said. "At least you're being noticed enough for someone to want to end you."

"That's a very morbid point of view, Artemis." Jack shuddered. "Are you turning into a real dhampir on me?"

I frowned. "Shut up."

"Why are you hiding away in *my* room?"

"Where were *you* running off to?"

"I don't have to tell you that," Jack replied with a smug grin on his face.

"Fine! I'll leave you to be attacked by Talisa's herb garden," I yelled, while pretending to move away from the windowsill.

"I was going to say I could just take you to my destination, but since you insist on being sarcastic, I'll just leave you behind," Jack said while turning his back to me.

"I'm not sure this place of yours is special enough to warrant my attention!"

"Then why are you so bent on trying to annoy me if you aren't so curious, hmm?" Jack winked.

I glared at him. "I liked you more when you didn't understand the meaning of cleverness, you jerk."

"I'll be right here waiting for you, my pale bundle of sunshine."

When I joined him, I punched the elf in the arm. I didn't care if the action hurt my hand; he deserved it. "Don't *ever* call me that again."

"Why not?" Jack frowned. "It's not as if Shadow heard it. If the man said such a thing to you, I'm sure you wouldn't punch *him*."

"I can hit you again if you don't start telling me about this little place of yours," I threatened.

"What little place?"

Jack froze as I turned around to see Callypso standing on the steps, amused.

"Jack was going somewhere and said I could come along," I explained, as I enjoyed Jack's sudden burst of nerves.

"Is that so?" Callypso joined us. "You wouldn't object if I came along, would you?"

"N-Not at all, Callypso," Jack answered while trying to straighten his posture.

"Excellent! Then lead the way." Callypso linked my arm into hers.

I heard Jack curse under his breath, and I chuckled. Callypso grinned at me, and I winked back.

"Where did you disappear to earlier, Cally?" I asked.

"Home, of course," she answered, her blond ringlets bouncing with each step we took. Jack walked a few steps ahead of us. "I needed a few provisions of my own."

"Like what? I've never seen you carry anything whenever you've visited me in the past."

"Not all elementals fight with their bare hands, Artemis." Callypso laughed. "I can't rely on using my abilities all the time. I may not be in hiding like the rest of my kinsmen, but neither do I want to give myself away to our enemies."

"The fact that she's coming with us is risky enough, Artemis," Jack chimed in.

"I know that!" I fought the urge to punch his arm again. "I was curious like you. I was just faster in vocalizing it."

Jack flashed a quick glare, and walked even farther ahead of us.

Callypso smiled. "You two are like siblings."

"It feels that way sometimes," I agreed.

"I know where we're going. Jack, you're taking us to the Grove of Kiare's Mirror."

"I am," he replied, not looking back.

"What's that?"

"It's sacred ground to Kiare, the goddess of water," Callypso elaborated. "It's a tool of many uses, including the foretelling of the future. Well, possible futures really." Callypso's attention shifted to Jack. "Why do you feel the need to return there, Jack?"

"The mirror works differently for me," Jack explained. "I have a hunch. I want to see if it'll play out."

"Why bring me then?" I asked.

"The mirror is how I saw your mother's death."

I stopped; Callypso almost tripped at the force of my halt. "Are you going to show me how she died?"

"To be honest, Artemis," Jack began, "I don't know what the mirror will show you. I have my own questions that need answers. I just have a hunch. Since you're with me, it may or may not play out."

"Did you inform Talisa at least?" Callypso asked.

"No, but she has known that when I disappear from the cottage around this time of night, I'm at the grove," Jack explained. "Right now, she has her hands full with Netira and Shadow. I have no desire to get any head-slaps today for interrupting her."

Callypso paused for a moment, and then nodded. "Yes, I suppose that is wise enough on your part."

"Ah. We've made it." Jack stopped in front of a large ash tree.

I was confused. "We have?"

"Still unfamiliar with the veils, Artemis?" Callypso asked.

I nodded. "During my time in Ellewynth there was never a time to escape to the veils."

Not until now.

"This will be a more interesting event for you," Callypso said, as we both watched Jack shut his eyes when his palm reached the bark of the ash tree.

"What's he doing?" I whispered.

"Opening the gateway," Callypso whispered back.

Once I did so, I realized we weren't in the forest anymore.

We were in a small clearing surrounded by oak trees, and I was stunned at the sight of the large rock wall with a well sitting at the center. When we walked closer to it, I realized the well was made of small multi-colored pebbles, giving the illusion of rolling waves.

I felt power in this clearing, and I was in awe of the beauty that surrounded us. I felt Callypso move away, and Jack patted my back.

"My jaw was hanging the first time I came here," Jack recalled. "Talisa snapped at me, of course. Said it was rude to gawk."

"That is definitely something Talisa would say." I laughed.

Jack led me to the edge of the well, and all three of us placed our hands on the rim. I felt a pleasant energy from the well, like small rippling waves. Callypso's eyes were shut, and Jack stared with deep intent into the water.

He held a hand over mine, and I raised an eyebrow.

"I need something from you," Jack said, while keeping his eyes on the water.

"What is it?"

He pulled out a thin, small knife from his back and held out a palm. "Every time I needed to use the mirror, I had to pay tribute. It's asking for a tribute from you this time."

"How do you even know this?"

"It is because he is a mage," Callypso explained. "Mages are different from others when it comes to the workings of magic. There is always a price that needs to be paid for them."

"So in this case, you need my blood?" I asked.

"So it seems," Jack nodded. "I'm only going to cut your digit. A few drops will suffice."

"All right."

Jack cut into my pointer finger, and I felt a sting; my hands were still healing from my stunt earlier this morning. He held my hand over the water of the well and pushed the skin together so that a few drops fell within. We all watched the droplets swirl in the water, and I saw something happening. I recognized the faces that formed after my blood disappeared.

I saw Jack in the mirror, but his hair was cropped short, and it was black. I heard him choke when Jack realized who he was staring at.

He wore the strange leather clothing that I saw the full-bloods who escorted Netira to the Woodland Realm wear, and he had a sword in each hand. Callypso was there with him, also wearing the strange leather clothing. Her hair was a deep blood red, like that of the full-bloods. They were both bloodied and fatigued, but they kept on running to this large tower made of steel. The skies were covered in darkness.

This was Blackwen City, the Dark Fortress.

What's going on here? I thought as we continued to watch.

The view shifted and now showed Netira, who was in a heated battle with several full-bloods. It looked as if she was in a prison; there were cells and chains everywhere. Talisa was with her, and she too wore the odd clothing. She was carrying someone I did not recognize—a male with long black hair and a silver cross earring hung in his right earlobe. He looked severely injured, but managed to keep conscious.

Was this Karesu, the vampire mage and Netira's lover?

Before I could study him further, the image changed once more. I saw myself and Shadow, and we fought full-bloods in a strange place. My hair was no longer a dark brown, but completely red. I was shocked to see that I was in the true dhampir form: silver irises, fangs elongated, and black leathery wings fully extended from my back. Shadow's hair was a similar red to mine; he looked as if he was one of the full-bloods.

I somehow found myself liking the look, and I then quickly erased the thought from my head.

"I will never look at Shadow the same way again," Jack snorted.

"Jack, keep silent," Callypso scolded.

I watched how well both Shadow and I worked while fighting together; it seemed that all the training sessions had paid off. The idea of having control while in the dhampir state was comforting as well; there was hope for me yet.

We ran up a long, spiraling staircase, and we all jumped when we heard a loud, piercing blast erupt from the mirror.

I shuddered as I remembered the sound—it matched the one from Arlina's pistol.

Jack was horrified. "That flintlock pistol again…"

Callypso held a hand to her chest.

I was puzzled.

"A flintlock pistol?" I asked.

"Yes," Jack answered. "It is a weapon used by merchants and sailors. We should keep watching, Artemis. I'll elaborate more once the vision is over."

I saw Shadow push me against the wall of the stairwell when more of the horrifying sounds exploded from the flintlock pistol of the unseen assailant.

"I'm going to break my promise, Artemis," Shadow said, looking solemn. "You're going to have to go to the top of the tower without me."

"I'm not leaving you behind!" I heard myself yell.

"You're going to have to," he insisted. "I need to take care of this bastard. *You* have to keep going. I swear I will find you when my fight is over."

"Shadow, don't do this."

The image began to shift; I felt my heart do a violent flip.

"Goddesses," I heard Callypso whisper.

Who was Shadow planning on fighting? I wondered, and I had a flashback of that damned dream.

I tried to get rid of the images from the dream as the mirror continued to show us more. I saw myself in a strange chamber filled with large onyx statues of women. In the center was a large black marble throne, and on the walls were jutted torchlights. In my hands were Mother's sai, and I noticed the jewels within the hilt were brighter than I recalled.

"Come out, Arlina!" I heard myself yell. "You've run from me long enough!"

There was silence. I saw annoyance form on my face. "I will admit the stunt you pulled in the tavern was unexpected, yet impressive. But why do you continue to hide when what you seek is finally within your grasp?"

I heard the flintlock pistol go off and watched as I rolled away. I saw the same woman who haunted my dreams, the same woman with the cold, gray eyes who fought my mother, the same woman who tried to kill me in Ellewynth, step from behind the throne and flash a devious smile.

"The filthy half-breed thinks to mock me in my own audience chamber," Arlina said, the thin and razor-sharp heels of her boots clicking with each step she took. "I'll have to show you what it means to disrespect me."

The image disappeared with another deafening bang, and the water stilled. I backed away from the well.

"Artemis?" I heard Callypso call.

"Is that what will happen when we get to Blackwen City?" I asked, avoiding eye contact.

"It's a possible future," Jack said. "That's the function of the mirror. They don't always come to pass."

"What's wrong, Artemis?" Callypso asked. "You've paled...more so now than you had during the visions."

"I just saw something that I hoped to never see again," I admitted. "I dreamt this morning of someone dear to me dying, and there was nothing I could do to stop it."

"Who was it?" Jack inquired.

I shook my head in refusal.

"Artemis?" Callypso asked once more. "Who did you see die?"

"It was only a dream," I said to myself, while rubbing my arms to rid them of the goose bumps that formed. "Only a dream..."

"Artemis, something in that vision triggered whatever image you're seeing now." Jack tried to have me look at him. "Who did you see die in your dream?"

I finally looked at him as the tears blurred my vision. Jack was taken aback and tried to apologize, but I waved him off.

"Shadow," I answered.

22

The walk back to the cottage was a silent one. Jack and Callypso were stunned when they heard the details about my dreams. They tried to dismiss it, but they knew I wouldn't. Those two of all people knew better than to label a dream as imagination.

Callypso held onto my arm in the effort to give me some comfort. I kept my focus on the steps I took along the earth. Jack was walking ahead of us again.

"You know," Jack began, "while I don't doubt that we will be encountering similar circumstances in Blackwen City, I don't think it'll turn out the way the mirror showed us."

"Why do you say that?" Callypso asked, intrigued.

"For one, none of us would leave Artemis alone in that tower, least of all Shadow," Jack responded. "Second...my hair will *never* be like that."

Callypso and I burst out laughing.

"I'm serious!" Jack yelled. "I like my hair the way it is!"

"I thought the color suited you," Callypso said. "Made you look like a true mage."

"Well, I guess I could survive with the color..." Jack muttered. "But it was *short!*"

"It's only a possible future, Jack," I chimed in. "Remember?"

"Yeah," he replied, unconvinced. Jack fell back in his step and stood to my other side. "Shadow's a tough man to kill, you know. He's already survived a ton of wars."

"I know."

"Does that explain the hand debacle?" he asked, pointing to my bandaged hands. "Tried to get rid of the feeling of his blood on your hands?"

I nodded. "It's part of the reason, yes."

"I'm sorry, Artemis." Jack patted my back. "I had a hunch that I thought would play out, and it didn't happen. I had the feeling you were going to come with me to the grove before we left and thought maybe the mirror would show another memory of the past, not a possible future."

"Why did it show us different scenes for a possible future?" I asked.

Jack shrugged. "I wish I knew."

"Kiare's Mirror is tricky that way," Callypso added. "I think perhaps the mirror was trying to quell the fear of you not holding up your end of the fighting."

"That's a nice way of looking at it, Callypso," I began, "but I don't think that was the mirror's intention. What we saw…it was a warning."

"A warning of what?" Callypso wondered.

"A warning that Arlina might not be our only enemy to worry about once we reach Blackwen City. This…accomplice…is one who also has a flintlock pistol, and one who Shadow seems to have a history with."

"I don't understand why someone like Arlina would have need of that weapon." Callypso frowned. "It doesn't suit the style she loves to use."

"But at least we know she still has it. Possible future or not," Jack pointed out.

"And we also know that we can survive the wounds it'll give," I added. "Netira is proof enough."

"It's still a dangerous weapon, Artemis," Callypso warned. "You'll have to use caution."

"Oddly enough, the pistol is not my main concern," I admitted.

"What is?" Jack asked.

"The identity of this other enemy," I answered. "Who is it?"

Jack sighed. "If it's true that we will have another enemy as bad as Arlina, then we're bound to find out once we go on our journey."

"Until that should happen, let us keep our focus on the first part of the journey, which is Westyron. That'll be a unique experience in itself." Callypso chimed in.

"So I keep hearing."

Netira was listening to Talisa and Shadow speak about the trip to Blackwen City. She still wished they didn't have to stop in Westyron. She did not like humans, and the humans of that city enjoyed persecuting "outsiders"—their term for anyone not of their race.

Netira excused herself once she felt odd pains in her chest. She knew Talisa and Shadow noticed the strange behavior, but they hadn't inquired about it. She was thankful for that.

Netira settled into her little sleeping space of the main room and kept rubbing her chest in the hopes of ridding herself of the pain.

What in Avilyne's hell is going on? Netira thought as she shut her eyes. *Karesu, what are they doing to you?*

"Karesu, I need a hand up here."

Karesu jumped at the sound of his grandmother's voice, and then put down an aged tome next to a stack of old parchment filled with his notes. It had been a few decades since he was first brought to his grandmother's study. Since then, Karesu never once regretted the decision of committing to his mage heritage.

Tying his hair back with a violet ribbon, he felt the coolness of his silver cross earring along his arm. Ever since the creation of the charm, the spirits were kept at bay, and he was able to rest peacefully again.

Making his way to the storefront, Karesu stopped short when he saw whom his grandmother was speaking to—the woman had warm violet eyes, and her long dark brown hair was plaited into a braid that hung over her shoulder.

Their visitor was Tamina Ravenwing, the eldest daughter of Blackwen's Mistress.

Karesu bowed and heard a scoff in response.

"That is never necessary," he heard Tamina say.

"Lady Ravenwing, he's a proper boy," Karesu's grandmother explained. "We show respect where it's due."

"I thank you, Minerva." Tamina smiled. "But again, none of it is necessary. I'm not a formal person, and we're not in City Tower."

"What can we help you with?" Karesu asked.

Minerva patted her grandson's back. "I need you to stay at the counter in case someone comes in and requires your assistance. Tamina Ravenwing and I have private business to attend to."

"Yes, Grandmother," Karesu said, suddenly noticing the girl who stood behind Tamina.

"You can entertain one another," Tamina suggested as she followed Minerva to the back of the apothecary.

Karesu studied the girl and deduced she was of a similar age to him. Her hair was dark brown and rested atop her shoulders. Her eyes matched the color of her hair, and he felt something different about her presence.

She was a vampire, yes…but there was something amiss in her aura that no other full-blood he'd encountered had.

"What are you looking at?" she snapped.

"Tamina is ordering something special for you, is she not?" Karesu questioned, intrigued by the girl who stood before him.

"What's it to you?"

"Tamina only does that when she's helping someone," Karesu explained. "Even from here, I can sense something different in you."

The girl's eyes widened. "You're like the older one? Some sort of wizard?"

"A mage," Karesu corrected. "Not as if anyone else in the city really believes in that sort of thing anyways."

"You'd be surprised," the girl said, now looking at the shelves of multi-colored glass vials. "I don't suppose…I don't suppose you have anything that can change the color of your hair, do you?"

"Why would you want to do that?" Karesu frowned.

Dark brown hair was a rare trait in Blackwen City, and he felt the color suited her well.

"Tell me,"—the girl folded her arms— "what's the difference you sense in me?"

"To be honest, I cannot explain," Karesu admitted. "Your aura is different from any full-blood I've ever encountered."

"It's...it's what Tamina is trying to help me with," the girl explained. "If she doesn't, I'll have to leave the city."

That's when it hit Karesu. The difference in her aura...she was a half-breed.

"You're a dhampir, aren't you?"

The girl froze. "You figured that out just from what I said?"

"I'm not a simpleton, but it does take me some time to solve mysteries." Karesu chuckled. "I'm sure there is more to you than that."

Her gaze narrowed. "I know that tone."

Karesu was puzzled. "What tone?"

"You're flirting." She wagged a finger in warning. "Don't even think about it."

Karesu frowned. "I don't flirt."

"That's what all males say." She sighed. "Look, if you and your grandmother can help me hide my dhampir heritage, then I would be more than grateful to you both. Don't start expecting that you'll get any more than that."

"Goddesses! Paranoid much?" Karesu laughed. "I apologize if it seemed I was making a pass at you. I was only stating what I felt to be a fact. If it offends you, then I would suggest you learn how to analyze things before you speak."

"Rude too." The girl flashed a smirk. "Typical."

Karesu rubbed his temples. As fascinating as the girl was, he wasn't pleased at the headache that now plagued him.

"If you're looking to alter the color of your hair," Karesu began, "and I can guess that you'd like it on a permanent basis, then no, we do not have anything like that."

"Nothing even on a temporary basis?"

"Temporary, yes," Karesu answered. "Permanent, however...you'll have to give me a few days."

"I can't pay you," the girl said, her expression solemn. "Forget that I mentioned it. Tamina's already doing enough for me; I can't ask her for more."

"It's no trouble, and you won't have to pay me."

The girl raised an eyebrow. "What's the catch?"

"Are you always so mistrusting of others?" Karesu asked, amazed at the annoyance he felt.

"I'm surprised you aren't the same considering your own situation," the girl answered. "Mages aren't welcome company here either."

"Yet here you are, standing in the store that's created by one," Karesu argued.

The girl giggled. "Calm down. I'm just stating a fact, as you put it earlier."

Karesu blinked at her. She was teasing him.

"Oh goddesses, Karesu!" he heard his grandmother exclaim once he felt her presence beside him. "Why are you so red?"

"I don't think he's used to someone challenging him," the girl said as her smile widened.

"I was just taken aback by someone...odd," Karesu answered, as he met a weird stare from his grandmother.

Tamina chuckled. She returned to the girl's side. "Netira, we should be on our way."

The girl glanced at Tamina and nodded.

"We shall see you in a few days, Tamina Ravenwing," Minerva said with a small bow. "The charm will be done by then."

"Excellent."

Tamina and Netira left the store, and Karesu was confused at the emotions he then felt. His grandmother chuckled.

"You were intrigued by the dhampir, weren't you?" Minerva asked.

"Strangely so."

"It's a shame when people of the city are persecuted because of their background." Minerva sighed as she rubbed her grandson's shoulder.

"I've never met a dhampir before," Karesu realized. "I always assumed the moment a dhampir was born in Blackwen City, the mother and the child were forced into exile. I thought that was the custom."

"That's...that's putting it in nicer terms, my darling," his grandmother said, her tone dark. "Those of her kind...they're usually killed the moment they take their first breath. The mother would share the fate soon after."

Karesu was horrified. "How did Netira escape that fate?"

"I'm not sure," his grandmother answered. "But I won't give someone a chance to continue the senseless murder. Dhampirs should be given a chance to live as well."

Our first stop was at a veil Talisa and Shadow had used back in the earlier war years. Apparently Tamina used it as well, so there was the promise of her clothing waiting for me and Netira to take.

The feel of Mother's sai were strange as the jeweled hilts stuck out from the edges of my boots. The energy from the dragon jewels was prominent whenever I touched the weapons, and I wondered if I was somehow storing my own energy within them. If they were still indeed connected to the specter, I wasn't sure if I wanted to know how it all affected her.

Needless to say, Callypso kept her distance from me even with her thick gloves and boots.

Shadow kept beside Azrael, who was clearly annoyed from having been turned from a warhorse into a pack mule. Jack had packed away more books from Talisa's library than any of us anticipated, so the mare had the misfortune of hauling them along with the other supplies Talisa felt it prudent to take. Shadow often whispered to Azrael in Elvish, and I could only assume he was showering her with promises of freedom in due time. At least her wound was better. She was certainly special...no other horse would heal as fast.

Shadow glanced in my direction now and then, and I could only flash a small smile in return. I could not stop the flashbacks of both the dream and the vision from Kiare's Mirror. Jack, Callypso, and I kept the events of that visit to ourselves; we didn't want any more potential issues brought to light concerning the already large list of problems we had. It sounded hypocritical since I demanded that everyone be open to one another, but at this point...I accepted that there would always be secrets.

When we reached the veils of the "safe house," I heard Shadow's sigh of relief. I didn't blame him, as I too wanted better-fitting clothes. Talisa was a bit larger than I was in build, and the extra loose cloth made me tighten the hold of my cloak for the fear that the wind would blow the garb off of me.

"Remember, we take what we need and then make haste," Talisa explained. "By now, Lord Celstian has sent out the hunting party for Shadow. I want to put as much distance between us as possible."

"I suppose crippling them is out of the question." Netira frowned. She watched the magic of the veil work and transport us to a clearing with a small wooden house complete with a stone well.

"They're only following orders," Shadow said, almost sad. "I won't have them killed on my account. We shall deal with them when the need arises, and without bloodshed."

"I shall wait out here," Callypso explained, standing beside Azrael while stroking her white mane. "I have all that I need."

"I'll stay here with you, Callypso," Jack said, while taking a few books from Azrael's back. "I don't need anything else either."

Shadow and I looked at one another and smirked, for we knew Jack would keep close to the elemental as much as possible. Netira shrugged and followed Talisa's lead into the house. Shadow and I did the same.

Talisa closed the door of the house, and the dust flew behind us. I coughed. Shadow waved a hand to move the dust clouds from his face, and Netira hid her face beneath her arms until the cloud subsided.

"Apologies for the lack of warning." Talisa used her pointed hat to fan the dust cloud away. "It has been a long time since this veil has been used."

"That's an understatement." I looked at the knick-knacks that lined the shelves and tables. "Just when was the last time you were here?"

"Before you were born, Artemis," Shadow answered while moving past me.

"Artemis, Netira, you'll find some of Tamina's old things here in this room." Talisa pointed to a small room to her left. "Don't take too long."

Netira and I went into the room and found two large trunks of my mother's clothing and other possessions. Thankfully Mother's clothing was better fitting for the both of us. Netira was also bigger than me in build, but the borrowed clothes from Talisa were still loose on her. While Talisa's garb hung on me, they gave Netira a disheveled appearance.

I found several ribbons I assumed Mother used for her hair and snagged a few for myself. Netira managed to find some daggers and spread them out on the floor. Despite not having being used for so long, there was no sign of rust on the blades.

"I'd hate to think what Tamina's better weapons were if she left these here," Netira commented while inspecting them. "I'd love to meet the one who made the daggers. I've never heard of rust-proof blades."

"At least they're safe enough for someone else to use," I noted. Netira was confused, and I tapped on the jewels from one sai's hilt. "They don't have any dragon jewels."

"Ah. Well, you should take one," Netira suggested. She picked a dagger half the length of my forearm with a thin enough blade so that I could conceal it with ease. "This one should work well enough for a beginner like you."

"I can use a dagger, Netira." I chuckled.

"You'll be an actual threat once you and I begin to spar. You'll lose the hesitation to take another's life by the time I'm done training you." She ignored my flinch and settled on two daggers for her own use. "Come. We don't want to keep Talisa and Shadow waiting."

I followed Netira out of the room, and we spotted Talisa with a large satchel in her hands.

"More healing supplies," Talisa explained when she noticed us staring at it. "And a few toys that don't require an explanation."

"Let's just say that anyone who tries to sneak into our camp will suffer severe consequences...it will make them wish they were dead," Shadow added as he entered the main room.

He had changed and looked much more comfortable than earlier. He also had strapped on a large leather quiver stocked with arrows, and held an elegant bow with what appeared to be a blade attached to one of its ends. "An old gift."

"That's the case with many of your weapons," I teased.

Shadow grinned. "It's how things work when you're kin to an Elder."

"I'm actually intrigued about these 'toys' you've mentioned, Talisa," Netira said. "I don't suppose there are herbs in there that give off the symptoms of plagues, hmm?"

Talisa winked. "I'll leave it up to your imagination."

"It is rather vast," Netira teased.

"Then think of the most vile way to die, and it still would not come close to what I have in my bag of tricks," Talisa said.

"This is why it's always better to befriend witches than to anger them," Shadow whispered to me as we left the safe house.

"Watching Talisa's interactions with Jack reinforced the idea enough."

Jack and Callypso stopped reading the books that were left open on the grass in front of them once we came out, and it didn't take long before we were ready to return to the forest of the Woodland Realm.

"If we follow the route that was agreed upon last night and we do not encounter any trouble, then we should reach Westyron within five nights' time," Talisa explained as we all followed her lead. "Any longer, and what minimal supplies we have left will be depleted faster than we can curse all of the goddesses."

"I do not worry for food," Netira said as her irises shifted to silver. Her wings stretched to full length as she removed her cloak. "I'm a capable hunter, and I'm sure Shadow is as well."

"You're going to hunt *now*?" Jack asked.

"If I am going to be useful to you, yes," Netira answered. She glanced at me. "Will you come, Artemis?"

I felt all eyes shift to me. I asked for her help, I know I did…but I couldn't allow the dhampir its freedom yet. I wanted a little more time of being plain ol' Artemis instead of Artemis Ravenwing, the dhampir and rightful Mistress of Blackwen.

Goddesses, I didn't want to think about being a ruler.

"No," I refused.

"I'll allow the refusal just this once," Netira warned. "The next time, I will not be so understanding. You asked for my help, and I intend to give it. You cannot deny who you are forever."

She then disappeared to hunt, and I saw Jack shudder.

"I'm glad she's on our side," Jack muttered. His attention shifted to me. "You know, I can't even remember the last time I saw you shift into dhampir mode."

I sighed. "Be grateful for that. The blackouts…I wonder if anyone saw me in that form."

"We'll be seeing that form soon enough," Shadow said.

I looked to the sky. "You all should keep your distance from me when it does happen. Whatever control I thought I had…it was all a lie."

28

Arlina didn't bother to hide herself with a cloak once she stepped onto the cobblestone streets of Westyron. Each human she passed cowered and moved aside when they encountered her. Arlina knew there were others of her kind here, as well as other "outsiders," but they were situated deeper within the merchant port city.

Latos and two others of her retinue accompanied her, as she had sent the rest of her remaining war party from the Woodland Realm back to Blackwen City. She wanted the traitor mage back at the Dark Fortress so that once he awoke he would find himself in the worst of the prison cells. Arlina had much she wanted to do to Karesu, and she was sure the pleasure it would bring would rival the satisfaction of finding Gavin again.

She *knew* he had to still be here; he had no other home. After what Arlina did to him that night…

"Mistress, where do you lead us?" Latos asked, interrupting her train of thought.

Arlina didn't bother to look at her subordinate. When she heard how Latos had acquired his injuries, she couldn't even glance at the imbecile. Latos was a capable enough warrior to hold his own against Shadow of Ellewynth, and he should have been able to kill the damned elf.

Arlina knew there was still some use left in him, however, hence the decision to keep him close for their little trip to Westyron.

She felt Latos' embarrassment for his loss deepen as her silence continued, and she felt that that alone earned him the privilege of an answer. Arlina stopped the others when she spotted a large tavern, the White Viper. It was as…charming…as she remembered, with its lively music hurting her ears and the smell of drunks and other pitiful lowborns stacked within the boarded structure wafting her way.

"I lead us here, Latos," Arlina said. "The three of you will stay out here. You're welcome to any straggling drunkards. It would be doing this disgusting city a service."

Latos and the others bowed their heads and stood watch as she entered the tavern. There were wenches digging into the pockets of those too drunk to move themselves off the floor. Several of the humans who sat at the bar watched her closely as she moved to an open spot and demanded wine. The bartender raised an eyebrow at her and eventually gave her a glass of deep red wine along with a small razor blade.

"I seen enough of yer kind in this here tavern to know ya want more than ya ask fer," the bartender said. He motioned his pudgy head to his right and pointed out a drunkard she could pawn blood off of. "Take more than ya need, and I ain't afraid to call the man upstairs, ya hear?"

Arlina smiled as she took the blade and cut into the now unconscious man's wrist. The blood droplets seeped into her wineglass with scraggly ripples. "On the contrary, sir, I hope that you will indeed call on him. He and I are old friends."

The bartender shook his head and walked away as she sipped the blood mixed with wine. Arlina was amazed, as the wine was actually succulent. The blood of the drunkard was enough to keep her satisfied for the evening. She would have to find out more about this wine.

It was rare to find something of the humans, besides their blood, to be considered "enjoyable."

A fight broke out. One of the humans was thrown into Arlina's side, causing her to drop her wine glass. It grew silent once she grabbed the man and hauled him onto the bar, her now drawn sai drawing blood from his neck.

She enjoyed the human's squirms; it made her bloodlust rise.

"I rather enjoyed my wine, cattle," Arlina hissed. "Perhaps your blood will compensate for it."

The click of a flintlock pistol drew Arlina's attention away from the human she had pinned and toward the bartender.

"Let 'em go, vampire," the bartender demanded.

"Or what? You'll shoot me?" Arlina was amused that the man couldn't even steady his hand. She understood then that he must have used the pistol only once or twice. "Do you have *any* idea what I'm capable of, human?"

"Arlina, calm yourself." Arlina felt her grin widen as she recognized the voice. "Let the imbecile go and step away from the bar."

Arlina turned around to see the one she had sought out: Gavin.

His black hair was much longer now, tied back with a dark red ribbon. His hazel eyes glared at her, and she noted he was wearing fashions similar to the full-bloods of Blackwen City.

How perfect.

"Gavin!" Arlina greeted him as she released the human. She raised her arms as if she was welcoming his presence. "How long has it been, brother?"

"Not long enough." Gavin frowned. "I am *not* your brother."

"Oh, but you are, Gavin." Arlina walked beside him and clapped his shoulder. "You may no longer be my brother-in-law, seeing as how my sister is rotting away in Avilyne's hell, but you *are* my brother by other means."

"Aerios blow you, not here!" Gavin spat. Gavin looked to his bartender. "Take care of the mess and close up for the evening."

"Y-Yes sir," the bartender said as he put away his flintlock pistol and began to throw the drunkards out.

Gavin motioned for Arlina to follow him and led her to one of the upstairs rooms, seemingly an office. She noticed the windows were boarded up, and Arlina couldn't help but smirk.

"I see someone didn't appreciate the gift I bestowed them." Arlina ran a hand through her short red hair. "That's not very nice, you know."

Gavin turned around, and his irises shifted to a deep red. "I should have known that you were never one for keeping your word! You were a deceptive bitch then, and you're still one now."

"I saw an opportunity and couldn't let it pass me by." Arlina shrugged. "You really should be thanking me, Gavin. You can run Westyron for as long as you desire."

"I just wanted to return to Westyron without having any more dealings with you damned Ravenwing women!" Gavin snapped. "I lost *everything* that night! You just had to add to it by turning me into one of you."

Arlina smiled. "You should have known it was coming, Gavin. You *were* bedding a full-blood, after all. I'm sure you would have enjoyed the process if Tamina had turned you."

Gavin folded his arms. "What in Avilyne's hell are you doing here, Arlina? Last I heard, you despised Westyron."

"I came to see how you were doing."

Gavin snorted. "I won't ask you again, woman."

"Always so serious!" Arlina frowned. Gavin's expression stayed the same, and she sighed in resignation. "Fine. I felt compelled to return to this poor excuse for a city. I have a hunch that someone we have in common will be stopping by here soon."

"Oh?" Gavin asked, intrigued. "And who might this be?"

"Your daughter."

Gavin froze. "Artemis is dead."

"You're still telling yourself that your daughter's soul was destroyed once you found out she was born a dhampir?" Arlina rolled her eyes. "Goddesses, you were such a pitiful human then. I hoped vampirism would have smartened you up a bit, but it seems I was wrong."

Gavin pounded the wooden desk he leaned against with a fist. "Artemis is *dead.*"

"Half-dead, technically," Arlina corrected. "Unfortunately for us, she lives. Turns out she's been hiding with the elves all this time."

"I thought you disposed of her as well as Tamina." Gavin tapped his fingers on the wood, irritated. "How'd you let an infant escape you?"

"If I remember correctly, *you* couldn't even dispose of those two. Don't you of all people dare to accuse me of failure!"

Gavin swore as he began to pace the office. "Will she be alone?"

"Hardly. She escaped me in Ellewynth, but I will not let that happen again. I'll anticipate her having help this time. I'm sure Shadow of Ellewynth will be one of those who will." Arlina felt the atmosphere grow cold, and she enjoyed the true anger that formed on Gavin's face.

"My, my. And here I thought the mention of your still-living daughter brought out such emotion from you."

"That prick still lives?"

"Yes. He is blessed by the goddesses themselves, it seems. Shadow returned from yet another war with the dragons with all of his limbs intact."

"If he comes into my city, he won't escape with his life," Gavin promised, while turning his back on Arlina.

"Fair enough." Arlina shrugged. "I only want the dhampir brat anyways."

"You are a clever one, I do have to say." Gavin laughed. "You knew I never wanted any dealings with you, and yet here you are, enticing me with an offer I just can't refuse."

"Believe me, Gavin, I still very much despise you," Arlina informed him. "Nonetheless, you were always one of my favorite toys. And so useful! You really were wasted as a human."

"I enjoyed my humanity," Gavin growled. "You stole that from me."

"Would you prefer if I ended your life?" Arlina asked, growing tired of the man's whining. "There's no other cure."

"No," Gavin replied. "I've accepted this curse you threw on me."

"Then shut up." Arlina rubbed her temples. "I can't stand men who whine."

"And I can't stand power-hungry bitches," Gavin retorted. He faced her once more, a smile now growing on his lips. "I suppose just this once I will ignore that fact."

"You will fight with me?"

"I want Shadow," Gavin explained. "What you do with Artemis is up to you. Once they enter my city, the fun can begin."

"Excellent!" Arlina beamed. "In the meantime, there is one more thing you can do for me."

Gavin raised an eyebrow, wary. "And what would that be?"

"You can tell me about the wine your bar serves."

I felt my body ache when I fell to the ground again. Netira crouched above me, with one thick twig against my neck and another poking into my chest. She moved only when I yielded.

"You're learning, but not fast enough." Netira sighed. "You're over-thinking your attacks."

"She does get distracted easily," Jack teased as he leafed through another page of the tomes he'd brought along.

"I wouldn't talk, Jack," I grumbled. "When was the last time *you* sparred with anyone, anyways?"

"Verbally? Quite recently," Jack replied. He laughed when I glared, and he marked a page before shutting it. "Very well, I accept your challenge."

I threw him my own pair of thick wooden twigs, and he raised an eyebrow.

"What?" I asked, feigning innocence. "You thought I was asking you to spar with *me?*"

"Evil woman," Jack muttered. "Be gentle with me, Netira."

Netira chuckled. "You should know that whenever someone tells me that, I only hit them harder."

I saw Jack gulp as she lunged toward him. I was impressed when he parried several of her blows. He even managed to dodge one of her attacks with a side step, and landed a hit to her back.

Jack beamed. "I told you I picked up a few things while staying at Talisa's."

Netira came at him again and knocked him off his feet. She pinned him to the ground just as she had done with me. I laughed and walked over to the two.

"Yes, so I've noticed," I teased.

"Never take your attention off of your opponent," Netira instructed as she helped Jack to his feet. "You'll end up dead before you can fully develop into your mage gift."

Jack stiffened at the mention of the mage gift. "I'm not sure I want to do that."

"Karesu was the same way once," Netira explained. She motioned for me to return for another spar. "Once he accepted his gift, he used it to bring much good into the world."

"He worked for Arlina," Jack reminded her.

"I did too, Jack," Netira said. "I don't excuse the evil I helped create. I did it because it brought me higher in Arlina's ranks, therefore bringing me closer to her. Unfortunately, the best laid plans are the first to fail."

"That's the truth."

Everyone turned and saw Shadow standing behind us, smiling while holding a pair of swords.

"Joining the festivities?" Netira asked.

"Naturally," Shadow answered. "Someone has to make sure Artemis keeps up her swordplay. It's best for one of her rank to learn as many weapon styles as possible."

I wished I were back in the days when I didn't know I came from nobility.

"Now *this* I have to see." Jack returned to his spot from earlier. "I've wondered if you had improved in that area."

Netira stepped aside and moved to sit beside Jack. "I'm sure Artemis is capable enough to wield a sword. She's surprised me so far."

"Remember when I said that she gets distracted easily?" Jack said. "That'll happen more now."

"I *can* hear you, you know," I said, taking one of the swords Shadow held out.

"Don't worry, Artemis." Shadow took a stance. "Jack's next."

"Wait, what?" Jack sputtered. "What's that supposed to mean?"

"It means that I will be teaching you swordplay as well," Shadow explained. "I'd rather be safe than sorry. You should not rely solely on the magic you've just begun to control."

"I don't think it's a good idea to trust me with a sword!" Jack whined.

"Don't be such a youngling," Netira scolded. "I'll teach you how to properly wield those daggers of yours as well. *I'd* feel safer that way."

Jack hung his head in shame while the rest of us laughed. I took my own stance before the lesson with Shadow started. Inside I groaned, for now I knew he wasn't going to hold back.

Talisa and Callypso circled the camp with the satchel Talisa brought from the safe house, and they dug little holes to hide the "special" herbs that would harm any who dared attack their camp. Talisa stopped once she heard someone approach, and she relaxed when it was only Shadow.

"Ah. I see the traps have been set already," Shadow said, taking care to watch where he stepped.

"Where are the others?" Callypso asked, taking a seat by the fire.

"They went to find some water for us," Shadow answered. "The sparring sessions lasted longer than we expected."

"How is Artemis progressing?" Talisa inquired.

"She's doing well…for a beginner," Shadow replied. "The only time we'll know for certain is when she goes into battle." Shadow rubbed his brow, his green eyes showing fatigue. "Somehow I can't help but feel that we will find trouble in Westyron, but we can't put off the trip."

Talisa sighed. "I know."

"Did she spar with the sai?" Callypso inquired.

"No. She's learning their fighting style from Netira, but Artemis has yet to actually fight with them."

"That is wise then." Callypso breathed a sigh of relief.

"You still believe they're linked to Tamina?" Shadow asked.

"I *know* they are," Callypso insisted. A cool breeze picked up, and both Shadow and Talisa watched her. "Apologies. I'm just…I'm a little anxious."

"We all are," Shadow said.

Talisa joined Callypso by the fire. She removed her dark blue pointed hat, and slowly plaited her long, white-streaked black hair.

"Shadow…" Talisa began. "Do you…you don't think *he* is still in Westyron, right? After all these years, do you think he returned there?"

Shadow stiffened. "That *is* his home. Perhaps he is."

"Who are you two talking about?" Callypso asked, puzzled.

Talisa stared into the fire, the glow of the embers shifting colors along her face. "We speak of Gavin. He is someone we once knew long ago."

"From the sound of it, he was someone you both didn't get along with," Callypso deduced.

"Gavin is Artemis' father," Shadow elaborated. "Tamina and he had a rather…well, to put it simply, a hasty love affair that led to marriage and then—"

"And then everything fell apart," Talisa cut him off. "To make a long story short, we only know that once he learned the truth behind the heritage of both Tamina and Artemis, he tried to kill them. Obviously, he failed. Shadow and I tried to explain to Tamina the kind of man he was before, but when you're in love with someone…you care only what *you* think."

"Oh goddesses…" Callypso gasped. "This man is still alive today?"

"He'll have aged, as he is human," Shadow said. "*If* he still lives, of course."

"Don't fool yourself, Shadow." Talisa frowned. "Gavin is too stubborn to die."

"You should tell Artemis," Callypso urged. Talisa and Shadow were silent. "You can't mean to be tight-lipped on the matter! Look what happened when both of you failed to mention Arlina to her! Ellewynth was destroyed because Arlina learned about her! Artemis should at least know the truth that her father could still be alive and in Westyron!"

"Artemis already has much on her mind," Talisa explained. "Would you have the girl lose her focus at the discovery of one parent still being alive? He tried to kill her, Cally."

Callypso glared. "If neither of you will tell her before the first of us take the evening watch, believe me when I say that *I* will inform her. Choose wisely."

Talisa and Shadow watched as Callypso disappeared into the one tent Talisa brought as a precaution for ill weather.

"She is right, Talisa," Shadow sighed. "We've kept enough from her already."

"*You* were the one who emphasized how important it was to keep her ignorant of the truth," Talisa reminded him. "For the sake of a clean slate, you said…for the sake of her sanity."

"And it backfired," Shadow recalled. "I won't lose her, Talisa. Not over this."

"Then I take it you'll be the one who will tell her," Talisa said, resigned.

Shadow nodded. "She has the right to know why I have the desire to end his life."

"You should leave that part out," Talisa suggested. "You can never win a woman's heart by telling her how much you want to kill the man who helped create her."

"Stranger things have happened," Shadow snorted. "Nonetheless, she has a right to know."

Talisa watched Shadow stand and face the now darkened forest; she assumed he was searching to see if the others were returning.

"Shadow, you didn't even glare at me for making that comment," Talisa said.

"Let's just say I've given up denying the truth."

She saw Shadow reach for the chain he kept hidden within his tunic. He held the silver band of birds holding a garnet within its center in his fingertips, a gift Talisa had given Artemis long ago.

"Will you ever give that back to her?" she asked.

Shadow let go of the ring. "I don't think I can."

I followed Netira and Jack with the gourds we brought for the journey, now all filled with water. Jack was complaining about how unfair it was that he had to train with Shadow, and I knew Netira was losing her patience with him. She glanced at me several times to help silence him, but I knew better.

Once Jack started, there was no shutting him up.

"I *don't* need to learn swordplay!" Jack whined. "However, I *do* want to learn how to properly wield a dagger, as Netira says."

Netira rolled her eyes. "I'm not sure that's a good idea anymore. I just might end up killing you."

Jack's jaw was agape, and I pushed it together for him. "Relax. It's a jest."

"I wasn't teasing," Netira admitted. "I might end up killing him after all the whining just now."

"I wasn't—"

I covered Jack's mouth. "I think he'll appreciate the tutelage, and he will keep his mouth shut as a way of showing his appreciation."

Jack glared at me as I moved my hand away. "But I hate silence."

"You should learn the beauty of it sometime," I teased. I rejoined Netira, who was walking faster just to escape the complaints.

Suddenly, she then stopped and held up a hand.

"What is it?"

"Shh!" she snapped.

I watched her dark brown irises shift to silver, and I understood something was amiss. Jack moved a hand to his back, and I saw a glint from the blade of a dagger. I reached for the sai in my boots and was met with the strange energy from the jewels. I shuddered as I felt the cold wisps of the energy seep into me.

Jack tapped my shoulder, breaking me out of the trance I was in.

"It begins," Netira whispered as she pulled out a dagger that once belonged to Mother.

"Are they Arlina's scouts?" Jack asked, also in a whisper.

Netira shook her head. "Their steps are lighter than a full-blood's."

"How many are there?" I questioned.

"I hear four...maybe five," Netira said as she shut her eyes. "Elves. That's the only explanation."

"How in Avilyne's hell did the hunting party find us so quickly?" Jack hissed.

"It's a hunting party, Jack!" I snapped. "Did you really expect us to avoid them forever?"

"Shut up, both of you!" Netira ordered. Jack and I grew silent, and Netira took off her cloak to reveal her black, leathery wings. "Get back to the camp. Warn the others."

"What about you?" Jack asked.

"I'm going to distract them." Netira grinned. "I'll try to lead them away from this path. I'll return to the camp when I'm sure they're no longer following me."

"How are we supposed to know that they've all followed you and it's safe for us to run?" Jack frowned.

"You'll be able to hear them leave." Netira rubbed her temples, annoyed. "Or at least Artemis will."

Jack was about to speak, but I clamped my hand over his mouth again. "You will find us, right?" I now heard the same footsteps Netira mentioned. "And you'll be careful?"

Netira nodded. "Artemis, I'm sure you know I can take care of myself."

"Couldn't hurt to ask."

"Indeed. I'll return when I can," Netira said as she leaped into the air and took flight.

Jack and I took cover behind one of the trees, and I heard the footsteps quicken; I knew they had spotted Netira. I could hear the footsteps move farther away from us, and I motioned for Jack to follow me.

24

Netira heard the scouts take the bait. She was disturbed, however, when she heard one fewer pair of footsteps follow her. One of them could have stayed behind; one of them could have realized she wasn't the only one around.

Netira prayed Artemis had more sense than that idiot elf mage friend of hers. She thought of how Karesu could help Jack grow into his gift properly, but she was sad the moment his image appeared in her mind.

Soon, she swore, as she continued to lead the hunting party away from the path. *Just keep fighting, my love.*

The camp was in sight, and Shadow was sitting alone by the fire. He stood up when he saw Jack and me, and he tried to wave us off. Sensing there was a reason behind the strange action, I pulled back Jack; he almost took me with him in a tumble.

"What gives, woman?" Jack snapped.

"Shadow was trying to tell us to stop, you idiot!" I yelled as I tried to regain my footing. "It's not my fault that you didn't see him."

"What in Avilyne's hell is going on?" Shadow asked as he drew closer to us.

"You first," I replied as I tried to catch my breath.

"You two would not want to be victims of Talisa's trap," Shadow explained. "Your turn."

"It's the hunting party Lord Celstian sent out," I huffed. "Netira's trying to lead them away."

Shadow's visage darkened. "They won't all have followed her."

"What do you mean?" I asked.

Shadow quickly grabbed the bow that was lying by the fire and notched an arrow. He aimed the bow directly at me; my eyes widened.

"Shadow, what are you doing?" Jack cried.

"Artemis, get down!" Shadow ordered. I ducked and heard the arrow loose. "Jack, get her!"

I felt Jack grab me, and we nearly ran over Talisa and Callypso as they stormed out of the tent.

"What's going on?" Callypso demanded.

"They found us," Jack answered.

Talisa went back inside the tent, and reemerged with a sheathed sword. "Shadow will be needing this."

"What about the rest of us?" Jack asked.

"This is Shadow's battle," Talisa explained. "We will not interfere."

"You all should leave," Shadow suggested while notching another arrow. He looked to the treetops and spoke louder. "And you should stop hiding! I have no desire to hurt you."

"How do you know I share the sentiment?" a male voice responded.

There was a loud thud, and an elf scout now stood behind Shadow. Shadow turned around and parried an attack by the scout with the blade end of his bow.

"I thought Lord Celstian wanted me returned alive." Shadow shoved off the scout. "I've done you no wrong."

"I do not serve Lord Celstian," the scout spat as he removed his hood.

The scout was as tall as Shadow and had similar dark blond hair, but the eyes differed; the scout had deep blue eyes, and there was a long scar over the left one. I didn't recognize him, but judging from the scowl that came from Talisa as well as Shadow, they both knew him on a personal level.

"Aellyas." Shadow frowned. "Still Destrius' pet, I see."

"*Lord* Destrius, deserter!" Aellyas snapped. "He didn't appreciate that sneak attack of yours."

Shadow snorted. "There was nothing sneaky about it."

"It was dishonorable!"

"Don't make me laugh at your sense of honor." Shadow rolled his eyes. "I'm not going to try to reason with you, Aellyas. If you're here, then that means you were given a particular task. I'm sure I know what that is."

"And what's that?" Aellyas asked with a smirk.

"To kill me before the rest of the scouts find you here. You'll try to convince them that I took the coward's way out—suicide," Shadow explained. "Destrius is a fool if he believes I would do something so pathetic."

"*Lord* Destrius!" Aellyas snapped as he raised his sword. He rushed toward Shadow. Talisa threw Shadow's sword to him, and he caught the hilt in one hand as he dropped his bow with the other. He continued to dodge the scout's slashes as he unsheathed his sword.

I was amazed at the blade; engraved within the steel was a style of glyphs I'd never seen before, and it seemed to have a faint green glow. I noticed Callypso staring at the sword as well, though more in recognition than awe.

"Cally?" I asked.

"Yes?" Her gaze was still on Shadow's sword.

"Are you all right?"

Callypso flashed a small smile my way. "Yes, yes I am. I'm just… intrigued."

"Care to share?" Talisa joined in the conversation.

"It's nothing."

Jack spoke up. "Who is this Aellyas?"

"Lord Destrius' dog," Talisa replied, disinterested. "And a capable assassin, I hate to say. Had he kept to the darkness of the forest, Aellyas might have been successful in his mission."

"But this is Shadow we're talking about." Jack frowned. "The man's a one-of-a-kind warrior."

"Yes," Talisa sighed, "but even Shadow can be caught off guard when the timing is right."

"Not for nothing, but why aren't we taking Shadow's advice about running away?" Jack asked.

"Once found by elven scouts, there is no escape," Talisa explained. "Yes, they are here for Shadow, not us. However..."

"What is it, Talisa?" I asked.

She sighed. "You'll understand soon enough."

Aellyas was now out of his cloak, since Shadow had cut off the clasp by the elf's throat. The two continued to circle one another in the hopes that one would tire faster than the other. Aellyas had the advantage, as Shadow's wounds from Ellewynth weren't healed yet, but with the way Shadow fought, it looked as if he hadn't been injured at all.

I flinched when Aellyas cut into the very arm Shadow had injured.

"Wounded, were we?" Aellyas taunted as he brought the tip of his sword toward him and pulled off a piece of ripped bandage with his fingertips. "It's true that even *you* can bleed."

Shadow grimaced, but kept his stance. "Anyone can bleed."

"I'll admit it would be a shame to kill you." Aellyas sighed. "Lord Destrius wanted to do so himself, you know."

"He never failed to remind me," Shadow replied. "He knew I was one of the first who believed the goddesses chose poorly in appointing him as an Elder."

Aellyas snarled as he lunged after Shadow, and sparks flew from their blades as they continued to parry one another's blows.

"They're evenly matched, given Shadow's condition," Callypso commented. "This could go on all night."

"Shadow won't last for long," Talisa explained. "He's more tired than he lets on."

Talisa was right, and Shadow favored the uninjured arm more than the other as he fought. He was forced to keep backing away, but then he smiled suddenly. Aellyas was confused, but it did not stop his barrage of swings.

"What are you smiling about, deserter?" Aellyas demanded.

Shadow dropped his sword. "I enjoy the image of you cursing night and day about how terrible the pain you're about to receive feels."

Aellyas hadn't realized he had backed Shadow to the edge of our camp, the same one where Shadow earlier stopped Jack and me from reaching. Shadow threw Aellyas down and I flinched at the sound of a loud pop. Talisa grinned as smoke rose from the ground.

Once the smoke cleared, we saw the scout. Aellyas' skin was instantly covered with thick, rosy boils. It was worse on his face and neck.

I gaped as the scout screeched. Jack took one look at Talisa and moved a few steps away from her.

"Goddesses, Talisa!" Callypso gasped. "I thought they were only supposed to feel as if they were plagued, not actually *given* one!"

"I may have taken a few more precautions given the new set of enemies we face," Talisa said, feigning innocence. "It's not the worst of my tricks, mind you. The boils will only last for a few nights. What comes afterward, however, will be far more unpleasant."

"And you're standing by your statement of that not being the worst of your bag of tricks?" I asked, horrified. She nodded, her grin wide.

"Avilyne's hell!" Jack cried. "You could have done that to me while I stayed in the cottage!"

"Yes, my dear apprentice, I could have," Talisa replied, her tone sweet. She patted Jack's cheek playfully as she would a child. "We hadn't yet reached the stage where I would teach you how to build an immunity to such things."

Jack spewed a string of Elvish curses while rubbing his skin as if he too had the boils. Aellyas' cries of pain intensified as we watched him roll around on the ground. Shadow stood up and held onto his bleeding arm, unaffected by Talisa's herbal trap.

"How is Shadow unharmed?" Callypso inquired.

"Shadow built an immunity to my herbs almost a century ago," Talisa explained. "He was my first test subject. Do you have any idea how many straps and restraints he destroyed during those tests? Kiare be praised that I had a merchant who didn't overcharge me for them."

"Why in Avilyne's hell would he do such a thing?" Jack asked, still keeping away from the witch.

Jack yelped when Talisa smacked the back of his head, despite the distance between them. "Because you never know what warfare you'll come across in battle. It was better that it was he who built the immunity with me, since we fought alongside one another more times than I can count. I didn't trust anyone else by my side when I fought with my plants."

"Curse you, Kiare's crone!" Aellyas screeched. He scratched his face to the point where blood and viscous yellow pus seeped out. "Traitors, all of you!"

"How original of him." I frowned. "I suppose traitor is better than *vampyra*."

"I don't even know him." Callypso blinked.

Shadow forced Aellyas to stop his writhing as he moved a foot onto his chest, pinning the scout to the ground.

"I will not harm any of the scouts that come after me," Shadow began, "but if Destrius sends more like you with them, then I will have no choice but to defend myself…even if it results in the death of an elf. I know you'll survive this, so go deliver my message to your master."

"There will be no need of that."

Everyone's attention transferred to four other cloaked figures, and my thoughts shifted to Netira. Jack glanced at me, and I knew he was thinking the same question I was—where was she?

The one who spoke sounded familiar. When the figure removed the hood of its cloak, I froze at the sight of my former archery instructor, Serlene.

Her blue eyes were as frigid now as they were years ago, and her blond hair was tightly pulled back into a plaited bun. I could feel the seething hatred within that single look she flashed my way.

"So it's true," Serlene said, her gaze still on me. "You deserted us for the *vampyra*."

Aellyas yelped as Shadow's foot pushed harder on his chest.

"Be careful with your words, Serlene."

"Don't presume to give me orders, Shadow," Serlene snapped. "Those days are long over."

"One of your own tried to kill me."

"So I see."

Serlene surveyed the ground and took a large step.

Talisa frowned when Serlene safely moved past the dangerous herb barrier.

"I hoped she wouldn't have noticed," Talisa mumbled.

Serlene stood beside Shadow and watched Aellyas. "I wasn't aware he was under orders from Lord Destrius. We will deal with him accordingly."

I restrained myself from calling her a liar on both counts. Talisa was far more subtle than I would have been.

"But...?" the witch asked.

"But we will not leave until Shadow complies with our orders," Serlene said. She faced Shadow. "You are to return with us to the ruins of Ellewynth. You are not to be harmed, per Lord Celstian's instructions. If you refuse, then we have no choice to but to take you by force. Either way, you will be forever marked as a deserter of the realm to us. Abandoning your status as a soldier to be at the side of of *vampyra...*"

"I'm aware of the declaration," Shadow said as he ignored the *vampyra* comment. He moved his foot from the scout's chest and stepped back to join the rest of us. "I refuse to return with you."

"Shadow, don't make this any harder on us." Serlene's hand was now on the hilt of her sword. "Don't force us to hurt you."

"I won't repeat myself," Shadow replied, now standing in front of me.

Serlene glared. "I never understood what you saw in that half-breed."

"Her name is Artemis!" Jack snapped. "She is a living being, just like you."

Serlene's attention shifted to Jack. "And I never understood what my sister saw in you. You're the spitting image of the last elf mage that threw us into chaos with the dragons!"

Jack couldn't hide his pained expression, and that was the final straw for me. I couldn't think as I felt myself move.

What happened after that became a blur.

25

"You...you punched me!" Serlene yelled. I suddenly saw her on the ground in front of me, clutching the right side of her now reddened face. "You *vampyra* bitch! You *punched* me!"

I was stunned when I felt the numbness of my hand, and I saw the other scouts draw their swords. Talisa and Shadow stood at each side of me, both ready to defend.

"First the *vampyra* burns down our city. Now she disrespects us further by laying her hands on one of our own," one of the scouts hissed. I wish I could throw all of their hoods down to see who was insulting me. "We should drag her back and let the Elders deal with her."

Now I *really* had it with them.

"I had nothing to do with the destruction of Ellewynth!" I yelled. "That was all Arlina's doing! For once in your miserable lives, blame the *right* person for the crimes!"

"You stole Shadow from us. That is your crime, *vampyra*," another one of the scouts added. "Shall we continue this pathetic dance?"

"He stayed and fought! Shadow still acted as a soldier. I had nothing to do with the attack!"

"You had *everything* to do with this, Artemis!" Serlene screamed. "I'm no imbecile! You and Arlina are both Ravenwing women! She came to do what the Elders should have done when Talisa brought you to us, which is to kill you. We were punished for letting you live among us...

as if we weren't punished enough for your ungratefulness. I would love nothing more than to silence you myself this very moment, but I have a duty to carry out. It's an idea you always failed to grasp, duty."

I was about to rush at her, but Shadow held me back. "Don't."

"I'm sick of her and that lot," I muttered. "I'm tired of their hatred. I won't stand for it anymore."

"I know." Shadow murmured. "It's about time you stopped feeling guilty about the attack on Ellewynth. It's about time you stood up to them as well."

"Then let me go. She has it coming."

Shadow sighed as he looked at Talisa. "Promise me you'll at least last a day in Westyron without causing any trouble," he said in a low voice.

I froze at the statement. "Shadow, you can't be serious."

"I'm *very* serious." Shadow frowned at Serlene, who was still rubbing her reddened face. "I'll return with you under one condition, Serlene. You must leave Artemis and the others alone. There will not be anyone sent to tail them, and yes, I'm well aware that you will report Talisa to the Elders. Even so, you will leave them be. Is that understood?"

Serlene eventually nodded her head in agreement. Jack and Callypso joined us while Shadow handed over his sword to Talisa, instructing her to take care of it.

"Shadow, you can't leave," I said, loud enough for only him to hear.

"Do you have so little faith in me to think I would really let them capture me, Artemis?" he asked. "You and the others must find Netira and continue on to Westyron. I will be back by the time you all reach the city."

"Shadow, you're playing a dangerous game," Talisa scolded. "I knew you would do it, but…Avilyne's hell."

"It's a necessary move, as much as I dislike it," Shadow insisted. "Something has to be done otherwise they'll just tail us all the way to Blackwen City. We would never escape them, and we can't afford their meddling. I also needed to make sure there were witnesses to Serlene's agreement concerning you all. She is less likely to go back on her word in the sight of fellow soldiers."

"What are you going to do to them, Shadow?" Jack asked. "You're not going to kill them, are you?"

Shadow was hesitant to answer. "I'm just going to send Lord Celstian a message to leave me be, that's all."

"Be careful," Callypso urged.

"All of you, stop looking so glum," Shadow ordered. "I won't be gone for long, I promise."

"Shadow, stop prolonging this!" Serlene snapped, drawing our attention again.

"I'm coming, woman," Shadow replied, walking away from us.

"Be safe," I whispered.

Shadow turned around to acknowledge that he heard me, and flinched when Serlene slapped iron cuffs on him. "Really, Serlene?"

"I know you, Shadow," Serlene reminded him. "I'm not taking any chances here."

"I'm sure Lord Celstian suggested the restraints," Shadow grinned. "You were never smart enough to make that decision on your own."

Serlene kicked at Shadow's heels, which forced him to the ground. The rest of us were ready to attack, but Shadow waved us back.

"I'll keep my word as long as the rest of you do not follow us," Serlene threatened. "Don't be surprised if you see us again, Talisa. The Elders will be disappointed in you as well."

"Good luck trying to find me, Serlene," Talisa challenged. "You never had great skill as a tracker."

Serlene glared at the witch while she forced Shadow to walk. He looked back at us, and I felt broken inside. The elves disappeared, and my hands clenched into fists.

How was Shadow going to get himself out of this one?

"Callypso, are they all gone?" Talisa asked, after a brief moment of silence.

Callypso nodded. "It seems they've kept their word."

"We have to go after them," I said.

Talisa shook her head. "I want to as well, Artemis, but we must continue to Westyron. We need to locate Netira first."

"You really think Shadow can escape them and find us?" Jack inquired.

"There is much that Shadow is capable of," Talisa said. "I knew he would do this the moment he began to fight Aellyas and I understand why he did it. If Shadow hadn't gone with them, those scouts would have meddled in our affairs and cost us the element of surprise with Arlina. They would have gotten in the way if he didn't surrender. We can't afford that."

"Talisa, he's done this before, hasn't he?" Callypso asked.

Talisa nodded.

"What did he do to his captors before?" Jack gulped.

Talisa sighed. "I'd rather not say."

"Elves consider it taboo to kill one of their own," I reminded them. "At least...at least the honorable ones do."

"The honorable ones are far and few in Arrygn." Talisa patted my back. "Shadow has his. To this day, he has not killed an elf. Now... now he will do whatever it takes to ensure our safety. Yours especially, Artemis."

Before I could speak, Talisa left to go to the tent with Shadow's sword. I felt someone grasp my hand; Callypso was inspecting it.

"Your hands seem to be better, and quite flexible despite the bandaging after your earlier sparring," Callypso assessed, while picking at the white strips that wrapped around my palms. "That was quite a punch, Artemis."

"It was a long time coming," Jack added with a grin. "And you stood up for yourself, finally! Kiare be praised, there's some hope for you yet."

"It was a blur." I shuddered. "I don't even remember punching Serlene."

Jack and Callypso looked at one another and blinked.

"What do you mean you don't remember doing it?" Jack asked. "You only have blackouts in your dhampir form. Avilyne's hell...what *do* you remember?"

"I was angry. I couldn't think," I answered. "Next thing I knew, Serlene was on the ground."

Callypso immediately took a step back from me. Jack did the same, with a sharp intake of breath. Before I could ask what was wrong, Jack gingerly took a sai from my boot and tapped a finger on the jewels; they were more luminescent than I remembered.

"How...how did that happen?"

"Your anger, Artemis," Jack deduced. "I warned you about it before we left the cottage."

"How in Avilyne's hell does my anger connect with the sai?" I snapped. "I didn't even use them!"

Callypso and Jack watched one another once more and sighed.

"It's worse than I thought," Callypso whispered.

"You're not answering me," I said.

"Artemis, the sai seem to draw power specifically from anger," Jack explained. "The dragon jewels brightened a bit when I had my moment of anger while I was trying to purify them."

"Cally, you said the sai are somehow still linked to my mother," I began. "What will they do to her when the jewels reach full luminosity? What will happen to me?"

"I pray that's something we never have to find out, Artemis," Callypso said, staring into the fire.

Epilogue

Tamina walked the streets of Westyron, looking for the one place she knew there: the White Viper. When she found it, she couldn't help but smile.

This was where she met *him*. This was where everything in her life had changed.

Drifting through the door, Tamina took a few moments to take in the sight of the empty bar. The memories of the past resurfaced, and she put a pale hand to her chest, as if to steady a heartbeat. When she found the staircase leading to the rooms above, she felt some excitement grow.

Tamina found the door she was looking for and drifted through. She saw the sleeping figure of her former husband behind his desk, and chuckled when she saw the windows boarded up with wood.

Hearing her laugh, Gavin stirred in his sleep. She moved closer to him, and when he opened a tired hazel eye, it focused on Tamina's form. His head snapped up.

"No…" He stood and moved away. "It can't be."

Why can't it be?

"Because you're dead," Gavin replied, nearly tripping over his chair. "You're dead!"

You thought that of our daughter as well, Tamina laughed, *but we both know she's alive and well.*

"Why are you here?" Gavin demanded. "You're supposed to be rotting in Avilyne's hell!"

How original of you, Tamina replied as she looked away. *I have my own reasons why I still linger in Arrygn.*

"Lingering spirits are a myth." Gavin continued to back away from her. "You're dead. This...this is just some sick dream."

Vampirism has done nothing for you, it seems. Tamina moved to the boarded window and tried to peek through the cracks. *I assure you, I'm no dream.*

"You. Are. Dead," Gavin said, emphasizing each word with his pointer finger. "*Dead.*"

Tamina flashed a grin with elongated fangs.

For now, my husband. For now.

Melanie Rodriguez holds a BA in creative writing from Green Mountain College in Poultney, Vermont. She says she's been compelled to write stories dictated by the voices she's heard inside her head since she was a child, citing the story line of her debut book Child of Blackwen: An Artemis Ravenwing Novel as one of the main reasons she majored in creative writing. It's an epic work of high fantasy narrating the coming-of-age story of a young half-vampire, half-human creature known as a dhampir.

A former New Yorker, Rodriguez is an avid reader and sports fan who now lives in Santa Fe, New Mexico, with her overly excitable shep-sky (a shepherd-husky mix), Shadow.

Made in the USA
Coppell, TX
07 July 2020